STATE LIBRARY OF WESTERN AUSTRALIA

To:	To:
From: HARVEY	From: HARVEY
Due Back:	Due Back:
ILL No.: No Renew	ILL No.: No Renew
To:	To:
From: HARVEY	From: HARVEY
Due Back:	Due Back:
ILL No.: No Renew	ILL No.: No Renew
To:	To:
From: HARVEY	From: HARVEY
Due Back:	Due Back:
ILL No.: No Renew	ILL No.: No Renew
To:	To:
From: HARVEY	From: HARVEY
Due Back:	Due Back:
ILL No.: No Renew	ILL No.: No Renew

Please initial below if you would like to record that you have read this book.

DIVERSIONBOOKS

Also by Nicole Elizabeth Kelleher

The Aurelian Guard
Wild Lavender

Diversion Books
A Division of Diversion Publishing Corp.
443 Park Avenue South, Suite 1008
New York, New York 10016
www.DiversionBooks.com

For more information, email info@diversionbooks.com

First Diversion Books edition May 2017.
Print ISBN: 978-1-68230-818-9
eBook ISBN: 978-1-68230-817-2

For Lucy of the beautiful smiles.
Not a day goes by when I don't remember her grace.

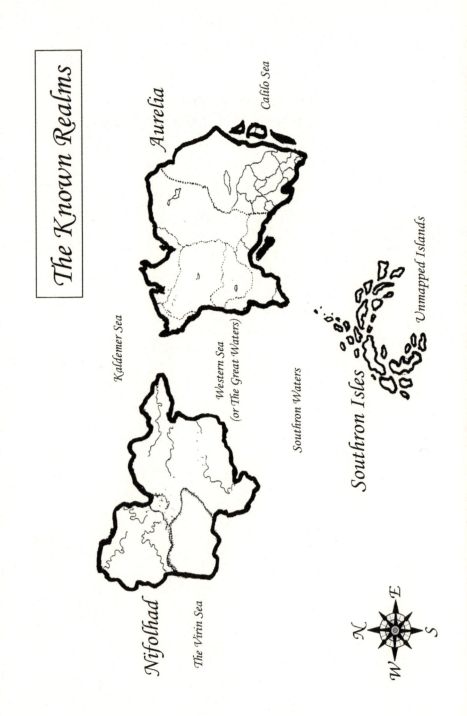

The Known Realms

Aurelia

Califo Sea

Kaldemer Sea

Western Sea
(or The Great Waters)

Southron Waters

Southron Isles

Unmapped Islands

Nifolhad

The Virin Sea

N E S W

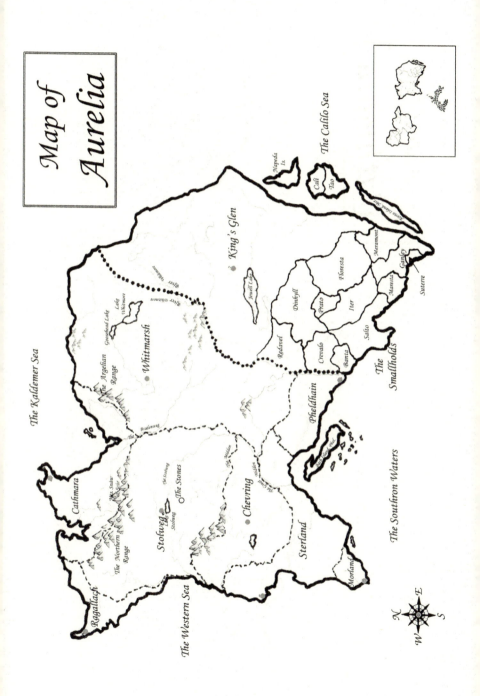

Map of Aurelia

The Catilo Sea

Napeda Is.

Cali
Tao

King's Glen

Jewell Lake

River Whitmoor

River Whitmoor

Lake Whitmoor

Greenhead Lake

The Argelian Range

Whitmarsh

Meramont

Floresta

Marella

Galley

Suterre

Dinhyll

Prato

Iter

Salto

Redavel

Crevalo

Banta

Phedthian

The Smallholds

The Kaldemer Sea

The Bradenwood

The Stones
Stofweg
Mt. Stobe
Stofweg

Mt. Snow Spir

The Stidon
The Coast

Chevring

Sterland

The Southron Waters

Cathmara

The Northern Range

Morland

Ragallach

The Western Sea

N
E
W
S

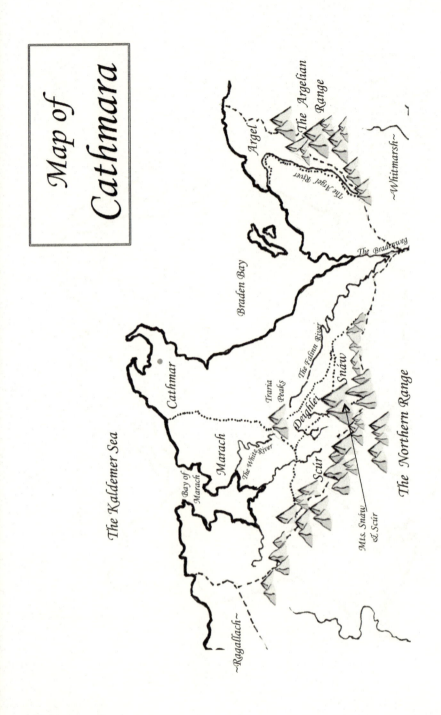

Map of Cathmara

The Kaldemer Sea

~Ragallach~

Bay of Marach

Marach

The White River

Cathmar

Braden Bay

Traria Peaks

Deighle

Scúr

Mts. Snáw
& Scúr

Snáw

The Falinn River

The Northern Range

~Stolweg~

The Braderweg

Argel

The Argel River

The Argelian Range

~Whitmarsh~

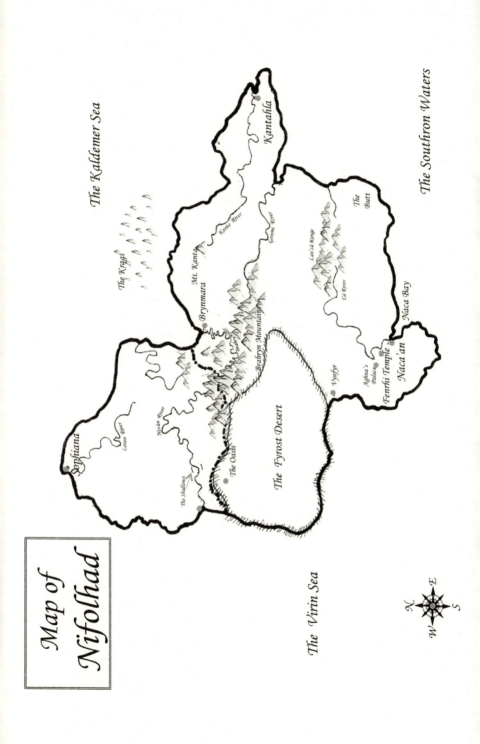

Map of
Nifolhad

The Kaldemer Sea

The Southron Waters

Kantahla

The Kraggs

Kantla River

Sorens River

Mt. Kantla

The
Butt

Brynmara

Lan'ca Range

Braebryn Mountains

Cá River

Soabryn

Cyrfyr

Aghina's
Palace

Naca Bay

Losan River

Nevian River

Fenrhi Temple

Naca'an

Sypfiana

The Shallows

The Oasis

The Fyrost Desert

The Virin Sea

N
W E
S

Prologue

In the Thirty-First Year of the Great Peace
Betwixt the Realms of Aurelia and Nifolhad
Tribute Day
King's Glen, Aurelia

Claire had fought bitterly to join her family for this visit to the royal court and to attend the triennial tribute. Now that she was here, she was determined to impress the queen. She glanced at her mother standing beside her, so proud and regal, though her gown was several years old and had been altered to appear fashionable. Few in Aurelia would suspect that the great Chevring House was struggling to maintain its standing in the realm.

Claire held herself straighter and lifted her chin in an effort to mimic her mother. Her grandmother had drilled her on one hard-and-fast rule: no matter the situation, keep your chin high, chest out, and shoulders back. As Claire had no chest of which to speak, she cast an envious gaze at Anna's figure, but couldn't find it in herself to be critical of her older sister. It wasn't Anna's fault that she'd been born first, but why did she have to waste her comely attributes by behaving like a boy? Claire almost sighed, but stifled the urge. She refused to act like a jealous child now that she was finally at court.

It had been Claire's grandmother, Lady Beatrice, who had cautioned against Claire's traveling to King's Glen. Unexpectedly, Anna—the *special* daughter—had convinced her family to let Claire accompany them for the first time. Claire had been thrilled, even though she wondered at her sister's motives. Just three years apart in age, they were constantly at odds. But what else could Anna expect, always being singled out for her extraordinary abilities?

Well, Claire had talents of her own. Unfortunately, they caused her to faint at inopportune moments, thoroughly embarrassing herself and her family. Anna had pointed out to their parents that it had been over a year since the last incident and, therefore, Claire deserved to join them. It wasn't quite the truth, but Claire hadn't informed them otherwise. She'd just gotten better at controlling her surroundings and minimizing the risks. When she had asked her sister why she had championed her, Anna had shrugged and said, "Perhaps you'll keep Mother so preoccupied with your well-being that she won't worry about me." Whatever Anna's reasons were, Claire was grateful.

"It's almost our turn," her mother whispered, drawing Claire's attention from the past. Chevring was one of the largest territories in Aurelia, and Claire's family had been a steadfast supporter of the royal house since its ascendance. During the Great War with Nifolhad, Chevring had been the sole provider of the King's Guard's destriers. Her family had prospered. But then the war had ended, and her late grandfather, and now her father, had been unable to stretch their resources in the peacetime economy. Claire had ideas—like beekeeping to take advantage of Chevring's many fruit and nut orchards, not to mention the plentiful clover which grew rampant throughout their land—but no one would listen to a nearly fourteen-year-old girl when she touted the lucrative honey market. In Chevring, if you were not fully committed to the horses, your voice was not heard.

Her parents had spent every coin in the Chevring coffers just to be able to afford the journey to King's Glen, and judging by the appearance of the realm's other representatives, her family's territory had been most hard hit. The bodice of Claire's gown was one that she had pieced together by dismantling two of Anna's passed-down garments. The skirt was made from an even older dress that her mother had worn when Claire was just a babe. Claire counted herself fortunate that she was tall enough to not have had to shorten the skirt and remove the beautiful needlework along the hem.

She glanced behind her and saw that her father was removing the muffling cloths from the hooves of their tribute: two Chevring steeds,

a rare set so similar that they could be twins, were to be gifted to King Godwin's sons. Her sister waited patiently with Lord Gervaise, their father, and Claire inwardly groaned. Anna's wild curls were already escaping her long braid. Claire was about to say something when her mother stiffened beside her. She turned her attention back to the King and Queen.

The Royal Hall was crowded with exquisitely attired lords and ladies. And the Royal Guards were resplendent with their gleaming swords and bristling muscles that warned one and all. A well-formed man knelt before the royal family. His hair was thick and flaxen-hued. When he stood, his muscles bunched and strained against his expensive-looking garments. Late twenties and too old for her, Claire decided. 'Twas a shame, for he looked rich enough that she wouldn't have to worry about wearing patched-together dresses. Unlike her sister, Claire had resolved to secure a betrothal before she turned sixteen.

The man's gifts of woolen fabrics and a great shield had surpassed all other tributes. The Queen's face, however, remained polite, if not aloof. Claire was determined to learn that practiced expression; it spoke volumes.

Behind her, Claire could hear her mother offer hushed congratulations to a young man who had come late to the hall. "...an honor to be chosen for the Royal Guard at such a young age. Lord Wolf must be proud."

At the mention of the Royal Guard, Claire turned to give the man a cursory study. She did not recognize the name Lord Wolf, and she prided herself on learning all there was to know about Aurelia's noble families. The newcomer wore a bear pelt as a cape and a sword belted at his hip. He appeared to have just ridden in, not even sparing time to brush the dust from his boots. A beard shadowed his face, but unlike the other noblemen present, he did not keep it neatly trimmed, choosing instead to wear it full. He must have felt her gaze, for his head turned to regard her in kind. Claire lifted her nose, dismissing his interest by looking to the Queen just as she cleared her throat to speak to the wealthy man kneeling before her.

"Our thanks, Lord Roger," Queen Juliana allowed. "Please express our wishes to your wife that her recovery is swift. We miss Isabel's bright smile at court." If Lord Roger meant to reply, he was cut off by the sound

of iron shoes on stone echoing through the hall. Claire's father had come forward, and Lord Roger and his fabulous gifts were forgotten. All eyes widened to take in the final and most spectacular tribute of the day.

King Godwin rose and stepped off the dais. He strode forward to greet Claire's father. They clasped arms, hands to elbows, displaying to all the respect and friendship they had for one another. It was then that Claire noticed that her sister had been given the honor of leading one of the destriers.

"Two, Gervaise!" the King boomed in admiration. "Are they twins, these steeds?"

"Not twins, sire, but brothers," her father explained. "Only a year apart, to honor your two sons, likewise separated by twelve moons."

A great cheer filled the hall when the King's sons rushed forward to claim their mounts. Anna handed the lead to the younger son and—oh, grief of griefs, Claire bemoaned—bowed low instead of curtsying! The ladies at court concealed their titters and remarks behind their bejeweled fingers. But the Queen had stepped forward, and the unrestrained chattering in the hall was cut short as she nodded to Anna and then to Lord Gervaise. It seemed that her sister's gaffe would be disregarded.

Claire couldn't bear to witness the exchange, so she scanned the vast room. Her eyes fell upon Lord Roger. He was glaring at her father and the King. When his gaze fell upon Anna, it twisted into something quite ugly. Claire felt a sudden rush welling inside her chest, that feeling that always forewarned her of one of her spells. Only this time, fear gripped her so tightly, she lost her breath. Her vision grayed, and she reached out her hand to grasp something, anything, to break her fall. A moment before she hit the floor, an arm reached out. She caught the scent of dust and leather and horses, felt herself being lifted by strong arms, and then her world went dark.

CHAPTER ONE

Wind

Seven Years Later
(Two years after the Nifolhadian incursion and the destruction of Chevring)
Cathmara, the Northernmost Aurelian Territory

Lark wondered why he had never before noticed the clouds of Cathmar as he lay flat on his back staring up at a sky so pale and thin that, if he could just reach it, he could rend it open one-handed. Mere wisps, the clouds were, nothing like the billowing masses drifting over the rest of the realm. The blue of the northern sky looked stretched, as if the expanse might rupture with the slightest breeze. Of course, there were no breezes in Cathmar. Only wind. Lark took a great gulp of air, his lungs unclenching as his own breath was returned to him.

He heard barking laughter above him, but turned instead to see Trian holding his own against his cousin Cordhin. It had been Terrwyn, Trian's older brother, who'd knocked Lark flat. That was the way of the Cathmarans: any reason to brawl was a good one. Lark loved Trian's family. And that Terrwyn attacked him so ruthlessly was testament to the fact that they counted Lark as one of their own.

His bear of a friend was locked in combat with Cordhin, neither one gaining nor giving ground. Though nearly as tall as Lark himself, Trian was a mere cub compared to his barrel-chested male relatives. Cordhin was greater in size and strength, but Trian was faster, both in body and in wit. It had been his friend's wit that had started this trouble.

Lark grimaced. He had been enjoying the thick grog the Cathmarans preferred, and was feeling quite at ease. He and Trian were due to depart

the next day, and Terrwyn wanted to send them off properly, pouring round after round into their cups.

Aside from being apart from his wife and daughter, the only disagreeable aspect of their journey had been Cordhin. The cousin was a constant needle, jabbing Trian at every opportunity with choice words and veiled insults, usually having to do with Trian's proportions.

Here at Cathmar, where girth of chest was more important than height, Trian was the brunt of many a jest—delivered more oft than not by his cousin. Cordhin had just proclaimed that Trian was the runt of the house, smaller even than some of the women. Trian, with his ever-calm demeanor, took each sting with a serene expression. Lark knew better.

To forestall the coming storm, Lark had suggested that Trian test him on his knowledge of the rugged dialect that was still spoken in the remote states of Cathmara. It had put Cordhin off, at least for a short time, while Lark provided translations to the words Trian threw his way. Then Trian gave Lark the word *dhin*. Simple enough. It meant "tiny" or "small". Terrwyn smothered a smirk that left Lark wondering.

"And *corai?*" his friend asked.

"Spear or sword, if I'm not mistaken," Lark answered, unaware that, next to him, Cordhin was turning purple. "And if put together," he continued blindly on, "you get *coradhin*, or 'little dagger.'"

Terrwyn blew out his grog. When Trian winked, Lark grasped the meaning of Cordhin's name, and his laughter echoed off the castle walls. Like all Cathmaran women, Cordhin's mother had a wicked sense of humor. Trian held up his pinkie and wiggled it to renewed gales of mirth.

And that was how Lark found himself staring up at the heavens. Cordhin had launched himself at Trian, and Terrwyn at Lark. Not because of familial honor, either. No, Trian's eldest brother and heir to Cathmara attacked Lark for no other reason than that he enjoyed a good scuffle.

Still on his back, Lark watched and waited; Trian had the upper hand even if Cordhin considered him beat. Engrossed in the struggle between his younger brother and his cousin, Terrwyn had stepped dangerously close to Lark's feet. If there was one thing Cathmarans respected, it was a man who could fight, even more so if the man fought dirty. And just like that, Lark swept Terrwyn's legs from under him.

The two thuds of Terrwyn and Cordhin's bodies hitting the ground

were nearly simultaneous, and it was their turn to regain their wind. Trian, the only one standing, was triumphant. In the end, Cordhin had no choice but to take his cousin's hand as he held it out to him.

They had just tucked in for another round of grog when Trian's sister Adara appeared.

"'Tis time, brother. Mother and Auntie await your presence." She raised her eyebrows at Lark when he rose to join his friend, a cool look of speculation flickering in her gaze. Lark kept his attention forward and his expression bland. When in council with the women of Cathmara, it was best to not appear too interested.

• • •

Across the Western Sea in the City of Kantahla
High Seat of the Steward King Diarmait of Nifolhad

It'd been an easy enough task to slip away from her main group now that the women from the temple were engaged with Diarmait's men. Harder for Madyan had been reaching the domed roof of the tower. She hung from it now, in her silken-rope harness, and crab-walked the curved stone surface until she rested above the window she'd been seeking.

Intrigue upon plot upon scheme. Was that what Nifolhad had come to? Madyan waited, unafraid of the extreme height at which she was suspended. This was her third and final night in Kantahla. At sunrise, she would rejoin her sisters and escort the tribute women back to the ship that would take them south to their home. Thus far, her nightly excursions had been for naught. She had learned nothing of the rumors about a bride destined for Prince Bowen, one who could put to rest, once and for all, any claims that Prince Ranulf to the north might put forth.

Like a spider, Madyan slowly edged away from the open window and carefully inverted herself so that she hung upside down. Two men had entered the council chamber, and she strained to hear their voices.

"…have to kill her husband first. Then, she'll be free, so to speak, to marry again."

"Widow or not, Phelan, I want her here in Nifolhad where she can pay for her crimes."

"Just as long as you don't kill her, my King," Phelan cautioned. "You'll need her for Prince Bowen."

"Bowen? Bah!" the Steward King exclaimed. "You worry too much, Phelan. She'll be alive enough for my son. The witches from the temple will see to that."

"Speaking of the witches, sire," Phelan hinted.

"Yes, yes, I know. They leave tomorrow. Amazing stamina—"

Their voices faded as they left the chamber. Madyan righted herself, scuttled sideways, and began the slow process of lowering herself to the roof of the castle's great hall. She'd freed the anchored end of her silken cord, releasing it from the architectural filigree holding her weight. From the great hall's roof, she wouldn't even need a rope to slip into her chamber's window. Ridiculously ornate, the castle had more ways in and out of it than a smuggler's cove.

Madyan finally had some intelligence to carry home to the one she protected. Together, they would decide on the best course of action needed to thwart Diarmait. If that meant rescuing an unknown Aurelian woman, so be it.

CHAPTER TWO

A Mother's Wish

Her brother and his friend Lark stood behind her as Adara rapped on the door to her mother's chamber. It was not a tentative knock, but a firm strike demanding invitation. Passing within, she gave Trian one last meaningful look before the door was closed again.

Adara's eyes swept the room, half expecting to see their father, but he would leave his youngest child's fate in the hands of her mother, Lady Baranne. She was currently deep in conversation with Adara's aunt, Lady Cafellia. Adara waited patiently while the two women discussed the sooth stones that had been tossed. Her aunt's bony finger pushed at the pebbles, pairing and rearranging them, before taking them in hand and tossing them again.

Adara smiled; her aunt wouldn't be satisfied until the outcome she wanted presented itself on the table. Lady Cafellia and her stones were oft consulted, and it was a great honor that her mother paid her by bowing to the old ways. Her aunt, childless, had once tried to teach Adara how to read the pebbles, but Adara had neither patience nor talent for them. And so the gift of sight that had graced their family, if it even existed, would end with her aunt.

Outside the door, Trian would be pacing. But not Lark; he'd be waiting patiently, steadfast in his support of his friend—married life and a child had matured him like nothing else could. Adara'd almost pressed her suit for him. Although rare, marriage to outsiders was not unheard of in Cathmara. Her parents often spoke of Lark with respect. He was the sort of man a woman could rely upon, with his lean muscles and dark looks.

Cathmara, the northernmost territory in Aurelia, was in itself comprised of six small regions, each ruled by one of the six remaining great families. There were once twenty or so Cathmaran states, but during the Great War, different regions bled together, and melded afterwards. Her own family's seat of Cathmar, the greatest of the six families', formed a great V on the northern coast. By royal decree, the Lord of Cathmar held the title of High Lord over all of Cathmara.

The other five states therefore had a vested interest in marrying into her ruling house. To the east lay the state of Argel, so named for the silver reeds which grew along its coast, and the precious metal found along its waterways. Three states sat below Cathmar, two named for Aurelia's highest peaks, Snáw and Scúr, and the third being Deighlei, with its ice plains in the shadow of the two mountains. The sixth state, and second largest, was Marach. The greatest ships in the kingdom were built there. Adara sighed. It was in Marach where her betrothed resided.

She noticed then that her mother and aunt were silent and waiting for her to approach. "My pardon. It was not impatience that caused my sigh."

"More like you were contemplating your union with the fair-haired Logan," her aunt guessed. "You need not fret, Adara. He will follow Cathmaran custom and reside here. Or perhaps in Braden, at Riverhome. Still, you'll not be too far from us."

Adara loved the port city of Braden almost as much as she loved the fortress. Her aunt winked; it had already been decided.

"Trian awaits, and Larkin with him," Adara supplied. "Should I find something to occupy his friend?" Lark was accepted as family, but that did not mean that he would be permitted to join a betrothal council.

"He is welcome," her mother allowed, surprising Adara. "Please, bid them enter. And you may remain as well."

Adara stepped to the door, pulled it open, and found Trian and Lark exactly as she'd pictured: Trian pacing and Lark leaning against the wall, unbothered. "They are ready for you. Both of you." If Lark was taken aback by his inclusion, he didn't show it. Trian, however, looked as if some horrible sentence was about to be settled upon his head. He stood tall and followed Adara into the lioness' den.

"Trian, my son," Lady Baranne greeted. "And Larkin." The two men bowed low, then shifted to pay their respects to Lady Cafellia, whose pebbles had been stowed away. After all were seated comfortably, Lady Baranne clucked her tongue. "What am I to do with you?" she asked in that way that only a mother could. She turned to her son's friend. "How much do you know about our betrothal customs, Larkin?"

"The firstborn, whether male or female, inherits the position and title." He steepled his fingers. "When non-firstborn children wed, the groom always relocates to the home of the bride. Terrwyn shall inherit title here, and already resides in the fortress with his wife and children. Aiden, your second son, has married Corsén of Argel, and lives with her family. Adara shall marry Logan of Marach, but the two shall remain in Cathmar. And Trian—" Lark began to conclude.

"—is not yet matched," Lady Cafellia provided.

"Therein lies the hitch," Adara quipped, eliciting smiles from all save Trian. He groaned.

"There is more to our customs than many realize, Lark," Lady Baranne hinted. "Matters of marriage and familial lines have always been left to the women."

"Left to the men, we would've died off by now," Cafellia half jested.

"There's much truth in that," Lady Baranne admitted. "Before Cathmara was consolidated, the feuding was petty and oftentimes brutal. Even now, no other region in the realm is thus organized, not even The Smallholds to the southeast. Here in Cathmara, it fell to the women to command and trade to keep our bloodlines strong. We were never content to wait on a man's proposal. We secured our own husbands. Corsén wooed Aiden, just as Adara pursued Logan."

Adara almost blushed. Almost. She wondered if Lark ever suspected that she had set her sights on him. She had planned to petition his mother for her blessing when news arrived that Lark had wed the *horsewif* of Chevring, now Lady Aubrianne of Stolweg.

"Each family in Cathmara has an extensive family tree: every root, trunk, branch, and leaf is noted," Lady Baranne went on. "Already, several noble houses have approached me for Trian's hand."

"Please, not from Snáw or Scúr," Trian blurted out, unable to remain quiet for once. And at this, Adara noted, Lark *did* show surprise.

"Yes, and from Deighlei as well," Trian's aunt replied, turning to address her nephew. "And Argel and Marach. We have even had envoys from a few of the Aurelian smallholds. It appears, dear nephew, that your prowess as a Royal Guard has reached every corner of the kingdom."

"But you would never consent to give Trian to one not of

Cathmara." Adara was suddenly worried for her favorite brother, and then she noticed her aunt's sooth stones were again on the table. "'Tis discouraged."

"That is not entirely true, Adara. Lord Marin of Pheldhain made an alliance with Lord Navis of Marach and married his niece to Navis's youngest son," Lady Baranne reminded. "Pheldhain needs ships; Marach now supplies them with the best." She turned back to Lark. "Many believe, erroneously, that we condemn outside marriages. In truth, it is only that our customs dissuade these unions. You see, outside of Cathmara, it is not touted that it falls to the woman to press her suit and win her groom. Just the opposite, in fact. As Cathmarans, we are forbidden to speak of our practices."

Adara was stunned. Lark was not Cathmaran! Trian sat up straight in his chair, looking from his mother to his aunt. Lark leaned back and stroked the clipped whiskers on his chin. "I understand," he said after some deliberation. "By honoring your customs, you ensure that the bonds between the states remain strong. Only a woman who truly loves a man of Cathmara would be persistent enough to win his heart. She would have to be resourceful, iron willed, and determined."

"Exactly," Lady Cafellia stated. "But she must come to this realization on her own. If it were to come to light that a *Cathmaran* intervened on her behalf, the other great families could block the union. But a few indirect nudges by an outsider, now and again, well, who would even know to object?"

Oh, how Adara loved these two women and their clever maneuvering. But how could Trian have fallen in love with an outsider, and she hadn't noticed?

"You have six and twelve moons, Trian," Lady Baranne intoned, pinning Adara's brother to his chair with her gaze. "If this girl for whom you pine is worthy, she will claim you of her own accord. If she does not, you must return in time for the autumnal equinox and choose one of the many who has properly sued for your hand. Whatever the outcome, you *will* be wed eighteen months hence."

"Love is possible, Trian," Lady Cafellia predicted, and though Trian and Lark missed the motion, Adara saw the sweep of her hand over pebbles. "I recommend that you use your time wisely."

CHAPTER THREE

Secrets

King's Glen, Seat of King Godwin and Queen Juliana of Aurelia

"You don't fool me," Claire flirted.

"Don't I?" Warin purred, inching closer, his hand skimming the silk of her sleeve. He gazed into eyes so like her sister's it was disconcerting.

"No, not at all," Claire responded confidently. Instead of retreating, she sat taller and leaned ever so slightly toward him. "Oh, I see right through you, that is for certain."

"And what exactly do you see, my sweet?" Warin had been at court these many months, and found Claire's forthrightness quite refreshing. This Chevring girl was better at courtly games than even the most seasoned lady-in-waiting. In fact, her repartee was so salted with truth that the noblemen at court hung upon her every word. Like a baker dusting his block with flour, she somehow smoothed every interaction with a heartfelt compliment. Then she would knead and pound and punch away with her words. But never once did any man leave her presence ired. Rather, one felt relieved, as if their life's burden had been leavened. Warin gazed at her with a directness that left most women quivering.

"A rogue," she accused. "A fisher of ladies. No hook for you; instead you cast sugary words like a finely woven net, catching as many fish as possible. Before they are aware of their peril, you've got them neatly filleted."

He pulled back infinitesimally, surprised yet again by her words, and glad for once that there were no witnesses. "And you, m'lady, prefer the spear to both hook and net, for your words aim to wound a man.

Look about this hall." He motioned to the assembled lords and guards. "We are each of us a pike, willing to jump from our lakes and streams into your hands. All would gladly risk suffocation for the mere chance of breathing the very air around you."

She stared down at her hands, and for a moment Warin thought he'd gone too far. But then she lifted her chin and laughed gaily, the sound of it tinkling through the hall, capturing the attention of all present. Each man wishing to be in Warin's place, tête-à-tête with the loveliest addition to the Queen's retinue—and every lady longing to be in hers, Warin reflected, with no false modesty. A pretty blush had stolen up her cheeks. He studied her.

Claire's striking resemblance to her sister, Lady Anna of Stolweg, was misleading. Yes, they were both tall and very much alike in face and form. But Claire was as graceful as a willow, and just as delicate. She and her sister shared the same brown eyes. But where Anna's sparked with gold, Claire's were deep and rich, like the fur of the fisher minks that played in the estuaries near his home in Pheldhain.

The sisters shared the same lovely brown shade of hair, but unlike the unruly curls of Anna, Claire's plaits were as smooth as ropes of Barbian pearls. He flexed his hand to stop his fingers from testing this belief. Caught up in his comparisons, he smiled upon realizing that she'd been taking his measure as well.

"Lark warned me about you."

"I can only imagine, m'lady. But pray, what did Anna recommend?"

"Caution," Claire answered cheekily. "But she also advised that if ever I found myself…in need of a net—" he grinned at her reference "—I could find no better friend to trust than you." Then she smiled at him, like only Claire could.

And there it was: the sensation of feeling better about oneself after spending time with her. Already, Warin knew their friendship would grow beyond that which he shared with Anna. "I wonder what it is with you Chevring women and the mystery that surrounds you."

"What do you mean?" Claire asked quietly, and he took note of the slight strain in her voice.

"Your sister and her special talents. And you," he started cautiously, "you recognize that which is left unspoken and then reply with what a person needs most to hear."

He watched her closely now. She had been sitting like a contented cat, pawing and playing with her captured mouse. But in her eyes, a sudden wariness emerged, a steeling of her senses as if she were preparing to flee, or attack. He touched her arm reassuringly. "Claire, Anna was right. You *can* trust me. You needn't worry."

"Worry, why should I worry?" Her voice was calm enough, but he heard the brittleness in her query just the same.

"Because you don't fool me either. I see you as well, though not in the way that you *see*, of course."

She opened her mouth to reply, but whether to deny his suspicion or to include him in her secret, Warin would never know, for she looked over his shoulder to greet the approaching Lady Caroline.

CHAPTER FOUR

Honey and Venom

Traveling upon the King's Road to Whitmarsh Castle

Claire had traveled this road several times before, but never once had her heart pressed so greatly toward her destination. Court had been more than wonderful, she reminisced, up to the very moment when Warin, over a month ago, had almost spoken aloud of that of which only her sister was cognizant. She had believed herself safe from discovery by maintaining a relentless pace at court: attending to Queen Juliana, dancing, even flirting. It was all pretense, a way to keep strict control over her curse.

Now that she was away from the never-ending intrigues of King's Glen, she was aware that the constant activities had also kept her from dwelling upon the loss of her parents. So, to keep her mind from resting, Claire searched for opportunities to occupy herself at every turn of the road.

This day's ride had been especially productive, and Claire lifted her chin, took a deep breath, and gazed at the late spring sky. The sun was already tilting to the west, and their party would pass one last night on the road before reaching Whitmarsh Castle, home to Lord Baldric and Lady Elnoura. Claire loved riding into the night, chasing the sun to the horizon. The day's warmth promised a mild evening, and the road they traveled was the fairest in the realm. Wide and smooth, it rose and fell gracefully through the plains and shallow valleys that separated High Court from Whitmarsh. Here were the farms and orchards that fed the populace of King's Glen. The scent of lilac scented the air, and cherry, apple, and pear blossoms made puddles of pink and white upon the orchard floors. Sarah, a Chevring girl of twelve and in training to be Claire's lady's maid, was comfortably, if not snugly, seated in the back of a wagon. Her cushions were the many bundles of fabric that Lady Elnoura and Claire had purchased while at court, her back- and armrests the baskets and bushels of provisions Claire had collected along the way.

Lord Baldric never begrudged Claire her many stops and starts. He knew her to be a reliable rider on her great Chevring steed, Rebel. When she paused to reap nature's gifts, it fell to Trian, one of the Royal Guards, newly returned from his home in Cathmara, to remain behind as her escort while the rest of their party continued forward at a leisurely pace. Trian would wait patiently while she dug up some root, or conversed with a farmer's wife on the merits of devil's nettle over shepherd's purse. He rode silently beside her now, as was his habit. Only once had he spoken to her, and that was to give her news of Lark and his recent return to Stolweg. Claire didn't mind his quietude, for it gave her the time she needed to work out what she had to accomplish in the coming days. Worrying out the myriad details of quotidian life kept her ever vigilant against an idle mind.

Rebel flicked his tail at a passing bee; his ears and those of Trian's horse pivoted in unison. Claire gazed over the low stone wall that ran along the road and saw a man in a wide-brimmed hat from which hung fine netting. The familiar drone of kept bees made its way to her ears. Claire harkened back to her long-ago dream of keeping honeybees at Chevring, and added the idea to her mental task list.

Rebel, already used to her frequent stops, slowed his pace. Trian pulled his steed to a halt while the rest of the party rode on. He dismounted, and politely held out his hand to assist her from her saddle just as he did each and every time she paused to forage. But as usual, she waved him off—thanking him first, of course—and leapt nimbly to the ground.

She stepped down the road, with Trian in tow, until she found an opening in the wall and the narrow path to the hives. After the initial pleasantries and the sharing of gossip from the King's Road, Claire asked the beekeeper what he'd been doing. The apiarist disclosed that his wife used bee venom to treat her aching joints. Noting her interest in his work, he offered to show her the delicate operation. She watched as the hooded man used his smoke to trick the bees into believing there was a fire. The insects gorged themselves on their own honey, and those that did not take to the air quickly enough fell into a lethargic state. He plucked one such bee from the group. "Ye must be careful not to take the queen," he instructed, pointing to a larger bee vibrating and moving in slow but deliberate patterns. The keeper took his victim away from the hive and set it on his board, then dissected it, using a very thin wire that had been sharpened to a needle point.

"Come a bit closer, m'lady, and you can just make out the poison sack behind the bulb end of the stinger. 'Tis a tricky business knowing who can tolerate bee venom."

"But how do you administer it?"

"Well now," the beekeeper stated with a grin, "there are two methods. The first takes a live bee, an' an angry one at that. Hurts, too. The next takes a bit more time, as you just witnessed, and more than a few bees to collect a droplet. The wife dilutes it with water afore application."

"My aunt mixes the venom into a balm," Trian piped in unexpectedly. He'd been so quiet that Claire had forgotten he was there, and she gazed at him in surprise. He cleared his throat before continuing. "It's less painful rubbing a balm into an ache than being stung, especially if the person is sensitive to such things. Although, my aunt has confessed that if the ache is strong enough, or the person overly difficult, a sting is more efficacious, not to mention more satisfying for the healer."

The keeper stood back and rubbed the whiskers on his chin. "Could be worth a try." He was so pleased to have gained this knowledge that he gave a crock of honey to both Claire and Trian by way of thanks. "The best honey in all of Aurelia," he boasted. Claire caught the amused twitch of Trian's lips. From their journey thus far, they had a collection of at least a dozen jars of the realm's best honey safely stored in the wagon.

She graciously thanked the farmer, offered a hasty farewell and some of her wildflower balm for his wife, and then she and Trian were riding to catch the others.

"My detour took longer than I anticipated. Should we not canter?" Claire suggested when Trian seemed content to keep a slow pace.

"They are not too far ahead, m'lady. And the Crown's Hart is but two hours away. We'll make the inn before nightfall."

It wasn't quite the answer that she'd sought, but the late afternoon was lovely, and keeping to a slower pace would ensure that she did not miss any chances to forage. "Is your aunt a healer, Trian?"

"My aunt? Oh, she only dabbles, m'lady. Her herb lore is not as extensive as yours. Aunt Cafellia has, er, other talents, and is a great advisor to my mother and father."

"She knows about bee venom. It's the first I've heard of it. How came you to be so familiar with the remedy? I imagine that the art of healing is not standard training for the Royal Guard."

Trian turned his gaze from the road ahead and focused on her. "Observation, m'lady," he replied, then turned back to the road.

In that brief instant, Claire had had the queerest feeling that she was about to swoon, for the very air about her seemed to shimmer. The steady hoof falls of their horses became a muted thudding; even the buzzing of insects seemed to cease. Only Trian's face had remained constant.

"May I beg a question of you, m'lady?" Trian asked, breaking the odd moment, and she nodded. "Why were you embarrassed when you gave the beekeeper your balm?"

"Why would you think—Oh, because I blushed." How could she explain about the importance of choosing a signature flower in her family?

"Your sister uses lavender in her recipe, does she not?" Trian asked.

"How did you...Yes, Anna prefers lavender. My mother liked roses, and my grandmother used lilac blooms. Each woman in our line must select a favorite."

"And you are not satisfied with your selection?"

"That, Trian, is my quandary. I have yet to choose."

He nodded at her as if he understood her predicament. "Seems a shame to limit yourself to just one."

All at once, Claire felt as if a great weight had been lifted from her shoulders. "Observation, indeed," she murmured to herself.

CHAPTER FIVE

Crossroads

Whitmarsh Castle and Onward to Stolweg

"The bolts of fabric have been divided and packed, Lady Claire. You were right about the mahogany velvet for Lady Anna. She'll be beautiful in that color." Claire was only half listening to Sarah. Her mind was on something else entirely.

"Lady Elnoura's maid helped me," Sarah chattered on. "It was right smart, the two of you buying together to get a better price in King's Glen." Sarah paused, and then her pretty brow creased with concern. "Are you all right, m'lady? Would you like me to fetch some tea?"

Claire smiled. "No, I'm fine, Sarah. Just eager to return to Stolweg."

"As you say, m'lady. I bid you a good night then." She gave a perfunctory bow, then yawned her way to her bed. Sarah was one of seven children who had been delivered to the safety of Stolweg after the destruction of Claire's home. Others from Chevring had joined the original seven survivors, men and women and children, those who lived farther afield from the castle, who were spared the treachery of her sister's first husband and the attacking forces from Nifolhad. One hundred and forty-three people and counting. A day did not pass that Claire did not watch for a messenger bringing news that another survivor had surfaced. Good to his word, King Godwin had sent men to rebuild her childhood home. The ringing of hammer and chisel against stone was a beacon of hope to the few still populating the territory of Chevring. Her territory, and her people, small in number though they were. For as her sister was now Lady of Stolweg, so Claire had inherited land and title at Chevring.

The coming reunion with Anna had Claire aching for the completion of this next leg of the journey. She missed her sister almost as much as she missed her new niece, baby Celeste. And being in familiar environs would allow her to relax the iron grip she had on her curse. King's Glen had been exhilarating, but hiding her secret had exhausted her. Except for Trian, Lord Baldric and his wife, and Sarah, Claire's daily interactions with others had been drastically curtailed. It'd been a relief. Unfortunately, the status quo was about to change.

That which had Claire preoccupied now was her additional escort. Upon arriving at Whitmarsh, they were greeted by none other than Warin. He'd traveled a rougher—albeit more direct—route and had beaten them by three days. Baldric had assigned him, along with Trian, to escort Claire and Sarah the remaining leagues to Stolweg.

A person need not be a seer to envision the idle banter and coquetry she would have to resume with him. The guard would no doubt wish to continue the conversation that had so closely touched upon her secret. Claire realized with regret that she would miss Trian's quiet ways. He had demanded neither wit nor wiles the few times they spoke.

A few days later, Sarah was fussing about the chamber, packing up their last few belongings while Claire studied her reflection in the looking glass. With her hair in a braid as tight as the hold she had on her curse, Claire tried to imagine how Warin might view her. At nineteen, she had grown as tall as Anna, and taller than many men. But Anna was the true beauty in the family, with her eyes lit with gold. Claire's own eyes were deep brown, and boring.

She shook her head and laughed at herself. Fine, she supposed that she was pretty. And the men on King Godwin's list of acceptable suitors—a list designed with Chevring's future in mind—could certainly do worse for a wife. It was just that she felt...she felt...

"Old," Claire reflected back at her own image. There, she'd admitted it. Her mother had been right in comparing her to Lady Beatrice, her grandmother. Ever calm; ever controlled; ever knowing what to do in any situation. Respectable. Reliable. An old soul. Those words had been used to describe Claire since she was a child. But when she studied her reflection and thought of the destruction of her home and the murder of her parents and friends, it seemed a thousand years of grief compounded in her gaze.

Her grandmother had once talked to her about loss, retelling the story of Claire's grandfather, a man who'd died decades before his wife. Theirs had been a great love. When Claire had asked her how she had survived it, her grandmother had put it simply: "When you lose someone who shares your heart, you wake each day, and pretend that you feel better. And even though you don't, you fake it. Then one day, you hurt a little less and understand that the person you've lost would want you to find joy again. I did. I found it in you and Anna."

Two years after the loss of her parents, Claire was still pretending. At least at court, she hadn't been alone in her superficiality. The flirting, the charades, the games; it was all a façade. As happy as she was to be reuniting with Anna, Celeste, and Lark, she was also steeling herself for heartache, because Claire was all too aware that she could not love a man the way Anna loved Lark. She wasn't as courageous as her warrior sister and would never risk it. The King's list of suitors, rather than making her nervous, was a comfort. An arranged marriage, one not founded in love, was all that Claire would ever dare to want.

"That's it, m'lady," Sarah said. The girl must've recognized the sadness in her mistress' eyes, because she reached for Claire and gave her a hug. The loss of family was a grief they shared, to be sure.

"Let us begin our journey anew," Claire said, and they departed the chamber they'd occupied at Whitmarsh Castle.

Too quickly, Claire bade Lady Elnoura and Lord Baldric goodbye. Sarah was once more comfortably ensconced in the wagon, and Warin and Trian stood by if Claire needed assistance with Rebel. For once, Warin left her to her thoughts as through the gates of Whitmarsh and over its fields and hills they passed, riding toward Stolweg.

More than a week later they came upon the Crossroads Inn. It sat at the juncture where the King's Road ended by forking into four separate routes. The northern branch led to Cathmara, cutting through the icy peaks of the Argelian Range, and the southern road led to the balmy clime of Pheldhain. Due west, their current route, was Stolweg. Claire looked to the southwest and sighed. That way led to Chevring. She tried to imagine taking that path and couldn't, although the King had assured her that not all was lost there. The castle's foundation was strong, and half and two of the walls yet stood. A curtain wall was being constructed, and an outer bailey planned.

A year, the King had promised, perhaps two, but no more, and Claire could return to her childhood home and assume her role as the Lady of Chevring. With the help of her sister, she would rebuild the breeding program which for generations had supplied Aurelia and its kings with war horses. For the first time though, the destriers would hail from not one, but two great houses: Chevring and Stolweg.

And with her return to Chevring, Claire would have to wed. Chevring required a lord as well as a lady. She forced herself to divert her eyes from Warin; he would be at the top of King Godwin's list of suitable husbands. Her regard chanced upon Trian. As she had been gazing to the southwest, so had his eyes traveled to the north and Cathmara. She wondered if he was pondering a love left behind.

CHAPTER SIX

The Inn

It had been Sarah who had persuaded Claire to sup in the common room. And Claire was glad for it, for she was having trouble shaking herself free of her melancholy. From what she could gather, the two guards who accompanied her were not strangers to the family who ran the establishment. What was more, while Trian was greeted warmly by the innkeeper, Warin was given only warnings. When the innkeeper's two daughters poked their heads around the corner to get an eyeful of the dashing guard, Claire understood why. The matter was put to rest when Warin seated himself next to her. He ignored the giggling girls no matter how hard they tried to capture his attention. Satisfied, the innkeeper marched away to arrange their meal.

"It appears that I will need your aid this evening, m'lady," Warin pleaded, "if I am to sleep with a roof over my head and food in my stomach."

"Does your reputation precede you?"

"Perhaps," he replied, "though it appears that Trian's does as well."

Claire turned her head and witnessed the two girls dragging Trian toward the head of the common room. "Let the man eat first," the innkeeper called to his daughters, "and then only if he agrees." Trian nodded congenially and made his way to their table.

"What was that about?" Sarah asked when he took a seat next to her. "They seem to know you well, m'lord."

"Not me, and not well," Trian replied. "Just my songs."

"Trian is the master of understatement," Warin touted. "It's not his songs; it's his voice. Any fool can put poem to tune. It takes an artist to give it life. Not that you can tell by looking at him, but Trian's singing could make an angel weep."

Trian looked uncomfortable with the praise, so Claire spoke in an effort to rescue him. "Pray, Trian, which song will you sing tonight?"

He opened his mouth to tell her, but Warin preempted him. "Another song about Cathmara, no doubt. Have you ever encountered a Cathmaran, Lady Claire? Other than Trian, of course." She shook her head. "A race of warriors all: men, women, and children alike. But every Cathmaran state has its tragic love story." Warin turned to Trian. "Is this one about a cliff, or a forest, or perhaps—?"

To his credit, Trian took Warin's jibes with grace. "Mountains," he cut in.

"Goodness, how can a song about mountains be a love story?" Sarah asked.

"In Cathmara, mountains abound," Trian explained. "But there are two that stand above all others: Scúr and Snáw. The song tells of how they came to be, and of the ice plains of Deighlei below them."

Before Warin could comment, the innkeeper arrived with their meal. Claire finished it quickly and, not wanting to appear rude, waited until Trian left the table to take his place near the hearth before trying to escape to her room. When Warin attempted to forestall her, Sarah rose and effectively blocked him. "M'lady, you must be exhausted. Let me help you to your chamber." Thank heaven for Sarah's interference.

They made their way through the crowded room. The Crossroads Inn was filled with travelers and locals alike, boisterous men and women talking and calling out to each other, rattling their plates and clanking their mugs. Claire doubted that anyone would hear Trian's quiet voice above the cacophony.

She had reached the landing where they had secured her sleeping quarters when the pipe and flute started. The entire room fell silent. She turned back just as Trian began his song, and sometime during the second verse, she sat upon the topmost step to listen.

'Twas in honeyed meadow he saw her fair
the bees about her waft and air
Of bronze and silk her hair seemed made
On such beauty his eyes had never laid

'Twas in honeyed meadow she lamented her fate
True love she waited, but lingered too late
Now pledged to one her heart maligned
Just sorrow and pain to hold and bind

'Twas in honeyed meadow he found her there
To know not her name, he could not bear
With care and caution more near he stepped
His heart did break for the tears she wept

'Twas in honeyed meadow her heart she found
Forgetting the one unholy bound
Together they fell 'twixt flowers and grass
And bespoke the love they'd found at last.

Trian's melancholy lyrics floated through the room, carrying such emotion that every person listened in hushed reverence. Claire couldn't drag her eyes away from him. Though he sang softly, the dulcet timbre of his voice brought life to his lyrics. She could almost see the meadow and hear the bees.

'Twas in honeyed meadow her betrothed did see
His promised bride with one more fair than he
More wicked than murder, far more worse
Upon their heads he placed a curse

But the heavens who made the sky and land
Had watched the lovers' fate be damned
Offended by hate, the husband they blighted
And improved his curse 'til love was righted

E'en now, o'er honeyed meadows they yet stand
Under cloud and sky, wait hand-in-hand
The one who cursed, entombed in ice is he
While their love stands true for eternity.

No sound was made, no scrape of knife on plate nor slosh of mead in flagon; only silence followed Trian's song. Claire watched as he returned to the table where they'd supped. Only Warin remained there, and before the noise of the inn resumed, Claire heard his words as he tilted his head in her direction. "And there's the angel."

She stood and turned before Trian could look her way, and noticed not that her kerchief, delicately embroidered with tiny blue and yellow forget-me-nots and damp from her tears, fluttered over the landing to the crowded floor below.

CHAPTER SEVEN

Sightings

Stolweg Keep

Claire surveyed the lush grasses growing all around. Earlier in the morning, within the curtain wall of Stolweg Keep, the vegetable plots had been weeded, the herbs trained in the manner that best suited their growth, and countless other tasks had been completed. She and her sister had packed a light meal and escaped the confines of the keep to ride out to where the horses were grazing.

Claire had not had a chance to wonder how the growing herd would be divided upon Chevring's completion, for Anna had made her intentions clear. As soon as the castle was habitable—meaning the stable was complete—the horses that had been displaced when Anna's first husband had destroyed Chevring would be returned to their place of origin. Claire would begin her role as the Lady of Chevring with no less than eight broodmares, two studs—including her Rebel—and all of their progeny.

Claire took a deep breath. She felt it before she heard it, and Anna's fingers tightened on her arm. A vibration traveled through the ground and up Claire's spine until her entire torso reverberated with it. Then the sound, like distant thunder, grew louder and louder until it seemed the ground would be rent open and thrown to the skies. She drew up her knees to set her chin upon them, wishing she'd removed her boots so she could feel the earth tremble through the soles of her feet. The rumble grew, and Claire followed Anna's gaze to the copse below them.

The herd galloped into view. A sight to behold they were, and when

Claire heard her sister laughing aloud with joy, she let loose the breath she'd been holding and joined her.

More than thirty horses poured into the valley. And when Rebel and Tullian beheld their brood, they snorted and stomped their hooves. Anna clicked her tongue, and Tullian shot off to join the herd. Claire did the same for Rebel, and together the two stallions shored up the equine flood.

"I'm so glad that Lark suggested this. It's just what we needed, you and I," Anna announced happily. "Still, Celeste—"

"—is perfectly fine with Lark. And Grainne. And Doreen," Claire stated, earning an elbow to the ribs. "You've been too long from the horses. Besides, you've been keeping Celeste all to yourself; Lark needs some father-daughter time."

"I realize that now, Claire. It's just that I never imagined that I could love anything more than the horses. Then I met Lark. And now we have Celeste. There was a time when I thought my life could be naught but what it had been with Roger. I sometimes can't believe how fortune has blessed me."

Claire took her sister's hand, and this time, she reached outside of herself and did something she normally avoided: she opened her mind, inviting a vision of her sister's fate. There was happiness and a growing family in Anna's future. "You'll be fine, Anna. You, and your family. I swear it to you."

"Oh, Claire! You didn't have to. You become so exhausted after—"

"Nonsense," Claire scoffed. She and Anna had talked about their legacies: Anna's fighting prowess and Claire's visions. Only the darker images Claire had seen had ever made her ill.

"Claire, just because you sense nothing of your own future doesn't mean you won't find someone with whom to share your life. You must have faith that you will find love just as I have. You only need heed Grandmother's advice and wait. I'll not let what happened to me with Roger happen to you. My oath upon it."

Anna rummaged through her bag, then withdrew a bundle of cloth. "A package arrived from court. From Queen Juliana, actually."

"What is it?" Claire took the log-shaped bundle.

"You'll see. The Queen's note said that it was time that it rejoined its siblings. But I believe they are too estranged to be reunited. Perhaps you could adopt this prodigal child. Go on, open it," Anna coaxed.

Claire set the bundle in her lap and untied the strings holding together the thick fabric. She lifted the folds away. "The missing dagger! Oh, Anna, by all rights, this belongs to you." But even as she spoke the words and held the blade, she felt how perfectly it fit her hand. Along both sides of the cross guard, in a bed of lapis lazuli, silver stars gleamed bright in the afternoon sun. The pommel was worn, and along the blade she detected the remains of some ancient writing.

"I already have Grandfather's dagger," Anna insisted. "I'd not part with it for all of my armor and weapons. And I can tell that you feel this blade. Its balance, its age, its—"

"—memories," Claire finished. She worried that Anna might think it an odd thing for her to say, but Anna grasped her meaning.

"I'm afraid its sheath is beyond repair," Anna added. "So the Queen promised to have one made by the royal tanner. He'll need the dagger back, so it'll be a month or so before you can wear it."

Claire held the beautiful blade in her hand and ran her fingers over the markings. "Did the Queen tell you what the runes signify?"

"She did, though she admitted that most of it has been worn away. But what remains is this: *with night do stars find strength.* Flip it over." Claire did. "This part is unclear," Anna continued, pointing to some partial runes on the blade. "She wrote that this symbol might represent the number six, and that this one—" she pointed again "—may indicate movement, or dance. Lark's mother may know more. Anyway, too much is missing to ever be sure."

Claire studied the markings, then wrapped the dagger in its cloth. Anna stood, putting her hands over her head and stretching. She let out two shrill whistles, and Tully and Rebel lifted their heads. "Let's get back to the keep," Anna suggested. "Doreen is baking her famous pasties!"

• • •

Warin had just stepped from the stables after his long ride through Stolweg. There was a nip in the late spring air, but it was not so cold that the evening was unpleasant. He stared up at the brilliant stars, procrastinating before finding Lark and Anna to report his findings. Earlier in the week, one of the foresters had observed riders in the western woods. Warin had volunteered to investigate but had sighted no one. And if any traces had been left, they'd been obliterated by the springtime storms.

He twisted at his waist and stretched his spine to shake off his saddle-bound stiffness. His findings, or lack thereof, could wait. He stepped into the keep by way of the kitchen and grabbed as many pasties as would fit in his hand. Doreen scowled at his theft, but laughed and shook her head after he gave a bawdy wink. He wasn't ready to meet with his friends in the great hall and so made his way to the battlements, wolfing down his meal in great bites along the way.

The sentry on duty was just passing by on his rounds atop the keep, and they nodded to one another. Warin paused when he saw someone standing near the parapet. Upon recognizing the lone figure peering at the dark landscape to the south, he stepped forward.

"Warin," she greeted pleasantly, as if expecting him, "I'm glad to see you safely returned."

"Claire," Warin answered, and took her hand in his to kiss her knuckles. She lifted her other hand to clasp his betwixt her two and studied him. Warin lost all awareness of his surroundings, transfixed as he was by her searching gaze. She released him, and the thin chain connecting them was broken. Her expression gave away nothing save the brief mix of disappointment and relief that flitted through her eyes. She'd come to a decision, Warin thought ruefully, one that did not involve him.

"'Tis not I, then." For a moment, he thought she might deny the truth of what he meant, then she sadly shook her head. A great student of history, Warin knew all about Claire and Anna's ancestors. Lady Anna was a conundrum in that she was both healer and warrior. But she lacked the one trait that had occasionally presented itself among her ancestors: the ability to foretell. He'd long suspected that this gift had gone to Claire.

"I'm disappointed to hear it," Warin confessed. "Do you know who?"

"No, I'm blind to my own fate, Warin. I always have been."

"Even so, it means much that you trust me with your secret. But are you sure? I—"

"I had hoped as well, for we've become good friends, haven't we?

But the fates have different plans for you, and I would not interfere with a love so great."

Warin gave her an incredulous look, and she smiled at him. "Oh yes, a love to rival that of Lark and Anna. But you'll lash out against it at every turn. In the end, you'll be so bound up by your own whip that you'll have no choice but to surrender."

Denial was impossible, Warin realized. What he desired most was what Anna and Lark shared. A love that would wipe away every meaningless tryst he'd ever had. He wanted to belong to someone. And Claire saw it all.

"But you'll find love too, m'lady," Warin assured her.

She looked away, then took his hand and led him from the battlements. "They'll be waiting for you in the great hall."

• • •

"What do you think, Lark? Could Prince Bowen have infiltrated our shores again? Warin found no evidence, yet he seemed unsettled."

"I think we're better off acting cautiously, rather than ignoring the possibility," Lark counseled. Anna came from behind the tapestry that divided the bathing area from their main chamber, finding him already abed. "We shouldn't risk riding out alone for the time being."

"I agree." She smiled when he raised his eyebrows at her. "What? I have a family now. You and Celeste have tempered some of my wild ways." He chuckled and patted the bed.

"Did you notice that Claire and Warin entered the hall together?" Anna mentioned, recalling the moment as she slipped under the blankets. Lark's body was so warm that she snuggled as close to him as she could. Her feet, cold from walking barefoot on the stone floor, rubbed against his, and she giggled at his sharp intake of breath.

"I wasn't paying heed." He sounded annoyed by the fact. Anna propped herself up on her elbow and studied her husband. He not only sounded vexed; he looked it as well. She ran her cold feet up his legs, and he mock shrieked.

"Out with it!" Anna demanded.

He grumbled and stalled until she put her hand tenderly to his cheek and made him gaze upon her. "If you know something, Lark…"

she started, then waited as patiently as she could. When he was not forthcoming, she tried threatening him. "My feet still need warming." She inched her toes up his thigh.

His shriek was in earnest this time, and he took one of her feet in his warm hands and began massaging the chill from it. "Just because Warin is at the top of Godwin's list," he began, "doesn't make him the best choice for your sister." Anna moaned when his fingers found a sensitive spot near the arch of her foot, and he concentrated his efforts there, making her moan again. "Others should be considered."

"Mmm." He had switched to her other foot. "Are you thinking of Tomas? He is too untried." Lark's clever fingers danced across the delicate bones of the top of her foot, and she thrilled at the heat growing in his dark eyes.

"Not Ailwen either, although I think highly of him," Anna barely managed to add, gasping in pleasure on the last word as Lark pressed his fingers deep into the muscles of her calf.

"You can't be considering Herlewin," she teased, aware of Lark's dislike for the greasy lordling. Lark's hands moved ever higher, and Anna all but wilted. "Ooh," she breathed. Her feet were no longer icy, and a delicious warmth spread deep within her.

"Who then?" she finally managed to ask, as his fingers sought to warm her more intimately. Lark growled and lifted her on top of him. She reached between them to massage him in kind. If he ever answered her question, Anna didn't hear.

CHAPTER EIGHT

Bloodline

Summer was unfolding around them, Claire realized. Her sister had finally settled into a routine, dividing her time between Celeste and the horses, and was much happier for it. And when, as they had now, the horses moved far enough from the keep to warrant camping under the stars, Claire stood in for Anna. It was good practice for Claire, as she would take half of their growing herd to Chevring.

The next foaling was not for several weeks, and Claire was able to focus on the abundance of flora around her. They now had dedicated storage at the keep for the roots, herbs, and minerals they collected. And although most of what they gathered was medicinal, Claire carried on the tradition her sister had started of reaping whatever foodstuffs could be found to add to Doreen's larder. Stolweg's stablehand, Will, was especially helpful, for Doreen was his mother, and he remembered where to find the asparagus patches he and Anna had once unearthed, and the old, long-forgotten fruit trees called pomerois. More important for Will was the discovery that Claire shared her sister's affinity for fishing.

"M'lady," Will interrupted, calling her back to the moment. "I thought we'd camp near the next stream tonight and see if any trout would like to join us for supper. I can show Pieter my favorite spots." Pieter was Sarah's older brother, and the stable boy who had fled Chevring with Claire more than two years past. He and Will had become fast friends.

Claire glanced over at Trian, who nodded. "Go ahead," she said. "While you're gone, I'll practice with my bow."

After their camp was settled, Claire checked on Rebel one last time before grabbing her bow and quiver. Passing by Trian's horse, she paused to study the handsome blood bay stallion. Being partial to the mottled gray of the Chevring breed did not leave Claire blind to the beauty of this red destrier. She ran her hands down the horse's muscled neck and admired the black points of his mane, tail, and fetlocks. The horse whickered almost silently, and Claire was reminded of Trian's quiet ways. She was curious if the nearly always dominant traits of Chevring steeds would win out if this horse were matched with one of her mares.

"His name is Culrua," Trian offered, appearing next to her as if from thin air. When Claire squeaked in alarm, he looked abashed. "My apologies, m'lady. I didn't mean to startle you."

"It's all right, Trian. I was lost in my own thoughts. And please, call me Claire."

"All right, Claire," he pronounced, as if her name were a foreign word and had never before passed his lips.

"He's beautiful," she observed. "Are all the horses of Cathmara so colored?"

"Most are," he replied. "Cathmarans like to keep to their bloodlines. Once in a great while, we'll recognize a trait in another that could enhance our strengths. Only then is an unconventional match made."

Behind her, Culrua shifted, bumping her so that she lost her balance. She tried to avoid colliding with Trian. Her ability to block unbidden visions had improved, but she wasn't sure if she would be able to stop one without preparing herself first. In the past, all it had taken was a simple touch, and she would swoon.

But there was no help for it; Trian had already reached out to steady her. Claire squeezed her eyelids shut and waited. She inhaled deeply, and caught the scent of dust and leather and horses. A distant memory teased the edges of her mind, with it came a feeling of calm and safety.

Claire opened her eyes and blinked. Nothing had happened. She gripped his bare wrist—skin touching skin—and concentrated. Not a single image to foretell his fate. He was studying her with concern, and she smiled, breathing a sigh of relief. "Thank you, Trian," she said, and excused herself to practice her shooting, leaving him to wonder after her.

CHAPTER NINE
Observation

The next morning broke crisp and fresh. Claire stood outside her tent and stretched. She was no longer a stranger to sleeping on the ground, but much preferred her comfortable bed at the keep. Will was busy stoking the fire. Pieter sat beside him spearing trout with water-soaked skewers made from the branches of a nearby poplar. Trian had suspended a buck, one he had downed the evening before, from a high branch to keep it from nighttime predators. He wasn't in the clearing, and Claire wondered what task had taken him away so early.

She considered her chores for the day; the killing of the deer added greatly to her duties. She waved to Will and Pieter when they noticed her, then made her way to the stream. Cattails were growing there, and it wouldn't take long to weave a few simple mats that she could use to wrap the butchered venison. She hadn't expected to bring home anything more than what they'd foraged and fished for, else she would have packed salt to keep the meat from turning.

She stepped into the shallows, bending down to scoop the refreshing water to splash on her face and neck. After she dabbed her skin with her handkerchief, she picked her way across the stream to where the cattails grew and drew the small knife she kept handy. One by one she cut at the leafy blades, tossing them neatly upon the bank until she deemed that she'd collected enough. When she straightened, she peered into the trees and saw Trian walking toward her, still some twenty paces away. He lifted his hand in greeting. His pace was brisk, and Claire tried to detect a snap of twig or a rustle of plant. She heard not a sound. Even more interesting was that he seemed to make no effort to be silent.

"Good morning, Claire," he stated, then extended his hand to help her up the bank. Claire hesitated before taking it, worried that she might sense something. But the absence of visions that had occurred the day before proved steady. Trian's grip was strong and warm, and when he released her hand, a faint lemony scent hung in the air. He espied her pile of cattail blades and nodded appreciatively. "We're of a like mind," he noted. "I came here ready to harvest this lot for the venison, and you've already done the work."

They stepped into the shallow streambed together, her boots splashing through the water, while Trian's long strides sliced through the current, making nary a swish. "How do you do it?" she asked, after they climbed the opposite bank. "How do you move so silently?"

"It would be easier if I showed you. Close your eyes."

Claire hesitated.

"If you want to learn, you'll have to trust me."

She searched his face for some ulterior motive, but only found a steady frankness staring back at her. She closed her eyes.

"Everywhere you go," he started, "I watch how you scan the landscape, seeking useful plants and roots. Think for a moment, then tell me about the flora that grows near the water."

"But..." Claire started to open her eyes, then stopped. In her mind, she retraced her steps to the stream. "Cattails, of course. Duck weed, fiddle-fern. Watercress, and scorpion's tail, and lemongrass. And..." Claire concentrated for a moment. "And mistletoe." She opened her eyes and peered up into the loftiest branches of the oak tree, pointing to the dark green ball of dense foliage. She wished she hadn't mentioned the last; it was customary in Chevring to kiss under mistletoe. Perhaps it wasn't the same in Cathmara. The brief moment when Trian's eyes met hers confirmed that their two regions shared the tradition.

Trian cleared his throat. "Good. You need only expand your vision to more than plants. Now, close your eyes again," he commanded, and she did as instructed. "Tell me, Claire, what color are my eyes?"

Claire frowned.

"No, keep your eyes shut," he pressed, when she began to open them. "Try to remember; you were just looking at them. Go back through our conversation, picture my expression."

"But, I wasn't..." she started, then stopped. "Brown," she said at last. "Light brown. Like the color of dried mud, only softer. And ringed with dark gray." Claire opened her eyes to check her answer, but he had closed his eyes as well. She felt like a thief as she studied his face, noting for the first time the chiseled jaw hidden beneath his full beard. His forehead was high, and his brow was strong but not overbearing. His hair was the color of sand, and a shade lighter than that on his face. His locks fell in long, shaggy waves around his head. There were two, no, three tightly woven locks of hair threaded with dyed strings matching the greens and browns of the forest. Warin had once told her that the different colors reflected a Cathmaran man's eligibility in regards to marriage.

Trian's eyes remained closed as she continued her perusal of him. She discerned now that his eyelashes were quite long, but one couldn't tell at first glance as they were so light at the tips. His skin was smooth, and already his nose and cheekbones were dusted with a light coating of freckles from the early-summer sun. Claire desired suddenly to know what the green and brown strings in his hair signified and if he was promised to another.

"Your eyes are brown as well," Trian echoed softly, his eyes yet shut, and Claire drew back her hand when she became conscious that she'd been about to touch one of the strands. "Like the color of oak leaves in the winter—those too strong to let go of their bond with the branch— and deep and warm. And, I'm guessing, they're open." He opened his own eyes then, and smiled.

She'd been wrong. "Not dried mud, but the dun color of a doe's hide in winter."

"I prefer mud," he said and chuckled. He set the bundled cattails on the ground. Then, placing his hands on her shoulders, he turned her around. "Now, study the trees, the rocks in the streambed, the foliage on the ground, everything."

"But what has this to do with moving silently?" She was much too aware of his hands resting warmly on her shoulders. He laughed again, and she decided that she liked the richness of the sound.

"The key is observation. The streambed is cobbled with large round stones, but there is sand too, soft and quiet: your feet can glide over sand and sluice through the water; but over the stones, you must step and splash. Now look ahead, where the oak stands. Though it is not yet the solstice, some leaves litter the ground. Crackling. Better to step wide of the canopy. To the left, a bed of ferns. Along our path's edge, moss grows—"

It was Claire's turn to laugh. "All right, all right. I get it. Observation."

"Close your eyes and tell me what else you notice. What do you hear?"

She did. She opened her mind to all that surrounded her. Behind her, the stream gurgled and splashed, drowning out everything else. But when she concentrated and filtered out the watery voice, there was more. "Insects," she noted, "crickets and flies. And there's a breeze; I can hear the leaves moving above us." She took a deep breath and caught the smell of the freshly cut cattails. The lemony scent still lingered in the air. "I smell wild thyme." She opened her eyes. "So, that is what you were doing this morning: collecting herbs for preserving the venison."

He nodded. "In Cathmara, we are taught to scrutinize everything around us even before we are taught our letters. This is your first lesson: observation. By the way," he asked, picking up the cattails, "what is scorpion's tail? You mentioned it earlier."

Claire pointed to a shady spot near the bank of the stream. "There. The tiny blue flowers with yellow centers. You can use the leaves for nosebleeds and eye infections. It's also called forget-me-not," she remarked, though she couldn't imagine why it embarrassed her to tell him the more common name. Who cared if there were ridiculous stories of romance attached to the delicate bloom? Trian seemed unaware that she was blushing and had looked to where the forget-me-not was grow-ing before returning his attention to her.

He next challenged her to walk as quietly as possible back to the camp, but to do so naturally and without a halting gate. Together they started down the path that would lead them to the clearing. Trian held to the side where the moss grew, and Claire followed as silently as she was able. He pointed to a newly fallen tree along their way. "There are sure to be dried twigs on the ground; search for the larger clues that hint at the smaller details."

Claire was beginning to understand why Trian was quiet more oft than not. It was not that he had so little to import, but rather that he could learn so much more by simply taking in everything around him. And when she was sitting in the camp, weaving her mats, Claire watched Trian carve the venison into portions they could carry back to the keep. She was looking forward to her next lesson and wondered impatiently when it would begin.

CHAPTER TEN

Loveroot

Claire woke before daybreak and absorbed the silence enshrouding the camp. A soft mist had rolled into their clearing, muting the already dim colors. Above her, there was a flutter of wing, a rustle of leaf. And over the steady *tick-tick-tick* of a wood beetle tapping out its song, she could hear the stretching of limbs as Will and Pieter stirred from their slumber. Trian's bedding had been packed, and he was nowhere to be seen. Claire rolled her blankets, collected her saddlebags, and then quietly stepped down the mossy edge of the path to the stream to wash away the last vestiges of the night. By the time she returned to the clearing, her tent had been dismantled, and Rebel had been saddled for her. He stood patiently next to Culrua and the other mounts. Their ears pivoted toward a break in the trees, and Trian strode into the campsite. Claire wondered how the horses had sensed him.

She understood then, as she walked toward Rebel, that Trian was a different man than she had first imagined. She had once believed him to be shy. The truth was that Trian carried himself with an air of gentle confidence and grace. He neither boasted nor complained. Claire would wager that his burly appearance was a veneer, and that underneath the leather and the beard and the padded tunic was a strong and lean-muscled man. Disguising one's true self was something that she could appreciate.

She clicked her tongue, and Rebel lifted his head and walked to where she waited. Slipping her foot into the high stirrup, she pulled herself up and into her saddle. The others followed her lead and, together, they pushed the herd toward Stolweg, Will and Pieter providing companionable chatter along the way.

As the morning passed, the day grew warm. When Claire stopped

to forage, Trian would wait, and she rediscovered that she quite enjoyed his company. Once, after she stooped to pick some herb, he asked what it was.

"Horsetail," she told him. "The stems, when stripped and properly prepared, can be used to staunch bleeding."

Over a patch of bee balm, she informed him that not only could the leggy plant's stems and leaves slow blood flow, they helped to reduce fevers as well. It became their habit to discuss the various uses of each herb and wild flower that she picked. Trian's memory was extraordinary, and soon he was helping her to carry that which they reaped.

Claire espied a patch of loveroot and reined in Rebel to dismount. When Trian questioned whether the herb was used for fevers or for wounds, Claire laughed. "No, not loveroot, Trian. It helps with digestion and, well, flatulence. It's sweet tasting; Doreen sometimes uses it in her cakes. Here, try some."

He cast a dubious gaze her way before chewing on a stem.

"It's excellent for cleaning teeth, too," Claire added.

Trian bent down to pick a few stalks for himself. When he noted her grin, his cheeks bloomed red. "For my teeth!" he swore.

"Of course," she humored him, then laughed. "I believe you!"

When she was not instructing him on plant lore, he told her of his home and the six Cathmaran states. He spoke of the silver reeds lining the banks of the Argel River. And of the great Bradenweg which cut through the heart of his family's lands.

Interlaced into each state's details were the stories of what Trian held closest to his heart: his family. He spoke especially fondly of his sister Adara, and of her upcoming marriage to a noble son of Marach.

"So, I will be leaving Stolweg soon," Trian explained as they rode under the archway of the keep's gate, "for my sister's wedding."

Claire found herself already missing the rides they would have shared.

CHAPTER ELEVEN

Rainbow

More than a month had passed since Trian had journeyed to Cathmar. Before his departure, he'd challenged Claire to learn how to walk as silently as he. She was trying her hand at it on Warin. Tasked with decorating the courtyard for the summer solstice celebration, they had dismounted to take some cuttings of the wild dog roses that grew along the tree line of the valley. Warin was twenty paces away, cursing at the thorny roses.

Claire's plan was to come up behind him undetected. The tall grasses that grew along the wood's edge would bestow no more silence to her step than a pile of dried leaves. So she waited and listened until she could discern the patterns of the breeze. The trees across the valley would stir and creek, then the grasses would undulate, sweeping in a circle like liquid swirling in a bowl. She would use the susurration of the grasses to mask her passage. She moved, and moved again, and moments later, she stood within an arm's reach of her friend.

When he cursed anew, she smiled. "Do we have enough weeds, m'lady?" he shouted.

"I imagine we do." He whirled around in surprise.

"How…You were…" he sputtered, then gritted his teeth. "Trian!"

"I don't know what you are talking about, Warin."

"Right. He's been teaching you, hasn't he? Tell me that it makes you happy, Claire, and I'll not say another word."

"It does," she answered honestly, taking his hand and plucking a thorn from his thumb. "And I do believe that we have enough *flowers* for the courtyard."

"Agreed," Warin stated, sounding relieved.

As they rode back to the keep, Claire catalogued their bounty:

soft blue hyssop and the brooding indigo of salvia, white-blossomed shepherd's purse, the pale pink dog rose and the vibrant red bee balm, and finally, the startling glow of goldenrod. Counting off the colors on her fingers, she found only purple lacking. Warin sneezed, and Claire remembered the large bundles of lavender he'd collected for Anna.

Perched on her saddle, she was surrounded by a halo of blooms. She felt like a bumblebee laden with pollen, except her cargo was a rainbow. Warin had refused to hang the bouquets on his saddle, and instead took hold of the sacks containing the fern cuttings and his bane, the thorn-armored dog rose.

When they returned to the keep, Claire hung the cords holding the bouquets about her shoulders. Warin followed her into the castle, holding the two sacks, and most of the lavender. Anna was in the great hall and looked up and gaped at the picture Claire presented. Warin set down his load and beat a hasty retreat.

"We've brought you some lavender, Anna."

"It looks like you found more than lavender."

"It's all for tonight. Most of it anyway. Some I'll need to keep for myself."

"Oh, Claire, are you finally choosing your flower? Do you know which it will be?"

"All of them!"

"That's a wonderful idea."

"It wasn't actually mine," Claire admitted. "You should have been there, Anna. All of those colors, mixing and shifting, and I recalled someone once telling me that it was a shame that I could only choose one. Do you think Mother would've approved?"

"She probably would have suggested it herself. Do you need help carrying them?" Anna offered as they were leaving the hall. "You're quite lost in all of those bouquets."

"No, I have them," Claire gratefully declined. She raced down the corridor and up the stairs, and as she turned a corner, one of the bindings loosened, and the hyssop scattered to the floor. No sooner did she stoop to pick up the wayward stems than the bouquet of lavender spilled. She was on her knees picking up two bunches instead of one when the shepherd's purse and bee balm slipped. Claire let fall a curse.

A pair of leather boots appeared unexpectedly before her, and she

cursed again. Before she could look up, two large hands reached down and started collecting the lavender. She sat back on her heels, a rosy blush coloring her cheeks, and stared into the face of Trian. His gaze locked with hers for a brief moment before he turned his attention to the hyssop. Her heart beat a little faster, and she concentrated on gathering the other flowers.

He stood, holding out his hand to help her to her feet. She took it and was fascinated by how small her fingers appeared in his. King Godwin's list came to mind, and she blushed again. Trian handed her two rescued bouquets adeptly tied together, not a single stem bruised.

"I did not think you would return until after the solstice. Your sister is betrothed, is she not?"

"She was," he corrected. "She and Logan made their vows a couple weeks ago. Weddings in Cathmara are simple affairs. It is the betrothals that are tricky." Then he bowed to her and, without speaking another word, continued on his way.

A feeling that Claire could not name fluttered in her chest. "Trian?" she called. He turned around. "I—I mean, well, thank you."

"I am entirely at your disposal."

And his voice, over a month absent from her ears, plucked at some chord within her. Before she could stop herself, she plunged forward, even taking a step closer to him. "You'll be at the celebration this eve?"

"Will you?"

"Yes," she replied breathlessly.

"Then I will be sure to attend, m'lady."

• • •

Trian couldn't keep his eyes from the flower-bedecked archway that would serve as the entrance to the courtyard. For once, he ignored everything around him save the anticipated arrival of the woman he hoped to wed. He risked a glance at his fellow guards.

There stood Lark—now Lord of Stolweg. And Warin and Ailwen. Then there was Tomas, the dashing angel-faced guard who seemed intent on taking Lark's place with the ladies at court. Trian let loose a quiet oath thinking on King Godwin's damnable list. He had a little over a year to make himself indispensable to Claire. He'd been lucky thus far in that he'd had no competition from the others. Warin was around, true, but it seemed to Trian that his friendship with Claire was just that—a friendship. Chevring Castle would soon be habitable, and then Claire's hand would be sought by every eligible nobleman in Aurelia. A grumbling, discontented sound emanated from deep within his chest. There was little hope that Claire would woo him when she had no inkling of the customs of Cathmara.

His view of the flowered archway was suddenly blocked by the others who had congregated there. He growled a curse in his Cathmaran dialect, for he'd missed Claire's entrance, and the other guards had not.

Warin made it to her first, and Trian could see by his gestures that he was asking her to dance. He nodded to her once, bowed, and as Claire slipped past him, put his arm around Tomas's shoulder and steered the young guard away.

Wondering at Warin's motives and disgruntled that the evening had not gone as planned, Trian decided that he might as well eat. Reaching for a slice of bread, he was surprised to find another vying for the same piece. He looked up from the buffet and into the eyes of Claire. She smiled at him, and he relinquished his claim. She tore the piece in half and offered him a portion. Trian set it aside, no longer hungry, and watched as she did the same.

She was even more beautiful than usual this evening. Her hair was pulled back from her face, but was left unplaited to swing free down her back. Here and there tiny blue and yellow blossoms had been artfully woven into her tresses: forget-me-nots. As if he ever could. Not once did Trian ever think he could love anyone but Claire, not since carrying her from the Royal Hall when she'd fainted all those years before. Her eyes flitted to his before she looked back at the table.

She was shy, Trian realized with a jolt. Her outward confidence, her need to control everything and everyone, was misdirection. He doubted that anyone had guessed, not even her sister. A sprig of forget-me-not was coming loose, and he couldn't help himself. He reached out and lifted one of her tresses, pushing it behind her ear. The bloom fell free, and he caught it without her notice.

This was going to be agony, Trian grumbled to himself, for he wasn't allowed to ask her outright if she would dance. He couldn't even invite her to sit and eat with him. He smothered a curse, deciding to fashion some compliment on how nice the decorations were, when he felt her hand on his arm.

"Will you dance with me, Trian?" Hope welled in his heart, and he took her hand in his and led her to the dancing area.

CHAPTER TWELVE
Out of Nothing

Claire lingered in the courtyard after the last of the revelers had departed, and then began picking up empty platters and stacking them neatly on the banquet table. It was hours past midnight, but the summer air was sweet and mild, and Claire was of a mind to be useful. Nearby, Trian was collecting empty mugs and cups. It had been a wonderful evening.

"I think we've done all that we can for tonight," Trian announced, striding toward her.

The stars above were bright, and to the east, the sky was deep purple. "It'll be dawn soon," she noted, and Trian followed her gaze as she lifted her eyes to the battlements. He hadn't taken the hint, so she pressed forward. "Would you like to watch the sunrise with me?"

"I can think of nothing I'd rather do." He held out his arm to her and led her to the battlements where they could watch the eastern sky from high atop the tower. The world was perfectly still below them, and they waited for the moment when the sun's rays would wake the land. Trian had placed his hand on hers, and the warmth of it reached her heart.

"Claire, what were you thinking about when you took my arm earlier? You held your breath. It happened again just now, when I touched your hand."

She turned to him. "I was only thinking that it is so easy to be near you. I don't need to prepare myself, or…" She was going to say put up her defenses. "…or do anything."

"Because of your abilities."

"But how—" she started. "Never mind, I know. Observation." He smiled, and a sudden breathlessness came over her, one that had nothing to do with her visions.

"And you see nothing when you touch me?" He had turned so that they stood toe to toe.

"Nothing at all."

"And this only happens with me? No one else?"

"Just with you." She found herself leaning closer to him. "No visions, no dizziness, nothing. I feel absolutely nothing when I touch you." He started to turn away. "Well, *nothing* is not quite the right word." On an impulse, she stood on her toes and gave him a quick kiss. She'd never kissed anyone before and wasn't sure if she had done it properly.

"That's at least something," he whispered, stepping even closer. Her heart lodged itself somewhere between her chest and her throat. "But I'd like to kiss you properly now, just to make sure."

"Make sure of what?"

"Mmm," he murmured. "To make sure that what you feel is more than nothing." Without waiting for her to respond, he leaned forward and brushed his lips against hers.

This kiss wasn't the quick peck she'd given him. His was a proper kiss. Claire reached up to cradle his cheek. She'd wanted to for so long. His beard was soft against her palm. Her head tilted, and her lips parted. He kissed her lightly at first, taking his time. Then he pulled her against him, and all she could feel was the hard expanse of his chest against her bosom. When his tongue finally courted hers, Claire surrendered completely to the embrace. Their kiss deepened, and a terrific heat grew inside her. She felt, for the first time, desire. She belonged with Trian, her own resistance to love be damned.

She would have gone on kissing him if he hadn't eased back. She gazed up at his face and was unembarrassed and proud that her boldness had brought them together. His hair was disheveled, and she giggled upon realizing that it had been the work of her hands. She smoothed it for him, and he grinned at her.

"We missed the sunrise," he noted, turning them back to face the horizon, his arm around her.

"There'll be others."

"I hope so," he said softly, and Claire felt that fluttering in her chest again.

• • •

The Eastern Shore of Kantahla

Prince Bowen gave his steed an appreciative pat on his neck. Of late, he'd become restless, riding out in the morning to await the rising of the sun. Somewhere out there, nearly due east, was Ragallach, the place his mother had been born, birthed his younger brother, and then died. Bowen now understood that his hatred for Roger had been misplaced. It wasn't Roger's fault that their mother had died and that Bowen had never had the chance to meet her. No, Bowen had finally come to discover, the fault lay entirely at Diarmait's feet.

And now that Roger was dead, Bowen regretted that he'd never given his brother a chance. The last time he'd seen Roger alive, he'd been bent on taking the glory of their Aurelian conquest from his brother's naïve hands. A day later and Roger had lost his lands and his life.

The blackness of the eastern sky was yielding to the inevitable, and the prince's eyes tracked slightly south to where he calculated Stolweg lay. The sun was probably lighting the towers of the great keep he'd once tried to conquer. And remembering the massive fortress, his mind turned to the hellion, Lady Aubrianne, and how she had unseated him in front of Phelan and their men.

Diarmait wanted her to pay, Bowen's spies had reported to him. And when the Steward King was finished using her, only then would he give his discards to his son. But Bowen had a better torture in mind for the lady. She had a younger sister, one that his dead brother had believed that Bowen and his men had used and then killed. Bowen knew otherwise; the young woman had escaped his clutches. "Lady Aubrianne's sister for the life of my brother," he vowed to the sunrise. The words had become his daily pledge.

CHAPTER THIRTEEN
Concealment

"Claire," Anna demanded, "what in the world are you wearing?"

"My new riding clothes. Why?" She smoothed her hands down the front of her tunic, and then adjusted the panels covering her wide-legged breeches.

"New? But the fabric is so faded. Surely—" Her sister stopped talking and grinned. "You wouldn't by any chance be riding with Trian today?"

It had taken Claire a week to fashion her new riding habit. Dull tones of brown and muted green fabrics, all cut from her oldest garments. "And if I am?" Claire had told Anna only a little of what Trian had been teaching her.

"As long as you stop sneaking up on me, I approve. You haven't been this happy in a long time, Claire. It warms my heart."

Claire paused in what she was doing. "I am happy," she assured her sister. "I only wish…"

"Only wish what?"

"It's only that…Well…Trian isn't…" Claire heaved a great sigh. "We don't seem to be progressing, if you follow what I'm trying to say."

"Yes, I see your problem."

"Was Lark very tentative with you?"—Anna snorted—"So, how can I tell Trian that I'm not going to shatter?"

"Perhaps you should show him instead," Anna advised. "However, as your older sister, I have to—"

"You don't have to worry about me, Anna. You know that Trian would never hurt me."

"I do, Claire. Now go," Anna ordered, pushing her out of the chamber. "Quickly, before Lark returns and sends Pieter with you."

Claire slipped out of the castle and across the courtyard. Trian was waiting for her in the stables, holding the reins to Rebel and Culrua. He examined her top to bottom, and Claire felt a flush spread all the way to her toes. They mounted and headed to the keep's smaller gate, the one that would take them over the bridge spanning the Stolweg River, across the fields and toward the western forest. But Trian turned north, and set their direction to the gray, stone-littered slopes that were the foothills of the Northern Range.

He had informed her that the next lesson would be in concealment and instructed her to choose a riding outfit that would blend in with her surroundings. Claire frowned. The green and brown of her habit would mark her as far away as the keep against the ash colored hills. At least Rebel would blend in.

She'd not ridden this way before and she studied the looming landscape. What appeared to be a narrow strip of green along the water's far bank was, in fact, a wide swath of both marshland and fertile grass declivities. The entire area was crisscrossed with rills, springs, and rivulets. From these little waterways cutting through the gray slopes of crushed rock beyond, deep, hidden gullies were created, each running at angles to the Stolweg before joining with the great river.

Trian led them into one such ravine, and Stolweg Keep disappeared from view. If someone were watching them from the battlements, it would appear as if she and Trian had vanished into thin air. The course they followed ended at a spring of clear water edged with gorse. Trian dismounted and tethered his horse in the tangle of the yellow-flowered shrub.

Claire waited for him to help her to dismount, though they both knew she was capable of climbing down herself. Trian reached up for her, and Claire felt again the whisperings of desire, the excitement that grew at his being so near. He lowered her to stand in front of him, and slid his hand to the small of her back, drawing her closer until their bodies met. He leaned in to kiss her, letting his lips dally, allowing the heat to slowly build between them. She wanted more from him than just kissing; her body yearned for it, but he seemed determined to not take advantage. And when Claire felt him pulling away, she reached up and held his face in her hands, needing more.

His face was a mask of patience, but his eyes betrayed his raw emo-

tions and smoldered with passion. "Trian," she whispered, "I want—"
Her words were cut off as he bent his head back to hers in a ravishing
kiss. She felt his fingers in her hair, pulling her head back and exposing
her neck. Slowly, he broke off, but his lips lingered against hers. She slid
her hands down to his broad chest and felt his heart beating as wildly
as her own.

Then, as his lips traveled from hers, she closed her eyes and gave
herself up to the sensation of his mouth and tongue on her jaw, behind
her ear, down her neck and across her collarbone. Claire pressed herself
willingly against him, her breasts aching to be cupped. No sooner had
this desire entered her thoughts than he did just that. She shuddered and
let go a soft gasp as his fingers sought to mold themselves to her shape.
His lips seared a path down her throat, stopping where the neckline of
her chemise covered the cleft between her breasts. Claire moaned and
held his head against her. He growled her name and lifted his head, as
if fighting to drag himself away. Their hearts raced, and he touched his
forehead to hers, withdrawing once again from the heat created by their
kiss. But why stop, she wondered?

Claire opened her mouth, to say what, she didn't know. How could
she tell him she wanted more, that she was ready to give herself to him?
Her feelings for him frightened and seduced her at the same time. Could
she tell him that she was falling in love when he had not said the words
himself? It maddened her that in the one instance she would give anything to read another's fate, she was blind.

"Claire?" Trian breathed, her name on his voice sounding like a
thousand questions. So she gave him the answer she assumed he wanted
to hear. She smiled, hiding her inner turmoil, and gazed up at him.

"Concealment, then," he began.

She nodded—at least she thought she did—and stepped away. He'd
told her what the day's lesson involved, and she took in the area to which
he'd brought her. "The colors I'm wearing won't help me one fig."

"The colors are perfect," Trian reassured her. "Look around. I
brought you to this spot for a reason."

Claire studied the shallow spring, more a puddle than a pool. It
made nary a gurgle as it flowed over its rim and cut a winding path in its
quest to join the Stolweg. She followed the water and tracked the prints
made by wild animals. Mixed in with them, the recognizable imprints

of shod hooves. "Two days old," she guessed. The mud around the hoof prints was thick and viscous, and dark like the earth girding the spring. "How much time do I have?"

"I'd say a little over an hour before Lark's men come through here. There'll be two of them if they keep to their regular rounds. Oh, and plain sight, Claire," he added, his eyes afire with mischief. "Also, that large growth of scrub over there is mine; it's not enough cover for us both."

She had little time, using everything Trian had taught her, to hide herself in the open with enough skill to fool two seasoned soldiers whose only task was to take note of anything out of the ordinary. She narrowed her eyes at Trian, and he winked at her, then began to erase the traces of their tracks. An outrageous idea came to her as she stared at the mud around the spring.

After Trian led the horses away to conceal them, Claire stripped off her tunic, her boots and her breeches. Clothed in only her chemise, she re-plaited her hair into several uneven sections, twisting and securing them in misshapen balls on her head. She sighed, looking at the muck and detritus near the spring, but then set about her task with frightening speed, scooping up stones and setting them closer to the edge of the pool. She lowered herself behind them and began layering on coat upon coat of mud to cover herself.

. . .

Claire heard the soldiers well before they came into view. Sometime after she'd finished disguising herself, Trian had returned. He'd signaled to her, using one of the many calls he'd taught her, but Claire did not respond. Instead, she held perfectly still, nearly buried along the muddy edge of the spring under the bordering gorse. A few well-placed branches concealed the telling lines of her hip and shoulder. The random knobs she'd made of her now mud-covered hair resembled the rocks strewn about the area.

The men were almost upon her, and Claire slowed her breathing in anticipation. If she were lucky, they would pass by without stopping.

One man, however, dismounted near the pool. He lowered his water bag into the now settled spring, refilling it not three paces from

Claire's face. She held her breath when, staring at a spot just above her head, his eyes began to narrow.

"Come on, let's go," his partner called. "We want to return to the keep before the moon rises. If I heard the stable lads correctly, Cook is making meat pies for supper."

"I'd almost forgotten," the soldier replied and, after searching the slope behind the spring one last time, walked back to his horse. He mounted, and they rode away, unaware that Claire had been under their noses.

Claire let go of the breath she'd been holding, but remained still. From behind the scrub, Trian turned around and stood a few feet away, staring at where the two men had disappeared. He walked to where Claire was hidden and, hands on hips, he threw his head back and roared with laughter.

Claire started giggling and felt the dried mud cracking on her face. Trian stretched out his hand to her. She grasped it, pulling herself free of the sucking mud.

"I assumed you would simply cover yourself in dust and hide in the shadows over there." He pointed to the western rim of the gulley where the sun was beginning its descent. "It took me a while to realize that you were right below me. I didn't expect them to linger, and they would have seen you when they stopped had you hidden under the ridge."

"What gave me away?" Claire asked as he helped her to stand.

"Even covered in mud, you smell of wildflowers." He kissed the tip of her dirty nose. "Come on, I have something to show to you. You'll be able to wash there." As he retrieved her clothing from where she had hidden it under some brush, she rinsed off her legs before pulling on her boots. Her long chemise, now weighted down by a thick layer of mud, fell nearly to her knees.

They walked for twenty minutes or so, down one gulley and up another, until they came upon a broad ravine wherein a stand of aspen grew. Trian had brought their horses here, and Rebel nickered at the sight of her.

He led her past the trees, then stopped, and her eyes widened. "A hot spring!" She threw her mud-encrusted arms around Trian's neck in a quick embrace. Before he could say a word, she bent to remove her boots. In just her chemise, she slipped into the warm depths.

It was heavenly, hotter than any bath she'd ever had, and Claire sank gratefully under the surface, gently teasing the mud from her skin and hair. When she came up for air, she stretched her toes and could just touch the bottom. The basin measured almost ten feet in diameter, and she submerged herself and swam to where Trian stood grinning down at her. He squatted and began picking out the stubborn bits of mud from her long hair.

"You're a beautiful mess." He chuckled as he removed his boots and rolled up the legs of his breeches before sitting at the edge of the spring. Claire supported her weight by slipping her arms over his outstretched legs.

"When did you find this place?"

"About a month ago. I don't think anyone's been here before. Few come this far past the northern bank of the river. The area is riddled with springs, some hot, some ice cold, others full of sulfur and gas. But none are as nice as this, or have such lovely fish."

Laughing, Claire pushed away from him, dousing his lap with water as she swam across the pool. Finding a submerged ledge, she pulled herself up, leaving her shoulders just visible under the water. Across from her, Trian stripped off his tunic and shirt; as she'd always suspected, he was lean and muscled. He slipped into the water.

The waning sunlight glazed the pool to a mirror finish, and Claire couldn't locate Trian as he swam underwater to her. She waited, her anticipation growing. And still he did not come up for air. The warmth spreading through her had nothing to do with the temperature of the spring. A minute slipped by, and unable to resist, she too submerged herself. She sank into his arms just as he came up, and when they broke the surface, their lips were already sealed together in a passionate kiss.

She ran her hands over the hard planes of his chest and the corded muscles of his shoulders. His skin was not yet heated by the spring and felt cool under her fingertips. She floated, held as she was in his embrace, the gentle currents bumping her against his body, then frustratingly away again. She reached out with one leg, hooking it around his thigh to anchor herself.

"Claire," Trian swore, dragging her tighter against him. He turned and sought out the ledge while pulling her onto his lap. "Claire," he growled again, holding her face in his hands and giving her a kiss so passionate that her bones felt as if they'd turned to silt and were drifting away. Then, he moved his hands lower to caress her through her shirt.

Trian grazed his teeth along her neck, then lifted her breast high as he bent his head to take her in his mouth. She moaned, and tried to touch him, but her hands got caught in the fabric of her chemise as it floated between them. She wanted to feel his mouth on her bare skin, not through the sodden linen. "Please, Trian," she begged him.

His mouth and hands left her, but only to untie the drawstring that gathered together the neckline of her shirt. He drew it down over her shoulders and pushed it around her waist. Then slowly, he brought his gaze to bear on her.

Claire's chest rose and fell, keeping time with her soft panting. She forced a semblance of calm over her features and stared back into his eyes. One of his threaded locks was plastered across his forehead, and she plucked it away, gently, tucking it back behind his ear while he watched her. His sun-dusted lashes lowered a fraction as he took in her nakedness. Pleasure knifed through her as his hand came to life, and, even before his thumb brushed across her nipple, she felt it harden to a peak, anticipating his caress. She gasped.

Trian exhaled, and his breath on her wet skin was cool compared to the steam around them. He dipped his head to touch his lips to her bare breast, and she shuddered as his mouth sucked and his tongue swirled around her.

She could feel his arousal against her thigh, and tried to press herself closer. "Not enough," she moaned, barely aware that she was speaking. "It's not enough."

"Shh, don't rush this." And his hand slid down and under and between her thighs, until his long fingers touched her and stroked her through the linen that had settled in her lap.

He bent back down to her breast while his fingers teased and caressed. And Claire let go her control and, with it, her inhibitions. She lowered her eyelids and did nothing but savor Trian's touch. When his knuckles grazed her, an incredible pressure began to build. Then, his thumb brushed against her, against the junction where she ached for release, and she nearly shattered. He stroked: slow, fast, slow again, making circles around and around. Her knees slipped farther apart as his fingers joined his thumb, massaging her with such intimacy that she wanted to scream. She tilted her hips, pressing herself against his hand, and the tension inside her grew until she felt she would come undone. And then she did.

She arched and threw back her head, fighting for breath as she pulsed with an aching sweetness. There was nothing left of her, and she hung limp in Trian's arms, half floating in the spring. He continued to touch her and suckle her, slowly gentling his caresses until all that remained was the feel of his lips trailing up her neck. It took every ounce of her strength to bring her head level, and she fixed her gaze on him. What she recognized in his eyes had her quivering all over again: raw hunger. And need. She shifted purposefully against him, and he groaned with unfulfilled desire. She tried to touch him, wanting to give him what he had given her, but he stayed her hands.

"No, remain still," he begged, his voice ragged, as if any movement would be his undoing.

She slumped against him, burying her face in his neck, feeling his rampant pulse on her lips. She placed her hand on his chest, unable to resist touching him in some way, and slowly, his pounding heart quieted. Trian plucked at the strands of her hair covering her cheek, gently swiping them back. Then he lifted her chin with no more than a finger, and kissed her lips.

Claire wanted to tell him that she loved him, had probably loved him since he had first escorted her to Stolweg. She opened her mouth to say the words, but stopped herself as her old fears returned to haunt her.

"The afternoon is growing late," he told her. "We should dry our clothes, then return before Lark sends out a search party." But he held her in his lap, not letting her go.

She sensed that he wanted to say more, so she waited, hoping to hear the words she herself felt in her heart. But he remained silent; so too did Claire hold her tongue.

CHAPTER FOURTEEN

Adaptation

Trian realized that something was amiss the moment he and Claire rode into the courtyard. Lark and Anna were conferring near the stable entrance. Then Gilles stormed out, Will and Pieter on his heels. The normally calm stable master threw his hands up and marched off toward the kitchen where his wife was sure to be. It was then that Anna and Lark noticed Trian and Claire, and the Lord and Lady of Stolweg walked quickly over to intercept them.

"What's wrong?" Claire demanded.

"Finally back from your picnic," boomed a voice that Trian recognized all too well. "Is this what you do every day? If I had known that the life of a Royal Guard was so blessed with leisure, I would have joined long ago. Godwin takes all of the hard-working noble sons for himself, with no care for how their families have to work to—"

"Cordhin," Trian interrupted, attempting to take control of his coarse-mannered cousin. If Cordhin thought to embarrass him here, in front of Claire, he could think again. "Why are you here? Is the family all right?" Cordhin, who had an eye for pretty women, had trained a leer upon Claire.

"They're fine." He attempted to brush off the hand Trian placed on his shoulder. "I am too, thanks for asking."

"What did you do this time?" Trian demanded, increasing the pressure of his grip and staying his cousin. Cordhin was always in some kind of trouble.

"Must you assume the worst of me?" Cordhin complained, half joking, half pouting. "What makes you think I've done anything wrong? No, don't answer that. Too many delicate ears about." He gave Claire a playful wink. "And who is this lovely flower?"

Trian sighed, for there would be no avoiding an introduction. "Cordhin, this is *Lady* Claire of Chevring, sister to *Lady* Anna and under the protection of *Lord* Larkin." He hoped that Cordhin might at least curb his remarks in the presence of so many titles. "This is Cordhin, my cousin." Claire had come to stand next to him.

Cordhin held out his hand to Claire. She hesitantly lifted hers, taking time, Trian knew, to ward her mind. His cousin bent over her hand, his lips poised to buss her knuckles. But he drew up instead, raising his eyebrows and staring at Claire's fingernails. When Cordhin noticed her disheveled hair and soiled clothing, he did exactly what Trian expected of him, and took the step that was one too many. "A lovely flower indeed, Trian," he flattered. "But from the looks of her, it appears that you have plucked her entire: bud, roots, soil, and all."

Before Trian could react, before even Lark could step in, Anna gut-punched Cordhin in a show of sisterly protectiveness. He doubled over with an *oof* before dropping dramatically to his knees. Anna took Claire by the arm and marched her into the castle. Gilles, Will, and Pieter were smirking with satisfaction.

Lark had started laughing, and was giving a scowling Cordhin a hand up. "You're lucky my Anna didn't aim lower."

"I've heard of these Chevring girls," Cordhin remarked, grinning at Lark. "That one hits as hard as a Cathmaran. A man has to respect a woman who can fight. If your Lady Claire is as tough as her sister, you've chosen well, Trian. Still, what was she doing today? Her fingernails were black, and I could have sworn there was mud in her hair."

Trian was not so ready to forgive his cousin's offensive words. He stepped forward, within inches of Cordhin. "You'll apologize to her."

Cordhin was not one to be cowed, but an easy look came into his eyes. "Aye," he agreed. "I'd not like to find out if she can hit like her sister!"

Lark put an arm around their shoulders, quite effectively separating them, and led them to the castle and into the hall. "You've missed dinner, Trian, but I'm sure we've some food left over. We can fill our stomachs while discussing why Cordhin is here."

• • •

If Trian harbored any hope of stolen embraces with Claire, it had been dashed by the arrival of his cousin. When they'd met in the stable before the others had joined them for the morning ride, Claire had asked him if it was true that he would be leaving Stolweg again. He had confirmed that he was and that his father wanted him to introduce Cordhin to the King and Queen.

Trian cast a frustrated scowl at his cousin now riding next to him; Cordhin saw and shrugged. They'd been talking again about why he was being sent to King's Glen. "It seems, Cousin, that even the Wolf cannot curb me. So I am being sent to court to become a Royal Guard. And you are to convince King Godwin that I will be no trouble to him."

"But you are heir to your father's stronghold," Trian argued. "He could not have set you aside."

"No, not aside," Cordhin confessed, "just on a shelf for a few years. Father believes that the King's Guard will temper me. Look what it has done for you and Lark. Besides, it's not completely unheard of that a lordling join the Guard. Who knows? Maybe it'll do me some good." He shrugged his shoulders in his typical fashion again, then trotted his horse over to Lark and Anna.

There must be something else motivating him, Trian determined, or Cordhin would not be so amenable to becoming a Guard. He eavesdropped on his cousin's conversation.

"He's beautiful," Anna was saying, gesturing to Cordhin's horse. "Are all Cathmaran mounts so colored?"

"Aye," Cordhin answered, "for the most part, they're blood bays like Trian's Culrua and my Blaze. About the same size, too. But every once in a while, we'll get a giant with some charcoal mottling on its rump and legs. There's no doubt where that trait comes from."

Anna laughed, and patted her great gray Chevring steed. Trian shook his head in astonishment that Cordhin was having a civilized conversation. Yes, he was positive now that something must have happened to him. It dawned on Trian then, and he smiled. Good or bad, he was willing to bet a woman was involved. Satisfied that his cousin was behaving, he nudged Culrua closer to where Claire rode Rebel.

. . .

"I like your cousin," Claire stated. They had stopped to make camp near one of Stolweg's broad and slow-moving streams. Trian groaned. "What? Oh, his rudeness yesterday? Don't worry, first impressions are oft times wrong. Besides, he seems a little sad to me."

"I grew up with him, Claire. My impressions—first, middle, and last—have not changed in over twenty years." He ran his fingers through his hair. "Still, he has not spoken another untoward word since yesterday. And he was behaving with your sister, a woman who struck where it hurt him most: his pride."

Claire glanced over to where Cordhin was standing. He was smiling and nodding at something Pieter had said. Lark joined them, and suddenly a wager was afoot.

"Fishing contest!" Anna announced, punctuating each word with exuberance. "We're to break off in pairs: Lark and I, Pieter and Cordhin, and you and Trian. Two hours to catch the biggest fish."

"What's the prize?" Claire asked.

"Crowing rights," Anna proclaimed. "That and the losers clean and cook, of course."

Trian rubbed his hands together. "When do we start?"

"Now, I suppose," Anna answered, and rushed off to follow Lark downstream. Pieter and Cordhin had already claimed the area closest to the tents.

Claire turned to Trian. "Upstream near the waterfall?"

Trian nodded, grabbing their fishing spears. "You were wonderful yesterday, by the way. I didn't have a chance to tell you, what with Cordhin arriving. I will never forget how you looked covered in mud."

"You sound surprised," Claire noted, remembering the times she had teased her older sister for coming home reeking of fish guts or covered in heaven only knew what. Anna had laughed and laughed when Claire had explained why she had mud in her hair, saying that their mother would have blamed it on her influence. Claire had always been such a proper lady. Now she wore breeches more often than gowns.

"Not surprised at all," Trian assured her. "Just pleased. It was something I would've done." They had stopped close to the waterfall. Trian reached out to her, running his fingers through her hair as the occasional breeze pushed a fine mist their way. "Before I leave, I want to start you on your final lesson."

Claire gazed longingly at his broad shoulders, at the muscular expanse of his chest, then stepped closer. "What is this one called? Appreciation?"

"No." He chuckled and pulled her to him. She pressed her body against his, savoring the feel of him. His finger wound around one of her tresses, and he watched as it uncoiled to fall straight again. "Today, I'm going to tell you about adaptation."

They sat next to each other on the bank, just out of reach of the waterfall's spray. And as they spoke, the fish swam unthreatened. Adaptation was the culmination of his lessons. "Imagine that you find yourself in a city. Will you be able to hear the trees shifting over the calls of the fishmongers or the haggling of the fabric merchants? What use it to note the trickle of the waste water in the gutter? Is there mud to be found to hide your presence, or a shrub? You must adapt to your surroundings, whatever form they take. Observe people instead of nature: watch how they move, listen to their accents, mimic them. Recognize resources such as the rickety sound of a cart's wheels on paver, or the lapping sound of water against a dock. Look not for things that will conceal you, but how you can adapt and go unnoticed—"

"—in plain sight," Claire finished, and he smiled.

"While I'm gone, I want you to practice mimicking Will and Pieter, the way their youthful limbs move with awkward grace. Watch the miller, his bluster when he struts and talks. When you next go to market, try to lose yourself among the vendors."

"When will you come back?" Claire asked finally, knowing she would count each hour until his return.

"Two months, maybe less. Will you...I mean..." He frowned and cast his eyes across the stream.

What had he been about to say? An idea teased her mind. *She* had been first to kiss him, to touch him. She'd been the one leading in their courtship dance. Trian only pursued once she initiated the next stage. He had paved the way for her small steps forward, yes, but he stopped shy of making any advancement himself. Almost as if—what?

"You'll be careful while you're away, won't you?" Some of her frustration accidently slipped out, and he placed his hand over hers. Claire sighed. "You know I will wait for you, Trian," she declared. "You must know."

He lifted her hand and kissed her palm. "I had hoped," he replied, his promise to her left unspoken. Claire looked downstream to hide the glistening of her unshed tears, but he touched her chin, drawing her face to his for a soft, lingering kiss.

She leaned against him in their sunny patch near the stream, their fishing spears still forgotten. His fingers ran through her hair, letting it fall in sections like sheets of water. "I love your hair, Claire. It makes me think of my home."

He twirled a tress around his finger and watched it unravel and fall straight again. "On the borders between Marach, Deighlei and Cathmar, there stands a group of mountains called the Traria Peaks. When the snows melt, the runoff flows in three directions: to the White River, which flows west into Marach Bay, toward Deighlei to feed the ice plains, and finally into the Falinn River. It is this eastern tributary where, just above the tree line, there is a waterfall. It doesn't crash to the earth as other waterfalls do, splashing and breaking against hidden boulders. This waterfall is unique. It descends, unblemished. You see, the rock behind it is hollowed out. Glassy streams of green and blue and gray, plummeting at least a hundred feet, doing so as smooth and as silky as your hair." He ran his fingers through her tresses once more, separating them and watching them sift seamlessly back together. When excited cheers erupted from downstream, they ignored them.

"Is there a song for it?" Claire asked, hoping that he would sing for her.

He smiled, but shook his head. "Not yet, though there should be, for the waterfall is special in more ways than its beauty. It is the only place in Aurelia where the great rímara falcons nest."

"I thought the rímara were but a memory, that they died off during the Great War."

"They still soar, Claire. At least they did a decade past. Years ago, my ancestors would capture the hatchlings to train them for hunting and battle. They are a part of my house as much as horses are of yours. I've seen them. Wingspans to match a grown man's breadth hand to hand, and talons as long as my fingers. They are as beautiful as they are fearsome."

Claire rested her head on his shoulder and listened as he spoke of the rímara, from finding the great raptors by following the Falinn River to its source, to warding off the adult falcons with smoke and flame in order to capture their young. He sewed poetry through his words, enchanting her with the beauty of his story. And in the way that only Trian could do, his words *were* a song, though they were not set to any melody.

"The path to the waterfall is treacherous," Trian told her, "and well hidden. Only when one is near it can they find the cascading falls. And not by sight, but by listening. For as smooth as it flows, in its passing, the water makes the air sing.

"There is a fissure in the cliff's face behind the curtain of water. I was eleven when I found it and was just able to slip through. Some thirty paces it went, twisting and turning before opening up again to daylight. At the tunnel's end, in the very heart of the Traria Peaks, there lies a hidden canyon."

He wrapped his arms around Claire, holding her against him. "I watched the falcons circle and wheel, riding the currents like no other birds can. One flew at me, cutting the air in a fierce dive. But I stood my ground, and the falcon pulled up, perching itself upon a limb not fifteen feet from where I stood. It shrieked at me, giving warning that I was too close to its nest."

"Did you ever go back?"

"A few times, when I was young, just to watch them. And then I grew too big to make it through the fissure. There were so few of them then. It just didn't seem right to tell anyone else. Until now."

She sighed, still cradled in his arms. "I've lost so much," she began. "I think about Chevring, and my parents. Some days, it takes all of my strength to keep pretending that everything will be all right. That such beauty remains in this world, untouched and unthreatened, helps."

Trian tightened his arms around her and kissed her hair. When another excited shout made its way upstream, Trian shrugged at their discarded fishing spears. "I suppose we're cleaning and cooking this evening," he said, sounding not at all disappointed.

They returned to camp, empty handed, only to discover that they were not alone in losing. Lark and Anna had also caught no fish. Claire was about to ask how it was possible when she noticed that her brother-in-law's shirt was inside out. Beside her, Trian chuckled. Cordhin noticed too, but was, for once, wise enough to keep quiet.

CHAPTER FIFTEEN
Gifts and Goodbyes

Claire stared ahead, shifting effortlessly in her saddle as Rebel trotted from between the trees and into the valley. Her hand curled around the warm object in her palm, a parting gift from Trian. Forty-one days ago—she'd been counting—they had met in Stolweg's chapel to say their goodbyes. He had reached into his tunic and pulled out a bundle wrapped in white linen. She'd recognized her kerchief at once, one of many from her fabric garden. Before she could ask him how he'd come to possess it, he'd unfolded the linen to expose a tiny leather pouch on a cord.

"To help you remember me," he had told her, placing the kerchief and pouch in her hand and asking her to open it only after he departed. Claire had lifted the pouch from its blanket and had seen that the flowers so delicately stitched on her kerchief were forget-me-nots. She'd pressed the linen square back into Trian's hand, giving him a meaningful keepsake of her own. "I'll come back as soon as I am able," he'd assured her, then kissed her one last time and was gone. Gone to King's Glen with his cousin Cordhin, where he would have to fend off the Queen's ladies and their game of hearts.

Claire closed her eyes and brought back his face to her mind, as sharp in detail as if he stood before her. When she opened her eyes, she opened her fingers as well and smiled at what lay in her palm. A drop of glass, round and clear, with a tiny blue sprig of forget-me-not suspended in its center. She wondered when Trian had commissioned the piece and how long he'd held onto it before giving it to her. When she heard another horse trot up next to hers, she slipped the bauble into the leather pouch hanging around her neck, then tucked it under her tunic.

"A few of the mares broke off from the main herd, m'lady," Pieter grumbled, pointing southeast to the rolling, wooded hills across the valley that cradled Stolweg's henge. "We'll have to take the herd into the woods to round them up. Should only take an hour or so. We've plenty of time."

They had been on their way back to the keep, still two hours away. Nightfall was twice that in coming. Claire was both eager and apprehensive to return. Word had come that Trian's arrival was imminent. But her disappointment mounted each day as she rode into the keep's courtyard and found him yet absent. Perhaps today would be the day.

"Meet me back here instead," she instructed, determined to be cautiously hopeful and ignore her growing sense of urgency to leave the valley. "The main herd won't wander from grazing near the henge. I'll remain here and watch over them."

Pieter studied the grasslands around them. "It would be better if we stayed together, m'lady."

"If you go alone, you'll be back in less than an hour. Those mares couldn't have gone far. I promise to stay near the henge." Pieter appeared unswayed. "Think about it, Pieter. There's no easy way to catch those mares without splitting up. It doesn't make sense to take the entire herd into the woods. If I wait for you here, I'll only be alone for a short time. And we can't *leave* without our deserters, can we? What would Anna say if we returned with three fewer horses?"

"*Hmpf,*" came his admission that he had lost the argument. "You have your bow, m'lady?" Claire patted her weapon where it was tied to her saddle. "Any sort of blade?"

"No," Claire replied patiently—if Trian would just hurry back to her, she would have her dagger, wouldn't she? Anna had given it to him to have it sheathed in King's Glen. "Don't worry, Pieter. We've never actually found any tracks on Stolweg land, no matter the rumors."

Pieter reached down and pulled a small dagger, a knife really, from his boot and handed it to her. Claire arched her eyebrow at him. "It comes in handy sometimes," he explained, turning his horse to the woods. "I'll be back as soon as I can. Stay here. Er, please, m'lady," he added upon realizing that he was issuing orders to Claire.

At her nod, he signaled his mount into an easy canter before disappearing into the trees. Claire studied the little dagger Pieter had given her, then touched the pad of her thumb to its blade; it'd been honed to a wicked edge. She tucked it in her boot as Pieter had done, then slipped from Rebel's back to the ground. "Keep an eye out for marauders, Rebel," she ordered before striding to the giant megaliths in the middle of the valley. Rebel only snorted.

The grass near the henge was high, and Claire, her arms held out from her sides, let it whisk against her open palms as she walked toward the stones. These last months, she'd been practicing everything that Trian had taught her; she couldn't wait to show him how adept she'd become at reading her surroundings. It'd become second nature to her. Even now, her passage through the field was silent, and she closed her eyes to allow her other senses to unfurl.

Upon her face, a gentle breeze buffeted her skin, mixing with the warmth of the early autumn sun. The sound of chirping, buzzing and clicking from a dozen different insects sorted itself out in her mind. Above everything, she heard the hissing of grass as the browning stems rubbed against one another in the breeze that funneled through the valley. The birds were twittering and calling to each other in the woods, and the echoes of the *rat-a-tatting* of a lone woodpecker punctuated the musical tones of the field wrens. Claire breathed in, smelling the fertile earth and peat that drifted into her nostrils before giving way to the dry, fresh smell of the field grass. Then, almost like an afterthought, she caught the aroma of crepe myrtles in full bloom, the trees themselves hidden somewhere in the woods.

Eyes yet closed, Claire breathed again, through nose and mouth, relishing the different smells, tasting them even, and taking comfort in their steadfastness. The crepe myrtle's scent lingered, and Claire was surprised by its underpinnings of spice. She took yet another drag of air, her brow creasing as she wrangled with the alien odor. But the breeze shifted, and the smell evaporated. A startle of wings broke in the trees behind her, a pheasant perhaps, and Claire opened her eyes to turn toward the sound. Rebel stomped and twitched his ears in the same direction.

Like a spider crawling up the back of her neck, an uneasy feeling crept through Claire. The world around her had gone silent. No bird called out its song, no insect rubbed leg to wing, only the drying grass whispered in the breeze. The pressure grew in her ears, and she had a sudden sense that the valley was out of balance. A flock of starlings exploded from the tree line, and Claire nearly jumped from her skin.

Her stallion had thrown up his massive head, likewise spooked. Then, over the silence, Claire heard—no, she felt it through her feet—the pounding of hooves. Breath held, she backed up toward the stones, stopping a pace or two away when a lone rider on a great bay steed came into view. Trian.

In the same instant that she caught the glint of sunlight on steel as he drew his sword, three men stepped from where the starlings had fled, their crossbows aimed at him. Claire stepped forward to scream his name, and a rough hand clamped down over her mouth. She struggled, smelling the strange and cloying spice from before. When another man stepped forward with a large, empty sack of some rough material, Claire bit down, tasted blood. Her captor loosened his grip in his surprise, and Claire dropped like dead weight to the ground, slipping through his arms. She scrambled up, tripping and catching herself as she ran toward Trian.

Panic gripped her, that same horror she'd felt when she'd been so helpless all those years at Chevring. She watched as two of the bowmen loosed their quarrels, the first dart missing Trian completely, the second sticking in his thigh. The third man aimed and fired his shot at the broader target of Culrua. The shaft found its mark, piercing the chest of the great horse. Trian's steed stumbled, forelegs crumpling beneath the weight of its body as its hind legs drove the destrier forward. Culrua's agonized scream echoed through the valley. Trian had barely freed his legs from his stirrups, and somersaulted from the saddle seconds before his mount's chest crashed into the earth, its neck bent at an impossible angle. Culrua's hindquarters lifted, flipping his massive girth over, slamming it to the valley floor in a resounding crash. The great bay horse was dead. Ten paces away, Trian had landed on his back. He, too, was unmoving.

Claire ran as hard as she could and heard the men behind her draw their swords and give chase. The bowmen paid her no mind as they reached Trian. Quarrels reloaded, one of them aimed at Trian's chest and shot. She heard them laugh as his body jerked up before slumping back to the ground. Her pursuers were almost upon her, and Claire frantically went over what she should do. Trian could not be dead. If she could just reach him…No, she would have to get help first. If they captured her, Trian would be lost.

She darted to the side and focused on reaching Rebel. The unexpected change in course put some distance between her and the men. She couldn't help Trian if they caught her, she repeated over and over in her mind.

A *swish-swish-swish* noise cut through the air. Suddenly, her legs were caught up in cords, and something very hard cracked against her shin bone. Claire flew forward, only twenty paces from Rebel. And when her horse started toward her, she saw that the bowmen were taking aim at her destrier. She whistled, two shrill bursts. Rebel reared, twisted around, and bolted up the valley toward Stolweg, the rest of the herd thundering in his wake. She watched her stallion long enough to see that the fired missiles fell short by ten lengths of his massive stride.

Quickly, Claire rolled onto her back. One of her pursuers had reached her, and she kicked up and out with both legs. He went down in a grunt of pain, holding himself where men were at their weakest.

With her legs trussed together, she could do naught but two-footed thrusts, so she set her mind to getting free. A shadow fell over her, and she looked up in time to see the flat of a sword arc down toward her temple. She heard the vibration of metal against skull. Then, she heard no more.

CHAPTER SIXTEEN

Lost

"I should've known it was you, Jessa," Pieter admonished the trouble-some mare, pushing the three horses forward through the trees and into the valley. "These other two ladies would never have wandered so far." He'd been gone longer than he'd intended, almost two hours by the look of the shadows made by the henge. Claire was probably worried. Either that or she'd found some plant to occupy her, or one of Trian's lessons.

She could be quieter than Anna or Lark when she put her mind to it. And she could hide anywhere, pretend to be anyone. Pieter had caught her aping his motions only last week! He gazed about the valley, noting that neither she nor her horse were in sight. The herd was like-wise gone. Clicking his tongue, he pushed the mares into a trot.

Lady Claire must have moved the horses north to the other side of the henge, so he trotted around the massive circle. It was then that he discovered a destrier in a heap on the ground. "H'ya!" he shouted and galloped to the downed animal. It was Culrua, and the once-great steed was dead. Already the whine of flies could be heard descending to lay their eggs.

Pieter sat higher in his saddle and wheeled around and around, frantic to find his lady. Just when he thought she must be safe with Trian, he espied a smaller mound some ten paces from the dead horse. He urged his mount forward. Two arrows, fletches pointing to the sky, came into view.

"Oh, Trian, no," he cried, searching for aide and for Claire. There was nothing Pieter could do for Trian, and he was smart enough to realize that he could not search for Claire alone. He charged out of the valley toward Stolweg. He hadn't galloped far when he recognized Lark and another rider racing to meet him. There was no time to stop and explain, and Pieter wheeled around, holding back his mount only long enough to let Lark—and Warin—catch up to him.

"What happened, Pieter?" Lark shouted over the thunder of twelve hooves. "We were on our way here when Rebel and the herd raced past us."

"Trian," Pieter shouted back. "I found him near the henge. He's dead!"

"Is Claire with him?" Lark shouted.

"I don't know where she is, m'lord!" He was riding faster than he had ever ridden in his life. Impossibly, his lord pressed his destrier Rabbit even faster, passing him by in a murderous gallop.

"Pieter," Warin shouted, still abreast of him, "hie to the keep. Bring back as much help as you can. And for all our sakes, do not let Lady Anna ride out alone. Now go!" Like Lord Lark, Warin pushed his mount to a hellish pace.

"You'll find Trian just north of Culrua," Pieter shouted after him. He wheeled his mount yet again, turning back to race to the keep. He glanced behind him once, but his lord and Warin were already lost from view.

CHAPTER SEVENTEEN

They galloped alongside one another, she and Trian, coming slowly to the rise of the hill. The strides of their horses were impossibly long, lifting them closer to the very apex of the ridge before coursing down the other side. No sooner had the ground leveled than Claire felt Rebel lifting again in a great leap. She turned to gaze at Trian, and he smiled at her.

"You have to let me go now," he told her. "It'll be all right, my love. Just let go."

"No." She was determined to stay with him. "I need you."

"You'll be fine," he assured. "Use what I've taught you and you'll get through this." Their horses surged again, but this time Trian's steed landed farther away from her. The distance between them grew. The hills swelled and dipped, morphing into great waves, lifting and heaving and carrying Trian away.

"Don't go," she begged. "I need to tell you something." He shouted to her, but she could not hear his words over the roar of the mounting waters. She and Rebel plummeted down, and Trian was gone.

The swelling noise was too much to bear, and Claire put her hand to her head. Her temple throbbed. She opened her eyes, and the room tipped violently.

It was dark, and the creaking was deafening. She was pitched from her bed. Sprawling on all fours, she slid and spun across the floor into the opposite wall. The back of her head hit the wood with a *thunk*, causing stars to explode in her skull. Before she could steady herself, the room bucked again, and she was tossed back toward her bed. She held on for dear life, letting go only long enough to grab the rough bucket conveniently tied to her pallet. The floor dropped away, taking with it her stomach, then together they rushed back up. Claire leaned over the filthy receptacle and retched, then retched some more until there was nothing left. Her pallet was secured to the wall with thick cords, and she wound her wrist around one and cowered in the measly bedding. She was asea, and from the roaring and creaking, and jarring and slamming, the vessel carrying her was in the midst of a raging tempest. The entire cabin shuddered violently, and Claire was thrown against the wall and knocked unconscious once more.

* * *

For some time, Claire lay awake with eyes closed and limbs unmoving. The orange-red glow against her eyelids indicated that it was daytime. The maelstrom had passed, and gentle swells lifted and settled in a rhythm older than time. She tried grasping at the dream she'd had. Trian, she thought painfully, was gone.

"Observe," she said on a breath so quiet that not even her lips moved. "Conceal. Adapt." She found little comfort in the words. Only memories made unbearable by the loss of Trian. "Observe," she tried again, citing the word like a prayer. "Conceal. Adapt."

"Eh? What's that?" a gravelly voice demanded. Claire kept her eyes closed, feigning sleep. "I know yer awake. Been awake this last hour. You've been dreaming of home, I'd bet. Maybe yer husband."

Claire opened her eyes, and pain sliced through her temple. The rank smell of bile assaulted her senses, and she saw that the bucket had sloshed its contents all over the floor. She examined her arm; it had been rubbed raw where she'd wrapped the rope around her wrist during the storm. The man's booted foot shoved a bucket across the floor; more water splashed out of it than remained inside.

She lifted her head to get a good look at him. He was across the cabin, squatting down, his back against the wall. Too far out of reach. She caught a glint of steel in his hand, and she turned her attention to his face. He had startling blue eyes and dirty blond hair that hung in matted clumps. His nose had been broken—more than once by its crooked appearance. His clothes were worn but of good quality. And he wore thick chains of gold and silver around his neck. He was younger than he looked, this seaman; the wind and sun had aged him. She glanced back at the small blade twirling fluidly between his fingers.

"Not taking any chances with you, m'lady." He deftly flipped the blade. "Know all about you and your ways. Your man might have put up with such behavior, but you won't last a day if you try any of your tricks here." He stood, and Claire assessed him. Long limbed, about her height, and graceful in the way he shifted with the rocking of the vessel.

Claire tore a piece of cloth from her threadbare blanket and dipped it into the bucket before dabbing it gently to her temple. She winced. "Where are you taking me?"

"Never you mind," he shot back, his eyes darting toward the door. "The cap'n would likely flay me, an' you after, if he knew we were talking. With me own knife, no less. I'm just here to make sure you don't expire before we make port. That's all you need to know."

She tried another tack. "You're not the captain?" So, Claire thought as the sailor stood a little straighter, he was pleased that she deemed him so lofty in the hierarchy of the ship. A bit of information to store away. Observe.

"First mate," he replied. "Though the bounty for capturing the mighty Lady Aubrianne might see me to enough coin to purchase m'own ship. Would've been a great deal more if those fool soldiers hadn't let the horses escape. At least they killed your husband. It's a good day when there's one less Aurelian nobleman breathing." He looked down at her in disgust. They were taking her to Nifolhad. And worse, they believed her to be Anna, the woman King Diarmait held responsible for killing his second born, Lord Roger.

Keeping his back to the wall, the first mate pulled a misshapen hat from his waistband, and stretched it to fit over his head. Claire dipped her rag into the bucket again, then wrung it out. Rusty drops splattered the planking of the floor. She feigned a tremor in her hand as she held the cloth to her temple. A quick wince and a suck of air through her teeth had the man reaching into his vest and pulling out a pouch. "Chew it first, then slap the cud onto the gash."

"My thanks," Claire offered, hoping to secure more sympathy. He left her, locking the door behind him. If he became enamored with her, perhaps she could she use it to her advantage.

• • •

Claire gave her prison cell a cursory scan, searching for a possible weapon. She found a few charts, an unlit oil lantern hanging from the ceiling, and an old sideboard secured to one wall. She remembered the knife Pieter had given her and checked her boot. It was still there. Around her neck, the leather cord and pouch yet hung. She pulled it off and slipped it into her other boot. The sideboard had two cupboards and a hutch with open shelves, but was empty save for a few dented mugs of pewter and a half dozen warped wooden platters, and more charts. In the far back corner, however, she discovered a worn strap. She tugged it to find an old leather pouch, half the size of a saddlebag. Empty though it was, she might find some use for it later and slid it under her sleeping pallet.

The floor was specked with her dried vomit. Claire tore another rag and did her best to clean the mess, if only to rid the small space of the stench. By the time she set the bucket with what was left of the filthy water near the door, her head throbbed. She slumped back onto the sleeping pallet.

The sailor's pouch was there, and Claire plucked it from the folds of her blanket. She opened it and smelled. Blood nettle, she realized in surprise. Its faint aroma told her that it was years away from being fresh. But anything was better than nothing. She dumped some of the dried herb into her hand. The leaves and stems were so desiccated they all but disintegrated. Chew it indeed. She would somehow have to moisten the herb and weighed her options: blood, vomit, and dirt-soiled water from the bucket, or spit. She opted for the latter. After making a poultice, she pressed it to her temple, then tore a strip of linen from the hem of her shirt and tied it around her head. She needed fresh air, so she staggered toward the porthole. Halfway there, she halted, grew accustomed to the rise and fall of the ship, then found her sea legs and took the last few steps across the cabin.

The porthole swiveled open like a vent, flooding the cabin with fresh, humid air. The sun was setting outside her window, and Claire wondered why they were sailing north. She heard the door being unlocked, and someone entering. Ignoring the footsteps behind her, she pretended to walk unsteadily to her bed. The first mate had returned. He placed a tray on the sideboard, then turned to ogle her. Claire stared back at him, and he looked quickly away.

"I brought your meal," he stated gruffly. "Make it last. You'll not get more until tomorrow evening. And there's more water here. And an empty privy pail." He retrieved the soiled bucket.

"Tomorrow? How many more weeks at sea?"

He narrowed his eyes at her as if trying to ascertain her motives. "Five. Six with foul weather." His eyes kept slipping to her breech-clad legs.

"How many days have I been here?" When he didn't answer, she added, "I'm just trying to understand why we are headed north." It was a risk revealing that she knew more than he believed, but she hoped to lure him into thinking that she trusted him.

He looked at the door, then back at her. "Too long by my reckoning. Four nights a'ready. The storm blew us off course, and broke one of the masts. Cappy's been in a foul mood since." Boot steps could be heard outside the door, and the first mate froze. They passed by, but his shoulders remained tensed.

Four nights, Claire considered carefully. The first mate must've given her water while she was unconscious, or she wouldn't have had the strength to move. He started to leave. "Wait," she begged. "Tell me your name."

"Why?" he asked suspiciously.

"So I can thank you properly." She pretended to be shy and looked up at him through her eyelashes. "For this," she added, touching the poultice on her temple. "And for keeping me alive these past few nights."

His eyes drifted openly over her hips and waist, and then to the curves of her bosom concealed under her fitted tunic. When he looked guiltily away, Claire wondered what else he might have done while she'd been knocked out. "Amal."

"Thank you, Amal," Claire said softly. She caught the excited gleam in his eye just before he slipped out of the room, securing the door behind him. If she could just get him to help her escape once they made port, she could be on her way back to Aurelia.

Claire snatched a mug from the hutch and dunked it into the bucket of water. It was potable, with no hints of herbs or poison, though from the slight tang of brine, she was sure the bucket had held seawater more oft than not. She pulled the cloth from the tray on the sideboard to reveal her meal: stale bread, moldy cheese, and something dried that may have once been herring. She was starving, but forced herself to not gorge on the food. In the end, she ate half the bread, half the fish, and all of the cheese. She divided the leftovers, wrapping one portion and setting it on the tray for later. She tore another piece of cloth from her ever-shrinking blanket, wrapped up the rest of the food, and stuffed it in the bag under her bed.

Next, she removed her overtunic, bundling it into a pillow for her sleeping pallet. Her stomach grumbled, so she refilled her mug, sat, and thoughtfully sipped her water. Four days at sea. If her captors had taken two weeks to transport her to the ship, then it had been eighteen days. They must've drugged her, for she could recall no part of their flight to the coast. She wondered at that and looked at her clothing. Except for her own blood and vomit, her breeches were unsoiled; it had to have been a waking stupor. *Eighteen days,* she thought again. Eighteen days since Trian had been killed. Claire set her cup down as the first sob wracked her body.

"I never saw it coming," she despaired. "Oh, Trian, I'm sorry. I never saw it." She hugged herself, remembering how much strength he'd given her. How he'd brought her from her self-imposed solitude after her parents had been killed. He'd told her that her curse was a gift. But what good was it? It didn't work when she needed it most, and Trian had paid the price. Her cabin grew dark as she gave in to her grief and, hours later, fell into an exhausted sleep. She welcomed her dreams; Trian resided there. She could feel his presence, urging her to be strong. But even asleep, she could feel the ship lift and fall in the gentle swells of the sea. And Trian's words filled her mind: *observe, conceal, adapt,* in time with the waves.

The weeks slowly slipped by. Each evening, Amal would arrive with her meal and water. He spoke little, sometimes not at all, but his eyes grew bolder with each visit. Her food selection improved. A few times, he pulled a piece of fruit from his pocket to add to the tray. Once, he smuggled in an extra blanket, though it was just as threadbare as the first. Claire had to do something soon to secure his help, for the ship would be making port in days.

Finally, one night, Claire made sure she was standing near the hutch where he always set the tray. Amal entered as usual, then paused. She took the tray from him, thanking him by name. She pulled back the cloth and broke off some cheese and bread, then held it out to him. "Have you had your meal? There is enough for me to share." He looked furtively at the door. "There is no other way for me to thank you, Amal," Claire explained to allay his suspicious nature. "Our voyage is almost over."

He stepped closer, then stopped. But his eyes raked over her legs, then rested at the juncture of her thighs. He left her then, without another word. She was suddenly conscious of how dangerous a game she was playing.

That night, she dreamt of Trian again. He came to her, holding out his hands. Soothing her fears and pain with soft words. His touch was gentle. His fingers smoothed her hair from her forehead. Claire sighed in her dream as she felt his hands trail down her neck to her collar. His calloused fingers teased her nipple. Claire breathed in and murmured his name; the scent of brine and spice filled her nostrils. Something was wrong; she wasn't dreaming. She was not alone, and it wasn't Trian who was touching her. She opened her eyes and, in the near darkness, pushed at the man looming over her.

"Shhh," he cautioned. "Someone might hear."

"Stop," she cried, struggling against him. "Amal, no!"

"Come now, m'lady," he hushed. "You're no innocent." He pulled at her chemise, tearing the seams at one shoulder, and pushed her back against the pallet. Claire was shocked to discover that he was half naked already.

"I said *no*," Claire repeated, as calmly as possible.

"No need to play the tease with me," Amal sneered. "I know this is what you want. And I won't care if you pretend that I'm your dead husband. Use his name even, just say it quietly." He pulled his breeches down, and Claire opened her mouth to scream. But his hand clamped over her face before she could. "Shut your mouth," he seethed. He had stopped moving and was listening. The slurring of water on the sides of the ship as it passed through the waves, the creaking wood, all the normal sounds filled the small cabin. Satisfied that nothing was amiss, he leaned close to her face. "Make another sound," he hissed in the dark, "and I'll cut your throat." She felt him fumbling to undo her breeches and she swatted at his groping hands. He grabbed her wrist and twisted it, then slapped her face.

She managed to lever him away from her with both arms, but he struck her even harder. He grabbed her by her hair with both hands, pushing her back against the pallet, then shoved his knees between hers. Head ringing, Claire pushed at him again, and was surprised by her own strength when he flew away from her. A wet *snick* whispered in the dark, then a gurgle. Amal coughed, and Claire heard a *thud* as something heavy hit the floor. She pulled up her legs, making herself into a tight ball.

Someone else had come into the cabin. Boots scraped across the floor, and she heard the unmistakable scratch of metal on flint. There was a soft glow, then a squeal as the lantern's shutters were opened, throwing wild stripes of light across the rocking cabin. Claire stared at the floor where Amal lay, lifeless, in a pool of his own blood.

She was thrown back in time to Chevring, when Roger's soldiers had threatened her with the unspeakable. Amal had tried to rape her; now he was dead. Claire was glad for it. "Thank you," she started, rising from her pallet and covering herself where her chemise had been torn. "Are you the Cap—"

Her rescuer advanced on her so swiftly that she had no time to dodge his blow. The back of his hand connected with her head, and she flew sideways into the hutch, crumbling to the floor. He kicked her in the stomach. "Whore!" he bellowed. "You will not say another word. Amal was the one man I thought I could trust to be strong enough to withstand your seductive ways. When I saw him filching extra food, I knew. What a waste of a good first mate."

He hunkered down in front of her, and Claire cowered under his hateful glare. He grabbed her by the hair and threw her onto her pallet. Two more men rushed into the cabin, crowding the small space. They stopped upon catching sight of her. Their leers left little in Claire's mind as to what they wanted. "Not one word more," he roared at her, "or I'll cut out your tongue and make you eat it. Diarmait won't care if you're mute."

She drew up her pathetic blanket, trying as best she could to hide herself from their stares. "Give Amal to the sea," the man ordered.

"Aye, Cappy," one of them replied, and they dragged Amal away, leaving a trail of blood. His breeches, vest, and shirt were left in a rumpled pile at the foot of her bed. The captain followed his men from the room, locking the door behind him.

Shaking on her bed, she took stock of her injuries. Her head throbbed, and her ear was ringing. She prodded her stomach. It was sore, but there was no sharp pain to indicate a ruptured organ or broken rib. Her elbow was cut and bruised where she had crashed into the hutch. Then, something the captain had said about stolen food came back to her, so Claire grabbed Amal's clothes. His vest wasn't wadded up; it had been carefully folded around a dirty pouch containing bread, more dried fish, and some figs. His payment for having her, Claire surmised. A pocket had been sewn into the vest's lining, and Claire discovered a small bag, this one made of fine linen and drawn closed with a silk ribbon. Within it, small brown berries. They were the size of dried currants, but smooth, not wrinkled. Perhaps four dozen in all.

Claire placed one on her tongue. She chewed it and swallowed. It was delicious. She pulled out her leather bag and stored her new foodstuff inside. She quickly searched the rest of Amal's clothes, but found nothing but a dozen or so small coins that she couldn't identify. She dropped them into the pouch that had once held the blood nettle that Amal had given her.

The sky outside her window was growing light, and she hid the clothing and bag under her pallet. It was then that she discovered that the dirty sack wasn't a sack at all; it was Amal's hat. She hid that as well. She worried then that the captain would return to collect Amal's things, so she took his shirt, tore a piece from its hem, then wedged it in the porthole's shutter as if it had torn when she stuffed his clothes through and overboard. Then, she took stock of her own clothing.

Her chemise was torn, but even with needle and thread, she would not take it off to mend it while amongst men such as these. She picked up her tunic and shrugged carefully into it. She had just laced it up when her door was unlocked and the captain stepped into the room. Claire shrank back against the wall, drawing up her knees to protect and cover herself.

Another sailor came in, keeping his eyes dutifully averted. Near the hutch, he found her leftover meal and removed it. The captain shut the door and stared down at her.

"I can't afford to lose another good man to you," he growled. "I barely trust myself where you're concerned. But the King, he has plans for you. So we're not allowed to sully ourselves upon you." He stared at her, and Claire was certain that he wanted her to speak if only to give him an excuse to make good on his earlier threat. She remained silent and kept her tongue safe.

"So that you understand your position," he continued, "you try to talk to anyone, and I'll hold you to my promise. Then I'll leave you in this room with three or four of my men." He narrowed his eyes at her, then scanned the space. "Where are—" His glare fell upon the fabric in the porthole. "Just as well."

He came closer, standing menacingly above her. "We make land in two days. Two more for word to reach King Diarmait's agents that we have you. And two again before they can send someone to retrieve you. Until then, not a single man will enter this cabin." He pointed to the water bucket. "Six days. You might want to ration that; it's all I'm willing to waste upon you."

CHAPTER EIGHTEEN

Forget-Me-Not

Voices. Incessant chattering. Always muttering in the background. And prodding him and poking. Why wouldn't they just leave off and give him some peace? Even now they were arguing over him. Except this time, he could make out some of the words.

"It's been weeks, Grainne," spoke a man whose voice was familiar but he couldn't place.

"I am aware of that fact, m'lord," the woman responded. "A cracked skull takes time to heal."

His bed dipped down as someone sat next to him. A cool cloth was placed over his brow, and he felt a gentle hand resting on his shoulder. The air around him smelled of lavender. Trian attempted to open his eyes and only succeeded in slitting them a crack. There wasn't much light in the room, and even that small amount was painful. He kept his eyes shut.

"But the fever's gone," the man argued. It was his friend Lark, Trian realized with relief.

"Yes, but that just means that the poison from the quarrel is out of his blood," she countered. "The only thing we can do now is wait. As I've been telling you, either the swelling in his skull will subside, or it won't. M'lord," the woman went on more gently, "sleep is his friend now. He'll wake when his mind realizes that his skull is done knitting."

Trian tried opening his eyes again. He blinked and was able to keep his lids levered apart. The hand on his shoulder patted him. "*Shhh*, take your time," another woman's voice soothed. He blinked again as his vision began to clear. Trian studied the woman sitting next to him. She smiled, but her expression was anxious.

"They're giving me a headache," he groused, his tongue thick in his mouth. She held a cup of water to his lips. It tasted as if it had been laced with honey and it soothed his throat as he drank.

"They're giving *me* a headache," she told him, just loud enough that the other two stopped their debate. He finally placed her: Lady Aubrianne of Stolweg.

"Trian! You're awake. Thank you, Grainne," Lark added, hugging the unknown woman and making her blush. He dragged a chair to Trian's bedside.

There were dark circles shadowing Lark's eyes. He hadn't shaved in days and his clothes looked like he'd been sleeping in them for weeks. "If I look as bad as you, Lark…" Trian started, expecting a chuckle. But Lark wasn't laughing, and neither was Lady Aubrianne. "What aren't you telling me, Lark? Lady Aubrianne?"

"Trian," his friend started, "it's Claire. She's been taken."

"Taken? But, Lady Aubrianne, she's…"

"Trian, no one has called me by that name in years," she cried. The other woman, Grainne, rushed to her side.

"Beg pardon, m'lady. Lark does mean your late sister Claire, doesn't he?" Lady Aubrianne stood abruptly and strode to the hearth. She kept her back to him.

No one, not even Lark, knew of Trian's feelings for Lady Claire. Her death during the destruction of Chevring still haunted him.

"Trian," Lark said, "you'd better tell me what happened to you when you were attacked."

"Attacked?" Suddenly, the quiet murmurings made sense. His aching skull, the pain in his leg.

Grainne had taken Lady Aubrianne's place by his side and pressed a cool cloth to his head again. She gave Lark a stern look. "Later, m'lord," she ordered. "He requires more rest. This won't help him."

But Trian needed answers, and Lark understood him well enough to ignore Grainne's edict. "Five minutes," she allowed. "And just the basic facts." And so Lark related how Trian came to be incapacitated.

CHAPTER NINETEEN

The Sea Bride

The first thing Claire noticed when she woke was the cry of gulls. The second was the stench. Whereas over the last couple days she'd smelled nothing but the scouring scent of saltwater, the air was now rife with odors: mold, refuse, and the telling reek of algae at low tide. But even if the odors hadn't screamed out that they had made port, the gentle bobbing of the ship was a sure sign. She raced to the porthole.

Outside, the sun had yet to rise, and no one was stirring on the piers save the wharf rats. The ship must have docked after she had fallen into an exhausted sleep. Huge mooring ropes stretched from somewhere above her. The time to escape was nigh; she only had to wait until the ship was bustling with activity.

Claire hadn't been idle in the two days since the captain had locked her in the room with what he believed was only a pail of water. She had portioned out her supplies, and even though Diarmait's men would be four more days in coming, she ate the last of her fish, bread, and cheese. She would need her strength. The figs and the dried fruit she saved, slipping them into the worn leather satchel. She planned on being far away when her future captors arrived.

Claire had refused to slip into self-pity. As soon as the captain had left her alone, she'd started planning. *Observe. Conceal. Adapt.* In the few moments she had had with Amal, and then the captain, she had studied them. How they walked, their gestures and mannerisms, even their accents. And at night, when someone had paused with a lantern near her door, they had exposed to her a crack in the frame. She had spent long minutes whittling away sliver after sliver. If she set her eye close to the tiny opening, she could see a small slice of the action on the ship, gleaning even more information to use for her escape. *Observe.*

She practiced the saunter of the sailors even now as she walked to the porthole and peered out into the growing light. The crew was waking, getting ready for the day. The sound of wood sliding against wood ended in a loud clatter as something heavy hit the docks—the gangplank had been dropped. Two men stepped nimbly down it and, as she observed them, walked in a jerking gait on the dock for a few steps before regaining their swagger.

Two hours more and she would act. She sat on the pallet, then grabbed the bundle from under her bed. She'd already bound her chest with strips of torn blankets. Over her own clothing, she pulled on Amal's, giving herself the much-needed bulk to disguise her curves. She considered his colorful vest; it might be identified as belonging to the dead sailor. Her study of the men on the ship revealed that most of them wore vests, each uniquely patterned. "Think, Claire," she ordered herself. "Yes!" It was as simple as figuring out how to escape her locked room. She turned the vest inside out and shrugged into it. *Conceal.*

She turned toward the door and examined her handiwork. The captain had been foolish in believing her secure. Though the door was locked, its hinges faced the inside of the cabin. Claire had removed the two lower pins. By pulling out the door near the floor, she could create a wedge that would be just wide enough for her to slip through. The topmost hardware would hold the door secure after she pulled it back into place.

Claire's plan was outrageously simple. She would wait until no one was outside the cabin, then slip out. The sailors and dockworkers would mingle while unloading the current cargo and loading the new goods, allowing Claire to slip into the queue of men. With luck and a little skill, she would be mistaken by both sides as belonging to the other. Once down the gangplank, she would deposit her load, then drift away unnoticed into the crowd. *Adapt.*

There was one task remaining; she'd saved it for last. As she lifted Pieter's blade, the idea that she was somehow betraying Trian filled her again. "Quit this foolishness. Trian wouldn't care. He would want you to survive." She grabbed a handful of her lank and dirty hair and wrapped it tightly around her fist. The knife work was quick at first, then it took some sawing as her blade dulled with the task she'd set it to. Eventually, every strand gave way. She stared at the last fistful of her hair, then dropped it into the privy bucket to be covered by her accumulated waste.

She slipped the blade back into her boot, then mussed her shorn locks. It was the same length that Amal's had been. Finally, she pulled the floppy hat from her waistband and stretched it over her head. From the lamp, Claire used some of the soot to soil her face, teeth, and hands. She frowned. Her fingers were still too clean, so she scraped more soot from the lamp, then rubbed it into her cuticles and under her nails until she had the desired effect. She used the last of the greasy ash to dirty her breeches and boots with dark smudges, concealing as best she could their Aurelian style.

From the tromping of feet on the ship's deck, Claire deemed it time to leave. She squeezed the pouch holding the glass bauble from Trian, drew what strength she could from it, then slipped it back into her boot. She adjusted the strap on her leather bag so that it crossed her chest and back, just as the sailors wore theirs.

Outside her porthole, the first wave of cargo had been carried from the ship, and dock workers began the process of lading the new. A steady stream of men and goods traveled up and down the gangplank. Claire stepped to the door, removed the hardware holding the hinge together, then peered through the crack. When her path was clear, she pulled at the bottom of the door and squeezed through the gap, closing it behind her. She stood straight and quickly assessed her surroundings.

"Don't let the cap'n find you lurking about that door or you'll find yourself sharing dinner with the fish," a voice growled behind her. Claire turned slightly, the strands of her butchered hair hiding the profile of her face, and then tipped up her chin and touched her forefinger to her cap as she'd seen the others do. "You dockers, always trying to find the easy way," the sailor snarled. "Straight ahead and you'll find enough to carry back down. Keeping busy'll keep you alive."

Claire shrugged and searched for something she could carry alone. Crates bigger than she abounded. But farther on, there were stacks of fleece-filled bags made of a rough, open-weave fabric. Claire found that she could easily heft the fleece to her shoulder. She grabbed a second bag for the other side, concealing her face even more. Then, she fell in with the line of men departing the ship. Ahead, she recognized the captain, set a grim line across her mouth, and walked unconcernedly right past him. After depositing her bundles in the growing pile on the dock, she turned to take one last look at the ship that had carried her to these foreign shores—ironic that she was christened *The Sea Bride*—and then she disappeared into the crowd, slipping into the flow of foot traffic filling the busy streets.

CHAPTER TWENTY
Damaged Goods

"The trail was easy to follow," Warin explained to Anna and Lark. After he dismounted in the stable, Will took the reins of his horse. Pieter stood by with an anxious expression on his face. "Speed was their purpose, not concealing their passage. When they hit the beach, they abandoned their mounts. I found cut brush strewn about, probably from hiding a small craft. From there, it would have been easy to row to a waiting ship. I'm so sorry, Anna, but your sister is on her way to Nifolhad, probably there already."

"It's Diarmait, Lark. He made good on his threats against me; only his men took Claire by mistake."

"I'm afraid you're right. I'll get her back for you, I swear it."

"I'm sorry, my friend, but you can't leave Stolweg," Warin countered. "Especially now. King Godwin will never sanction it."

"He's right, Lark," Anna counseled.

Before Lark could protest, Warin added, "I'll go."

"Fine. But can't you go alone, Warin."

"I must," he averred. "If I don't leave now, Godwin will get wind of the abduction and forbid any rescue attempt. He'll push for a diplomatic resolution. You know it as well as I. But if I am already gone…"

"I'll go, too." Warin turned to find Pieter listening in.

"Absolutely not," Anna stated. "You are not responsible for Claire being taken; there was nothing you could've done. Claire sending you to retrieve the mares likely saved your life." Warin glanced at Lark.

"I doubt you could stop him, Anna," Warin coaxed. "Better he's with me than running off on his own. I'll keep him safe." Warin could tell by the way the stable boy tensed that Pieter was about to add to the argument. He laid a heavy hand on the lad's shoulder and tightened his grip. Anna still wasn't convinced, and any show of exuberance on Pieter's part would tip the balance in the wrong direction. "Besides," Warin added, "I have a plan." He reminded them whence came the wealth of his family.

"But smugglers?" Anna worried. "Can you trust them?"

"Of course," he answered easily. "I used to sail with the men from the Southron Isles. It's a rite of passage for any Pheldhainian. They've charted every cove and inlet in Aurelia. And Nifolhad, too. By now, the ship that took Claire has made land somewhere along their eastern coast, probably Kantahla Bay. It's the closest port to Diarmait's stronghold; I should have no problem slipping in. Besides, I've already sent word to my brother; he'll have my ship and crew waiting for me.

"Claire's alive. I'm sure of it," Warin continued. "Diarmait could've had her killed in the valley. He didn't." Warin needed not add that Diarmait most likely had special plans for her. "I swear to bring her back, Anna. But before I go, I would like to speak with Trian."

Lark led the way. Behind them, he heard Anna instructing Pieter to pack his belongings, then meet her in the armory. Warin and Lark were almost inside the castle when he heard Anna call out his name.

"One more thing," she said, catching up to them. "When you find Claire, give her this." She handed him a sheathed dagger. "And be careful," she cautioned. "We need you to come back, too." She kissed his cheek, her eyes growing bright with tears, and then continued on her way to the armory.

The leather sheath was one of the finest Warin had ever beheld. A great destrier surrounded by intricately tooled stars merged the symbols of what would be Claire's new coat of arms: the Chevring escutcheon and the ancient symbols from the line of women from which Claire and Anna came. He turned it over in his hands to discover that part of the leather had been cut clean through on one side. Warin pulled out the blade. It was an old dagger, and one that he recognized well, for it matched the weapons and armor held by Lady Anna. Where the cross guard met the blade, there was a shallow gouge in the metal.

"That blade saved Trian from sure death," Lark explained as he navigated the corridors leading to Trian's room. "He was carrying it under his tunic, and it turned the quarrel's tip from his heart."

Warin slipped the blade home, detecting a small hitch as the uneven metal snagged on the rent leather, then followed Lark to the room where Trian was recovering.

"Warin," Lark cautioned before they entered, "he isn't the same. He's lost part of his memory. What he had with Claire is gone, though Grainne is sure that it will come back in time. I'm starting to believe it, too. He holds one of Claire's handkerchiefs and refuses to let it go. But Grainne is worried that if we push him too hard, it will hinder his recovery. He needs to come to it of his own accord."

"Understood."

"There's one more thing. What I am going to tell you, I've sworn an oath to never share with anyone. You see, Cathmaran betrothal rites—"

"Please, Lark," Warin interrupted, "please tell me that his family isn't making him adhere to their ridiculous rules about courtship and marriage." Warin grinned at Lark's astonished face.

"But how came *you* by this knowledge?"

"Well, my mother's uncle's third son's fourth daughter—"

"Your *cousin*, in other words."

"My cousin," Warin conceded. "She married a Cathmaran from Marach—they met when she traveled to Cathmara with her family to purchase ships; they now reside in Pheldhain." Warin stopped suddenly, realizing where Lark was going. "How much time does Claire have before Trian is forced into a betrothal with another?"

"Less than a year. Claire must return to press her claim by the autumnal equinox. Otherwise, he will be lost to her."

Warin leaned against the wall outside of Trian's chamber and released a long, worried whistle. "Does she know of the three challenges?" Lark's perplexed expression answered his question. "If his hand is in contention from any other—and I guarantee that it will be from the other houses in Cathmara—she'll have to prove herself by winning him. Is Claire even aware that she must petition his mother?"

Lark shook his head. "We've had word from Trian's family. He's to return home in two weeks to complete his recuperation. There's not enough time to help him to remember what he had with Claire, but we can start the process. When Anna is with him, she discusses the time he's spent here, days when Claire was also present." Lark put his hand on the door to Trian's chamber, but paused before entering. "Warin, his memory will return. But the poison in his leg weakened him."

Warin thought back to when Lord Roger had been alive and to the clearing where poison had almost taken Warin's life. Even now, he shuddered to recall how it had inhibited his ability to move. He followed Lark into Trian's room expecting the worst.

Grainne was there, bustling about. The first thing Warin noticed was how clean the air smelled, not closed and dark, but bright with the scent of fresh herbs and flowers. This was Claire's chamber, and he took in the rows of drying plants hanging from dowels. The shutters on the side windows were open, allowing the rich October air to permeate the space. A fire burned steadily in the hearth, keeping the cooling afternoon warm. From the great mullioned window, the golden light of autumn fell across the bed where his friend rested.

The once-robust guard stared back at Warin with empty eyes. It was as if an essential part of him had bled out into the valley where his head had struck the rock. His cheeks were hollow, his chest smaller, even his once-full beard seemed scraggly. Warin sat in the chair next to the bed, stretching out his legs and folding his arms across his chest in an insouciant manner. Lark beckoned Grainne from the chamber.

"What do you want, Warin?" Trian asked testily, sitting up in his bed.

"That is the very question I have for you," Warin drawled. "What is it that *you* want?"

Trian slumped back against the cushions and stared across the room at the window. Warin waited patiently while his friend found the words. "I want what was taken from me," he declared angrily.

"And what was that, my friend?"

Trian turned, his eyes bright with desperation, and in his clenched hand was a blue-flowered handkerchief. "I don't know," he said, sounding lost. "And they won't tell me. It has to do with Lady Anna's sister. And this." He held out the wrinkled square of linen. "Can *you* tell me?"

Warin took the kerchief and smoothed it over his palm. "I'm afraid, my friend, that what was taken was a part of your heart."

Trian looked almost relieved to have heard it spoken aloud. "Yes, that's exactly how it feels!"

Warin handed the kerchief back to him. "Do you know the name of the flower embroidered there?" Trian shook his head. "It's called forget-me-not. And when you remember how you came by that kerchief, you'll have once again that which you seek."

"And the rest that was stolen?"

Warin smiled and leaned forward. "Ah, well, I'm going to find it and bring it back to you." He stood up to leave. "My oath to you, Trian."

"Why?" Trian asked. "Why would you do this for me?

"Two simple reasons. One: I have never had what you have lost— that alone is painful enough. And two: because you are my friend and you would do the same for me." Trian seemed to accept Warin's reasons, then relaxed deeper into the cushions, falling into what Warin hoped would be a less troubled sleep.

CHAPTER TWENTY-ONE

 Nlaca'an

Thank you, Trian, Claire thought. He'd made her stronger than she'd ever imagined she could be. She rolled her shoulders forward and walked in an ungainly manner through the marketplace. All around her, the scents of strange spices assaulted her nose. And the colors! Never before had she dreamed of such colors. Silks and damasks and the finest woolens in hues she'd never dreamed could be produced surrounded her. The rainbow of flowers she had used to decorate the courtyard during the summer solstice came to mind, and unbidden memories of Trian, of dancing, of their first kiss. And just as she could turn off her ability to sense things about other people, Claire closed off her own recollections lest they overwhelm her in this public place. She would mourn Trian once she was quit of Nifolhad. For now, she needed drink and nourishment.

She spent her morning on the outskirts of the market. The produce available there was of baser quality, but the vendors were less inquisitive. Unlike the busiest booths, with the barter and banter loud and involved, the outside booths offered no such camaraderie. Claire took a coin from her pouch, one that she had seen a man use to buy a crock of wine, and approached the same merchant. The seller kept his head down, and like the previous patron, Claire pointed to one of the crocks and held out her coin. The man didn't even look up from what he was doing as he took the money and shrugged for her to take her wine and leave.

Claire found another stall with cheese and bought more than she ought to have, not knowing the worth of the coin she used. But, she was getting used to the process. The next time she stopped, she pointed to a loaf of bread and handed over her money. As she turned away with the loaf, the vendor shouted at her, causing those around her to stare. Claire turned, feigning annoyance. The man held out his hand when Claire returned to the stall, and she realized her error. She'd given too much for the bread and had forgotten her change. The merchant dropped it into her outstretched palm, gazing around at the others to show them that he was an honest man. Claire slipped away as more customers were drawn to the booth.

She found a quiet spot away from the market, but not far enough away that she couldn't slip into the crowds and disappear at the first hint of danger. She tore off a chunk of bread and ate it, then did the same with the cheese. She wished that she had some fruit as well, but those booths had been in the center of the market. She took a swallow of the wine. Her eyes watered, but she choked down the vile liquid. It was worse than drinking vinegar. There was a fountain trickling nearby, so she surreptitiously dumped the contents of the crock into the dirt, then filled it with fresh water.

Claire returned to the spot where she'd eaten her bread and cheese. For the rest of the day, she listened to the accents, trying to mimic them under her breath, and studied the mannerisms of the people around her, all the while trying to discover some means of conveyance to the north and Sophiana. Once there, she would petition Prince Ranulf for his aide in returning her safely to Aurelia.

She espied a shadowy figure huddling in an entranceway directly opposite of where she sat. The person stepped into the sunlight; it was a woman. She was covered head to toe, and she looked back and forth, then hurried down a deserted alley to finally disappear around a bend along the cobbled street.

Claire looked around. The market crowd was comprised only of men, she realized in alarm. There wasn't a single woman to be seen. Where were they all? Some of what Amal had said came back to her: "Pretend you make it off the ship. You can't hide. You are a woman in men's clothing. Where could you go?"

The vendors began packing up their wares. Night was not far off, and with night, Claire would need shelter. A large group of men were leaving the market, and Claire slipped into the throng.

One after another, men started peeling away from the main group, going down one side alley or another, until only twenty or so remained. They were stretched out, not talking to each other, so she felt secure enough to stay with them. As the sky darkened and the number of men filtered down to less than a dozen, Claire lagged farther and farther behind the group. Ahead of her, rectangles of light spilled onto the cobbled walk. She passed one open door, and peered inside. A tavern. And then another. The deeper into the city she went, the seedier the drinking rooms became. She passed by another and, for the first time, espied more women. These were not the bawdy tavern wenches of Aurelia, whose vocations were respectable, but women of a different sort.

There was no one behind her, nor ahead; Claire was alone in the labyrinth of an unknown city. To her right, one last spill of light indicated an open door; the muted illumination was inconsistent, as if it came from a low-burning hearth. She stopped to get her bearings and heard a sharp suck of air through teeth.

"A mite fresh for these parts, you are," came a coarse, but definitely female voice. "Shouldn't you be at home with yer mam?"

Claire turned around to head back the way she had come, but stopped when she noticed a furtive movement near one of the darkened alcoves. If she kept onward, perhaps the alley would spill into a larger street. She chose to continue up the pitch black alley.

"What's the trouble?" the woman in the doorway sneered, angling so that Claire could see her features in the dim light. Her front teeth were rotten, and her upper lip was split clean through and long since healed. "Looking for your mam, lil man? Or is it a dif'rent sort of teat you need?" The woman reached into her bodice and pulled out her breast, blue veined and ponderous. Claire whirled away from the sight. The shadow behind her had shifted; whoever it was had used the distraction to move closer. Claire headed deeper into the darkness. The wench's cackles buffeted her from behind, pushing her forward that much faster.

She stepped stealthily up the cobbled passage and waited for her eyes to adjust. The buildings had grown closer together, and it seemed to Claire that the walls were leaning forward, staring down at her as she progressed deeper into the shadows. She found an alcove on her right and slipped into its dark embrace to peer back the way she'd come. She waited, her heartbeat loud in her ears. Finally, there was a shape, blacker than the shadows surrounding it, keeping to the left side of the lane. Claire had two choices: wait and confront her pursuer; or blindly move forward, aware that somewhere ahead, her path would likely come to an end.

The figure was only paces away. Claire was reaching down to pull out her only weapon when a dim light suddenly silhouetted her stalker. The light grew, and the figure—one that Claire could see was cloaked—jumped to the side and hid in a recess directly across from where Claire stood, holding one finger to his lips.

Claire pressed herself deeper into her niche, sliding down to make herself as small as possible. The raucous laughter of several men echoed down the alleyway and, as they approached, the light from their swinging lantern caromed off the sharp angles of the frontages. They passed by, then walked around the next twist of the lane, and the lamp's glow faded with their voices. Claire looked for the man who had followed her, but her sight had been compromised by the lantern. She inched forward and waited, allowing her hearing to take the lead. It was the humid exhale that had her darting to the side just as she felt a hand brush her arm.

She pivoted on her toes and was about to flee back down the alley, and to the taverns, when a whispered call reached her. "Wait! They know you've escaped the ship. They are searching the city."

"Who are you?" Claire demanded, her voice a mere wisp of smoke in the night.

"Come with me or be captured," the voice exhorted. Claire liked neither option. Another wash of light spread across the walls behind them. This light was purposeful, and Claire heard urgent voices.

"Follow me. Quickly!" Her pursuer turned and raced up the dark alley, away from the men behind them.

Claire made her decision and took off, close on his heels. When they came to a sharp turn, the man surprised her by stopping at a slatted wall. He reached up and pushed at the barrier, exposing a hidden entrance. They darted through, closing the door behind them and sealing themselves in pitch blackness. Claire was blind.

"Mind yourself," the voice cautioned, coming from farther away and above her. "On the right, there's a groove cut into the stone; it rises with the steps and will guide you in the dark."

Claire found it and moved forward. Soon she was racing along as fast as the man. From his slight build, she had assumed that he was young, a boy even. He was nearly silent, but her training allowed her to detect the sound of his footfalls, breathing, and even the hiss of his cloak against the stone wall. There was a creak of wood and hinge, and suddenly Claire was up and out into the fresh air. She stopped and stared out at a crystal-clear evening. Already, the stars glowed brilliantly in the night. Spread below her was an immense city with storied buildings crowded so close together that passage between seemed impossible. Everywhere the walls were made of stone and rock, the rooftops of flat clay tiles. Claire looked to the east. The bay, with its many ships, waited, an uninterrupted slick of ink save for the spike of moonlight cutting over the glass-like surface of the water. That it was the hunter's moon was apropos of her current predicament. "What is this city called?" Claire asked her mysterious guide.

"Naca'an. And that is Naca Bay, whence you escaped."

Claire gazed out, amazed by how far she had traveled over the course of the day. "How did you find me?"

"I nearly didn't. You are very good. Too good almost," the guide replied without truly stating how. "Follow me. We must make the western edge of Naca'an before sunrise."

"How far is it?"

The figure moved along the edge of the rooftop. "If we had wings, several leagues. As we don't, we are forced to pick our way. Stay close; we'll rest in an hour."

"Who are you?" Claire demanded again, but her guide was not one for answering questions and had already slipped away. Their trek was easier to manage than she had imagined it would be, slinking like cats along the spine of the city. Thanks to Trian, her endurance was much improved, and after an hour, Claire pressed to keep going without rest. When they finally stopped to share some of Claire's water, she again asked her guide how he had seen through her disguise.

"By accident. When you drank of the fountain water, you tilted your head and exposed your neck," the cloaked voice told her. "Rare is the man who has no apple." Claire's guide raised the crock of water to take another swig, baring his throat to the rising moon.

"You're a woman!" Claire exclaimed, and her guide shrugged. "Who are you?"

The woman ignored her, passing the water back to Claire, who lifted it to her lips and drained the rest. She opened her satchel to store the empty jug. "Leave it. We'll have water and more in the morning." They rose from their crouched positions and started again, weaving back and forth along the rooflines, always moving westward.

CHAPTER TWENTY-TWO

Sacred Fruit

The moon had risen and set, and still Claire followed her guide at a relentless pace, the entire time doubting that she could trust the cloaked woman. The quiet bore down on her, making even her heartbeat clang like an alarm ringing through the city. When her guide stopped and stood at the edge of a rooftop, she beckoned Claire forward and pointed out into the night.

"Our destination is just beyond the trees," she whispered. "It is the most perilous stretch. We will be forced to leave the safety of the rooftops and travel on the ground. We'll rest here a moment before continuing." They sat down, and she handed her water sack to Claire, not bothering to hide her curious stare.

Claire took it and drank. She wiped her mouth on her sleeve, then stared back. "If you have a question, ask it."

"You surprise me. We have been taught that the women from Aurelia are soft. Well, not you, exactly. The tales about you are well known. Still, there are few in Nifolhad who could keep apace of me. And those who can are without your skill. You were so quiet, I found myself searching behind me, believing you had gone."

Taking a cue from her guide's behavior, Claire offered no explanation and turned to the west. They were on the far edge of the city; the roof upon which they rested looked over an immense forest. Beyond the trees, a hill rose, and on top of it a great palace was perched. She gazed again at the city over which they had raced. Above them, the stars were yet bright against the black night, but to the east, the sky had brightened to the darkest of indigos.

"I've been instructed to not talk to you other than giving you directions to follow, but you need to know what is ahead. There are wardens in the woods," the woman warned. "They guard the forest both day and night."

"Whose palace is that to the west?" Her guide was not forthcoming, so Claire tried a threat instead. "Perhaps I would be safer on my own."

The woman's features tightened. "It was Princess Aghna's seat. I suppose it belongs to Diarmait now. He's not there," her guide tempered when Claire swore. "Besides, the palace is not our destination."

"Then where are we going?"

"To sanctuary," she replied, divulging no more. "But the forest, you must—"

"Stop it," Claire ordered. She'd had enough. She was safely delivered from the streets of Naca'an. All she needed now was a place to rest. If her guide couldn't guarantee that much, she would retreat and squirrel away for the coming day in one of the many hiding spots she'd noted during their race over the city. It would be nothing to lose the woman and start out on her own, traveling northwest to where Prince Ranulf still held power. She could take her chances with him. "If you want me to remain with you, tell me where we are going." Her guide remained unmoved. "I don't even know your name, and you are asking me to blindly follow you. I could have lost you a dozen times over. In the woods, the next time you turn to look for me, I won't be there. Now, where are you taking me?"

Her guide squared her shoulders. "To the Fenrhi," she finally informed Claire. "To our temple, west of the palace."

"Who are the Fenrhi?"

"We are women," she declared proudly. "We live outside the rules of the men of Nifolhad. They leave us in peace because we leave them in peace. Now, it will be light soon, and we must be through the forest before dawn. If the wardens hear us, they will hunt us. Our passage must be silent. We must be invisible to their eyes and less than a breeze to their ears."

"Then perhaps I should go first." Her guide was alert, but Claire detected traces of weariness creeping into her eyes. It had been a long race. Claire, too, was feeling the fingers of exhaustion digging into her muscles. She reached into her pouch and pulled out some of the dried berry-like fruits that she'd taken from Amal's belongings. Their sweetness would give her a much-needed burst of energy, and she popped a couple into her mouth. She held out her palm, presenting a few to her guide.

The woman's eyes widened as if she were afraid someone would see. "Where did you get those?" she asked, her voice reverent.

"On the ship. Why?" Claire chewed the fruit. "What are they?"

"They are dried pihaberries from the pijala tree. They are sacred." She stared at the fruit in Claire's palm, as if unsure what to do. "Thank you, but no; I have naught with which to pay you."

"Pay me? I expect no payment from you."

"You would if you understood the value of what you offer. The fruit has become almost impossible to procure. Pijala trees grow only in the northwest. If Diarmait knew that the captain had such a bounty, he would kill the man and his entire crew."

"So, I was not the only illicit cargo on that ship," Claire observed humorlessly. "Why are the trees sacred?"

"Not the trees, the fruit. The pihaberries are revered for their many properties, including renewing strength in body. They are purported to give visions to those with special gifts, and to protect the mind against trickery." The woman frowned and studied Claire for a moment, as if struggling with some decision. "Put them away, and hide them once we reach the temple, or they will be confiscated. You may find that you have need of them one day."

Claire took her guide's hand and dropped the fruit into her palm. "I demand no payment from you," she repeated. "If you are as tired as I was before eating these, then you jeopardize our flight. Eat them. Do not be so foolish as to think I will not desert you if you are detected."

The woman bowed her head and placed a single berry in her mouth. The others she tucked into the folds of her sash. She chewed with her eyes closed. When she finally swallowed, she looked over the roof to the ground below, then eased her body over the edge. "The vines here are strong enough to hold us both. Come, Lady Aubrianne, I'll lead us to the tree line, then you can take point."

"You trust me, then," Claire stated, dropping down to the wall and climbing after her guide.

"You shared the bounty of the pijala. Offered it without price. Such a thing is not done in Nifolhad. So I will pay you back with trust and with honesty." She stopped her descent, hanging on the vines. In the dark, Claire felt the weight of the woman's scrutiny. "My name is Madyan." She dropped the last few feet to the ground before skirting along the shadowed side of the street, slinking north. Claire followed.

Closer and closer the trees loomed, stretching their branches and scratching the mortared stones with their twiggy fingers. The western buildings of Naca'an created a natural barrier against the forest. But soon the structures were replaced by a thick stone wall, one that rose higher and higher the further north they moved. Her guide stopped, their path having dissolved into the growth of trees. "The wardens live *in* the trees. It is too dark in the forest for them to see us. Likewise, we cannot see them. But if they hear us, they will find us."

"And if they do?"

"They will kill us and feed our corpses to their pigs." Claire shivered, the words were spoken so matter-of-factly. "Are you ready, Lady Aubrianne?"

"Almost," Claire whispered. "Lady Aubrianne is my sister. My name is Claire."

"You've honored me twice now," Madyan noted, her voice barely distinguishable from the rustling of the breeze through the forest's canopy. "Now, we really must hasten."

Claire stepped silently between the trees. She moved confidently, taking her time, picking the spots where her feet would fall. Her ears were open to the sounds of the night; her eyes adjusted to the murkiness of the woods. This time, it was Claire glancing back every few minutes to make sure Madyan had not fallen behind. She paused repeatedly to reconnoiter. Their pace was steady and silent. Just when Claire believed they would reach the temple without incident, she drew to an abrupt halt. She listened, but heard nothing. She peered through the thick trees and up into the branches, and again, nothing. But her instincts were screaming that danger was near.

Claire took a deep, silent inhalation. On the soft breeze coming from the west, she caught the scent of sweat and burning oil. Someone was coming. She led Madyan north, into a growth of maple, then up into the ladder-like branches. There, they concealed themselves and waited.

Scanning the forest floor, she heard the men before she saw them; Madyan mouthed the word *wardens*. There were two of them, one holding an almost completely shuttered lantern. They walked slowly, searching back and forth.

"Close that lantern," one of them hissed. "If she's made it this far, you'll give her warning." The light was snuffed instantly, and only a soft shuffling of feet could be heard below the branches where Claire and Madyan hid.

"This is a snipe hunt," the lantern holder carped. "If the woman were fool enough to come through the forest, we would've heard her by now. We've searched since dusk, and I've heard nothing but leaves rustling and your labored panting for hours. I say we go back now, before there's nothing left that's warm to eat."

"We should go at least as far as the wall," the other man advised. "If Diarmait's witch is awake when we return, we'll want to have an honest answer for her. Quit your complaining; come on, it's not much farther." They disappeared into the trees.

To be safe, Claire waited ten minutes, then slipped from the branches. Madyan dropped silently next to her. "Diarmait's witch?" Claire whispered.

"A truthseer," Madyan retorted angrily. "We must hurry now. The wardens may have gone to the wall without haste, but their path home won't be so cautious. And the night's ink is fading fast."

But Claire was already moving northwest, slipping silently from tree to tree, listening and smelling. There was barely any light in the forest, but despite the dimness, she searched the ground and the branches above as she moved. A truthseer, she marveled. Did such a person truly exist? Nifolhad was a strange land indeed. If Trian were here with her— she nearly stumbled when his image came to mind. She pushed her pain away again, somehow knowing that in a realm with truthseers and sacred fruit, there would be more to survive in the coming weeks than these woods.

CHAPTER TWENTY-THREE
The Bathhouse

Claire's head was still heavy with sleep when she finally woke. She ran her hands through her hair, remembering too late that it was matted with the dirt and blood from her journey. She'd been given a sparsely furnished room, nightclothes, and refreshment, and then had been left alone. Her hands were cleaner than they'd been before; most of the lantern soot was gone. She touched her face. The grime there too had been wiped away. Her mouth was dry and gummy, and she recalled drinking the tart, sweet nectar that had been set out for her. She'd been too tired to eat. At least she had remembered to secure the pouch of pihaberries behind her bed. That was all that she could recall from the moment she'd entered the temple to waking in this room; she'd fallen asleep as soon as her head had hit the pillow.

Claire absorbed her surroundings; it was light outside the small, high-set window behind her. By the soft quality of it, Claire deemed it to be morning. She frowned. Had she only slept a few hours? She felt as if she hadn't moved in days. Her mind was struggling to shake free of the grogginess she'd felt when she had first opened her eyes. Her clothes had been laundered, then placed in a neat pile on the chair next to her bed. Could she have slept the entire day and night, and was now waking to a new morning?

She rose and stripped the sleeping gown away, for even if her own garments were in tatters, at least they were hers—most of them anyways. She left Amal's clothing on the chair. Her boots, now clean of the filth of the last few weeks, rested next to the door. She tucked her pihaberries into the waistband of her breeches, and then crossed the room to check the door.

Though it was reassuringly unlocked, it didn't necessarily mean that she wasn't a prisoner of the Fenrhi. One door and one small window covered by an intricately carved screen were the only two possible points of egress from the odd wedge-shaped room.

Claire had almost forgotten her other belongings: Pieter's dagger and, more importantly, Trian's gift. Her panic was short-lived when she saw the knife, her leather bag, and the small leather pouch holding her precious bauble. She plucked the pouch from the table and dropped its contents into her palm. The glass-shrouded forget-me-not blossom sparkled in her hand as fresh as the day Trian must have picked it. She kissed the token before slipping it back into the pouch and hanging it around her neck.

Someone had come into her room while she had slept, cleaned her boots, washed her garments, and rearranged her belongings. While she pondered this, she heard a soft rapping on the door. "Enter," she beckoned, hoping it would be Madyan.

A slim woman garbed in a pale gray tunic and leggings entered. "Good day, m'lady," she greeted, then walked to the table to set down a small tray of bread, cheese and fruit. "I am called Milla. I have been sent to serve you while you are in the Fenrhi's care." She stood in front of Claire and bowed her head, her eyes downcast, then returned to the table where she straightened the already neat tray.

"Where is Madyan?" Claire asked.

"She is fine," Milla assured. She glanced over her shoulder at Claire, managing to keep her chin tucked down so that Claire could not regard her face. Then, Milla closed the door and turned to her. "A name spoken to another by one from the temple is a gift. Please, do not use hers so freely. It would be considered ungrateful of you. I am only telling you this because you are unfamiliar with our customs."

"But you have given me your name," Claire pointed out.

"I am a simple initiate. The name Milla holds little value," she droned. Her words were rote and definitive of her status.

"Milla, look at me, please." Keeping her eyes to the floor, the woman lifted her chin haughtily, as if unused to being commanded. She was perhaps Anna's age. "I will value your friend's gift and keep her name secret."

"But why do you assume that she is my friend?" Milla asked suspiciously.

"You must be friends because you, too, know her name. And I will respect her, and you, because you have taught me something new," Claire pointed out, trying to remain patient. "And while I do not require a servant, I could benefit from a teacher during my stay here, however short my residence may be." Milla tilted her head in contemplation, flashing her eyes up at Claire for the briefest of moments. Her irises were large and hazel and, Claire saw, breathtaking. "I only wanted to thank my guide. I would not be here if it were not for her aid."

"I am only an initiate—" she started, then paused when Claire let loose a beleaguered sigh. "Fine," she conceded, in a tone equally as terse as Claire's had been. "I will endeavor to be of help."

Claire laughed, so sarcastic was Milla's delivery. This was no down-trodden servant by any means. "And our mutual friend?" she prompted.

"I do not know where she is, m'lady. Resting, most likely." There was a touch of amusement in Milla's voice. "But I am sure she is all right; she is very resourceful." She studied Claire's dirty bag with a frown and sniffed the air. "I have brought you fresh bread and cheese, m'lady. Can I take away your spoiled food?" Claire nodded and Milla plucked the bag from the table. "I am instructed to tell you that you will be meeting Mother this afternoon. She leads the Fenrhi. I am sure you would like to breakfast and bathe first. I will wait for you in the hallway while you eat, then take you to the bathing rooms."

Claire was relieved that the woman had gone, for if she was to bathe, she would need to hide the pihaberries first. She did not trust this place. Odder still was the way Milla had said "Mother." She pulled the small pouch from her breeches and searched the chamber. She settled on securing the tiny bundle to the slats on the underside of her bed. When she stood, her stomach protested that it had been too long since she had eaten. Claire took a piece of cheese and nibbled at the mild white chunk. She paired it with the thick brown bread, eating while she surveyed her chamber. After grabbing a handful of grapes, she left her room to meet Milla.

As they walked, Claire attempted to memorize the route: down a short passageway, though an archway, and into a courtyard. She stopped in the center of the open space, then turned and gazed at the egress from which they had just come. Each entrance had its own symbol; she committed hers to memory.

Milla, having noticed that her charge was no longer following, turned around. "Your room is in the guest quarters." She pointed to the design above the door. "That is the symbol for 'welcome' here. And there," she pointed to an entrance across the courtyard, "that way leads to the baths."

Milla tapped her foot impatiently while Claire studied her surroundings. "After you meet with Mother, I will take you on a tour of the temple. For now, you really must bathe." Claire resisted touching her head when she caught Milla staring at what was left of her hair.

The moment they stepped under the archway leading to the baths, Claire could feel the steam on her skin, warm and humid. The soft, musical *plink*ing of water drops filled her ears. Moisture beaded on the smooth, flat stones that made up the walls and floor.

Milla passed her, leading her down a short, dimly lit corridor. At the end of the hall, there was a small round foyer surrounded by six narrow, arched openings. Claire followed Milla to the right and under the first arch.

Like her chamber, this room was strangely shaped. In the middle of the floor, there was a reservoir filled with steaming water. In fact, the entire floor was warm. The baths must've been situated above a hot spring, one that had been contained and directed to the manmade basins.

"Take as long as you need," Milla said quietly. "We have a couple of hours before your meeting—"

"—with your, the, Mother," Claire finished, uncomfortable using the moniker.

Milla nodded, then pointed to a tray set next to the stone pool. "Oils, salts, and soap," she explained, "from the herbarium. You'll find sponges and cloths as well, and cool water to drink. There are fresh linens in the corner with which to dry yourself. If you put your clothing in the basket near the wall, I will bring fresh replacements suitable for your audience with Mother." She bowed, backing her way from the room. Just before she departed, she paused. "I will make sure to return your garments to your room once they have been mended."

"Thank you," Claire told her, and the woman was gone. Next to the low basket on the floor, there was a rectangular opening in the wall.

Claire stripped out of her torn clothes and set them in the basket. She sat near the edge of the bath. A submerged shelf ran around the pool, and Claire lowered herself onto it, the water coming up to her chin. She stretched out her legs, searching for the bottom of the reservoir, and found it a couple feet down.

When she dipped under the surface, the grime of dust, oil, and brine lifted from her skin. She ran her fingertips over her scalp and winced when she touched the still-sore spots where she'd been hit on her head. Now that it was so short, her matted hair easily untangled under the water. It must be frightful to look at, she mused, having been hacked off with her dagger.

When she could no longer hold her breath, Claire surfaced. She ran her hands over the stonework of the bath. It was an impressive feat of engineering, even if the builders had shaped the room so oddly.

Something about the bathing chamber niggled at her. Of course! The courtyards, this room, even the shape of her chamber, they were the same. Six bathing rooms: if the walls were removed, the open space would be shaped exactly like the courtyard. Her guest accommodations were slightly larger, and she could imagine three such rooms clustered together, echoing the repetitive shape. Each building and outdoor space was hexagonal and interconnected with the next in a complicated series of honeycomb patterns. Just how large was this temple?

She would have to check her theory later. For now, she wanted to be clean. There were various oils in glass bottles and scented salt crystals in marble bowls. She unstoppered one bottle at a time, sniffing the delicate scents of floral, spice, and citrus. And finally, a perfume that brought tears to her eyes: lavender. She set the bottle down, shaking, and buried her face in her trembling hands. Anna.

A sob racked her body. The tremendous weight of all that she had lost crashed down upon her: Anna, Lark, and Celeste; her friends Warin and Grainne and Doreen and young Sarah. Poor Pieter; she prayed that he was safe. And finally, Trian. She allowed herself to grieve for him, reliving his murder in her mind's eye and breaking apart inside. She had permitted herself to love, and her worst fear had come true. Never again would she feel his touch or hear his beautiful voice when he sang. Never again could she be so unguarded with another. Worst of all, he had died never knowing that she loved him because she had never said the words.

Claire sat in the bath, drawing her knees up to her chin and wrapping her arms around her legs. For a long while, she simply wept.

It was the scent of lavender that finally brought her from her despair. And when she rinsed the tears from her face, she grew angry. She was through with crying. Trian was gone, just like her parents, but her sister was still alive, and her niece, and Claire would spend every minute working toward returning to them. She selected a citrus scent from the tray and poured some into the steaming water. Then, she plucked one of the sponges that had been placed next to the bottles and began scrubbing herself clean. Until she was home, she wanted no remembrances to distract her. And as soon as her resolution was made, her hand brushed against the leather pouch that hung about her neck. Trian's forget-me-not.

She wrapped her fingers around the soaked leather; it would shrink tightly around the glass as it dried. Good, she thought angrily. Though the pouch would never leave its home from around her neck, she wouldn't take the glass from its leather cocoon again. Simply knowing it was there would lend her the strength that she would need to return to Aurelia. It would forever be a talisman against risking her heart by giving it to another.

There was a soft scraping noise. Drawn to the sound, Claire turned and watched as the basket disappeared through the hole in the wall. She picked up a cloth and poured some of the cool drinking water over the fabric. She folded it, placed it over her closed eyes, and leaned back. She would not meet this Mother with tear-swollen eyes.

Claire considered everything she possessed. She would always have the skills taught to her by Trian. And there was her other talent: her sight. She could read people when she chose to and could divine general impressions without even touching them. She had practiced blocking the visions so often that it was now second nature. Today, she would open her senses when meeting this Mother and gather what information she could regarding the Fenrhi's intentions toward her.

The shushing of wicker against stone drew her attention back to the wall: the basket had been replaced. Within it: fresh clothing. Claire stepped from the bath, dried off, then dressed herself in the strange new garments. They had not given her a gown, but leggings that belted around her waist and tapered at her ankles. There was a fine linen shirt and a long-sleeved tunic that reached to her knees. It was open down the front, with side slits cut to her hips. The tunic and breeches were the color of dried, pink roses. Finally, she slipped her feet into a pair of leather slippers. It was then that Claire discovered one more article of clothing in the basket: a very long, amber-hued sash embroidered with intricate patterns—honeycombs overlaid with elegant swirls and loops in various colors. It had been seeded with many tiny pearls. Beautiful, but its purpose evaded her. As she held it in her hands, Milla entered the room. She took the sash from Claire and, holding the center of the length against Claire's middle, she carefully wound it around and around Claire's waist.

"The smaller belt holds up your leggings and is worn under your tunic, the way you have it on now," Milla instructed. "This sash is worn on the outside of the tunic by wrapping it around your waist. The colors of your garments indicate that you are a guest here and not an initiate. The outer sash tells us that you are to be given special respect and honor."

"And the design?"

"Honeybees are the symbol of royalty in Nifolhad," Milla stated, and Claire heard the tightness in her words. "The honeycomb and its queen are sacred to the Fenrhi. Mother gives you a great gift, honoring you with such a sash." Milla turned Claire around, making slight adjustments to the cloth band. "Perfect," she finished, then frowned when she noted a damp blotch on the tunic just above Claire's heart. She gave an exasperated sigh. "Perhaps Mother will not notice it. Come; she is waiting." She picked up Claire's boots, and preceded Claire out of the bathing room and into the maze of the Fenrhi temple.

CHAPTER TWENTY-FOUR

The Mother

As Claire deduced, the temple was comprised of groups of hexagon-shaped buildings, each leading to another series of rooms or courtyards. Some of the archways were etched with symbols similar to those near her section, but there were others as well. As she proceeded to her audience with the leader of the Fenrhi, Claire found that she was the center of attention. The smiles were always welcoming, the bows respectful, the curious glances never rude. Many of the Fenrhi wore gray, like Milla. Other women stood together, wearing pale blue, mossy green, or black, as Madyan had. They kept to like-colored groupings, and their reactions to her seemed to be determined by the hue they wore.

The women attired in gray invariably nodded or bowed deferentially to her. The Fenrhi gazing upon her with an assessing frankness wore black. The warmest smiles came from the women donning shades of mossy green. And those who stared at her with eager curiosity wore blue. "Milla, what do the colors you wear signify?"

"All Fenrhi begin with the color gray," Milla droned, head bowed and eyes downcast. "It does not change until an initiate is placed. But until one is placed, she must serve in Earth Caste. It can take months or even years, although a lucky few are placed within weeks.

"Green is worn by our caregivers," Milla provided, the longing evident in her voice. "And you are already aware that the shadow women wear black. They comprise the Umbren Caste."

A few women in gray came from under an archway; all were carrying empty trays except for an older woman who was herding her charges before her like a shepherdess. When the others bowed, this woman only inclined her head. Her sash was embroidered with the same intricate honeycomb pattern that adorned Claire's. In the temple, it seemed that even nobility could serve.

"What does blue represent?"

Milla stopped and flicked her gaze about her to make sure they were out of hearing of anyone else. "The women of Kena Caste, they wear blue. You would be wise to avoid them." She turned and walked to the archway whence the women in gray had come. "Here we are," Milla informed her, after their route had twisted and turned through the temple to finally open to an expansive courtyard across which a small but beautiful temple soared toward the sky. "I will wait here to help you find your way back after your audience with Mother is concluded."

Claire crossed the courtyard to the main entrance. She stepped under its arch and into a wide passageway. The ceiling was coffered and intricately carved with symbols similar to those on the multitude of arches throughout the Fenrhi complex. She continued on, then pushed open the heavy double doors before her. Directly in front of her sat a regal woman swathed in a honey-colored robe: the Mother. Flanking out from either side stood a dozen women all dressed in blue. So much for avoiding the Kena. Claire sighed, and the Mother smiled.

"Come forward, please," she beckoned. "I have long wanted to meet you."

Above them, there was a narrow balcony that ringed the entire hall, with six more doors, all evenly spaced. Intricately carved panels of wood surrounded the lower level.

When Claire did step forward, it felt as though she were caught in a river's current. Strange, she thought, and focused on the woman in the honey robe. She pushed forward. There was a gasp from one of the women in blue. The others were frowning.

"Thank you for welcoming me to your temple," Claire acknowledged straight away, "and for giving me sanctuary here."

The woman stood and walked toward her, and Claire detected movement on the balcony above. Women in black were stationed there, ready to protect the head of the Fenrhi. "Leave us," the Mother ordered, and they disappeared like mist on a sunny morning. She turned to the Kena and waited.

"But Mother," one woman started, stepping forward.

"Thank you, Rhiannon, but you may leave as well." The woman in blue stared at her, a crease between her brows. Claire felt as if she were being buffeted by a strong wind and braced herself as if it were real.

"Rhia!" the Mother admonished, and the woman bowed and then turned on her heel, the rest of her caste trailing after her. The pressure Claire had felt dissipated. She shook her head, not quite believing that what she had felt had even happened.

The Mother had turned back to her. "Come, Lady Aubrianne—" so, Madyan had kept her name secret "—we will sit in my private chamber; it is much more comfortable." Claire followed her through a door across the domed room. There was a round brazier with glowing coals set in the center of a sunken pit. Large, silken pillows were strewn around the perimeter. The room, paneled in silk and brocade was, of course, six-sided. And Claire watched, suddenly wary, as her host sat on a cushion next to a small table. She poured two glasses of a golden-hued wine and handed one to Claire.

"I am sure there are many things you wish to know." She took a sip from her cup and waited.

Claire lowered herself to the cushions, quietly regarding the woman called Mother. She was older than Claire had first judged, though her skin was flawless. Like her robes, her hair was honey colored. Her irises were light blue, bright and clear, and with a gaze possessed of a wealth of knowledge. "What should I call you?"

The woman blinked in surprise, then laughed. "Not the question I expected, as you've already been told that I am Mother. Does this trouble you?"

"My apologies," Claire protested gently, "but I cannot call you by that name. I had a mother and would not give her title to another. I mean no disrespect."

"No, I suppose you don't. Let me see." She drummed her fingers in thought. "Perhaps Ni'Mala. It is name I once used."

"I understand that the giving of a name is important to the Fenrhi," Claire said. "So I will tell you mine." For the first time since meeting her, Ni'Mala did not appear so confident. "A mistake was made when I was abducted. I am not Lady Aubrianne. I am Claire, her sister."

"This explains so much," Ni'Mala stated with an excited glint in her eyes. "You were not who we expected, for we have heard much about your sister. Thank you, Claire, for your gift. May I tell others of your identity?"

"Please do," Claire urged. "In Aurelia, we do not put so much value behind keeping our names secret. I only kept up the charade when I was in custody of Diarmait's men. I believed it prudent to let them go on believing that I was my sister."

"Indeed," Ni'Mala agreed. "You might not be here speaking with me in my chamber if they'd discovered their error. More likely, you would have ended up in the sea. Though I should warn you, Diarmait would have been just as satisfied with you." Ni'Mala took another sip of wine, then sat back in comfortable repose. "So tell me, Claire, what else would you like to know?"

"Tell me about the castes, if you please."

"To tell you everything about the castes would take days," she began. "So I will begin with the basics. First, you must be taught who we are. We are called the Fenrhi. We search for initiates, and sometimes initiates search for us. We come from great families and from destitute ones. My own father sold me to the Fenrhi when I was a child. Beginnings do not matter here; only what one can become. All initiates start out in Earth Caste. Most stay there, but some go to Sylvan and others to Umbren. Only a few initiates are accepted by Kena.

"The clothing of Earth Caste is the color of dust," Ni'Mala went on. "There are noblewomen and peasants alike in Earth Caste. They act as the temple's laundresses, cooks, farmers, anything needed to support our life here." She took another sip of wine. "The Earth Caste is the hardest working of our castes; they also have the most freedom. They are welcome in every part of the temple. And if they show a talent for it, they become our artisans."

Claire drew her fingers over her sash and smiled. "And they are the teachers of the initiates," she guessed.

"You understand better than most outsiders, Claire. Now, if an initiate exhibits an aptitude for healing, she is marked for Sylvan and wears the color of moss. The Sylvan tend to the herbariums. They are our healers."

"The drink I was given when I arrived," Claire recalled, "was it dosed with some herb?"

"A sleeping drought," Ni'Mala explained. "Do you imagine, after what you have been through, that you could have slept when you first arrived here?" Claire shook her head. "Our healers recognized that. They tended to your wounds whilst you slept. Sleep, they believe, is one of the greatest weapons against pain and ailment."

Claire touched her temple. The swelling was gone and a scab had formed. The Sylvan women must have dosed her considerably for her to not feel their attentions. Claire looked at Ni'Mala. "Tell me about those who wear black."

"The color of the Umbren Caste. Though if you examine it closely, it is not truly black; their garments are woven of many dark hues. Had your sister come here as an initiate, she would have most likely been marked for Umbren." Ni'Mala leaned forward to pour herself more wine. She handed her cup to Claire, then took Claire's and drank from it. "This has not been tampered with, my word on it."

Embarrassed, Claire put her lips to the cup and sipped. It was sweet and delicious.

"It is a smart woman who is always cautious, Claire, but a boring one as well. Now, where were we? Ah, the Umbren. They alone move freely outside the temple. They are our seekers and our hunters. They act as escorts for the other castes if they must leave these walls. When fate forces us, the Umbren do what is necessary. And you may be interested in hearing that they have already approached me regarding you. You made quite an impression on your guide. If you decide that you would like to join us, they will argue for you."

Join the temple? It hadn't occurred to her, and Claire frowned at the idea. Most of the women chose to stay within the temple grounds; Claire couldn't imagine herself so chained to one place. She wanted to return to Aurelia, didn't she? "Why would the Umbren argue for me, and against whom?"

Ni'Mala smiled. "Kena, of course. Rhiannon may be upset now, but she will come to accept what an asset your talents would be for the Fenrhi."

"My talents? What do you mean?" Claire asked, almost afraid to hear the answer.

"There are many names assigned to the gift you possess. Seer is the name the Fenrhi use, and abilities such as yours are celebrated here. Kena

Caste is the second highest of all of our castes. I myself was marked with indigo before becoming Mother to the Fenrhi." She lifted her sleeve.

Up and down her forearm and over her hand and fingers, blue lines swirled in strange patterns, just like those on Claire's sash. The designs were a part of Ni'Mala's skin, as if dyed deep into the tissue. There were dusty gray lines as well. And here and there, Claire caught glimpses of amber under the surface. Odd that she hadn't noticed until it was pointed out to her. When Ni'Mala said that the women were marked for their castes, she had meant it literally.

"When you entered the hall," Ni'Mala continued, "Rhiannon had some of her ilk try to read you. You repelled them without even realizing what you were doing. You pushed back, so to speak, injuring one of the Kena."

Claire drew in a sharp breath. "But how? I never touched anyone."

"It is not your fault, Claire. After hiding your gift your entire life, it must be strange to hear another speak of it so openly. And no, I am not reading your mind. I promise. I'm simply aware that a talent such as yours is not considered a gift in Aurelia. You could *choose* Kena, or Umbren, or even Sylvan, I think. And I say 'choose' only to a few. Most women who come here are selected by a caste after they prove where their talents lie; a very few show aptitude for more than one.

"I did not expect you, Claire. This goes to show that even a Mother can be surprised. We had heard that Lady Aubrianne had been captured and brought to our shores. We were prepared to help her return to her family. But you, Claire, you have no husband or child in Aurelia. You could stay with the Fenrhi. I am offering you a place here, and not as an initiate. You would have to be taught our ways, of course, but you could choose your own caste. You could explore your talents, hone them, learn from the Kena, or the Umbren if that is your wish. Possibly both. And in return, I am sure there is much you could teach us."

Claire could not quite believe her ears. The Fenrhi *celebrated* the very thing that made her so different from everyone else. She frowned again. Something about this bothered her.

"It is quite a bit to take in," Ni'Mala acknowledged. "You should take some time to consider what I've said. In the meantime, do you have any other questions for me?"

Claire looked at the brazier, unsurprised that it too was in the shape of a hexagon, and it dawned on her: Earth, Sylvan, Umbren, Kena, and the Mother. Five castes. If her suspicions were correct, there had to be a sixth group. What was Ni'Mala hiding from her and why?

Ni'Mala narrowed her eyes, as if divining the direction of Claire's thoughts. Whatever the purpose of the missing caste, Claire would have to discover it on her own. She cleared the mystery from her mind and gave Ni'Mala a forthright look. "May I look at your marks again?" Claire asked, holding out her hand. Ni'Mala drew back her sleeve, and Claire followed the intricate lines on the woman's wrist. "So amber for your caste, and blue for Kena. You have gray here as well, but nothing for Umbren or Sylvan."

"All Mothers must serve." Ni'Mala indicated the gray marks. An ember in the brazier sparked, shooting ash in all directions, and she leaned forward to stoke the glowing coals. Her hair fell away from her neck, exposing even more markings on her nape: intricate patterns of blue and the thin trails of gray. With a start, Claire made out another color: dark red. Before Ni'Mala could turn back to face her, she smoothed her features. "You are still troubled," Ni'Mala remarked anyway.

"I am," Claire confessed. "You are not telling me everything and it makes me uneasy." Ni'Mala waited patiently, and Claire prayed that her next words would conceal the fact that she was cognizant of the existence of another caste and that its color was red. "You seem to know quite a bit about Aurelia, but I too have studied history, including that of Nifolhad. I know how women are treated here. Why are the Fenrhi exempt?"

"Ah," Ni'Mala responded, "the reasons are as simple as they are complicated."

"I don't mean to be rude, but you *are* asking me to join you. It is only fair to explain what I would be joining."

Ni'Mala thrummed her fingertips on her knee for a moment. "Here is the simple truth: in return for services to the realm, we are left alone. We welcome any who come to our gates: lowborn or high, servant or king. Even you, an Aurelian. Our artisans are given commissions by the many noble families in Nifolhad. Our healers freely give aid to any person who requests it. As for Kena and Umbren: merchants want confirmation that a supplier is honest; messages must be delivered in secret."

"But why does Diarmait leave you alone?" Claire persisted. "A large group of women, living independently, freely. It seems contradictory to what I've heard about him."

"As I have already informed you, *we provide services to the realm.* Not only to Diarmait, but to Prince Ranulf as well. If a price is agreed upon, we could even be engaged by someone from Aurelia. But we never participate in the political schemes of the noble and royal houses. And for that, they leave us in peace. We remain neutral."

"But by helping me, aren't you interfering with King Diarmait?"

"He is only the steward king," Ni'Mala corrected. "And yes, we have interfered. But not in the contention of the throne of Nifolhad. Diarmait wants his son, Prince Bowen, to be named King Cedric's successor. But many in the realm support Prince Ranulf. The Fenrhi will neither help nor hinder either party in their pursuit. Your presence, or what should have been your sister's, will not give Diarmait the throne. His motivation for wanting your sister is personal and has nothing to do with naming his son as heir."

"Diarmait's men are coming to Naca'an. Will you allow them to search your temple?"

"Most assuredly," Ni'Mala answered. "But you *are* safe here. They will find no trace of you. However, until you decide whether or not you wish to join us, you must remain hidden from the world outside the temple walls."

"And if I wish to return to Aurelia?"

Ni'Mala regarded her for a long moment. "We will cross that sea when it is time. Come, I will show you out," she concluded, leading Claire to the audience hall. They walked together in silence to the double doors, and Claire kept thinking about what would happen if she chose to leave the temple. Or even if it would be allowed. Ni'Mala would have assisted Anna in returning to Aurelia. She hadn't offered the same to Claire.

"If you need to speak with me again," Ni'Mala instructed, "you can pass word through your helper."

Outside the doors, Milla was waiting for her; she bowed low when she saw the Mother. "I want you to explore the temple," Ni'Mala said. "Milla, please make our guest comfortable here. If she is to join us, she must learn about our purpose. You are to be not only her guide in the temple, but her teacher as well."

"You honor me, Mother, but I am yet an initiate. I would not wish to disgrace you or Earth by pretending that I am capable of—"

"Nonsense," Ni'Mala interrupted. Milla bowed her head. "See to her needs." And with her command, Ni'Mala turned around, closing the doors to the hall behind her and signaling the end of Claire's audience.

Milla stared at the two heavy doors. Finally, she turned, a disingenuous smile pasted on her face. "Are you hungry, Lady Aubrianne? I can bring your meal to your room."

"I am hungry, but I'd like to dine with the other women here." Mainly to study their habits and further her knowledge of the temple's layout, Claire thought. Out of habit, she smoothed her hands down her tunic to make sure she was presentable. Then she patted her braid, checking for loose strands, remembering too late that she had sawed off her hair. "I need two things first, Milla," she started, heading—she hoped—back in the direction of her room.

"If it is in my power," replied Milla.

"Could you procure a pair of shears for me?"

Milla peered up and arched her eyebrow at what remained of Claire's tousled, lobbed tresses. "What is the second thing that you require, Lady Aubrianne?"

"That you call me Claire. Lady Aubrianne is my sister."

"Done, and done," her guide consented with a sincere smile, finally looking at Claire without reservation. Together, they went back to Claire's room and, though she did not realize it, Claire began to feel just a little bit better.

CHAPTER TWENTY-FIVE

Smugglers

Warin stared at the glassy surface of the sea. They'd made excellent time sailing to Kantahla, but it'd been for naught. The ship bearing Claire had never arrived in Nifolhad's second-largest city.

After departing Stolweg, Warin and Pieter had ridden hard for Pheldhain. Sparing no time for his parents, he'd secured his brother's aid in obtaining a craft to take him to Pheldhain's Southron Isles. He'd made contact with Captain Grieg—the man who'd taught him all he knew about ships and smuggling—and was sailing for Kantahla Bay in less than a day. Strong winds, fair skies and seas, and Warin was off the ship and on land in a little less than six weeks from the time he'd left Trian supine in his bed.

The word in Kantahla was that Diarmait had gone to Naca'an. The captain's smuggling contacts related the story of a ship named *Sea Bride*. She'd been due in Kantahla, carrying some important cargo, but had been blown off course and had to make port in Naca Bay weeks later than expected. Worse yet for the captain and crew, they had allowed Diarmait's cargo to be stolen. Diarmait had had the captain flayed and every crewman bound to the ship before setting the *Sea Bride* aflame, anchored in the middle of Naca Bay, as an example to all.

Warin's captain had been quick to complete his business in Kantahla, and they'd had three good days asea before the wind gave out. Five days the ship sat dead in the water; five additional days where Claire was without a friend in a country where women were considered less valuable than farm animals. Warin stared off to the west, his eyes squinting against the setting sun. Somewhere out there was the southeast coast of Nifolhad. He heard footsteps approaching and leaned against the rail.

"How are the supplies holding up?" Warin growled when Captain

Grieg came to stand next to him. The rest of the crew had been giving Warin a wide berth. Even Pieter, with his thousands of questions about the adventures of being a smuggler, had left him alone.

"It doesn't matter," Grieg replied. "We won't be stranded here long enough to find out." He pointed portside. In the far distance, toward Aurelia, dark clouds were piling. "I'd say we'll have wind soon enough to run around the Butt. Then it'll be a matter of two or three days to Naca Bay. You 'n the lad'll be free to find Diarmait's missing cargo."

Warin clapped the captain on his back. No sooner was his mood lifted by the news than the rippling sound of wind ribbons set the crew into action. A song rose above the whistles and calls and the slapping of bare feet on deck, and Warin dove in to help, even lending his voice to their melody. As they hoisted the mainsail, he prayed that Claire was safe.

CHAPTER TWENTY-SIX

Dances

Though Milla was neither more nor less friendly toward Claire, she proved to be an excellent teacher. Claire reclined on her bed and contemplated the woman, wondering if Milla was reporting her activities to Ni'Mala.

It had been weeks since her audience with the Fenrhi Mother. Claire had been almost everywhere in the temple, an ingenious construction of rooms and buildings meant to confuse outsiders by leading them in circles. When King Diarmait's men had finally arrived to search the temple, they went from cluster to cluster, always returning to where they started. The proud men that they were, they would not own that they were flummoxed and, fearful of Diarmait's wrath, reported that the temple had been thoroughly searched. They had never even reached the guest quarters.

For her part, Milla appeared to enjoy showing the different areas of the temple to Claire. Earth Caste had the greatest number of rooms and space, and Milla, being most familiar with the area, had shown Claire the kitchens, laundry, gardens (shared with the Sylvan), weaving rooms, potsheds, and the many other areas essential to the operation of the temple.

The Fenrhi's home was more of a small city. One without streets, but filled with walkways, corridors, and courtyards. Every building was attached to another. And when Claire recalled her nighttime journey through Naca'an, she decided to secretly take to the rooftops of the temple. What she saw amazed her. The palace was beautiful, a construction of domes and filigreed spires reaching deep into the night sky.

High walls rose up all around the complex. To the south and east, they acted as a bulwark against the forest. To the west and north, the walls separated the Fenrhi from the lands of the royal palace, where Princess Aghna had once resided.

During the day, Claire tried to keep track of the different corridors in the temple, but it was difficult. Milla would often take shortcuts to reach their destinations. Such was the case when they'd gone to the herbarium of the Sylvan Caste for what Milla called "training." Her guide clearly liked this caste the best, and Claire couldn't blame her. It was a remarkable place, one where Claire felt completely welcome.

She and Milla had gaped at the extraordinary number of rows of growing herbs, many of which were unfamiliar to Claire. In another section, there were vast rooms filled with not only herbs, but minerals and powders, and insects, reptiles, and birds—some still alive, others preserved. They happily spent three days exploring the Sylvan workrooms. And the women in green were enthusiastic about Claire's thirst for knowledge, patiently answering all of her inquiries. When she overheard a woman complaining of aches in her joints and that a tincture of meadowsweet would be prescribed, Claire mentioned the benefits of bee venom. An excited hush fell around the room, and the women asked her to return in the morning.

Claire and Milla arrived the next day to find a table had been set out, atop which rested a board with long pins and a piece of polished marble. Next to it was a tightly woven hamper: one that hummed. Bees. All around, women waited with parchment and quill, ready to take notes. When Claire explained that she had never actually performed the miniature surgery, a wave of disappointment cascaded over their faces. So she pushed up her sleeves and went to work. After the third attempt, she was successful at removing the stinger and venom sac. Milla stood off to the side, looking on with great interest, so it was her teacher to whom Claire motioned first to give the operation a try. Milla was deft in her movements and successful on her very first attempt. Afterwards, she and Claire stepped back to allow the Sylvan women access. They repeated the procedure over and over. After the last bee had been dissected, they crushed the stingers and venom sacs in a small marble pestle. A crystal vial was procured, and the women chattered excitedly as it was held up to the light. One fat drop of strained bee venom rested at the bottom. The cost? Twenty-three bees.

She and Milla visited the Sylvan often after that, but that particular day would always be special to her. It was perhaps the first time she had felt anything other than despair over the loss of Trian. The Sylvan were healers. And somehow they had helped her to forget her pain, and her heart had healed a tiny fraction.

The Fenrhi had kept her going from dawn until dusk, she realized as she sat in her chamber, and she was grateful, but tired. She yawned and stretched, then picked up the leather-bound book that the Sylvan women had given her in thanks. It was intricately tooled with the same designs that abounded throughout the Fenrhi complex. On her sash, in the fabric panels decorating the audience hall and sitting room of Ni'Mala, and even dyed into the skin of the Fenrhi. And when Claire asked if they had any meaning, her Sylvan friends expounded on the nature of the queen bee. Her dances of alarm, of gathering, of mating, of tending, and of birth were all means of communicating with her workers.

Claire opened the book. Its once blank pages now bore the notes and sketches that she had made while in the herbarium. Her first entry had been on the procurement of the bee venom, and with her sketches, Claire was reminded of the time spent with Trian and the beekeeper. Instead of crushing her heart, she was comforted by the memory and the peace it brought her. Trian would approve of her joining the Fenrhi, she believed, if only because the act would bring her some solace. She closed the book and lay back in her bed. Tomorrow, Milla was taking her to train with Umbren Caste, and Claire was excited to learn all that they could teach her.

* * *

"You may leave us now, Milla," the Mother decreed.

Rhiannon scowled after the door to the audience hall closed. "I don't trust that one," she spat.

"Come now, Rhia. You don't trust anyone that you can't manipulate. Is it her fault that she has a drop or two of royal blood in her? Half of Diarmait's servants are related to some bastard of his. Why, even you—"

"Please do not speak it aloud!" Rhiannon shouted, earning a reproachful *tut*. "Forgive me, Mother," she begged, dropping to her knees.

"My dear girl, you are always forgiven." Rhiannon made her face a mask of contrition before tilting her chin to the woman before her. "Your efforts are bearing fruit, my sweet Rhia. Lady Claire has not mentioned returning to Aurelia even once." The Mother leaned forward and gave Rhiannon a gentle kiss.

This again, the Kena woman laughed to herself. Like the Aurelian girl, Ni'Mala was easily manipulated. All Rhiannon needed to do was pretend that she loved her, that she could be hurt by the mention of Diarmait. She had feigned these weak emotions, and the Mother remained blind to her intentions.

Rhiannon reached around the Mother's waist, pulling her down to the cushions where she knelt, then sent out a pulse of goodwill and love, in part directed to the fawning woman before her, but also toward the Aurelian. One day soon, this current Fenrhi leader would be ousted. Rhiannon sensed great power in Claire, but the Aurelian had no idea how to wield it. Rhiannon would show her and, in doing so, bind her inexorably to her side. A strong Mother, one completely beholden to her, would make the Fenrhi powerful again and change Nifolhad forever.

CHAPTER TWENTY-SEVEN

Adara

Cathmar

"You look awful!" Adara charged. She had just returned from Riverhome in Braden; her husband Logan was, at the moment, speaking to her older brother and father about strengthening their holdfasts. All of the lords of Cathmara would be assembled here in a few weeks to discuss the strange sightings of ships on nearly every coast of Aurelia and the bolstering of their territory's defenses. At the moment though, Adara was not concerned with the safety of Cathmara, nor the realm. That which worried her now was the wellbeing of her younger brother Trian. "Truly awful," she repeated. His very lack of response made her even more fretful—an emotion that irritated her greatly. "Get up," she ordered. "Let's take a walk. I want to visit the beach."

Her brother was turned away from her, staring at his hearth in empty contemplation of nothing. He was about to refuse, so Adara wisely preempted him. "Come now, brother. You need to be out in the fresh air; heaven knows it's stifling in this room. The brisk February breeze will do you good. Do all three of us good." She placed her hands protectively over her small but growing abdomen and smiled down at him.

"A nephew?" Trian asked quietly.

Adara took his hand and placed it on her stomach. "Or a niece." Her brother was the reason she had been summoned back to Cathmar Castle. Her mother had determined that if anyone could rouse Trian from his waking slumber, it would be the family member who was closest to him.

"Your stomach is so hard," he marveled. "I imagined it would be soft. Are you sure you should venture outside?"

She smiled and placed her hand over his. "It's perfectly safe. Especially if I have you to steady me."

"I'm afraid it will be the opposite," Trian warned. "You'll end up supporting me."

"Then we'll just brace each other." She let Trian stand on his own, not extending her hand to help. Her mother had already conveyed to her that he could walk, that his strength was returning. It was Trian's mind about which Lady Baranne was concerned.

They headed toward the beachhead, one of their favorite childhood haunts. Along the way, Adara detected a hitch in Trian's noisome step, a limp that would only resolve itself with time and exercise. The breeze gusted with greater intensity near the sea's edge, however, she and her brother knew of a protected spot on the leeward side of a great boulder. She set down the bundle she had carried, straightened up, and discovered that her brother was frowning at her.

"You should've let me carry that for you," he chided. "In your condition—"

Adara wasn't about to make it easy on him. That he'd been so coddled was certainly part of the problem. Everyone in the family was treating Trian as if he were likely to shatter. She raised her eyebrow at him. "*You* should have noticed that I was carrying something."

"Mother summoned you to play nursemaid to me," he accused, but did so wearily.

Adara pulled out a blanket from her bag, spread it out, sat down, and patted the space next to her. Trian eased himself down, then leaned back against the sun-warmed boulder. "I take umbrage with your accusation. As if I would ever be a nursemaid, especially to you, brother. However, I do believe it's time for some hard truths right about now. Some that I will tell you, and some that you need to tell me." She rummaged through the bag, pulled out a skin of cider, some cheese, a loaf of bread, some salted and dried fish that were a favorite of hers, a honey and nut tart, and some slices of rare roast venison.

"What? It's not all for me." She arranged the foodstuff on the blanket. When Trian reached for the fish, Adara pulled it away from him. "I *am* eating for two, remember?" But she broke the loaf of bread in half, tearing it open and stuffing it with cheese and venison before handing Trian a portion. Between bites, she told him about her new life with Logan. That he was a kind husband and that they had even fallen in love. And now that she was with child, their bond had grown even stronger. When it was time for Trian to tell her about his troubles, she brushed away the crumbs from their meal and leaned back against the boulder, closing her eyes and lifting her chin to the late February sun. "Your turn, Trian." Giving him time to sort out what he needed to say, she listened to the rhythmic pounding of the surf, counting the waves and timing the spaces, determining that low tide had just begun. It was Trian's nature to be thoughtful before speaking, and she was relieved that his character had not changed so much.

"I..." he started. "You see, it is not..." He sighed heavily.

"From the beginning," Adara put forth. "You were attacked..."

"I don't remember it! I came to, beheld Lark, and wondered where I was. They immediately realized that something was amiss. Lark told me that he and Anna were married, had a daughter even. After a week or so, I recalled some of it—enough that I was no longer surprised—but the details were gone. And then, they asked me about Claire."

He turned to her. "My last memory of her was hearing that she'd been killed by Bowen and Roger. My dream of a life with her ended that day. When Lark told me that she was alive and that she and I were in love, there was not a single recollection. There still isn't."

Adara reached out and stilled his hands from twisting the knot of fabric in his grip. "May I look at that?" He handed over the cloth, surprised that it was twined around his fingers. She spread it out on the blanket in front of them. "Was this Claire's?"

"So I've been told."

"Forget-me-nots," she noted, and her brother gave a short, angry laugh. "If you can't bring her back to mind, little brother, then why are you holding this as if it's a lifeline?"

"I've no idea. I just can't let it go. But there's nothing. I have no memory of our becoming close. You would think that I would feel loss. Something. Anything."

"You do," Adara soothed, pulling his head to her shoulder, stroking his hair like she had when he was a little boy. "Your heart feels the loss. Your head may have forgotten, but not your heart."

"It was Warin who pointed out that part of my heart was taken."

"Did he now?" Adara mused, for it was well known that Pheldhainians were all romantics. "What else did your friend tell you?"

"He told me that when I recalled how I came by this kerchief, I would remember what was stolen. And he promised to find it for me and bring it back to Aurelia."

"I hope he does, and soon." Adara relinquished the kerchief. "The question now is what are we going to do with you in the meantime?"

"I don't know."

"Well, for starters, you can stay out of that bed of yours. Exercise every day. Every. Day. I want that limp gone before I leave."

They rose, and Trian folded the blanket. He stuffed it in the sack, then slung the strap over his shoulder. "You're not leaving for a while, are you?"

Her heart broke at the hope in his voice. To be sure, he needed a stronger hand than that of their coddling aunt or worried mother. "Not until after the council has concluded and decided Cathmara's course." She turned him so that he faced her. "Trian, I mean it. You and I will walk together every day. Your infirmity is not becoming of our father's house, and you know it. From this moment forward, you will stop feeling sorry for yourself and begin remembering who you are and what it means to be Cathmaran." She smiled when he came to an abrupt halt, silencing the sound of his feet crunching down upon the beach pebbles. "So along with daily exercise," Adara continued, "I will tutor you in the ways of our house. Lesson one: observation." As he caught up with her, he did so *almost* silently. And even without looking at him, Adara knew her brother was grinning.

CHAPTER TWENTY-EIGHT
Shadows and Enlightenment

The Fenrhi Temple

Claire had woken early, eager to once more join the Kena women in their training room. She simply could not understand why Milla always begged off attending these sessions with her, choosing instead to wait for her outside the entrance. The women were, without fail, kind and welcoming, even the once-hostile Rhiannon, though she saw the Kena leader not often.

When Claire arrived, the instructors promised her that she would witness something special, a demonstration of a rare gift among the Kena. So she waited patiently to the side of the room and watched the assembled group.

Two young members of Kena leaned against one wall. Directly across from them stood a matching pair of gray-clad initiates. The instructor asked one of her pupils to begin. At first, nothing happened. Then oddly, the woman opposite the student abruptly sat on the floor, eliciting clucks of approval from the instructors. The other gray-garbed woman remained still, and the teacher *tut-tutted* the other pupil. Finally, the initiate began to sway—her feet shifted, her arms lifted over her head, and she turned in circles, dancing around the room, faster and faster, whirling until she was breathless. Though the instructor praised the second student, she clapped loudly and brought the room back under her control. As for their practice subjects, they resumed their places against the far wall, looking discomfited.

One of the instructors walked over to them, extolling their helpfulness, persuading them to be proud of themselves, joyful even. And Claire watched as the two anxious faces relaxed. The instructor informed them that by helping the Kena, they were helping all Fenrhi to be safe. Then she excused them from the room, and the pair walked out the door, smiling and congratulating one another.

Claire almost applauded the two young Kena. It was a revelation of just how powerful these women were. Earlier that week, Claire had determined that she was best suited for either Kena or Sylvan. But now, how could she wish to wear anything but blue?

After the demonstration, one of the teachers approached Claire and offered to let her try her hand at the technique. She jumped at the opportunity. The Kena trainees were still standing in the far corner of the room listening to the other instructor. The teacher standing next to Claire explained that some of their members had the ability to compel another into completing certain actions. A nudge, a harmless little push, a suggestion that could, if used properly, bring peace to conflict, resolve grievances, even help to heal those with no tangible injury. She then nodded in the direction of the students and encouraged Claire to try to reach out and push an idea into one of the young women's minds.

Claire wasn't confident at first, uncertain of what to attempt, but then the more adept student of the two yawned as if bored by her instructor's critique. So Claire focused on her, reflecting that she must be very tired to show such disdain. When the girl yawned in earnest, Claire's instructor smiled encouragingly, then coaxed her to try more. Claire decided that her test subject would be happier if she took a nap. She kept thinking it in her head, imagining that her thoughts were the girl's, and finally, the young woman stepped away from the group and dropped to the floor. Within seconds, she was asleep! Claire almost whooped with joy, it felt so incredible to do such good for the Fenrhi. She could not wait to tell Milla that she had made her choice: Kena Caste.

On their way back to her room in the guest quarters, Claire was euphoric at what she'd accomplished. Milla remained strangely quiet. They were passing near the baths when a figure in black called to Claire. It was Madyan.

Milla paused, staring straight ahead as if she'd heard nothing, and Claire followed her Umbren friend into a shadowed alcove. Madyan took Claire's hand and placed a dried pihaberry in it. "I meant to return this to you; I didn't need it," she said. "Some of us watch, m'lady. When your dance commences, you'll not lack for partners." She insisted that Claire eat the pihaberry right away, even waiting until Claire swallowed it before disappearing back into the shadows.

Milla escorted Claire to her room as if the interruption had never occurred. She set out Claire's nightclothes—something she hadn't done since Claire's arrival. When she departed, Claire discovered the pouch containing Trian's gift lying on top. She plucked it up and held it to her heart, not remembering when or why she had ever taken it off.

When Claire woke the next morning, she felt more refreshed than she had in weeks. She found her cache of pihaberries, ate one, then prepared for another day of training with the Kena. The next morning, she ate another, and again every day thereafter. She started recalling things, little by little, each day: Anna, and Lark, and Celeste. And most of all, she remembered Trian, their unspoken love for one another, and everything that he had taught her.

On her last day with the Kena before rotating her training back to the Umbren, there had been no initiates to command. This was a group who shared varying levels of the ability to foretell. Claire soon discovered that most of the Kena possessed only a fraction of her capabilities. Some could not perform without the collective support of the others. Rarer still was the Kena adept in more than one area. Rhiannon and Ni'Mala were two of a handful who possessed multiple talents. Claire instinctively hid the full extent of what she could do, allowing them to believe that her visions were only rudimentary images. And as for her ability to push at another's will, she made sure that she was never again as successful as that first attempt.

Since resuming her intake of a daily pihaberry, she'd become aware that, whenever she was with the Kena, waves of goodwill seemed to wash over her. Claire could only describe the sensation as a relentless tide of contentment that pulled and sucked her under the surface of the Kena's camaraderie. It was an easy enough feat for her to simply focus her mind on floating above the swell, enjoying the benefit of the pleasant feelings instead of being drowned by them. The Kena were none the wiser.

As Claire's memories returned, so too did her dreams—invariably, they were about Trian and left her feeling off-balance. She sat on her bed and rubbed her temples, trying to dredge them back up. Her dreams always began the same way: Trian riding toward her in the valley, an impending sense of disaster, Claire screaming a warning but no sound issuing from her mouth. Then, she was running to him, only when she looked down, it wasn't over fields of grass but the baked tiles covering the roofs of Naca'an. The roofs rose higher and higher, and Claire climbed, trying to make it to the city's boundary. If she could just reach the edge, Trian would be waiting there. With each dream, the border loomed closer, but Claire always woke before attaining her goal.

Tugging at her cropped hair and trying to recall that which eluded her, she growled angrily. She hated the idea that Trian—or rather her mind—was trying to tell her something important. She was positive that her dream alluded to the Fenrhi castes. It nettled her thoughts throughout the day, just out of reach, and teased her sleeping mind at night.

Before changing her clothes, Claire dropped to her hands and knees, then extracted the pouch of pihaberries from its hiding place. She plucked at the thin ribbon gathering the neck of the bag, gently tipped the contents onto her bed, and counted out thirty-two dried fruits. After popping one into her mouth, she hid them again, and moments later, Milla entered her room.

She picked up Claire's embroidered sash, and Claire lifted her arms as her companion wrapped the long piece of fabric around her waist. Milla was securing the ends when Claire noticed the markings on her wrists.

"Milla! You've been accepted by the Sylvan Caste!" Claire studied her friend: the intelligent hazel eyes, the delicate nose, the proud line of her mouth, and her flawless complexion, everything conveying to Claire that despite Milla's submissiveness, the woman was of noble blood. A ghost of a smile graced the woman's lips, as if she had finally succeeded in some great endeavor. "This is wonderful news," Claire congratulated. "It's what you wanted, isn't it?"

"One of many things, m'lady. And I have you to thank. It started when you included me in the demonstration with the bees. Doing so is not allowed here, but no one thought to naysay you."

"I'm so pleased for you, Milla. Truly." She would miss her friend when a new initiate would be assigned to her and, curious about the strange induction into the castes, she asked if the marking rite had hurt.

Milla held out her arm, and Claire studied the beautiful dots and tiny dashes that peppered her skin in graceful loops and whirls. The deep teal of the ink was vibrant against the irritated skin surrounding the designs. "The Sylvan have herbs to numb and deaden feeling. The swelling and redness will subside in a day or two." She turned her arm to show Claire the full pattern, and Claire discovered that a second design in pale gray curled with the first. "When the Sylvan invited me to join them, I asked if I could continue to serve you until you choose your path."

"So, you are both Sylvan and Earth. Isn't that a great honor?"

"Yes, and now I will not have to leave you until you are ready to leave me. And if you choose a caste and it is Sylvan, we can train together as sisters. One day, I hope to repay you for how you've helped me."

I *have* a sister, Claire reminded herself. She had almost forgotten her family in Aurelia, a fact that continued to unsettle her. "Milla," she started, wanting a few minutes to reflect on her own, "I'd like to finish a sketch in my journal before breakfast—" it was their habit to eat together in whichever caste's dining space they were visiting "—I'll follow you in a few minutes."

"It's falconry with the Umbren this morning," Milla reminded her, before leaving her room.

Claire was on the verge of remembering something of import and sat on her bed and closed her eyes. She pictured her last encounter with Madyan, how she had placed the pihaberry in her palm, then turned and disappeared through the archway. The flair of the woman's tunic as she turned, and the soft shift of leather on stone as she pirouetted on the ball of her foot. She remembered the soft scent of some perfume that wafted in the air as Madyan's hair lifted and swung out like the skirts of the women at court when they danced. And then, Claire glimpsed them. The tiny patterns of dots and swirls etched irrevocably on the back of Madyan's neck. Deep red, appearing like the skittering scratch of a thorn as it snags and jumps over the skin. The marks were simpler than the dances of Earth, Umbren, Kena and Sylvan Castes. Was this the proof of the sixth division of the Fenrhi? Its color as rich in hue as the sanguine fluid coursing through her veins, the name of the red dance surely must be Blood Caste.

Claire wondered what Madyan had meant when she'd confided that there were some who watched. Could Milla have been watching Claire for someone other than Ni'Mala? Certainly not Kena, for Milla avoided them whenever possible. And something told Claire that Milla had her own agenda here in the Fenrhi temple. By accepting the gray markings, the woman had opted to remain by Claire's side until she chose her path. But she had said *if* Claire chose a caste, not *when*.

Having tarried too long in her room, Claire rose from her bed to join the others for breakfast. When she arrived, Milla was there, holding a place for her at the table. They quickly finished their meal and then headed to the area of the temple where the Umbren resided.

The hours flew by as Claire was taught how to properly use the tools of a falconer: jesses, bells, and hoods. She learned that the young falcons remained with their handlers at night in a process called manning, whereby the once wild birds became accustomed to sharing space with their trainers. The teacher warned the women to avoid believing that they had a bond with the raptors. The birds of prey could not grow to love their masters like a dog, rather they sought only the easiest method to obtain food. It was a cold truth, but a lesson that had to be learned and perhaps applied to more than just the falcons.

• • •

That night, Claire thought about the raptors, and in doing so, the memory of Trian and his story about the rímara falcons stirred. Unlike her time with the Sylvan, where she shared her knowledge of healing, she never once divulged the many things that Trian had taught her. Those lessons were a part of him, a part that Claire held close to her heart and could not share.

She ate another pihaberry, extinguished her lamp, and hoped her mind would be open to that which had been eluding her in her dreams.

CHAPTER TWENTY-NINE
Blood Caste

He was there, in her dream. Claire raced over the fields. As before, the fields became tiled rooftops, and the path she followed arced again and again, never keeping to a straight line. The rooftops of Naca'an turned into the domes of the honeycombed Fenrhi temple. In her dream, it was to the east that she ran. Trian was standing at the very edge. This time, he didn't disappear over it as he had before.

Claire slowed, taking care not to rush too quickly to him. In this dream, he waited. Then, she saw it: the blood. He was shirtless, arms stretched out. He regarded his hands and the trails of blood making fantastic designs over his skin. He backed away from her as if he didn't recognize her. She wanted to reassure him, and when she stepped forward and placed her hand on his bearded cheek, his eyes widened. As Claire pulled away, his beard turned into a blanket of bees. They spread out, multiplying over his neck and chest. And where Trian's heart was, where he'd been fatally pierced, Claire found her. The queen. She moved with purpose, a weaving and whirling choreography. Trian's hand came up, and where there were yet no bees, Claire felt his fingertips brush her cheek. So brief was the touch, it mayn't have happened at all. He lifted up and away then, separating into a thousand different pieces, swarming and swirling and made up entirely of the black-and-yellow insects. The swarm held its shape for a moment, a blink really, then spread out and up into the night sky to vanish among the stars.

"Don't go, Trian," Claire pleaded as she shot up in her bed, trying to hold on to the vestiges of her dream. "Trian," she whispered to the small window separating her from the crescent moon. Every moment of her dream was fresh in her mind. She had made it to the wall, but she had not looked over. She had not seen what Trian had been trying to show her.

It was time to remedy that, she decided, with a determination she'd not felt since escaping the *Sea Bride*. The pihaberries had opened her eyes to the truth of the Kena, and more. Barefoot and in her sleeping attire, she stood in the center of her room and opened up her senses. The moon was no thicker than an eyelash in the sky; its faint glow would not pick her out in the night, especially with the low clouds scudding across it. Claire could smell the dust shifting and settling in the air. She listened. The wind was strong and gusting. The Fenrhi temple was filled with chimes. She could hear them even now: the high tinkling of glass and metal underscored with the beautiful, mellow tones of hollow wood pipes. Simple to lose herself in the noise of the night.

Claire was about to go when she heard a strange sound. A muted, frenzied noise came from near the remnants of her evening meal. She lifted away the napkin from her tray and discovered that a bee had been trapped beneath it. The winged nectar hunter lifted away and out the tiny window and into the night. Claire turned, slipped out her door, up one of the downspouts that funneled rainwater into underground cisterns, then out onto the rooftops of the sprawl that was the Fenrhi temple.

She took a moment to get her bearings, then, with an ease that would leave them envious, she eluded the detection of the few Umbren who were set on guard. Claire kept low, tracing the circuitous route around the domes. She moved quickly, steadily, shifting her speed to race along with the pale shadows of the clouds as they passed under the weak lantern in the night's sky. She halted at the edge of the temple's grounds. Someone was waiting. A lone figure, hunched, and cloaked in shadows.

"Tell me, Madyan," Claire ordered, sitting next to her friend, "tell me about this place. Tell me about Blood Caste and who they are."

• • •

Into the night, Madyan whispered to Lady Claire, "Who are they? They are all of us. Earth, Umbren, Sylvan, and even a few Kena, though that happens less and less of late. Blood Caste is both the stile and the floodplain. It's what allows the Fenrhi to exist under Diarmait's rule."

Madyan gazed at the woman sitting next to her, watching the comprehension come into her eyes, and the fury building there. She explained that during King Cedric's time, Blood Caste was rarely called upon. But since the steward king began his reign, the rooms were never vacant.

"In the past, each caste would ask for volunteers, and women would go willingly, perceiving it as duty to the Fenrhi. You see, we are given such license here, allowed to live as we wish, to not fear like the women outside of the temple walls. The men of Nifolhad take us, m'lady. Sometimes with kindness, more oft with violence. We volunteer our blood to them."

"This is insanity, Madyan. The Fenrhi are only trading one prison for another."

Madyan's shoulders slumped. "It wasn't always so. Generations ago, the Fenrhi shared their blood in hopes of gaining a child. It was a place of creation. There were no beatings, no torture. But even before King Cedric was killed, the balance had begun to shift. When Diarmait took over, only the strongest of the Fenrhi, those who were confident that they could survive the assault, only they went forward. The Kena would be there afterward to soothe the mind even as the Sylvan healed the flesh.

"But the Kena have changed the rules," Madyan continued. "All of us are deemed strong enough. Even women I would never imagine could withstand such violence to their persons go willingly. Happily, even."

• • •

Claire recalled the semblance of well-being she had felt when amongst the Kena. The elation she herself had experienced when she'd successfully manipulated another. Now, the unnaturalness of her actions only made her ill. But it was much worse; she knew that now.

"Rhiannon is training her caste to plant seeds in the minds of those weaker than they," Claire surmised. "And to what end? So that these women will happily prostrate themselves before Diarmait and his ilk?" The red markings on Madyan's neck came to mind. "Oh, Madyan," she grieved. "I'm so sorry."

"It was *my* choice!" Madyan cried with a vehemence Claire had not heard from her before. "They did not force me. I went willingly and for my own ends. Like you, I have a supply of pihaberries—though I suspect that you will no longer require yours. You are strong enough on your own. Stronger, I think, than even Rhiannon. She only succeeded with you before because she was willing you to be happy, something a heart and mind desires more than anything."

Claire studied Madyan for a moment. "What else?"

"A Fenrhi's time in Blood Caste is supposed to be limited to one week. But when I was there, I noticed an Umbren who had *volunteered* over two months ago. She behaved as if she'd just arrived." Madyan stared at the building below. "They are now taking women who have just joined their castes. There is no longer a period of grace—one's mark had a year to heal before the red dance was added."

"You protect Milla," Claire deduced, finally understanding the bond between the two women with fresh eyes. "Why? Who is she?"

"Her name is a gift that only she can give." Madyan smiled when Claire grimaced.

"What needs be done?"

"We must escape this place," Madyan decreed.

"But, how? Ni'Mala will not allow us to quit her so easily."

"The way out is simple: it is through there." She pointed to the rooms that housed Blood Caste, then mapped out the plan to Claire.

It could be done. Claire could envision it. But she would have to influence the minds of others to affect their escape and give them time to distance themselves both from the Fenrhi and Naca'an. She thought of her dream, of Trian, and of the queen bee over his heart. He would have wanted her to do whatever was necessary to survive. "All right, Madyan, I will help."

CHAPTER THIRTY
Dreamwalk

Castle Cathmar

Adara awoke to a determined rapping on her door. She levered open her eyes and stared across the room at the glowing embers in the hearth. Dawn was still hours away. She rose, swinging her legs over the side of her bed and resting her arms protectively over her abdomen. The nighttime summons could only mean one thing: Trian. Of late, he'd taken to sleepwalking. A watch had been set on his door, and those on guard had been instructed to wake her if he left his room. Adara was the only one who could rouse him and return him to his bed.

Logan woke upon hearing voices and looked up groggily from his slumber. "It's been almost every night this week." He shuffled to the hearth to add fuel to the embers.

When he went to retrieve his breeches, Adara stopped him, gently pushing him back to their bed. "You don't need to come. Stay here and keep the blankets warm for me."

"Are you sure?" he asked, sitting on the bed and leaning forward to lay gentle hands on her belly.

Adara smiled when he kissed her protruding stomach. She ran her fingers through his bed-mussed hair before tilting up his chin. "I'm positive. Besides, you can make it up to me once our babe is born." She pressed her lips to his in a gentle kiss. When he tried to draw her to him, Adara pushed his arms away and laughed. "Perhaps when I return—if you keep the bed warm, that is."

She threw on her cloak, slipped on her shoes, and crossed the room to the door. Behind her, Logan plunged under the blankets. "Hurry back," he called after her.

In the corridor, one of her younger cousins waited. He had drawn the short twig this evening, and had been the one on guard. "Where is he?" Adara asked, assuming that Trian would go to the stables again, and so headed in that direction.

"The battlements, m'lady." Adara turned on her heel, and as fast as she dared, she followed her cousin to the open roof. They reached the top, and she bade the young man to wait, not wanting to startle her brother. The last few nights, he'd been talking in his sleep, and Adara had only been able to hear a few of his words. She'd told their Aunt Cafellia, who had then urged her to try to draw out his sleep-time discourse.

Adara stepped into the cool night air. The moon was just a sliver. If not for the multitude of stars lighting the sky, she would not have found her brother. He sat facing southwest, legs crisscrossed on the flat top of the redan, his back to the Kaldemer Sea. He was mumbling something about blood. His hands roved restlessly over his face and chest, and then, all of a sudden, his eyes widened and he threw his arms out, staring into the night sky. When he finally turned to her, awareness seeped back into his gaze.

"Adara," he worried. "You should not be up this late. Your babe needs you to rest."

"My babe is just fine, Trian. He's strong." She helped to steady him as he came off the wall. "Do you recall anything of your dream? When I came upon you, you were speaking of blood."

He shook his head as she walked him back to his room. "Blood," he said. "I remember having blood on my hands. Nothing more." He paused. "I don't think that I was alone in my dream."

"Hmm. Maybe you'll recall more in the morning," Adara hoped, then kissed his cheek before he entered his chamber. "Goodnight, little brother."

She had taken but a few steps when he called out to her. "Bees. I remember bees." He touched his fingers to his heart. "She was here, dancing."

"Who was?"

"The queen."

He closed his chamber door, and Adara turned and walked the opposite direction from her own chamber. Before she could return to the warmth of her bed and the comfort of Logan, she first had to speak with her aunt.

CHAPTER THIRTY-ONE

Sacrifice

Naca'an

As the sun began to rise, Bowen paced back and forth in the chamber that had once belonged to his cousin. He hated this palace. It seemed that the very rooms haunted him, ghosts of King Cedric and Princess Aghna. If only she had not been murdered that night he'd gone to see her. She'd rebuffed his proposal, and, in his ire, he'd attacked her.

At first, he had believed that it was he who had killed her, but then he saw her corpse. If she hadn't spurned him, he'd likely be as dead as she. For surely he would have shared the poisoned wine in her chamber.

The scuffing of shoe on stone outside the door had him turning to greet one of his many half-siblings. "You risk too much summoning me like this," she complained, and even though her face was hidden by the great hooded cloak, Bowen recognized her by the arrogance in her voice.

His reaction was instantaneous; he grabbed her by the neck, shoving her against the closed door. "Careful, sister. You'll not speak to me in such a manner. If I demand that you slit your own throat, you'll do it. Now, tell me, what news in Aurelia?"

"As expected," she answered, rubbing her neck when he released her. "We have spies placed in most of the territories. Your plan, using the destruction of Chevring and its scattered people as means to put my Kena in key households, has proved successful."

"Everywhere?" He hated depending on others to obtain what he wanted, but he would need the Fenrhi on his side if he were to succeed in his plans.

"Almost. The people of Cathmara are distrustful of outsiders. And King's Glen is still closed to us, as is Stolweg."

"And the Aurelian woman?" he asked. "Any word?"

"No, my prince. She has not been located."

• • •

Madyan held perfectly still for several minutes after Prince Bowen and the woman departed. Neither of them was aware that on the other side of the silk-lined wall, a secret compartment and passage had been built. This early morning meeting was not the first on which she'd eaves-dropped, but it was the most intriguing. Why would Bowen need to place spies in Aurelia? And why had Rhiannon lied to him about Lady Claire's whereabouts?

• • •

Claire sat in her room, contemplating everything that had happened in the last two weeks. That Milla was more than she appeared was no great surprise. She was important enough to Nifolhad to warrant having Madyan as her sworn protector. And not just Madyan. There were others as well: the so-called watchers.

The time of their escape was upon them, for Milla had volunteered for her week in Blood Caste. They had decided that Claire would choose Sylvan, then volunteer as well. She would go with Milla and try to *sway* those in charge to let slip from their minds Claire and Milla's presence. If they were fortunate, they would have a full week to make their escape. Madyan would procure Umbren traveling clothes, three swift horses, and the necessary supplies. Together, they would ride northwest and into Prince Ranulf's vast domain. From there, they would need to con-vince him to give them asylum.

This afternoon, Claire was supposed to meet Milla in the mews again and was running behind. She yanked open her door and ran into a wall of blue: Rhiannon and two of her minions. Rhiannon was doing nothing to shade the hostility pulsing from her mind. Claire gasped and took a step back. The other two women from Kena glanced nervously at each other, then at Rhiannon who, despite the animosity flowing out of her, had her expression set in angelic repose.

"Good afternoon, Claire," she greeted cheerfully. "Mother has requested your presence in her audience hall. Come with us, please."

There would be no ignoring the summons; she followed the women through the honeycomb of the temple. When she entered the hall, Ni'Mala sat on her dais conversing with four women, one each from Sylvan, Kena, Earth, and Umbren. Ni'Mala gazed at Claire for moment, then stood. "Come, Claire. We'll both be more comfortable in my private chambers where we can speak uninterrupted about your future." Waves of aggression pounded at Claire's back, and as if sensing it as well, Ni'Mala stopped and frowned. "Rhiannon, you may remain here while Lady Claire and I converse."

"But—"

"I will call on you if I need you, Rhia, but right at this moment, you are doing your very best to intimidate Claire. Not only is it counterproductive to what we are all trying to accomplish, it is *not* working."

Claire couldn't help but smile at the flummoxed woman in blue and trailed Ni'Mala into her chambers. After they were seated and refreshments poured, Ni'Mala regarded her for a long moment. "Tell me, Claire, are you able to discern if I am lying to you?" When Claire frowned, Ni'Mala encouraged her. "Go ahead, you may tell me. I already know that your gift is greater than mine, perhaps even greater than Rhia's—this explains much of her hostility toward you."

Claire took a sip of the wine, searching her mind for a way to stall. There was no avoiding the question. "No, I can't tell. You could be lying or simply not being entirely truthful."

"Hmm. I see you are wise enough to know the difference. But you could simply read me. You have the gift of sight, yet you block yourself from using it. And it is this very skill, blocking, that has demonstrated to us that your mind is unusually strong. Agile too. We've never met anyone before who could control this gift so naturally. Most go insane from the endless visions." Ni'Mala's piercing gaze kept Claire uncomfortably riveted, so she took another sip of wine. "Do you feel…pushed?" Ni'Mala inquired. "Right now, I mean?"

"No, not in the least."

"That's good. I confess that we discovered just recently that you are immune to that sort of encouragement. Rhiannon had been expending quite a bit of effort to influence you to join them. And for all of her *persuasion*, you have yet to select where you wish to be placed. I am starting to doubt your desire to reside with the Fenrhi at all."

Claire took another sip of wine, set her nearly empty cup down. She hadn't realized how thirsty she was. "But I am trying, Ni'Mala. Just this morning I was considering Kena." Ni'Mala set her cup next to Claire's and refilled both. "Then I decided on—"

"Enough, Claire! Unlike you, *I* can tell when someone is prevaricating."

Claire reached for her wine and lifted it to her lips. While Ni'Mala had picked up on her untruth, she did not actually know what was on Claire's mind. Misdirection was needed here, a reason for her lack of veracity. "Perhaps, Ni'Mala," she bluffed, her cup still raised, "perhaps I should join Blood Caste." She watched as Ni'Mala leaned back in surprise that Claire had ferreted out the existence of the sixth caste. Claire waited for a reply, then tilted her cup once more.

"How long have you known?"

"From the first day I met you," Claire answered honestly. "There was something missing from the four castes, five counting yours. Everything pointed to a sixth. Then I started noticing the different skin designs, all in blue, green, gray, black, and your gold. And, hidden where it could not easily be seen, red." Now was the test; she had only admitted part of the truth. Would Ni'Mala sense all that she was withholding? She took another sip of wine.

Ni'Mala studied her in thoughtful contemplation. "It is not so simple for me to maintain the balance here, Claire. You yourself know that influencing the mind does not work on everyone. Especially those in power or those with enough wealth. There are ways to subvert our methods. And the noblest houses in Nifolhad are unaffected by the Kena. I suppose the same would be true in Aurelia. Those born of the blood have a natural immunity."

Ni'Mala poured herself more wine, then refilled Claire's cup. Claire's fingers flexed infinitesimally toward her drink, but stopped. She wanted to keep her wits sharp.

"You see, Claire, it costs the Fenrhi a great deal to be left alone. Every caste must pay something: Earth Caste with its artistry, Sylvan

Caste caring for any seeking their help, Kena for its counsel, and so on. But it is those who wear red for their one week who pay the dearest. They are the Blood Caste; they give themselves."

"There must be another way," Claire persisted, picking up her wine and sipping. She set down her empty cup and focused on Ni'Mala's words.

"Every initiate is made aware of the existence of Blood Caste before the Marking Rite. They have the option of foregoing their sacrifice before they are indoctrinated into a caste. If they so choose, they are free to leave the Fenrhi."

"And do what, exactly? Leave the temple? Walk into the hands of the wardens, or the men of Naca'an?" Her ire had been pricked by Ni'Mala's callous indifference to the welfare of the women she purported to protect. "Not really a choice."

Ni'Mala gave her a hard look. "If an initiate opts to remain here, she is given time to come to terms with Blood Caste. Only when she deems herself ready do we allow her to give her sacrifice. Besides, this is not Aurelia, Claire. Women here are not free to walk the streets, visit the markets. Their marriages are arranged. Their lives are controlled. The Fenrhi exist to protect them when we can. King Cedric is dead. Princess Aghna is dead. Diarmait has thrown us back into the dark. But there is always a choice: leave here, and possibly die; or remain, and sacrifice a little blood for the greater good."

Ni'Mala's words were so cold that Claire tipped her cup once again to her lips; it was devoid of wine. She leaned back into the deep cushions. How she had finished her third cup? Or was it her fourth?

"Everyone has a choice, Claire," Ni'Mala insisted, rising from her cushions to lean over her. "Everyone but you."

She tried to focus on the pale blue eyes staring down at her.

"Claire," Ni'Mala soothed. "I summoned you here for a special purpose. The hour of your Marking Rite has arrived." Claire heard someone behind her; she tried to turn her head, but her muscles wouldn't obey. "Shhh," the Mother hushed, running her fingers over Claire's cheek and down her neck. "So lovely. It will be interesting to see what the Artists will make of you." Rhiannon came into view and smiled down at her.

"Get away from me," Claire yelled, but her voice sounded so weak, as if she were underwater. Ni'Mala took a step back.

"Ma'là, but she is strong," Rhiannon hissed. "One more draught,

I think." She poured yet more wine down Claire's throat. Claire was helpless to do anything but swallow.

"Close your eyes, Claire," Ni'Mala shushed, coming closer again. "It is time to determine your caste." Her cool hand brushed down over Claire's forehead, closing her eyelids.

Claire hadn't the strength to open them, but she could feel Rhiannon's breath on her neck when she murmured into her ear, "It'll be Kena; then you'll be mine to use as I see fit."

"Perhaps, Rhia," Claire heard Ni'Mala reply, feeling her cool hand caress her cheek. "It is not for you to dictate. We will let the Artists choose." Rhiannon gave a muffled retort, one that Claire could not decipher, then her mind when blank.

CHAPTER THIRTY-TWO

Marked

"Wake up," Trian gently nudged. She was so tired; her arms and legs felt as if they were encased in lead. Even her eyelids refused to open. "Wake up now," he repeated softly, brushing his lips against her forehead, then her temple, touching his nose to hers. He kissed her then, and Claire responded, pressing gently at first, for it was the only action she could manage in her lassitude. The embrace ignited the passion that always smoldered between them, and with the passion, Claire felt her strength grow. She kissed him back as ardently as he kissed her. Oh, how she'd missed him. It had been so long since she'd been cradled in his arms.

He drew away, and she opened her eyes: Trian. He gave her the smile he'd always reserved just for her. "I cannot stay, Claire. Before I go, there is something I must tell you."

"Trian," she sighed against the lips she'd drawn back to her own. "Don't go."

"Shh, just listen," he whispered, "It's time for you to embrace what you are. That which makes you special is a gift. Trust yourself to know when to wield it."

He broke free of their embrace and pulled away, his image blurring and disappearing. It was only a dream, and the harsh reality of losing him hit her once more. "Wait," she whispered. Then, she lapsed back into an unnatural sleep.

• • •

"Claire, please." It took a moment for Claire to realize that someone was speaking to her. "Claire, you must wake up!" It was Madyan.

154

"I can't stay, Claire," Madyan begged. "Eat this." She felt something being pushed between her lips, two small lumps. "Chew them, hurry. Now swallow." Claire did as she was told. She managed to just make out Madyan's face hovering over her in the dimly lit room. She felt her head being lifted, a cup tipped to her lips, then a liquid: water. Claire swallowed again. "I'm so sorry, Claire. It was too late when I found out. I would never have believed the Mother capable of this. I was so wrong." Madyan's tone was bitter. "I must go, but I *will* come back."

Her head was gently lowered again. "Wait," Claire rasped. "Why can I not move? I can't feel anything." Claire heard the panic in her voice, but if she didn't get an explanation, she would lose her mind.

"You've been drugged so that you wouldn't feel the Marking," Madyan rushed on. "One of the Artists, she watches with us. That is how I was able to come here. But, Claire, I have never before seen such work on anyone."

"What do you mean?"

She lifted Claire's arm and held it in front of her face. Claire blinked, trying to regain her focus, then stared in horror. The skin on her arm was covered in angry, red welts. Visible underneath the swollen discoloration were designs: small dots, like needle pricks, trailing in lines down her arm to her fingertips. The ugly red mottling did nothing to hide the swirls and waves, the spirals upon spirals curving and running in different patterns along her skin. And the colors: blue, gray, black, and green.

"Where else?" she croaked, insisting again when Madyan gave no answer, but simply set her arm back from where she had lifted it. "Madyan?"

"Everywhere," she intoned. "Claire, no one has been marked like this, not in generations. The Artists sometimes intuit more than one calling in an initiate and ink with more than one hue. But this? I don't understand it."

Claire closed her eyes in an effort to shore up the building tears. Madyan placed her hand on Claire's head. It was a soothing touch, one meant to calm her. Skin to skin; so, they had even shorn her head.

"Not your face, Claire," Madyan assured her as she pulled back the light linen cloth covering Claire's body. Claire was too numb to blush and too angry to be modest. Madyan studied her, scrutinizing every inch of her skin. "Your scalp is marked," she started, and then continued with the litany of vandalism. "Most of the design work is on your arms and the backs of your hands. But your neck, chest, and torso, and your back, I imagine, are also inked. There's more on your legs, too, and the tops of your feet. It's almost as if…"

When Madyan's words trailed off, Claire opened eyes. "What is it, Madyan?"

"There are stories of the first Fenrhi," she replied. "Their lore states that the Artists used sigils to help to channel the bearer's gifts, making them more powerful. Today, the designs are naught but designations, symbols with no more meaning than a drawing on a tavern sign." Madyan's head jerked toward the door. "I must leave before I am discovered here. The pihaberries will stop Rhiannon from overpowering you in your weakened state. The Artists should allow Milla to attend to you soon, for you are in one of the rooms reserved for those who need time to recuperate. In this place, you should be protected from Rhiannon, at least until the paralysis wears off." She covered Claire once more, then stepped away from where Claire lay on the high, padded table. Crossing the room to the window set high in the wall, she pulled herself up and out. A moment later, her head dipped down. "What they did, Claire, however unforgiveable, is beautiful. You are breathtaking." And with those final words, Madyan was gone. Claire stared at the ceiling, feeling the tears roll down the sides of her face, their saltiness stinging her sensitive skin. Eventually, she closed her eyes and drifted back to sleep.

• • •

"It is not permitted for you to be here," an angry voice ordered. Claire woke to the sound of an argument. She kept her eyes shut. "Don't even try that on me, Rhiannon," the woman spoke, her words clipped. "I am not an initiate, nor am I one of your addlepated followers."

"Tell me which caste was chosen for her," Rhiannon demanded haughtily. "Or just let me look at her arms, and I'll be on my way." Claire noted the wafting scent of fresh herbs. Her protector was Sylvan and had stepped into Rhiannon's path. She took some comfort in feeling the linen cloth tucked tightly around her, and what was more, her scalp was warm, so likewise covered. Wondering if she could move, she flexed her thumb and felt the light pressure of her nail where it came into contact with her thigh.

"It is forbidden! But you are well aware of this already," the woman intoned. "The girl has not even had a chance to see her own reflection, and you want to spy on her. No. It is time for you to leave, Rhiannon. Or must I call for reinforcements? Should the schism between the castes yawn even more? All for one woman's curiosity?"

Claire felt a dramatic shift in the air around her, but quickly realized the pressure was in her mind. She blocked the urge to move, to open her eyes, to engage Rhiannon. For that was what Rhiannon was trying to do.

"You have one day," Rhiannon threatened. "I will return tomorrow morning and have my questions answered."

"She needs at least a week to recover," her guardian persisted.

And Claire, wanting to have as much time as possible to regain her strength, focused on the idea that a week to recuperate was reasonable. Gently, quieter than a mosquito hovering just out of reach, she pushed: one week.

"Fine," Rhiannon spat. "But when I return, I'll strip her myself if need be. And she's awake, in case you didn't notice."

There was a scuffle. "Don't worry. I won't touch her." Claire sensed Rhiannon standing near. "You should know that you can never return now. Not the way you are. I've seen it," she whispered. "If Lady Claire of Chevring ever returns to Aurelia, there will be blood and death." Then she was gone, and so was the monstrous pressure that had filled the room.

Claire heard a shuffling and then a relieved sigh, and she opened her eyes and beheld her Sylvan protector. "Thank you," Claire stated, quite forgetting that this was probably one of the women who had marked her. The woman's expression, a queer mixture of remorse and excitement, confirmed it. Then Claire remembered her: she had been among the four discontented women who had been with Ni'Mala immediately before Claire's audience.

"This is one of the few places left in the temple that is protected from the Kena, even from Rhiannon." Another woman entered the room, this one garbed in blue, and Claire tried to sit in alarm. "Do not worry," she went on softly. "The Artists are loyal to all and therefore belong to no caste. We only create what we dream should be. Our dreams become our designs. And in you, we dreamt of many things."

The woman in blue then drew back the linen sheet from Claire's shoulder and lifted Claire's arm to examine her skin. Together, they supported Claire as she sat upright, the sheet draped across her bosom. The woman in green set a bundle of linen next to her. "Clothing."

"Where are my things?" Claire asked.

"There." She gestured to the neat pile on a table across the room. "These garments are made with the softest of linens. Your skin will be sensitive for some time. Would you like to see yourself now?"

Claire nodded, brushing away their attempts to assist her.

"There is a looking glass behind you, and a hand mirror," the Sylvan artist explained. "If you need our help, we will be nearby."

Only when both women left the room, shutting the door behind them, did Claire take her first good look at her arms and hands. She gasped. The swelling and redness had faded from her skin to reveal an intricate blending of scrolls and loops down her arms. A double figure-eight symbol was predominant. Tiny dashes in green, blue, dust, and charcoal formed multiple lines, swirling and cresting to her wrists, then separating again to trail down each finger. It was as if a seamstress had embroidered the inks into her skin using combinations of whip, straight, and seed stitches. Claire brought her hands closer, marveling at the brilliant colors, and saw, finally, that which had eluded her when her skin had been swollen and red. Just underneath all of the fantastic whorls, a geometric grid had been indelibly drawn upon her: hexagons, hundreds of them, all linked together like a honeycomb. The color was the palest of yellow—no, it was the amber color of honey. She'd thought her thumbs alone had been spared from being marked, but the honeycomb pattern continued, only smaller, forming a golden ring around each thumb. When held together, they formed that same figure-eight pattern.

Carefully, she swung her legs over the side of her raised bed, letting her naked toes dangle above the floor. The tall looking glass was directly in front of her, but angled away. A stool stood in front of it, and on top of it, a hand mirror that she could hold to view her back and posterior. She set her hands on the bed to either side of her hips, testing the strength of her arms. When she was satisfied that she was strong enough to catch herself should she stumble, she stretched her feet to the floor and shifted her weight to her legs. Her knees, though wobbly, did not give way. She shuffled the few steps it took to stand before the looking glass.

Minutes passed—time that she spent staring at her feet—before she found the courage to lift her chin. Calmly, she closed her eyes and focused her mind on examining herself in the way that Trian had taught her. She opened her eyes, forbade herself to rush, and swept her gaze over her figure, starting with her scalp. Her once-short locks, which had been growing out nicely over the past months, were completely gone. She touched the soft stubble. The markings stood out in contrast to her pale scalp. Madyan had been right. The designs, though Claire was at a loss to explain to herself why, made her feel beautiful. Her mind was infused with a sense of strength, tranquility, and purpose that she had never felt before.

After examining her head, she allowed her eyes to drift slowly to her face. Here, her skin was untouched, almost. Peeking out from where her hairline would grow back, tendrils of green and blue reached toward her temples, her cheekbones, and the lines of her jaw. Lower, the same designs—always underlain with the pale honey color of a Fenrhi mother—reached from behind her neck, coming from her nape and trailing down over her shoulders and collarbones like tresses of hair in the same blue and green, and interspersed with dusty gray and sooty black.

Claire steadied herself, then plunged her gaze to her chest and torso. Where her breastbone was, a much more vibrantly colored honeycomb emerged. Over the brilliant amber, there were four figure eights in the color of each caste. She'd seen the symbol before, but the locale eluded her. She lifted her hand to trace the shape. When her fingertips touched her skin, Claire sucked in a sharp breath. Her reflection wavered, replaced by a vibrant memory. She was in the lush valley where the great henge of Stolweg sat, and her hand was held by another's. Trian's. She heard the soft sound of the breeze, the insects, and Trian's laughter as they walked together. It was the day when they had decided to explore the stones. Claire could smell the crushed blades of grass under their knees as they knelt on the ground and touched one of the sun-warmed stones near its base. Trian bent to kiss her, and did, and she smiled up at him. Then they turned back to the stone. Claire reached out, tracing the timeworn runes. She could feel the pebbly surface as her fingertip followed one of the circles up and around, then back down to the starting point before repeating the mirrored motion. And suddenly, Claire was gazing at her reflection, naked, standing in front of the looking glass, her finger tracing the same symbol on her breastbone. She'd had a vision, one like she'd never had before, and she frowned at its import. Had touching the markings caused it?

She resumed the study of her torso. Emanating from the central honeycomb inked on the skin covering her breastbone, lighter combs reached out and covered her breasts, then trailed down her center to her stomach. It was here finally, that Claire beheld the evidence of the Blood Caste. Around her waist, draped over her hips, a chain of red had been drawn into her skin. The links met just below her navel, then a single strand trailed lower, losing itself in the triangle of tight curls. The crimson chain links were tiny hexagons—*They would be,* she thought dryly. She pivoted around and, using the hand glass, gave her back a cursory inspection. The same tendrils of dust and soot fell down along her spine, intertwined with blue and green. The red chain went all the way around her midsection, so artfully made as to perfectly resemble an actual belt of crimson links. Her buttocks were free of any mark, not even the light, honey-toned comb pattern was visible.

"No thanks for small wonders," she sniped, reaching for the linen robe that had been given to her. No sooner had she donned the garment, tying it loosely with a sash, than her keepers returned. An entire contingent of them. Claire climbed onto her bed, crisscrossed her legs underneath her, and waited as the four women positioned themselves in a semicircle around her. They remained silent, and so too did Claire, deciding that as they were the ones who had vandalized her, they could begin the explanations.

Claire's attention was jerked toward the woman in blue and, noticing her smug expression, she narrowed her eyes. She imagined a bubble around her thoughts, and allowed it to stretch and expand, pushing out at the woman, wiping away her pleased smile. The others were watching closely, evidently approving of whatever it was that Claire had accomplished. But the patronizing, all-too-knowing smile didn't return. To her core, Claire believed this to be a good thing. The woman's wary gaze held more than fear; it held respect. These women, these neutral Fenrhi, had some ulterior motive, some scheme in place, one in which she was the means to their end. She liked it not one bit.

The Sylvan woman stepped forward. She held in her hand a small jar, and Claire recognized it as one of the many she had used to make her balm when she had spent time in the herbarium. "We four have never marked anyone so extensively," the woman began.

The gray-clad woman stepped forward and, taking the jar from the other's hand, gave it to Claire. When she spoke, her voice was a raspy whisper. "I'm called Gudrun," she started, gifting Claire with her name, and Claire placed her age at near seventy. "She of the Sylvan is called Hedra, and that's Jenai in black. Radha, from Kena, is our youngest member."

"Member?" Claire asked.

"Of our group. Of the Artists. There are four of us: one from each caste. There will always be four."

"But there are six castes," Claire pointed out. "No blood artist? No one to represent your Mother?"

"We all are each marked with red, so the Blood Caste is represented. As for the Mother, we all serve her, as she serves all Fenrhi," Hedra droned on as if by rote. "The honey markings do not belong to her; she belongs to them."

"Hedra is only partially correct," Gudrun continued. "*We* have never marked anyone so extensively. But I am born of Blood Caste and have always resided in the temple. When I was very young, I beheld the woman who was named Mother then. She was a sight, let me tell you. Over seventy years have passed and never after has another been so marked. Not her successor, nor the current mother."

"Over the years," Hedra picked up, "the caste markings have become mere decorations. It was not always so. The Artists had more say in where an initiate would be placed. They would dream their dreams and create their designs. We did not plan what we did to you. We were inspired, each of us."

Gudrun and Jenai bobbed their heads, smiling and congratulating one another. Only Radha remained silent and apart from her sisters.

"Why have you done this to me?" Claire demanded. "You have a Mother. I doubt Ni'Mala would approve of this."

"Mother is more and more influenced by Rhiannon," Radha

explained. "She *believes* in Rhiannon's methods. The Mother no longer serves the Fenrhi; she serves herself. She feeds her ambitions as she fills the temple's coffers with the gold given to her by the men who frequent the halls of Blood Caste. She has even permitted Rhiannon to select from the initiates, sending them from the safety of these walls to the palaces of Diarmait." Radha was all but seething as she spat out her next words. "Of late, those sent do not return. The Fenrhi—"

Jenai gently placed her hand on the other's sleeve and drew her back into the semicircle. "Come now, Radha, let Gudrun explain." Radha calmed, either by Jenai's soothing tone or her soft touch. Claire found it intriguing that the two castes that seemed most at odds throughout the temple supported each other here.

"You have yet to tell me why this has been done to me." Claire didn't bother to hide the anger in her voice. "You poisoned me, then covered me with Fenrhi symbolism. It's tantamount to rape. So, unless you want to be subjected to that of which I'm now capable, you'd best explain yourselves." While she had spewed her wrath at the women, they had all taken a step back. There was fear in their eyes, all except Radha. Radha's gaze was full of warning, but warning against whom?

Gudrun shuffled a bit closer, her hands raised in placation. "*We* did not poison you. That was done by the Mother. When they brought you to us, we had no choice," she argued. "Had it not been us, Rhiannon would have had someone else perform your Marking, someone she could control. She would have taken you for the Kena to do with you what she willed. She can never do that now. We've saved you from her."

"Saved me?" Claire asked aghast. "Look at what you have done to me." She swiped her hand over her bald head. "You could have marked me for Sylvan, or Umbren, or Earth. But no, you've turned me into a damnable rainbow." She ran her fingers over the top of her other hand; a strange sensation crept through her as it had before. "How am I to…? I will never be able to…" It had been the word *rainbow* that had triggered the vision, that and the touching all of the colors etched on her fingers. For suddenly, Claire was running down a corridor, festooned with fresh flowers. First one bunch broke its bindings, scattering to the floor. They were blue. The other bunches fell one by one, but the flowers were now the colors of the castes.

Claire reached down to sweep them together, the scent of spice and honey strong in her nose. She was reliving that first moment when she became aware of the attraction between Trian and herself. And in recalling his name, his hands appeared to help her. Yet this time was different. Trian held her hand and, lifting it, lightly brushed his lips against her knuckles before turning her hand over and pressing a kiss to the underside of her wrist. She watched his head lift away to study the colored patterns on her skin. Trian stared at the markings for a moment, then he smiled at her as if nothing were amiss. Claire blinked, and the vision was gone.

"—so you must accept that it is a gift we have given you," Gudrun was saying. Not one of the women seemed to have noticed that she'd been somewhere else, even if that place was only in her mind. Anger grew deep inside her, a rage that she could barely suppress. How dare they do this to her?

"Enough! Who among your little quartet can tell me what was done to me and why?" Radha stepped forward. "The rest of you, leave," Claire ordered. When Gudrun hesitated, Claire glanced at her pinkie finger, the one marked with the dusty tones of Earth Caste. She didn't know why doing so would intimidate Gudrun, she just *knew* on some instinctual level that it would. She raised an eyebrow at the other women, waiting.

"As you say," Gudrun acquiesced, pulling Jenai and Hedra from the room.

"And close the door behind you," Claire demanded, having had enough of Gudrun's dance around the truth. She eased back toward the head of her bed, tucking her legs under her blanket as she did.

"Can I get you something?" Radha offered. "Water, perhaps?" At Claire's nod, she poured a cup. "Just water," she promised. "But you know that."

"You have no idea what I know," Claire retorted, but took the cup and drank from it. Radha sat opposite her at the foot of the bed. Her back was to the window, so she did not notice the shadow that flitted past. "Now," Claire began, "tell me, and without all of Gudrun's embellishments, what you have done to me, and why."

"Gudrun, the others, they need you," Radha explained. "So we marked you in the old ways, using the patterns that would strengthen your already innate abilities. The four of us worked both together and independently, each imbuing our design with the strengths of our separate castes, while uniting to create the underlying strength of the honeycomb. From Hedra, the Sylvan ability to help heal people, to intuit what they need, what danger their illness or injury poses, its cause and its remedy; from Jenai, Umbren Caste's protectiveness, their unfailing desire to act as a shield against harm; and from Gudrun, more than just a desire to be of service, but commitment to doing one's duty no matter the cost."

Duty? Claire had misunderstood Earth Caste, or had been made to misunderstand it. When she observed the women wearing their dusty gray raiment, "service" had been the word that always came to mind. But to Earth Caste, it was more. It had always been their duty, their duty to the temple, their duty to the Fenrhi. "And what did *you* give me, Radha?"

Radha smiled, pleased with herself. "When the Fenrhi began, they formed the different castes to support one another. But the castes are mere fragments of what they once were. Duty became service; enricher became healer; shield became stealth; and for Kena Caste, enlightenment became control. I gave you that purest, most basic essence of the Kena: the skill to see. Nothing more. You have always had these abilities; the marking rite only roused them from their dormancy.

"You've traveled in a vision, haven't you?" Radha then asked. "Do not worry that it happens unbidden. Just as you were able to control your ability to sense things about others through touch, or to block unwanted ideas from manifesting in your mind, so too will you learn how to control these new visions."

"So you have only given me more headaches," Claire observed. "I could *see* well enough before."

"Pardon, m'lady, but I did not mean *see* in the common sense of the word. I meant that your eyes are now open. To the past, the present, the future. To interpret. To understand. You are now aware of what the others want from you. I believe that you have known it all along." Claire pressed her hand to her chest, felt the undeniable power that radiated from her core. "You are beginning to comprehend how the honeycomb acts to bind the castes together. Each is only as strong as the other. No one caste can stand alone, not without the honeycomb."

"And not without a mother," Claire finished, and Radha nodded.

"The Fenrhi can trace its roots farther back than the most noble of families in Nifolhad," Radha expounded. "The Mother once went by another title: 'Queen'. We were a matriarchal society, living harmoniously with men. But generations ago, the balance shifted. Then the Great War with Aurelia started. By the time the Great Peace began, the Age of the Queens was barely a memory. Kings ruled Nifolhad. And so The Mother came into existence. With each generation, the woman raised up to bind the Fenrhi became weaker and weaker. Ni'Mala's power is diluted. Her tenure has ushered in a time of great imbalance between the castes. If we are to survive, we must grow strong once more. We must all commit to one purpose. But we need a fulcrum. Upon you, we have bestowed the strengths of Queen."

Claire opened her mouth to deny this, then shut it and narrowed her eyes at Radha. "Gudrun, and the others," Claire started, "they want me to replace Ni'Mala—" open eyes, indeed "—and you, Radha, what is it that you want?"

"I want more. Replacing Ni'Mala with another Mother will only help the Fenrhi. The others are shortsighted. To change the Fenrhi, to find our Queen again, we must change Nifolhad."

Claire sighed, swung her legs over the side of her bed and slipped to the floor. She poured herself more water and drank it thoughtfully. "I find this tedious, Radha. And I grow weary of the hints and riddles that you Fenrhi so enjoy. If you want my help, I suggest you try a new tack. It's something we Aurelians like to call *getting to the point*."

"As you wish," Radha conceded. "If directness is what you want, then may I point out that by saying *we Aurelians*, you have announced your intentions in regards to the Fenrhi?"

Claire smiled, for that had indeed been her aim.

"I urge you to reconsider your decision. I do not wish to simply elevate you to Mother of the Fenrhi." There was a tap at the door, and Milla entered with a tray. She set it on the table, then pulled something from her pocket. She extended her hand to Claire; dangling from her fingers was Claire's tiny leather pouch. Radha gave Milla a cursory glance before going on. "You are from a noble line; I have studied your bloodline farther back than your great aunt, the one called Lady Jeanne. But are you learned in your own history, m'lady?"

"I can cite my ancestors. All of them," she replied proudly. "What could you know of my line?"

"Go through the names, generations before Lady Jeanne, and you'll recognize that some of your ancestors have similar names to those found here in Nifolhad. Before the Great War, and the many wars that have plagued our two realms, before the intermittent peace, there grew one great royal house in Nifolhad, one where a brother and sister were expected to rule together. But discord formed between them. The sister stayed here and begat the line of Queens. The brother sailed for Aurelia and married into a noble family. It was he who was married to your ancestor. Ironic, isn't it, that the strength and nobility of a man started your line? Daughters after daughters after daughters, through the generations, and all of your ancestors, and all of your future progeny, all possess the blood of a Nifolhadian prince named Aghnar."

"Aghna," Claire put together. Behind Radha, Milla stiffened. Had the princess lived, she would have been Queen of Nifolhad, and her uncle, Steward King Diarmait, would not be causing so much strife, both here and in Aurelia. Claire's eyes widened at the implications.

"Ah. You now appreciate more of our purpose. Your blood is more than noble. Like the blood of our murdered princess, that which flows through your veins is royal. We need you to become our queen!"

Quiet as a mouse, Milla had prepared a plate and brought it to Claire. She went back to the tray to pour Claire more water.

"The day has grown late, and you need some time to consider what we're offering. Milla will see to your comfort; you can trust her."

• • •

"Foolish woman," Milla criticized after Radha departed. She sat on the bed next to Claire. A moment later, the panel was lifted away from the window, and Madyan slipped into the room. "You heard?" Milla inquired.

"I did," Madyan said scornfully.

"Does she really believe that I have a claim to the throne?" Claire asked them.

"She does," Madyan replied. "And it is true."

"But I don't want to be the Queen of Nifolhad," Claire declaimed. "I don't want to be the Queen of anywhere."

"Nor do we wish it," Madyan concurred. "There is another who holds that right."

"But who? Princess Aghna was the last of her line, and she is gone. Is there another, a sister, perhaps?"

"No, there's no sister," Madyan answered, then stepped back.

Had it been right in front of her all this time? "Aghna," Claire guessed, turning to Milla.

"I am pleased to meet you, Cousin Claire. For we are related, are we not, descended from the same blood hundreds of years past?"

CHAPTER THIRTY-THREE
Milla's Tale

Aghna stood, prepared two more plates and, after handing one to Madyan, began her tale. "When my father, King Cedric, died, I was sure that he'd been poisoned by Diarmait. Afraid that I would accuse him, my uncle kept me isolated from the rest of court. One by one, he replaced those advisors who'd been most loyal to my father, and therefore loyal to me. Even my ladies were removed, sent back to their families, or married off—at least that is what I hoped. Only one remained in the end. One of Diarmait's daughters, half sister to Bowen."

"I didn't realize Diarmait had other children," Claire observed. "Strange that we have not heard news of this in Aurelia."

"Diarmait only ever valued his two legitimate sons. He has had many wives in his quest to beget more male heirs but has only succeeded in siring girls."

"How many daughters does he have?"

"Last count? Seventeen, including those from both his wives and his mistresses."

"Seventeen! Where are they all?"

"Alas, his only use for his legitimate daughters has been to gift them to various nobles in Nifolhad, betrothing them nearly from birth to the men of the greater families, linking them to his house in a tight web of blood connections. And his many wives? Diarmait gave them each several chances to bear him sons, at least in the beginning. As each one failed to produce male heirs, they disappeared, never to be seen again."

"And this half sister to Bowen, what made her so special that Diarmait kept her near?"

"Her name was Jalara, and she was as malicious as his two sons." Aghna's gaze grew far away, and she lowered her voice to a mere whisper.

"I remember every detail of the day I escaped as if it happened yesterday. There was a great feast held in Diarmait's honor. Disgusted by the entertainment, for they had ordered several of the Fenrhi to dance attendance on the men, I rose to leave. Jalara was enjoying the abuse paid to the Fenrhi, and, as I wanted to be free of her for once, I did not demand her company.

"But Diarmait took note, and he berated Jalara, had her thrown to the floor to be kicked and ridiculed. I escaped from the hall to return to the sanctuary of my quarters. When I entered my chambers, Bowen slipped in behind me.

"He grabbed me, Claire, my own cousin, he… he…He tore at my gown, and used the tattered silk to bind my hands. I kicked him when he tried to…I kicked him. He was so shocked that I fought him. That I dared to resist. He grew incensed and attacked. It only took one punch to my head to fell me, but he was too far gone to stop. I tried curling up into a ball—"

"—to protect yourself," Claire finished, remembering the men on the ship.

Aghna swallowed. "I cursed him while he, my closest cousin, reached down to remove his breeches."

"You never told me," Madyan worried. "I would've—"

"He was unable to do anything more, for Jalara burst into my chamber. She screamed at him, pounded her fists against him. And he backed away from her. There was fear in his eyes, and I was amazed at her power over him. She, the same woman who had just been humiliated, pinned him with naught but her glare. As she pushed him from my chamber, Bowen begged her to not tell Diarmait. She closed my door and set the latch, then walked over to where I lay bound on the floor.

"I remember thinking that perhaps I'd judged her too harshly, that perhaps there was more to her than her cunning looks and her malicious slights. She hovered over me and, as I shifted to give access to my bound wrists, she swung her leg back and kicked me. Her toe caught me on the thigh, and then she kicked again, and again. How many times she kicked me I will never recall, for when she connected with my temple, I lost consciousness.

"I came awake to the sound of singing," Aghna began again. "Jalara was dancing and chanting to herself. She saw me watching her and hissed. She raved about being forced to hide her beauty, and about no longer having to grovel. She wanted to force her half-brother into making her his wife. If Bowen refused, she said she would threaten to tell others that he had killed me, and he would never be king."

"How did you escape her? And Diarmait?"

"Some of my gowns had been laid out so that I could choose what to wear the next day. When Jalara noticed them, she ripped off her head covering. She didn't even wince as a thick lank of hair was pulled out. Then she went to my looking glass, stripping as she walked, peeling away her leaden gown. She stared at her figure and smiled, then began telling me of her scheme: 'We are so alike, you and I. We could be twins. Even our eyes are the same color. So why is it always your eyes of which the poets extol? They never look my way. Never. But they will write about me now, won't they?' I offered her the dresses, all of them. Her face contorted, and she flew at me. This time when she kicked, her naked feet did no harm.

"I rolled to avoid her, and my wrists came loose. The garments on my bed distracted her again, and she left me alone. When she put on one of my gowns, I was astounded that we indeed looked like sisters. Same height, same carriage, same hazel eyes, even her hair was the same color as mine. She helped herself to the meal that had been left for me. She drank my wine. First one goblet, then a second."

Aghna paused and took a shaky breath. "It began when she started drinking her third. Her gloating expression changed to one of discomfort. She started coughing and shuddering. She screamed, a strangled sound that I will never forget. When she turned to me, her mouth looked as if someone had held her face in a fire; her lips and chin were covered in sores. I watched as her fear gave way to panic. She rushed to the looking glass to watch her skin welter and blister until she was unrecognizable.

"Do you know what the last thing she said to me was, just before she fell dead? That it wasn't fair."

Claire took Aghna's hand. "How horrible."

"It was an ugly death, one meant for me. I admit, though, that I was not sorry for her. It sounds bitter, but at the time I was glad of it. And later, grateful. Jalara had always hated me, and in my arrogance, I never cared. Her death opened my eyes in more ways than one.

"There she was," Aghna finished, "on the floor, in my gown, her face horribly disfigured. But her eyes and hair, so like mine, gave me my only chance. I dressed in her clothes, packed a few belongings: coins, jewels, and my father's ring. Dressed as I was, it was simple to slip from the royal wing of the palace, then insert myself into the group of Fenrhi women returning the next morning to their temple. They realized that I was not of their group, but they didn't contest my presence. I was just another bruised and beaten woman who needed help."

Claire studied her. "Who else knows that you are alive, Aghna?"

"Besides you, just Madyan. And until we are safe, I will persist as Milla. Even when we cross into Sophiana."

"Why have you waited so long to come forward?" It bothered Claire that Aghna had not tried to escape the Fenrhi earlier and go to Prince Ranulf. "Why stay hidden, allowing your people to suffer?"

"Here," Aghna offered, holding out her hands, "take them. I have trusted you, and now I need you to trust me. The fastest way for you to do so is to see me for who I am." When Claire stared at the proffered hands, she hesitated. Looking *into* someone was something she worked hard to avoid. "Go on, Claire," Aghna pressed. "I want you to understand. I am running out of time, and so are you."

Claire took Aghna's hands in hers, reached out with her mind. Impressions of the princess's life came to light. The lessons, the grooming her father gave her so that she could one day rule with Prince Ranulf by her side. Claire saw Aghna's youthful infatuation with him, and how it had grown to respect. By remaining hidden, letting all around her believe she had perished, Aghna hoped that Ranulf would be safe from an assassination attempt. Claire beheld as well that Aghna's dream for Nifolhad was of a country run by a queen and king determined to find peace with Aurelia. She let go of Aghna's hands.

"Well?" Madyan asked.

Claire heaved a great sigh. "When do we make our escape?"

CHAPTER THIRTY-FOUR

The Plan

Claire stared at the ceiling of her tiny recovery room. Four days had passed, and she had reviewed their escape plan over a dozen times, coming up with unseen variables and working out the solutions with Aghna and Madyan. If all went as planned, they would be ahorse by the next evening and riding northwest to seek sanctuary with Prince Ranulf.

As schemes went, theirs was simple enough. Madyan had volunteered to go to Blood Caste again and would join Aghna in the queue of women. She and Claire would change places before entering the hall. Claire had volunteered to go herself, but Radha had been keeping too close an eye on her and had forbid it. Her week of recovery was not yet complete, and when she pressed to go, Claire sensed Radha's growing suspicion.

For now, Claire needed to rest, and sleep eluded her. She could not stop picking apart the myriad details of their plan. Aghna and Madyan would report to Blood Caste, along with four other Fenrhi. They would don the crimson robes with their deep hoods and form a procession beginning at the Mother's palace. Moments before entering the section of the temple that housed Blood Caste, Madyan would stumble, purposely landing near a shadowed alcove. Similarly clothed, Claire would switch places with her and slip in with the others.

Once inside the hall, it was an easy enough task for Claire to *suggest* that she and Aghna were viewed as a pair—a gentle push. Madyan's earlier reconnaissance had revealed that two women at once was a common enough request of the guests of Blood Caste. Then, Claire would have to influence the man who had paid for their entertainment. She would plant the seeds that he had enjoyed his night in the temple. In reality, he would be sound asleep until morning. Aghna and Claire would disappear into the night and out onto the rooftops, where Madyan would be waiting to escort them to their horses. It was the next part of their plan that disquieted Claire: two other women would take their places before dawn—Madyan had assured Claire that they were part of her secret group of watchers and were committed to making the sacrifice.

Once clear of the temple, the trio would ride, day and night, until they reached the lands of Prince Ranulf. Claire, with gentle nudges to the minds of any who sought to stop them, would see them safely to their destination.

The Artists' attempt to install her as Mother would fail. In the end, Radha would only find herself with a rightful queen. And Rhiannon and Ni'Mala? Well, they would never even glimpse the designs of the six castes that had been inked upon Claire's skin. Claire smiled at the thought of thwarting so many claims on her future.

Her future. An ache clamped down on Claire's heart, and she held the small pouch that hung from her neck. Uncinching the opening, she prised the glass pebble from the hardened leather and held it before her eyes. The forget-me-not blossom was unchanged. Closing her fingers around the glass, Claire settled back against the cushions of her bed. She tried to recall Trian's voice, and how his quiet words had always been a balm to her restless mind. Finally, sleep came to her. Her grip relaxed upon the bauble, and it slipped from her fingers, settling upon the intricate amber patterns inked above her heart.

CHAPTER THIRTY-FIVE

Jump

Cathmar

"You're sure?" Lady Baranne asked.

"Of course not," Lady Cafellia answered. "My stones only give me impressions, you know that. But over time, impressions turn into trends, and a watery truth emerges. The casting of Trian's fate has always been an exercise in contradictions." She threw her stones again. "Trian must fall in love with a stranger; doing otherwise will cause great strife."

"And this queen he's been dreaming of, and the blood?"

Lady Cafellia shook her head and tossed her stones anew. "I do not know. It's too early to see." She looked up. "Wait, here he comes."

• • •

"I'm not ready," Trian insisted. "You gave me eighteen months, and by my reckoning, there are five to go before I am forced to wed."

"I don't see any benefit in waiting," Lady Baranne argued. "Warin has searched nigh eight moons for Claire—a woman you cannot even recall loving—and has found no evidence that she yet lives."

Trian had heard this argument from his mother many times in the past few weeks. She was worried for him and wanted him settled. She believed the best thing for him was a good, strong woman from Cathmara. But regardless of the pressure exerted by the great families from the Cathmaran states, his mother would never yield to them if Trian held to his current line. So he stood and endured, this time not even trying to justify his certainty that he should wait until the end of his allotted time. He couldn't even understand it himself, why he preferred his solitude. The chances were slim that Warin would find Claire, that Claire would find him in Cathmar, and that he would find his memories.

As his mother continued the debate, his mind wandered. He was lying to himself. Trian knew exactly why he wanted to wait. But it would be impossible to explain to his family that he loved the ghost of a woman who visited him in his dreams. Even though he could never recall her face upon waking, she was so real to him. The way she spoke to his soul while he slept, she *had* to be the elusive Claire. Trian felt more awake dreaming than he did, even now, standing in front of his mother and his aunt.

"You're doing it again, Trian!" Lady Baranne admonished. "You are physically present, but your mind is somewhere else. You need a wife. And children. Then you will come around. Now, your brother Aiden's wife has a cousin. She is comely enough, and smart. And Argel is so close, we would see you often."

Trian held his tongue and earned a scowl from his mother. She narrowed her eyes, and the staring match commenced. Finally, she threw up her hands in exasperation. "Fine," she growled, standing up. "But in five months, on the autumnal equinox, you *will* decide, or I will do it for you."

Trian bowed to his mother, then kissed her cheek before she stormed across the room. He leaned over to kiss his aunt and noticed her amused expression. "Best beat a hasty retreat before she changes her mind," his aunt counseled, but held his wrist before throwing the stones she always held close. She studied the pebbles for a few seconds, then slid a glance at Lady Baranne.

"Trian, do you know how your great-grandfather came to be married?" He shook his head. "Best find out, then. Now go," she ordered, and winked.

Trian was out the door and on his way to his chamber, the hour growing late, when he was waylaid once more. This time by Adara.

"Well?" she asked.

"We need to talk," he answered. "About Great-Grandfather."

"Great-Grandfather? Oh, yes, I can imagine just how that would buy you more time. Auntie?" Trian nodded. "That means she's on our side. Go and get some rest, Brother," she ordered. "I have some research to do. I'll go over everything with you in the morning." She spun on her heel and headed toward their father's study.

When Trian reached his chamber, he removed his clothes to wash. He examined the area on his leg where the arrow had pierced his thigh; the scar was prominent. He flexed the muscle and felt only a twinge of pain.

He climbed into his bed and, holding the kerchief in his fist, he rolled to face the great open window in his chamber. The night sky was clear and star-filled, and he wondered if he would dream of the woman he hoped would turn out to be Claire.

· · ·

The Fenrhi Temple

Across the Western Sea, Claire turned in her dream-filled sleep; she was no longer in the Fenrhi temple, nor was she alone. Trian was with her. He lay, turned away from her, facing a broad window through which she could see the stars.

She reached out and traced the delicate curve of his earlobe with her fingertip. There was a scar behind his ear, one that she didn't remember him having. She touched it, tentatively stroking, feeling the smooth, hairless flesh on his scalp. She knew the exact moment he became aware of her presence; his breathing changed. His hand reached back and captured hers as he rolled toward her. He stared at her, searching her eyes, then he gathered her up in his arms and held her close to his chest.

"What troubles you?" he asked, and she trembled with longing upon hearing his voice. The pain in her heart was acute; she wanted to wake. Trian kissed her forehead. "Just tonight," he begged of her, "please. Do not take yourself away from me yet." Then he drew her tighter into his arms, and Claire's heart broke.

She succumbed to her desire to touch him, to recall every muscle and bone, and she ran her hands over the flat planes of his sculpted chest, tripping her fingers along the ladder of his ribs. He smelled so clean and strong. And alive. She leaned forward and kissed him. He kissed her back, gently at first, as if this ghost who visited her dreams was as afraid as she that the other would dissipate in their arms. Their kiss intensified until passion took them, and not even the shattering of the sun could wrench her from her slumber. Claire tasted him, ran her tongue over his, boldly questing into his mouth as he did hers. She moaned when she felt his hands sliding down her back, cupping her buttocks and pulling her up hard against his rigid length. Then, his fingers traced down and between, seeking the quivering flesh between her thighs, touching her, tracing a lazy pattern over and over until she felt as if she would break into a million pieces. He probed the opening of her wet and swollen sheath, and slowly inserted his finger into her yearning body, establishing a rhythm, in and out, timing his thrusting hand with the rocking of her hips. He kept pushing her, lifting her higher, until she felt she would crumble. And then he set his lips to her breast, drawing her nipple into his mouth. When he touched his thumb to that place he knew would unravel her, Claire came apart.

So cruel, this dream. So real. But she was beyond caring as she opened her thighs to him, pressing herself against his throbbing staff. She reached down to stroke him, and he groaned his pleasure. She had never had the chance to give this to him before and, even though it wasn't real, she was determined to see him as pleasured as she. But he rolled them, sliding next to her, stroking her hair until her breathing slowed, returned to normal. And because her dream Trian seemed content to gaze at her, she returned his study with her own, fixing him in her mind, fearful that she would not be able to recall his face upon waking.

"Tell me what is wrong," he whispered.

"Tomorrow," she replied, putting to words that which she hadn't voiced to the others. Compelling another person terrified her, and even the best-laid plans never went as expected. That she would do whatever was required of her was at the heart of her troubled mind. She could and would injure another if forced to protect herself and any others for whom she cared. "Tomorrow, I might have to hurt people. What will that make me?"

"It doesn't matter. You must be everything that you can be; accept who you are. Use what you are. Stop being afraid and jump. And when you make the leap, I will be waiting to catch you." He touched her hair again, running his fingers through the long strands. "So beautiful," he remarked reverently.

His stroking of her long hair was a crushing reminder that this wasn't real. In her dream, the dawn was unfolding outside. She closed her eyes against the inevitable rising of the sun, intuiting that its arrival was paralleled in her waking reality. When she opened her eyes to glimpse him one last time, he was already gone. She was awake. Her hand lay upon her chest, and underneath it was the glass pebble with its tiny blue flowers encased within.

"I won't be afraid, Trian," she vowed, rubbing her shorn scalp. "I will jump. And I will do so knowing that if I crash, you will be there to catch me."

CHAPTER THIRTY-SIX

Push

"A fairer pair I've never seen," one of the men crooned, leering at Aghna and Claire. "Well, what are you waiting for?" he snapped. "You've been instructed to serve us, so serve us." He gestured to the table in the corner, and Claire and Aghna obediently moved to do his bidding.

Aghna shot Claire a swift glance as she poured some wine. Everything in their plan had gone exactly as expected. Everything except the fact that, instead of facing and subduing one man, they had been sent into a room with two.

"I know you don't want to use your gift, Claire," Aghna whispered, "but you might have to now. We won't be able to overpower both men."

"Quit your muttering," the other man shouted from where he'd been sitting with his companion on the cushions. Only his friend was no longer sitting, Claire realized as Aghna ducked out of his reach when he tried to grab her from behind. The wine sloshed in the goblet, marking the tiles like drops of blood. The other man rose and began stalking Claire. She edged away from him. He was tall and muscular, and if it were not for the lecherous gleam in his eye, Claire might've thought him handsome.

The ensuing game of cat and mouse was exciting him, and he leered at Claire. "Come closer, dove," he ordered. The other man had caught Aghna by her hair and was pulling at her clothes.

Stop! Claire pushed. The man holding Aghna released her and froze.

The other blinked at Claire, then shook his head. "Who are you?" He took a step toward her. "What have you done?"

"Stay back," Claire ordered, desperately pushing the idea into his mind. "Stay away from me."

He froze midstep, his anger building. Anger and more: the struggle to regain control of his will. "I think not," he hissed, taking another step. "Release whatever hold it is that you have on my friend, and perhaps I'll let you live to greet the morning." And then he was upon her. His hands wrapped around her neck as he shoved her into the wall. Claire lost her wind from the impact. His hands left her neck and grabbed at her robe, trying and succeeding in pulling her hood away, then ripping the garment from her shoulders.

"Where have they been hiding you?" he asked, spellbound by the extensive markings on her skin. "Quite the painted beauty." His body pinned her against the wall while he worked at his breeches, pushing them down.

This was the moment for which she'd been waiting. Claire brought up her knee as hard as she could, smashing it into his groin. He groaned and doubled over. She made for the dagger concealed in her boot, but was unable to reach it in time. She hadn't kneed him hard enough, and he was coming at her again with a blade of his own. He raised his hand to stab her, and Claire braced herself to ward off his blow. But he fell, arm still raised, first to his knees, then forward. Aghna stood behind him; the other man was staring in horror, still unable to move. She had used his dagger to save Claire, driving it between her attacker's shoulders.

"I wasn't able to stop him," Claire gasped.

"You couldn't have. He must have royal blood in him. I'm sorry, Claire, I should have prepared for that possibility."

They turned to the other man. His eyes darted back and forth between them, anger and fear equally visible in his panicked gaze as Aghna pulled the blade from its deadly sheath and returned it to his belt. "You know what you have to do, Claire," Aghna urged while wiping blood on the man's hands.

Claire managed to shake off her shock. "You fought with your friend. He was not sharing us with you. You fought and killed him. You will forget everything else that has happened here. Forget us both," Claire ordered. "You will wait here and confess that you have killed your friend." Aghna opened the door and peered down the corridor. "Now, sleep," Claire finished, and turned to Aghna. "I have no way of knowing how long the suggestions will last."

"It won't matter. He'll be put to death for killing someone of royal blood."

Claire paled and stared one last time at the man collapsed on the cushions, then she and Aghna slipped from the room, silently making their way down the corridor to where Madyan was waiting on the roof. A high, narrow window was set in the wall ahead of them. When they reached it, Aghna tapped twice against the carved screen. There was an echoing *tap tap*, and the screen was lifted out and up. Claire wove her fingers together for Aghna's foot, boosting her friend through the narrow gap. Then she leaned against the wall, raised her hands to the opening, and gripped the wrists that reached for hers. Claire ducked her head, and was hauled out and onto the roof.

Madyan levered herself over the edge and replaced the panel. "Your hands are covered with blood, Princess. Are you injured?"

"No. There was an unanticipated complication. We had to improvise," Aghna answered coldly. "We will no longer have the week that we'd hoped to have before our absence is noted. But perhaps we've caused enough of a diversion to give us a couple of days before the Kena regroup. We'll tell you all about it once we are quit of this place."

"Then follow me." Madyan led them at a pulse-racing pace across the rooftops of the Fenrhi temple, not stopping until they reached a darkly shadowed section of the roof adjacent to the outer wall girding the temple from the forest. She distributed their packs. "We each have the same amount of water and food," she informed them. "Only dried fruit and meat, and honeyed biscuits that will not spoil on our trek. We must travel light."

She indicated three more parcels, handing one each to Aghna and Claire and keeping the smallest for herself. "Traveling clothes. You can change here before scaling the wall. Your personal items are already in your packs."

As Claire and Aghna changed into the Umbren clothing better suited for stealth, Madyan scooped up their castoff garments. She slunk away, keeping her head below the edge of the wall.

"She's going to destroy them in the kilns," Aghna explained. "They are always lit, and the fabric will burn quickly, leaving no trace that we have passed this way." Aghna and Claire had just pulled on their new Umbren cloaks when Madyan reappeared. After peering over the wall, she threw two knotted ropes over the edge.

"As we planned," Madyan reminded. "Climb down, make for the

far edge of the western woods. The wardens are fewer in number there, but you must stay alert. Aghna, I trust Claire to keep you safe. She is better equipped to avoid the wardens than I. I'll catch up to you."

Claire had just touched the ground and released her tether when Madyan hauled it back up. The ropes would be incinerated along with their discarded clothing. Madyan would reach the ground another way. She got her bearings, then led Aghna into the shelter of the woods. Reaching the far edge, they waited for Madyan. When she finally appeared, they moved northwest, always keeping three or four rows of trees between them and the open grasslands. When there were no more trees, they raced across the dark fields to the waiting hills.

Madyan led them to where their mounts had been secured in an abandoned croft. Claire could discern in the dark gloom of the night that the beasts were itching to move freely. She'd never ridden anything but Chevring steeds, and these horses were smaller, more finely boned. She put the light, padded saddle on her horse and led it from the shelter. Together, she and her friends rode into the foothills surrounding Naca Valley. Claire, first and last a horsewoman, found her mount's gait as smooth as any Chevring steed. Her mare must have felt her silent praise, for she gave a low rumble that Claire felt through the saddle, and pushed her pace up another notch. Aghna followed close behind, and Madyan brought up the rear.

CHAPTER THIRTY-SEVEN

Warin was ready to leave Nifolhad. He had combed through every trace and clue regarding Claire's whereabouts and was frustrated beyond all measure that each had proved to be a false trail. The visit to Naca'an had been the most disheartening. They'd stayed over a month, listening to the gossip about the torched ship in the middle of the bay, of the bodies of half-burned men who'd washed ashore for weeks. He and Pieter had searched for hints of Claire, but nothing was divulged save that Diarmait had lost some valuable cargo, and that the cargo was a woman.

After weeks of hearing the same information, they'd sailed down the coast, visiting the fishing villages and hidden smuggler coves south of Naca Bay. Bringing Pieter along had proved fortuitous, for he had a way with the children of Nifolhad; they seemed to trust him and were more talkative than their adult counterparts. But the gossip they shared was disparate and varied. The stories ranged from Diarmait finding his cargo and killing the crew that brought it to Nifolhad all the way to the crew killing the mysterious woman and throwing her overboard. Warin's favorite rumor had been the one that he'd heard near the small fortress city of Vynfyr: a secret cult of powerful women had rescued Claire.

Unbelievably, this last rumor was the most widely held, growing more far-fetched with each telling. One child related that the woman was lifted away from the ship by a swarm of bees, carried over the rooftops of Naca'an, and deposited in a giant honeycomb. Nifolhadajans spoke the same language as Aurelians, but it was a country that was still riddled with the old tongue and its many dialects. Warin and Pieter were never completely sure if the stories they heard were fantastical or if they had simply misinterpreted a word here or there.

They were once again in Naca'an, waiting while the ship was provisioned for their journey home. Warin hadn't yet come to terms with his decision to return to Aurelia. He'd left Pieter with the captain and had gone to get drunk. He sat alone in one of the outlying taverns near the city square and ordered a bottle of the strongest brew the inn could provide. A jug of what had to be the worst-tasting wine ever produced was set before him. One gulp and Warin recognized that he was drinking the dregs of some barrel. He drained his mug anyway, then reached to pour another. But the jug was pulled from his grasp, and a similar vessel set in its place. He scowled and glanced up at a woman, probably the innkeeper's wife. In the busy common room, no one was paying attention.

"We call it *mala'eth*," she said, indicating the jug. "It's stronger than the grappa." She poured some into his mug, and Warin tasted the finest honeyed mead he'd ever had. He felt the effects of the heady drink almost immediately. She slipped the jug into a silken bag. "This is no place for an Aurelian smuggler. Take this and return to your ship."

"Leave me be," Warin grumbled. He heard a buzzing noise, and flicked his hand at a hovering bee, most likely attracted by the food and drink. When it landed on his shoulder, he jumped up, nearly upsetting the table.

The woman gasped, saw the innkeeper approaching, and leaned in. "Take your drink; hurry back to your ship. She who you seek has already escaped the Fenrhi temple. She—"

The innkeeper angrily shoved his way to the table, hand raised to strike his wife for her audacity. Before he could, she waved her hand about her head and spoke to him, "*Api*." And hearing those two simple syllables, the innkeeper's eyes widened, his skin paled, and he backed away, bowing to Warin as he went. The woman lowered her head and quietly withdrew, beckoning him to follow her to the alley.

When they were hidden in the shadows, Warin turned to her. "What did you say to your husband? What does ah-pee mean?"

"Honeybee," she provided. "The honeybee is the sacred symbol of the Fenrhi. It has marked you as one in need of assistance. We have been watching for you."

"Assistance," Warin repeated, incredulous that after months of finding no hint of Claire and even less help, the simple act of an insect flying near him would open doors he'd thought barred against him. "What is the Fenrhi?"

"Not what. Who. Powerful women. They once practiced the ancient arts based on six basic principles: enrichment, duty, protection, enlightenment, sacrifice, and unity." The woman peered at the door before leaning forward to speak more softly. "It is believed that the six tenets have not been completely forgotten."

"What do you know of the woman for whom I search? Of Diarmait's lost cargo?" Warin asked next.

"The Aurelian? She is lost to Diarmait, though he still searches for her. She is said to be skilled in the old ways. You seek a woman wanted by many. The Fenrhi wish her to join with them."

There was a rustling noise further down the alley. "You must hie to your ship and sail to Sophiana. Make haste or you'll miss the tide."

"Wait," Warin pleaded, grasping her wrist. "Please, I need more information. The woman, she is my friend."

But the innkeeper's wife pulled away. Before she ducked back into the tavern, she turned. "If the woman survives the Fyrost, you will see her again in Sophiana." And then she was gone. Warin slipped away, not bothering to double back and confuse any pursuer, for he was leaving Naca'an for good.

He made it to the ship just as the tide began to turn. Pieter was anxiously waiting. Warin grinned at him, then turned to Captain Grieg. "We sail to Sophiana with the tide," he proclaimed, and once more, they were asea.

CHAPTER THIRTY-EIGHT

Jia'ma

"What's the old Nifolhadian word for wind?" Claire asked while rubbing down her mount. They had ridden hard the last seven nights, stopping to rest and finding shelter just before daybreak. Claire had questioned her two companions on what they could expect once they reached Ranulf's fortress. The interrogations were invariably short-lived. Aghna and Madyan simply did not possess enough information about the goings-on in Sophiana. Prince Ranulf had gone on with his life, believing his betrothed dead the last several years, though his continued bachelor status gave Aghna some hope.

Aghna shook her head and laughed, guessing why Claire was asking. "Wind? There are many different words for wind in Nifolhad. But I believe the one that would suit your mare best is *jia*. The *jia* is the wind that blows from the south, a swift wind, strong and enduring. It scours the great desert of Nifolhad, wearing down everything in its path."

"Jia," Claire repeated. "And the word for mare?"

"*Ma*," Aghna supplied.

"Well, Jia'ma," Claire murmured to her mount, "will you carry me safely to our destination?" She gave her mare one last scratch before settling her belongings next to Madyan and Aghna's. Cover was not yet a problem for their party of three, for there were copses and hidden ravines aplenty in the hilly land they traveled. Aghna was seated on her blanket, checking over their supplies. They had been careful with their food, using almost nothing from their stores. Instead, they had taken turns each dawn to capture whatever small game they could find in the early morning hours while the other two foraged. Claire's favorite was the garnet-colored root that grew as big as her foot. There was nothing like it in Aurelia. Under the tough skin was a crunchy, turnip-textured meat, only much sweeter. Aghna showed her how to peel the skin, then slice the tubers into long, square strips. They remained fresh for days— weeks, if left unpared.

"If you are set on naming your mount," Aghna concluded, "Jia'ma is as good as any. 'Tis a strange custom you Aurelians have."

Claire smiled. "I could say the same of Nifolhad, you know. You are so reluctant to give your names, and when you do, it's considered a gift. Why?"

Aghna was thoughtful for a moment. "It is not the case with the men here. But for women, words are so scarcely spoken. This wasn't always our way, Claire. Only as our role, the role of women I mean, evolved to one viewed as lesser than a man's did this habit of gifting our names begin. A show of trust, as you saw with the Artists. Or a show of power, as with Ni'Mala and Rhiannon."

"But why do you not name your horses?" Claire asked.

"We do not name the things that we may someday have to eat," Madyan asserted pragmatically, then glanced at the three horses chomping on the fresh grass growing near their hidden camp. Claire shuddered.

"Such meat should not be wasted just because the initial use of the beast is over," Madyan went on. "If you have a sheep for wool, do you not eat the mutton once the beast is past its prime?"

Claire had no response to this. She glanced at Aghna, but her friend was busy staring off to the southeast.

"No doubt our absence has been noted," Aghna finally stated. "Pursuit is guaranteed. But like us, the Fenrhi must conceal themselves by day. Madyan was wise in choosing our route."

"How so?"

"Because only a madman would cross the Fyrost," Madyan answered. "This is where we are now." She used the tip of her blade to draw a compass and three dashes in the soft earth near their feet. Next she drew a hexagon almost two feet away, to the southeast of the three marks.

"The Fenrhi temple," Claire presumed.

Madyan drew in some mountains, then drew an *x* northwest of the range. "Prince Ranulf's fortress and domain." She smoothed out a great space south of their destination and west of the mountains.

"The swiftest route is by ship on the Virin Sea, but we dare not risk it." She notated with wavy lines where the western water was located. "These are the Brabryn Mountains," she said, and pointed to the range she had already drawn in the dirt. "Difficult to cross, but we could manage it. A mountain passage would take three weeks, then another two to reach the city of Sophiana."

"Five weeks," Claire calculated aloud. "Why not skirt the mountains to the east?"

"Still five weeks," Aghna answered for Madyan. "That way is easier, but more treacherous. The eastern path takes us too close to Kantahla and Diarmait's largest fortress."

Claire frowned. "What is this Fyrost, then?"

"It is the wasteland of Nifolhad," Aghna explained. "Few who have walked into the great desert have ever walked out again."

"In the summer, the *jia* that blows from the south licks at your flesh like tongues of fire," Madyan explained. "But spring yet holds sway. And there is treasure to be found in the Fyrost in spring. Especially if you have a guide who can steer you across, one who has passed in and out of the sands before."

"You are acquainted with such a person?"

Aghna and Madyan smiled at each other.

"Can we trust him?" Claire asked.

"You already do," Aghna revealed. "Madyan's parents were Fyrjians, travelers with the wind. She was raised in the desert. Lived there until her family was killed. She escaped and found her way to the Fenrhi."

"And you can lead us safely across?"

"Yes," she vowed. "Though the dunes constantly shift, the desert is the same now as it was a thousand years ago. There are hidden places rooted deep below the sands."

"How long will it takes us to reach Sophiana?" Claire asked. "How long will it take us to cross the Fyrost?"

"Two weeks," Madyan replied. "Any longer and it won't matter; our mounts won't last. Without horses, we won't either. Then, once across, another week to Sophiana. Two weeks faster than the other land route, but many times deadlier. Only by ship is it faster."

"Our route is unlikely to be taken by anyone else," Claire surmised. "Can the horses make it through this wasteland?"

"You tell me, Claire. What do you see?" Madyan asked, turning to regard their mounts.

Claire studied the horses, comparing them to their Chevring counterparts. "They are smaller than the horses of Aurelia. They—"

Madyan snorted, and Aghna took Claire's hand. "Don't let your preconceptions blind you. Open your eyes, Claire. Reflect on their purpose."

Aghna's directive could have been spoken by Trian. Claire drew her hand from her friend's, then stood and walked to her horse. Aghna and Madyan followed her and watched as she ran her hands down her mount's forelegs, inspecting the bones and the hooves. "She's a light horse. Finely boned. But her hooves are broad." She ran her hand over her mare's barrel chest. "Full chested, lean flanks. Light, so as not to become bogged down in the dunes; wide hooves to keep atop the sand. Large ears to cool her blood. Her nostrils too, though they have a dual purpose: cooling and bringing air to the lungs housed in this great chest. She's perfect for crossing a desert."

"Wind, you called her," Aghna stated. "It is an apt name."

"Jia'ma," Claire corrected. "But two weeks? Will she last?"

"She will, as will the others," Madyan swore. "The desert winds will buffet our backs and push us across, and these horses will be our ships. They've been bred by my ancestors for as long as your family has produced your Chevring steeds. Like me, they were born and raised in the Fyrost. If we are separated, tether yourself to your mare. She'll be your only chance to find water."

Aghna walked back to where they had drawn their map in the dirt. "Ni'Mala will send Fenrhi through the mountains. And she will send her people east, past Kantahla. She may even send a few unfortunate souls into the desert; they will be swallowed up and erased by sand." She kicked at the map with her boot, obliterating its existence.

"When do we reach the Fyrost?" Claire asked.

"Tomorrow morning," Madyan replied. "As we do now, so then shall we only travel at night. Especially in the desert."

CHAPTER THIRTY-NINE

Bones

The Virin Sea, Four Days South of Sophiana with Fair Wind

Warin stared across the waves at the bleakness of the Fyrost Desert. Its dunes caressed the sea for leagues. He could smell the sand and dust even from the great distance his captain had put between the ship and the coastline. It was known by all true sailing men that these waters were treacherous. The hidden shoals shifted at the whim of the desert winds, making them as impossible to chart as the desert dunes themselves. Even now their ship slipped past the skeleton of one such scuttled rig as it reached up from the depths, its ribs so darkened and worn by the water's cold embrace that the beams looked charred. The ships were not the only victims of the desert. It was once calculated that nine of every ten caravans crossing the Fyrost were swallowed up by its dunes.

Weeks ago, when they'd sailed from Naca Bay, Warin, Pieter, and the captain had met to confer about the latest intelligence regarding Claire. Warin had pulled the jug of honeyed mead from the sack, then poured a cup for the captain and himself. To Pieter, he gave a taste. *Mala'eth*, Grieg had told them, meant "mother's milk," and he'd only tasted it once before. And when Warin had shaken the bag, another item had rolled out onto the chart table: a small crock. He knew, even before he removed the cork, that it would be filled with Claire's balm. No sooner had he opened it than the scent of wildflowers filled the cabin, chasing away the constant odor of salt and sea. He shook out the sack again, hoping for some clue as to Claire's location. But there was nothing except the all-important proof that Claire had made it to

Nifolhad and survived long enough to mix up a batch of her balm. For Warin and Pieter, it was all they required.

• • •

"She's a terrifying place, she is," Captain Grieg remarked, coming up to stand next to Warin and Pieter. "No place for a smuggler from Pheldhain."

"She?" Warin asked with a smile; his captain was a romantic and a poet. Warin winked at Pieter.

"Oh, aye," Grieg professed. "She pushes and pulls and changes the landscape to suit her whims. That stretch of coast will be completely different next week. Of course, the Virin helps a mite with that. How's your skill with the Nifolhadian tongue?"

"I've not had any complaints," Warin responded smoothly. Beside him, Pieter's face washed crimson. The captain laughed and slapped Warin on the back, nearly pitching him into the sea. Warin waited a moment, then answered, "I'm versed in the rudiments of the old dialects, though my accent is awful."

"Do you know the meaning of 'Fyrost'?"

"Fire and bone," Warin supplied, and Grieg nodded and cleared his throat. "Prepare yourself, young Pieter. I believe our good captain is about to spin a yarn."

"There's truth in legends," the captain insisted, then began his tale. "Fire and bones, you said. Well, you can see the bones poking up from the Virin's depths. But in the desert, the storms are deadlier. Nifolhadian lore bespeaks the story of the goddess of the sky with eyes as blue as what you see above. One day, she observed a beautiful man working the soil, trying to make the sere earth grow lush with plants and trees. She came to him, and asked him why he toiled so hard where nothing could ever thrive. He smiled at her and complimented her and played to her vanity. He was a cunning man and, when he studied his plants and trees, he saw the one thing they lacked that would make them flourish: water. So he set himself to seducing the sky goddess, always aware that she could move the heavens. He lamented his plight, then lavished praise upon her, extolling her beauty, her kindness, and her strength, thus tricking her into falling in love with him.

"One day, he invited her to a great gathering of his people. And at this gathering, he married the goddess of the forest instead. His desires came to fruition when the sky goddess' heart broke and, in her despair, her tears rained down upon his land, nourishing his plants and his wife's forests. But the trees grew too tall and pierced the sky goddess, wounding her deeper still. Her despair turned to rage, and she summoned her brother, the wind god.

"The wind god let his sister throw him across the heavens. He ripped over the man's fertile lands, stripping away his forest and his bride, taking his plants, even the soil itself, and strewing all far afield. This was how the rest of Nifolhad was created. In the end, all that remained was the man, surrounded by his people, standing in the middle of a great wasteland. And still the scorned goddess raged. She pulled fire from the sun and cast it at him. But her wind brother took pity on the man and drove the sand against him, ripping the painful burning flesh away and ending his agony.

"The anguished sky goddess next turned her ire upon the man's people, for they tried again to plant and make things grow. And again, the wind god took pity, and the people were blown away to settle upon the newly formed lands elsewhere in the realm. The sky goddess gazed upon the bones of the man she had loved, and the desolation she had caused. Her grief was so great that she threw herself into the sea, ending her own life. To this day, the wind god pushes the sand into the Virin, hoping the water will one day cast his sister back to him."

Warin chuckled. "Remind me to introduce you to my good friend Trian." He stared thoughtfully at the barren shore, grimacing at the whirlwinds of dust and sand. "And the meaning of 'Nifolhad'?"

"Dark land," Grieg replied, "born of the sky goddess' rage."

Pieter frowned at the land to the ship's port side, and Warin set his hand on the boy's shoulder. "She'll make it, lad."

But somewhere, Warin still worried, in the madness of flesh-stripping windstorms, Claire was crossing the Fyrost. If she survived, he would see her within the week.

CHAPTER FORTY

Foresight

There was so much life in the desert. Everything Claire had been taught about such climes led her to believe that the Fyrost would be nothing but a vast expanse of desolation filled with choking dust and pounded by the relentless heat of the sun. She stared out at what she had once thought was a barren landscape.

Madyan had revealed to her the true beauty of the arid dunes and had taught her where to find nourishment and water. The reed-like leaf pushing out of the sand to a mere ankle's height hid a treasure under-ground: bulbous roots with spongy flesh that could be squeezed for precious moisture. And would anyone in Aurelia guess that snake meat was so succulent? Even better were the snake eggs with their rubbery shells. Birds, lizards, and insects abounded. Claire could have sworn she glimpsed a rabbit early one morning before they'd made camp. It had been a lean creature, long-limbed with a narrow head and stiff, pointed ears. She'd set snares while they rested each day, but thus far, had had no luck.

With Madyan as their guide, they navigated the dunes with ease. She had explained that there were anchors in the desert—fixed points in the shifting sand where one with an intimate understanding of the wasteland could find shelter, food, and even water. She drew out their route each morning, making sure that Claire and Aghna had their rest-ing places committed to memory and testing their knowledge along the way until they could draw the course themselves. It was necessary in the event that they were somehow separated.

They traveled in a series of hops, straight lines more than not, though many detours were taken to accommodate the endlessly chang-ing desertscape. Madyan pointed always to the night sky, reminding

Claire and Aghna to seek out the Weeping Sisters, a constellation of five stars whose cluster denoted true north. Paired with the Boar's Eye, the brightest star that appeared on the eastern horizon, Madyan invariably found their path and led them to shelter before daybreak.

They were traveling almost due west now, and Claire twisted in her seat to study the sky behind them. Though still dark, the eastern horizon was a stark silhouette against the heavens; dawn would soon best the night. She patted her horse's neck as her mount trotted a few paces to catch Aghna's mare. They rode single file, Madyan always taking point. Claire's friends became more and more distinct as the eastern sky lightened behind her. Finally, their Umbren guide dismounted and climbed the steep slope of the slow wave of sand before them, disappearing over its crest. A few moments later, her head popped up twenty paces away. Claire and Aghna dismounted and led all of their horses to where Madyan waited. When they crossed over the dune's lip, the sand dropped off sharply to the left and right, but directly in front of them was a series of stone ledges. With guidance, their horses' descent down the broad steps would be just manageable.

"These are too regular to be natural," Aghna noted.

"My father believed it was a temple," Madyan explained. "One built long ago to summon back the goddess of the sky. The steps are not always visible. Fortune favors us, for the winds have swept most of the ruins clean of sand. We'll find shelter below."

Claire studied the terrain before them, but only saw a massive, curved wall of stone. They drew the horses through a break in the structure, and she was astonished by what lay before them. An oasis! Her mare snorted and shook her mane, scenting the moisture coming from a cluster of palm trees. When Madyan let loose her mount, Claire and Aghna did the same. The horses kicked up and bucked in their excitement to find the water source hidden in the palms and reeds.

After nearly two weeks of sucking moisture from roots, Claire couldn't wait to feel the water on her skin. She tore at the gauzy linen that protected her face from the winds and sand and darted after the horses. Aghna whooped as Claire raced past her.

"Just stay on the path," Madyan yelled after them before giving chase.

Claire looked down and, indeed, there was a path. It was made of time worn stones, wide and flat. The scrub palms tried to encroach, jutting their gigantic fronds into its space, but the pavers held the plants at bay. Here and there, a few reeds had managed to thrive in the joints of the interconnecting stones. Even running, Claire could smell the water. She kept going, as eager as the horses to reach the cool promise of the pool. The path ended at a narrow band of reeds.

The horses had taken a different route, and the crushed greens left behind as they hied to the water smelled obscene after the choking sere of the desert. Claire stood as still as she could, soaking it all in. Behind her, she could hear her friends as they came up to the water. The stones continued, surrounding the pool and forming an almost perfect circle.

Her companions stood to either side of her, each, like Claire, immobile, as if they needed permission somehow to enter such a sacred place. Claire lifted her chin, giving silent prayer to the sky goddess Madyan had told her about—a deity she did not believe in, yet found it necessary to pay homage to.

The ever-serious Madyan was first to break their reverent silence. "Come on," she cajoled, though Claire needed no such prodding. Madyan started with her cloak, stripping off her garments one by one. Aghna did the same, and Claire wasted no time following their lead. Bare to the water, the sky, the reeds and each other, the young women stepped off the stone brim and into the palm-shaded depths of the pool.

The waist-high water lapped against Claire's midriff. She was naked for the first time since leaving the temple and, though she hadn't forgotten that she was marked, for it seemed at times that the inks lived and breathed with her, she had not consciously dwelt upon them. She turned her wrist, marveling at the way the water sluiced over the patterns. It trickled, ran, and formed droplets, ignoring the colored paths dyed into her. Upon noticing it, Claire suddenly realized that her skin was still just skin. For the first time, she was not ashamed of the lines staining her flesh and finally accepted the gift that the Artists had given her.

"You're beautiful," Aghna whispered in awe.

Madyan concurred, and Claire felt the makings of a blush steal over her skin. But it seemed to her that the markings protected her from such a concept as modesty. The designs were a shield. More, even: they were a constant companion. One that would always stand with her, never to abandon her. Her skin, wet from the pool, sharpened the details of the markings. The honeycomb pattern became a trellis for the vines of black, gray, blue, and green, all made more vibrant by the water.

"My mother once claimed that this was a healing pool," Madyan recollected. "Seeded by the tears of the sky goddess, the minerals in the spring soothe and give strength." She dipped her hands, ladling the water, and sieving it through her fingers.

Aghna grinned. "Healing or not, it is just as effective at cleaning off the dust of the desert." She dove into the center of the pool.

Madyan was about to dive in after her when she slipped. Claire grabbed her, taking hold of Madyan's arm. When her fingers wrapped around her friend's darkly inked skin, their surroundings transformed into a field of barley.

"Where are we?" Madyan wondered, eyes wide. "How can we be here? I can still feel the water around us. I can smell the minerals and hear the horses."

"It's a vision," Claire answered. Madyan did not see the figure coming at her from behind. Claire's heartbeat quickened; her nerves sang. Something here was wrong. She'd never had a vision of herself; she had somehow tagged along with Madyan. She yanked at her friend's arm, dragging her to the side before letting go. As soon as contact was gone, Madyan dissolved from view just as a woman, knife in hand, raced forward. She stabbed at where Madyan had stood, then she was gone as well.

Claire blinked as the oasis came back into view. Had it been real, her friend would be dead. Aghna tread through the water as quickly as she could to reach them. Madyan was slower to realize where she was, and stared at Claire in confusion.

"Are you all right?" Aghna demanded.

Claire took great gulps of air. "I've always been blind to my own future."

"Don't panic," Aghna reassured her. "It must have been Madyan who took you there, when you touched her. I had wondered if you would be able to share your sight."

"Could you see what was happening?" Claire asked.

Aghna shook her head. "If it weren't for Madyan blanking out like she did, I would have never even have noticed. Radha warned me about this possibility. She told me that your sight is yet evolving."

"Then she knew all along that we were leaving the temple."

"I think so, too," Aghna agreed. "Why else would she teach me how to help you? If you would like, I'll share all that I learned when we finish bathing."

Claire nodded, and they washed away the dust and sand from their arduous trek, afterwards shaking out their garments and then washing them as well. When their wet things were spread out in the sun, they changed into dry clothing, and Claire and Aghna sat down on their blankets in the shade of a grouping of palm trees. Madyan stood apart, having again claimed the first watch. She stared up into the palm fronds before nimbly climbing the branchless tree. The broad green fans rustled, and a small lump sailed down at them.

"Dates!" Aghna exclaimed, as the ripe fruit peppered their blankets. "These are a rare delicacy, for they only grow in the Fyrost. Try one."

After eating a few, Claire dove in without preamble. "So, what else did Radha tell you? And why didn't she just tell me?"

"You were recovering, and I was still serving you…She wanted me to report back to her, and her alone." Aghna bit into another date. "You mentioned that you've never seen your own fate—are you at least reliving past moments in your life?"

"Yes."

"Radha said that the strongest visions are those of events that have already transpired. These visions will give you a kind of expanded hindsight. They most often take the form of dreams, but not always."

"That last vision hasn't happened yet," Madyan interjected, climbing back down the palm tree. "I've never been to that place with you. What can it mean, Claire?"

"You saw what I saw, yes? There was a barley field, still green and fresh."

"It was not the desert, that much is sure," Madyan replied. "This being the end of our time in the Fyrost, I think it is very close to where we will be in the next day or so. The terrain was familiar—low, crop-covered fields. The sky was bluer and not as washed out as it is here. Those fields and distant hills are part of Ranulf's territory. And the barley was still young, so whatever we saw, it will happen sooner rather than later."

Aghna looked from Madyan to Claire. "What else?"

Claire closed her eyes. There was something; she could just see it.

When she'd had the vision, she'd first thought that only Madyan had been there. Her eyes opened. "You were there, too, Aghna. And there was another woman."

"Others as well," Madyan announced. "Hiding in the trees behind you, Claire. I couldn't tell how many. Did you recognize the woman behind me?"

"No, but she meant us ill. She had a knife. Madyan, I think she was Umbren." Silence followed that pronouncement. Finally, Madyan stretched and yawned.

"Let me take first watch for once, Madyan," Claire insisted.

• • •

Claire shielded her eyes as she gazed across the desert floor, in her mind replacing the sand with the fields of barley that had appeared in her vision. In the distance, she saw farm buildings, for grain storage perhaps. But between two of the buildings, there was movement. A horse and a man? Aghna was to her right, holding their mounts. The air had been so still—no rustle of wind through the crop. Only the smell of the barley grass, and of her own sweat mingling with the dust of the desert. Tomorrow, then, or the day after, for she still carried the odor of the Fyrost.

Claire focused more intently, but the vision had faded too quickly. However, in the remembering, Claire heard a soft hissing cut through the air. She recognized it for what is was. She'd heard its whisper when Trian had been killed. Quarrels in flight. Forever in her mind the cowardly weapon of an assassin.

Later, Claire roused Aghna to take over the watch. She didn't make conversation with her friend as they sat quietly together supping on their meal. Aghna was as caught up in her own thoughts as Claire. When they finished, Aghna covered Madyan's portion of food, and then stood, motioning for Claire to follow.

They walked to the pool's edge, sitting and dangling their feet in the water. "It seems we are both troubled by the coming days." Aghna spoke so softly that Claire had to lean closer to hear her words.

"Why don't you tell me about your worries?"

Aghna sighed. "Ranulf, of course."

"Ah."

"Ah, indeed," her friend echoed, giving a wry smile. "When we were promised to each other, it was for the realm. Ranulf spent time at my father's palace; later, I traveled to Sophiana. We…we liked one another. We had similar hopes and dreams for Nifolhad. I came to know him, his values; he came to know me, and mine. When we last parted, more than friendship had grown between us." She blushed.

"There were no professions of love," Aghna went on, "but there were words of fidelity, of support. Love was an unexpected gift, one that we both hoped to nurture." She smiled the softest of smiles; Claire had felt the same with Trian. How beautiful and tender and aching those first stirrings had been; that soft smile had once graced her own lips.

"Ranulf was in Sophiana when my father was murdered. Diarmait commanded that our betrothal be broken. He cast suspicion on Ranulf, though I never believed it possible. He forbade me any contact with him."

"And you never heard from him after your father's death?"

"Just once. He tried to smuggle a letter to me, promising to protect me from my uncle and to honor our betrothal. But the messengers, an entire family, were captured and executed. The letter was burned before my eyes, unread."

"Then how did you—"

"What my uncle did not realize was that one member of that family survived. They'd been caught on the southern edge of the Fyrost. One of the daughters had been sent from camp to forage; she returned in time to witness the massacre.

"You see, Claire," Aghna continued, "Ranulf wrote the letter, yes, but he also read its contents to the messengers before they left Sophiana. The surviving daughter waited almost a month before making her way to the palace and to me. She disguised herself as a maid and hid in my chamber." Aghna smiled. "She had so much anger in her, but felt honor bound to complete her family's mission. She told me that she would go back to the desert and bury her people. I made her swear to return to the palace if she could. Months passed, and I feared she had perished.

"Then one day, I was sitting in my garden under a tree when a date from the Fyrost dropped into my lap. No one else noticed. A few minutes later, when my keepers turned their attention elsewhere, I stole a glance up into the branches and leaves."

"Madyan," Claire guessed.

"Yes, Madyan. Later that night, when I was alone in my chamber, she found her way to me. I sent her to the Fenrhi, where her skills would place her with the Umbren. I gave her pihaberries to protect herself. She has been my spy in the Fenrhi temple, telling me about Rhiannon and the Mother and the Blood Caste. And when I fled the palace, she was waiting to guide me to safety. I asked her how she'd heard of my plight."

"Those who watch," Claire deduced, and Aghna nodded.

"I owe Madyan for my life many times over, Claire. She is my family now, as I am hers. We count you as a sister as well. Together, we will make it to Sophiana, and then I will ensure that you are sent safely home to Aurelia. So you can trust me, Claire, and tell me everything that happened in the vision."

Claire gazed about her, then up at a sky whose color was the faded blue of an indigo cloth washed one too many times. On three sides, the dunes rose up above them, and the air shimmered with heat. Their little oasis was but a drop in the vastness of the desert, and she and her friends were mere specks.

"They are going to kill you, and Madyan. Soon after we leave this desert: tomorrow or the next day. I heard quarrels, or maybe arrows, in flight." She shook her head. "It was so fast, Aghna. And I didn't realize that I could have such visions. I wasn't paying attention like I should have. Trian would not have been impressed." It was the first time she had spoken Trian's name aloud to anyone, and she touched the pouch on her chest.

"It's all right, Claire. You say his name often when you sleep. Who is he?"

"He was my Ranulf. More, even."

"What happened to him?" Aghna asked gently.

"He was killed by the men who brought me here."

"Claire, we three are bonded, having all witnessed our loved ones die before us. And now we can use your vision to forearm ourselves. Go, get some sleep if you are able. This evening we will discuss what we can do to better our odds."

"Thank you, Aghna. My visions have never helped me in the past. But you've given me hope that perhaps we can change things for the better." She walked back to where Madyan slumbered, and when she finally fell asleep, she dreamt of other men, two of them. Both tall and dark, with lean, muscular frames, one with green eyes and the other with blue. When Madyan woke her, the sun was sinking below the horizon, and Claire had a nagging suspicion that she was acquainted with at least one of the men.

CHAPTER FORTY-ONE

Borders

Mounted, they followed the great dune cradling their oasis. The ever-migrating peaks eventually leveled in their endless rise before stretching out into a high, flat, windswept expanse. The three riders continued on into the night, turning northwest to where the desert plain gradually rose toward the horizon. The sand thinned, and the soft, sifting earth was slowly transplanted by hard, packed dirt. Rocks and boulders appeared next, but still no vegetation. On and on their horses climbed, carrying them up a rise so great that it stretched from east to west as far as they could see. The stars, once teeming and so distinct in the pure desert sky, now shimmered in the purple black above them, winking on and off behind a tracing of high, thin clouds. Hours later, they crested the great rise and were finally quit of the Fyrost.

Low in the sky and late in rising, the crescent moon was stingy with her light. Claire removed the veil that covered her face: the odor of choking dust had been replaced with the scents of fertile earth and vegetation and animal life. She could hear the soft fluttering of wings below, and she glanced to the east. At this elevation, dawn's light would be less greedy with its entrance than it had in the great basin that was the desert.

Madyan pointed to a break in the rolling hills far ahead to the northwest. "That is our route to Sophiana, through that valley. But first we need to be off this rise, lest the sun announce our arrival. The path below is sure, and the horses will know better than we how to pick out the route." She clucked to her mare and started off.

While they descended, Claire continued thinking about Trian. His stories of home, his exploits, his family. In her heart, she knew that it was time for her to say goodbye to him and stand on her own. No more dreams. And as her recollections of him wound down, Claire was surprised that she did not feel the sense of betrayal she'd imagined she'd feel upon letting him go. Nor did she believe she was abandoning him. He would always be in her heart as long as she recalled all that had made him hers. It was simply time to move on.

The gloom had brightened, and there was game stirring in the sparse vegetation that grew on the slope. Ahead, Madyan brought her bow to ready, nocked an arrow, drew, and released. She dismounted to retrieve her kill and returned with a plump coney.

She pointed to a clutch of trees and shrubs some distance away. "We'll rest there. Now that we are out of the desert, we can travel in the daylight, at least in this area. The terrain is yet too rough for farming this side of the Névan River. Once we reach the trees, we can rest for a few hours, then continue until nightfall. There are places enough to squirrel away the night. Tomorrow, we can make an early start and cross the river before the sun rises."

"Tomorrow, then," Claire predicted, remembering how the shadows had fallen in her vision. "And if tomorrow, it'll be afternoon before we are intercepted. Is there any way to avoid the farmlands altogether?"

"Unfortunately, no," her friend replied, mounting up again. "They stretch from the Brabryn Mountains to the Virin Sea, following the meanderings of the Névan. Prince Ranulf's land is comprised of good, fertile, river-basin soil. And if we want to steer clear of the forts and watchtowers, we'll have to stick to the less guarded fields."

"So, my vision might have been for naught."

"Not true," Aghna argued. "We know that we are expected. We can take measures to protect ourselves. Even from quarrels."

• • •

In the brightening day, they found shelter and risked a small fire to roast the coney. Claire had found sage and wild onions growing along their path, and had seasoned the skinned rabbit before spitting it and roasting it over the campfire.

They had made better time than expected, their mounts having more endurance than anticipated. Madyan suggested that they rest for five hours, allowing a two-hour nap for each of them, and overlapping parts of their watch. She passed around some dates as a treat, but saved a large portion of them, stating that the rest were to be presented to Ranulf as a betrothal gift from Aghna. They all laughed until Aghna realized that the fruit was all that she would be able to give him. At least until she claimed the throne.

"I want to remain veiled when we arrive in Sophiana," she blurted, surprising Claire and Madyan. "At least until I can determine where Ranulf's heart lies. It's been years since I supposedly died. He may have found someone else. His beliefs may have changed. He may no longer want the same things for Nifolhad as I." No amount of reasoning would budge her, and the women fell silent as they took turns resting.

• • •

They resumed their trek, stopping at nightfall in a place that Madyan's family had used before: an easily defendable cave near the river. One that had an escape tunnel, should it be necessary, though they would have to leave the horses behind. She spoke of her nomadic ancestry, and how her family had traveled with the seasons, traversing the Fyrost and the lands both north and south of it for generations. It came as no shock when Aghna noted that Madyan's father had been Lord of the Fyrost, a descendant of the man who'd angered the sky goddess herself. Some of Madyan's people yet roamed the wasteland, though they were scattered and without a leader to guide them. That evening, while Claire took her turn keeping watch, she wondered what Madyan would do once Aghna was settled.

It was well before dawn when she roused her friends. They ate the leftover coney, making a broth to which Madyan added a cut up tuber that she swore was edible, though it lacked any discernible flavor. It thickened the broth at least, and, as they finished their meal, Madyan sketched their route in the dirt of the cave floor.

They would ride hard for the river, hoping to cross it before the sun rose. There was a place called the Shallows—an expanse a mile long where the river made a constantly shifting false delta before converging back into a swiftly flowing watercourse. It was the only place where they could swim the horses across that was not near a settlement. Once quit of the Shallows, they would press through the farmlands, again riding hard. Their goal was to reach the wooded hills to the north before the sun dipped in the west. In the hills, they would be able to shake any enemy who chanced upon their trail. But first, they needed to traverse the barley field.

Claire was about to mount Jia'ma, when Aghna stopped her. "To you both, my family," she espoused.

"To our escape and to the safety of Sophiana," Claire added.

"And to your safe return to Aurelia," Madyan finished.

Then Aghna handed Claire and Madyan two pihaberries each, wanting to be as prepared and alert as possible. They mounted, riding three abreast, and made for the Shallows.

● ● ●

It was midmorning, and they had encountered only the occasional field worker. Still, they gave each laborer a wide berth. They passed several wooded areas and farm buildings, but had had no difficulties. Hours had passed when a prickling sensation crawled up the back of Claire's neck as she spied three small structures ahead. On both sides of the broad field through which they rode were trees. Danger in the woods on either side and behind, and danger ahead. The only way forward was through, and then on to the rolling hills. Madyan cast a wary glance Claire's way. They took flanking positions on either side of Aghna, kicking their mares to a gallop and racing forward.

They had passed by the trees when Claire recalled that they hadn't been ahorse in her vision. They were riding too recklessly. She shouted to rein in, but it was too late. Madyan's horse stumbled, pitching her through the air. Claire and Aghna pulled back on their reins, and Claire watched her vision unfold, unable to stop it.

As Claire raced on foot to where Madyan had landed, Aghna rode off to catch her horse, and Jia'ma followed on her own. Luckily the ground was soft, and Madyan readily gained her feet. "Before you learn to climb," Madyan extolled, her chest still heaving, "you must learn to fall."

Her friend stood before her, and no one loomed behind. For a moment, Claire was relieved, and then the barley, still in the windless day, shivered and shifted a few paces behind her friend. Madyan's eyes narrowed on the trees behind Claire.

"They're coming," her friend whispered.

"From both directions."

Madyan dodged to the side, racing to reach Aghna. Claire dove toward the moving barley. Arrows, not quarrels as she'd thought, whistled through the sky. She left Aghna to Madyan's protection and focused on the rising figure before her. The woman had just lifted from her crouch when Claire tackled her back to the ground. But her attacker was Umbren trained, and she twisted from underneath Claire's weight.

They both made it to their feet, and the woman hefted her knife, dancing forward, taking jabs at Claire. Claire melted away from each thrust, gracefully leaving only open air as a target.

Enough, she thought. "You don't have to do this. I don't want to hurt you."

"You can't hurt me," the woman boasted. "They're protecting me even now."

"Who?" Claire demanded. She had not forgotten the figure behind the farm building in her wrestle with the woman, but there was still no sign of him.

"My Kena sisters, you fool," the woman spat. "You can't stop us. You may have fooled Ni'Mala, but never me. I won't desist until you are mine."

Claire heard the hissing of more arrows, but they missed their marks. Madyan and Aghna were using the horses as a shield. Madyan's horse had gone down. Then Claire saw him, a man racing from behind one of the buildings. He held a drawn sword in one hand and carried a stave in the other. All of this she absorbed in an instant, just as Trian had trained her, and determined which was the greater threat. The Umbren woman.

Claire stepped within range of the knife. As it came forward, she slid to the side and brought her hands down on the woman's arm. She reached into the mind of her attacker and found the person she knew would be there: Rhiannon. With all her will, she pushed at the image. Behind her in the woods, someone screamed. The Umbren woman crumpled to the ground. "I'm sorry," Claire murmured. "I'm sorry that I hurt you."

The woman managed to grasp Claire's tunic. "It wasn't you who hurt me," she whimpered. "I would never have done the things they made me do. You freed me." Blood trickled from her nose. "She wants you alive. My blade was poisoned to weaken you. But the arrows will kill. Hurry, you can still save your friends." Then, her eyes glazed over.

Claire stood, noting that the *swish* of arrows in flight had stopped. Behind her, from the trees, twenty armed men emerged and raced toward Madyan and Aghna. Aghna was on the ground. Claire scooped up the Umbren woman's knife and charged at the men streaming from the trees. The man with the sword angled his course to intercept her. He was ten paces away when she finally stole a glance at him. His face was covered, but he had blue eyes. He winked at her, tossed her the staff, and raced past. Claire caught the pole and followed him into the coming mêlée. Madyan started to join them, but Claire yelled for her to stay with Milla—she had just barely remembered to not say the princess's true name.

Her swordsman had already felled four men when Claire arrived with dagger and quarterstaff. She managed to take down another with a deadly throw of the Umbren blade. But then three men attacked her unexpected hero at the same time. Claire tried to help him but was cut off. Four soldiers were attempting to surround her; they held thin spears in their hands. Poison-tipped, no doubt. She focused on those advancing toward her. Rhiannon had to be nearby. Claire imagined pushing a great wall toward the trees, imbuing it with the strength of a gale-force wind. Her thoughts met with a resistance that was almost physical, though it developed fissures as she maintained her pressure against it. And then, the resistance broke. The advancing men hesitated, and her unexpected fighting partner, having rid himself of his assailants, strode to where Claire was struggling to keep her own at bay.

More men arrived, but the rallying attackers faltered when a thunderous noise reverberated through the air, causing the ground to tremble. They began to retreat, racing to the cover of the trees. Claire turned toward the source of the noise, and stared at the cavalcade galloping toward them. She and her swordsman raced to Madyan and Aghna. Madyan went on the defensive, bow at the ready. Aghna stood, pulled an arrow from her chest, and held it out.

"He's a friend," Claire shouted over the noise of the approaching riders. The four of them stood shoulder to shoulder, facing the oncoming force. Two columns of armored horsemen split and encircled Claire's group. Her friends turned outward, facing the thirty or so riders.

"Ranulf's men," Aghna provided.

Her swordsman chuckled. "Out of the pan...as Doreen is wont to say. Don't you agree, Claire? It is you, isn't it?"

"Good afternoon, Warin. How did you recognize me?"

"You are a perfect mix of Anna and Trian when you fight." Warin laughed outright this time. "If I had known there would be this much action when around you, I would have left off chasing your sister years ago."

Aghna gasped, but Claire laughed, a good, hearty one from her belly. Warin would always be Warin. And after everything that she'd endured, it was a relief to discover that some things in life were permanent. "Tell yourself that again if we survive these new dance partners." She stepped forward to greet the riders. Warin kept apace, and Madyan and Aghna followed. "These are my friends," Claire added, "Milla—" Madyan gave a short nod, giving Claire permission to tell Warin her name "—and Madyan. Ladies, this is Warin of Pheldhain, and of the Aurelian Royal Guard."

Warin bowed to them, then noticed the arrow in Aghna's hand. "Nice weapon. Are you hurt?"

Aghna knocked on her chest where the arrow had lodged, letting Warin hear the dull thump of wood under her clothing. "Forewarned is forearmed. Our only casualty is Madyan's horse."

One of Ranulf's men rode forward, coming to a halt five paces away. He gazed at them, taking stock, especially of Warin, before settling on Claire.

"That's Ranulf's captain," Aghna said quietly.

The captain made a show of sheathing his sword even though Warin kept his steel at hand and Claire her stave at the ready. Claire studied him. She had mistaken him for a much younger man; he had seen at least fifty years. "Princess Claire of Chevring," he greeted. "Prince Ranulf has been expecting you. I am his captain and advisor, Lord Etain." He addressed Warin, ignoring Madyan and the still-disguised Aghna. "I assume that you have a horse nearby. I'll send a man to—"

Warin gave a shrill whistle, and a young man came from behind the shed, leading two mounts. Etain's men allowed him through their circle.

Claire removed her veil and, espying her, the boy dropped the reins and raced forward.

"Pieter!" Claire greeted, then hugged him when he reached her.

Etain sat his horse, peering down his nose at the reunion. He cleared his throat. "By my count, princess, you are one mount short. Would you care to ride double with me?"

Beside her, Warin bristled. He had yet to sheath his sword. The captain's hand drifted toward the hilt of his own. "As lovely as that sounds, the *princess*—" Warin started.

"—will ride her own horse," Claire finished. "And it is Lady Claire, not Princess."

Lord Etain only smiled. "I've been sent to welcome you to Sophiana and to escort you to Prince Ranulf." He turned toward the trees, then signaled to the men on his right. They wheeled away on their horses, charging into the woods. "I see that we have arrived just in time."

"Oh, I don't know," Warin said with a casual flip of his hand toward the nine dead or wounded men on the ground. "I believe we were doing just fine." Rather than take offense, Lord Etain chuckled. Claire relaxed her hold on her quarterstaff, and Warin sheathed his blade.

"Lord Etain," Claire began, "we accept your gracious offer to escort us to Prince Ranulf. If we could have but a few moments to collect our things."

"As you command, Princess. I'll send some of my men ahead to settle a camp at the base of the hills." He returned to his men. Claire watched as he pointed to where their skirmish had been, and four soldiers went to tend to the wounded.

She and her friends walked back to their horses. Madyan began stripping her belongings from her mount.

"Madyan and I can ride together," Aghna proposed. "We'll have to keep a slow pace as my mare is already overtaxed."

"Our horses aren't," Warin pointed out. "You and Madyan can take one of our geldings, and Pieter can ride your mare."

"No offer to let me ride with you?" Aghna observed, echoing Lord Etain. "I appreciate the chivalry."

"It's not chivalry, m'lady," Warin countered, giving her his most disarming smile. "I only fear that your wood would abrade me from behind."

Claire, used to Warin's wit, waited for Aghna's reaction. Her friend narrowed her eyes at him. "Who says I would ride behind?" She turned and winked at Claire before going to assist Madyan.

"I could grow to like your friends," Warin said to Claire, rounding on her and setting his hands on her shoulders. "My oath, but it's good to finally find you." And then he pulled her into a hug so fierce it would shame a bear.

Claire hugged him back, tears filling her eyes. "It's good to see you, too, Warin. I've missed you." She stepped back, removed her head covering, forgetting for a moment her markings and shorn head. But Warin only smiled at her, reaching out to rub the short, spiky hair. It was the perfect thing to do, and she turned and took his arm.

Pieter, bringing the horses, gaped at her, then shook his head. "Wait until Lady Anna gets a good look at you! You've turned into a warrior just like she did!"

"What trouble did you get yourself into, Claire?" Warin asked, taking in the colored designs on her skin. "And why on earth did you not wait for me to join you?"

"I'll explain later," Claire promised. "But first, tell me, is Anna safe? Lark and Celeste, too?"

"Hale and healthy when we left them months ago," Warin replied, but his tone was uncertain. "Claire, don't you want to know what—"

The sound of a sword being pulled from its sheath cut him off, and he turned with Claire toward the noise. Lord Etain's men had completed questioning the survivors. Instead of binding them to take to Sophiana, the soldiers were executing them. Warin started to protest, but Claire stayed him. "It's nothing less than they deserve," she said, imbedding each word with ice as she thought of the hidden archers.

"Claire?" Warin asked uncertainly.

She mounted her horse, then gazed down at him. He seemed a little lost, so she bent down and placed her hand on his cheek. "It's all right, Warin. I'm still the same person I was before. And a little more as well." She sat up, clicked her tongue at Jia'ma, then cantered to where Lord Etain waited.

CHAPTER FORTY-TWO

Warin hadn't known what to expect upon finding Claire. For months, he'd prayed that she was safe and whole, but prepared himself for the very worst. And now? Well, he wanted nothing more than to drag her off her horse and give her a good shake. There was something off about this neat little triangle of women. Madyan was obviously Milla's protector. Claire seemed concerned for her, too. But why worry so much about a woman who behaved like a servant? Because she wasn't really a servant, he deduced. He drew alongside Claire's mount; Lord Etain flanked her other side. Warin leaned in and quietly asked the one question to which he most needed an answer: "Do you trust me, Claire?"

There was a flicker of impatience in her gaze. She nodded to Lord Etain and unapologetically excused herself to confer privately with Warin, then pulled her horse away from the main group. Warin shrugged at Ranulf's captain and turned his horse to join her. Madyan and Milla trailed behind him, though they kept their distance so as to be out of hearing. Pieter brought up the rear.

"Lord Etain isn't very pleased with you right now," Warin noted when he pulled up next to Claire. She smiled, leaned over to view the cavalcade some fifty paces to her left. Etain's back was fire-poker straight as he conferred with a man who had just returned from the raid into the woods. When Claire leaned back, relaxing her seat, Warin rephrased his earlier query. "I suspect some adventure is afoot. Do you trust me enough to include me?"

"Warin, except for myself, you and Pieter are the only people here that I *do* trust. Madyan and Milla are my friends, but they still have their own agendas. Your goal and my goal are one in the same: to return as soon as possible to Aurelia. For that, I need them and Prince Ranulf."

She gave an exasperated sigh. "I can't believe you had to ask, Warin! Perhaps I should ask you the same."

Her ire would not cow him. "You don't need to ask, Claire. You know that. And you can be angry with me, but you can't blame me for wondering. The Claire I remember would never have dismissed the value of a man's life as you just did. Do you imagine that Trian would suffer Etain's decision? I don't know what happened here to make you—"

"Not here, Warin," she cut back. "You are right, you have no idea what I have been through. Those men back there, they are of the same ilk as the men who cut Trian down with their quarrels." He tried to speak, but she held up her hand. "Please, ask me anything you want, but I beg you, do not speak to me of Trian."

She continued glaring at him. "Fine. For now, tell me how you were abducted." So he listened as she recounted the past year.

"They changed how my mind worked," Claire confided, when she spoke of her time at the temple. "I *wanted* to remain with the Fenrhi. I *believed* that Anna would have preferred me to stay. Even now, I can't count the weeks that passed where I lost myself. It was Madyan who helped me to remember. And when I did, I pretended I hadn't so that I could learn everything they could teach me." She turned back to him. "Warin, it is frightening what they can do. And it terrifies me that I can do the same."

"What do you mean? You can control people?"

She nodded.

"Try to make me do something, Claire. I bet you can't."

"It's not some player's trick to enjoy at a fair, Warin." She looked appalled. But he insisted, assuring her that she would be unable to manipulate him. He watched as she focused on him, frowning as each second slipped by. "How many pihaberries did you eat?"

"How did you know?"

"There are only two ways that can help a person resist the manipulation of the Kena: if blood from the royal line runs in their veins, or if they consume pihaberries. How came you by them?"

He grimaced and hinted at the long tradition of smuggling that the Pheldhainians enjoyed. "We learned long ago that the fruit helped a person keep a level head when negotiating prices on goods. Especially in Nifolhad." He glanced at her. "What else can you do, Claire?"

212

So she began to explain what the colors on her skin represented, and how each Fenrhi was marked for a particular caste. "But I was different; I was marked for everything."

He regarded her for a long moment. There was much she was holding back, but at least it wasn't because she didn't trust him. "Your hair has seen better days."

She punched his arm, hard.

"Ow!" he complained, but she was laughing. After a few minutes, he asked her how she came to flee the temple. She told him about the women who wanted her to usurp Ni'Mala. When she spoke of the Blood Caste, she did so sparingly. "And Milla? What is her role in all of this? She is more than a companion helping you to Sophiana, isn't she?"

"Oh, Warin, it is refreshing to speak so frankly with another. You can't believe the games these Nifolhadajans play. It is enough to drive a person insane."

"But you're still not going to tell me who she is."

"I gave my word; you'll just have to be patient. We need her, though. She swore to get me, and now you and Pieter too, home to Aurelia."

"Speaking of Aurelia," he started, then reached behind his back, "I've been carrying this around with me since I rode from Stolweg. It's from your sister." He hesitated before handing her the dagger.

But she took it from him, and he watched as her thumb rubbed the spot where the leather had been rent. She didn't unsheathe the blade, and she didn't ask how its sleeve had been damaged. "Thank you." She strapped the dagger to her waist.

"You're now the most well-armed princess I know," he jested.

"Actually," Claire confessed, "I have Pieter's blade in my boot. Remind me to return it to him."

Warin stared ahead. He needed to get Claire to Cathmar with all possible haste, but she had closed off any talk of Trian. "By the way, why did Etain call you a princess?" he said to avoid the subject.

"It seems that Anna and I are direct descendants of the ruling house of Nifolhad. Many generations ago, there was a rift in the royal family. The sister remained here to rule. The brother emigrated to Aurelia. He was our great-great-great-I'm-not-sure-how-many-times-great-grandfather."

"I always wondered how your line began. You do understand what this means, don't you? It's the reason Diarmait wanted Anna. Bowen's claim to the throne was enhanced by Roger's marriage to your sister. When Roger died, Diarmait must have wanted to marry Anna to Bowen, or maybe even marry her himself. They got you instead." He smiled. "I'll be damned. All over this realm, you were referred to as Diarmait's lost cargo. But just as many times, people referred to you as his claim."

"If that's the case, we need to leave Nifolhad as soon as possible. For, surely, he is aware that I'm on my way to Sophiana."

"It may not be that easy," Warin warned. "Ranulf probably knows who you are as well. And he needs a princess to replace the one he lost."

CHAPTER FORTY-THREE

Prince Ranulf

Claire had much on her mind when, nearly a week later, their procession rode through the city of Sophiana. People of all ages came outside to cheer them. So stark was the contrast to the city of Naca'an that Claire experienced a moment of confusion. She glanced at Aghna, who was staring in surprise at the waving people. There were men and women standing together along the streets. Gone were the women's head coverings and veils. The children, too, looked happy as they ran alongside Claire, throwing blossoms to her as if she were already engaged to Ranulf and installed as Queen of Nifolhad.

Warin chuckled upon hearing Claire's groan. They had discussed Warin's revelation with Madyan and Milla, and found that the two women had already come to the same conclusion. They determined that Ranulf had to have had a spy in the Fenrhi temple. The four friends—for Warin had been able to seduce even Madyan to laughter with his wit—had tried to determine who had been responsible for passing Claire's whereabouts to Warin. In the end, they assumed it had been one of Madyan's watchers, though they knew not who or how.

Riding side by side, they followed Lord Etain as the street climbed to the castle. Warin rode his gelding, Aghna her mare, and Madyan rode a horse that had belonged to one of Diarmait's ill-fated soldiers. On either side of their group, tall buildings ranged the street, and cheering faces appeared in the windows. Soon, the riders were moving through a storm of flower petals. Claire cast a nervous glance at Aghna. But she remained serene, playing the role of Milla. "This should be for you," Claire murmured so no one else could hear.

Her friend leaned closer. "It's fine, Claire. Truly. Do not worry so much."

The grade grew steeper, the buildings fell away, and the street wound back and forth up the great rise upon which the castle sat. Lord Etain signaled for the cavalcade to turn away toward the barracks. He remained, along with five other men, as escort. "If you would like to refresh yourself before being presented to Prince Ranulf—" he pointed to a pavilion "—you can do so now, Princess."

Claire rolled her eyes. There was only one response to such a ridiculous notion. She tapped her heels to Jia'ma's flanks and set her mare into a brisk canter. Madyan and Aghna did the same. Claire heard Warin shout to Etain over the clopping of hooves, "You really expected her to wash up for Ranulf? You do realize that you are dealing with a Chevring woman, don't you?"

● ● ●

"That's Ranulf in the center," Aghna said with a tilt of her head toward the tall man who stood in front of a group of people, and then checked that her veil was in proper order as they slowed.

Warin, having caught up, sounded a long whistle. "Damn, but that man is handsome. Remind me to never chase the maidens when he's around."

Claire couldn't argue. He was the most beautiful man she'd ever laid eyes upon. His skin was flawless, olive toned with a shadow of stubble on his cheeks. His eyes blazed green. His hair was the same length as Warin's, wavy too, but a dark mahogany. He had at first appeared youthful, but as Claire dismounted and stepped up to him, she detected the thin lines etched around his mouth and a slight graying of hair at his temples, no doubt brought on by the responsibility of protecting his people against Diarmait. For all that he presumed, she couldn't help but admire and respect him. And when a slip of a woman raced up, his smile was genuine as he took a step sideways to let her stand beside him.

She was a perfect female version of Ranulf, and Claire sensed in her an innocence that had yet to be marred by Diarmait's machinations. A clatter arose behind Claire as Etain and his men arrived.

Lord Etain dismounted and walked quickly to stand before Ranulf, going to a knee. "My Prince, I present Prin—"

"—Lady Claire of Chevring," Warin cut in over him, saving Claire the trouble. The young woman next to Ranulf stared at Warin with wide eyes.

Etain made a gesture to correct Warin, but Ranulf waved him off. "Thank you, Etain," he said finally, his deep voice slipping from his lips like honey. "And you are?" he asked.

"He is Warin of Pheldhain, representative of King Godwin and a Guard of the Realm," Claire answered. "He is my companion and friend, as is Pieter, and these are my Fenrhi friends Madyan and Milla." Madyan had decided that it would be easier for all if she gave her name to Ranulf; the chance was negligible that he would recall her face from when he had met with her family.

"Late of the Fenrhi, I have heard," Ranulf corrected.

"Your information is especially current, m'lord," Aghna responded.

Ranulf glanced her way for the first time, and his welcoming mien faltered, just for a moment, before slipping back into place. "I will take that as a compliment, Milla." He gestured to her veil. "You are free to remove your coverings; we do not abide by such restrictions here in Sophiana."

Perhaps, Claire thought, this was why he had frowned. It was the perfect opportunity to find out if Ranulf's ideals had remained in line with Aghna's. "Milla is shy," Claire apologized. "I'm sure that, given time, she will reveal herself. But at the moment, we are all tired and dusty from our journey."

"Of course," Ranulf acknowledged. "I've rooms prepared for you in the high tower." He turned to the woman next to him. She was bouncing on the balls of her feet, near to bursting with excitement. "But first—or she'll never forgive me—let me present my sister, Princess Anwyl."

Anwyl raced forward and took Claire's arm, all but dragging her through the gates and into the courtyard. Claire had wanted to walk with Ranulf, allowing Aghna to listen in. She would have to wait for another opportunity, and tried to focus on what Anwyl was saying.

"...prepared rooms. I supervised, of course; my brother wouldn't appreciate what women need. You have the best view in the castle. There's a bathing room. And the sitting room is large enough for a party. I picked flowers for you from the gardens. We'll have food and wine brought up for you. And I sent some gowns up so you'll have fresh clothing." She glanced at Warin and frowned. "We weren't expecting you to be traveling with an Aurelian Guard, nor with the boy. I suppose we can find them suitable—"

"We've searched this land of yours for months to find Lady Claire," Warin interjected, "and we're not losing sight of her again. We'll sleep in the sitting room, on the floor if need be."

"Oh!" Anwyl exclaimed. "Well, only if it's all right with Rani."

"Rani?" Claire asked with an innocent smile. Prince Ranulf grimaced.

"Rani, short for Ranulf," Anwyl answered, oblivious to her brother's discomfort. Claire heard Warin chuckle, earning himself a glare from Anwyl. "Only special people are allowed to call him Rani," she told Warin. "Let's see…me, of course, and our mother did when she was alive, and perhaps Princess Aghna before—"

There was a long and awkward silence as Anwyl realized her gaffe. Claire seized the opportunity and patted Anwyl's arm. "I have heard that she was a lovely princess," she prompted, knowing that Anwyl would take it from there.

"Oh yes," Anwyl concurred. "She was lovely. I only met her once, years ago. She was shorter than you, and me too, I guess. But she had the most beautiful eyes. And she was incredibly smart. As smart as my brother. And kind, too." She turned and frowned at Milla for a moment, then leaned in to talk in a quieter voice, one that everyone could hear anyway. "Princess Aghna would not have let your friend cover herself. She would have wanted the rest of Nifolhad to be as it is in Sophiana."

Claire smiled when Anwyl launched into a lecture about her brother and all that he had built and protected. "You mentioned something about food," Claire patiently interrupted. "Do you mind having it sent to our quarters now?" She hoped to have some discourse with Ranulf and needed Anwyl occupied elsewhere. "We've been eating nothing but snakes for weeks."

"Oh! Right away," she answered and, to Claire's surprise, embraced her before running off.

"Ranulf," Claire begged, taking his arm, "would you show us the rest of the way?"

He placed his hand over hers, then led them forward. "Snakes?"

"Yes. And roots, too," she added. "I'll tell you all about it later. For now, I'm quite curious about you." She made sure Aghna was close enough to hear. "In Aurelia, you are viewed as someone who wants to make great changes in Nifolhad. Is this true?"

"It is. I would lead this realm out of this repressive age. Nifolhad has fallen far from King Cedric's vision. Diarmait has created a nightmare realm afflicted by suspicion and hatred."

"What would you change?"

"I would start with outlawing the abuses against women," he began. "I would give the men in this realm a chance to do what is right. Not all male Nifolhadajans—and I'm not just referring to those in Sophiana— view women as chattel. In Naca'an and even Kantahla, they pretend when in public, but are loving husbands and fathers in the privacy of their homes. They are afraid of recriminations from Diarmait's soldiers, so they play along." He stopped and turned toward Claire. "I am not ignorant of what is happening in the Fenrhi temple either. This Blood Caste, while it has been around for generations, is an evil I'd remove." He began walking again. "King Cedric understood that he could only do so much, which is why he wanted the marriage between his daughter and me. He believed we could accomplish things that he could only imagine. So when I make decisions about how I rule Sophiana and my people, I consider not what King Cedric would have done, but what Princess Aghna would have envisioned."

"Why?" Claire asked. "Why not just remain here, in Sophiana, and leave the rest of Nifolhad to Diarmait?"

The prince came to an abrupt halt; the green of his eyes intensified as he gazed down at her. "Because I can't leave it alone. I have to continue their work. If I relax my guard, Diarmait will destroy everything I've built here. We repel his soldiers from our borders every week. They force the Fenrhi to control the innocent. Last week, one of our mills was destroyed. The family butchered. And when I'm gone one day, who will protect my sister? Who will protect the rest of the people here? There's only one solution: I must overthrow Diarmait. To do that, I must be declared king and rule with a strong queen by my side." He studied Claire for a moment, as if weighing her worth.

"We've arrived," he informed them, and pushed at the entrance to reveal an expansive sitting room. "That door leads to the sleeping quarters, and the other to the bathing area. Hot water has already been brought up. Shall we meet in three hours and converse after you are refreshed from your journey? I'll send Anwyl to show you the way." He swept away before Claire could respond, leaving her and her friends standing in the corridor.

Warin turned to Pieter. "I need you to find out where they've put our horses." Pieter nodded, then bounded away. "If you ladies will please wait a moment while I check our accommodations." Once satisfied, he returned and ushered them in and closed the door. "Well, that was an interesting conversation. Why the interrogation?"

Claire turned to Aghna for permission, and her friend shook her head. "I'm sorry, Warin. It is not my place to say." She turned. "This ends today, Milla. You witnessed our reception by the people. I'll not pretend to be a willing bride. I respect what Ranulf is trying to accomplish enough to extend him that much courtesy."

"She's right, Milla," Madyan added softly. "No more of this. Now that you are free of the Fenrhi and safe from Diarmait, you shouldn't waste any more time. Quit avoiding your fate and live your life." For Madyan, it was quite a speech.

Aghna snarled, removed her head covering, and headed for the bathing area, slamming the door behind her.

"I'll wait in the hall for Pieter," Warin announced. "And Claire," he added a bit harshly, "perhaps you should heed Madyan's words as well." He turned on his heel, and another door was slammed.

Claire shook her head at Madyan. "What does your advice have to do with me?" Her friend shrugged her shoulders and went to look out the window. Warin was angry with Claire, and she had no idea why.

The arrival of food and drink stemmed any more thoughts on Warin's annoyance. Claire was famished. She made plates for Warin and Pieter first and had Madyan take them out to the corridor. Then she helped herself to the food. As she finished, Aghna reappeared, wearing a thick robe. She looked contrite.

"There are three basins," she explained after Madyan returned. "One for each of us. And plenty of hot water waiting near the hearth. I'm sorry I didn't offer to let you go first."

"It's fine, Aghna," Claire assured her. "I know this must be hard for you, watching Ranulf play court to me. But I have to say, the way he spoke about you, I feel that he will never love another so well. Tonight then? We can end this?"

"Yes," Aghna relented.

Madyan exhaled in relief.

Between the three of them, they managed to save enough hot water for Warin and Pieter. Claire hid in the sleeping chamber when Warin came in, and so managed to avoid him. She didn't even know why she was doing it, and that, more than anything, bothered her. She shook off her vexation and looked about the chamber. When she found the gowns that Anwyl had selected for her, she called to Aghna and Madyan. Madyan eyed the sumptuous and richly beaded garments with something akin to fear. They were, quite literally, made for a queen. In the end, Claire chose to dress in the clothes the Fenrhi had first given her. The sash, with the honeycomb pattern to indicate nobility, was enough. Madyan eschewed her traditional Umbren garb for flowing pants and tunic the color of eggplant. Anwyl's selections had been extraordinarily precise in fit and utility.

When Aghna gazed upon the silken fabric and decorative stitching with wistfulness, Claire insisted that she wear one of the queenly gowns. Madyan agreed, so Aghna bowed to the pressure of her friends. She selected the simplest raiment, then threw a floor-length cloak about her to hide the gown. Madyan helped her to put a veil in place and cover her hair with the cloak's hood.

There was a knock on the bedchamber's door, and it opened a fraction. "Ready?" Pieter called though the crack, and they filed from the room. Warin exited ahead of them, not allowing Claire to catch his eye. In the corridor, Anwyl met them and led them through the castle to its great hall. She rattled on about the various aspects of her home, but Claire wasn't paying attention. Instead, she memorized the route and possible means of escape.

The hall resembled the audience room at the Fenrhi temple. It was a broad, circular space—not hexagon-shaped, Claire noted, relieved—with a domed ceiling. An upper gallery girded the entire room. There was a raised dais directly across from the main entrance. It was there that Ranulf waited, along with Lord Etain, and another woman who Claire recognized immediately: Radha.

"We didn't know," Aghna swore.

Anwyl stepped up onto the dais, taking her place next to her brother. There was nothing for it but to approach. Ranulf seemed sweetly nervous. But Radha bore an expression of one who had found a rare jewel. Claire stopped before Ranulf, and when Warin stood next to her, she was grateful for his support. She wanted to reveal Aghna before Ranulf could speak, and save him the embarrassment of her having to decline his proposal.

"Let's not waste time," Radha jumped in, preempting Claire's wish. "Princess Claire, by now, you can't be ignorant of how a marriage could save Nifolhad. Can we assume that, even though you are stubborn and did not wear one of the gowns made for you, you will agree to wed Prince Ranulf and rule with him as his queen?"

Claire opened her mouth to speak, but again was cut off.

"Lady Claire cannot marry Prince Ranulf," Warin intoned. "She is already pledged to another, and will marry and reside at Chevring with him as lady and lord."

Ranulf jumped from his chair and off the dais. Three strides and he stood before Warin. "You are her betrothed!" he accused. "Is this true, Claire?" Claire was at a loss for words; she never imagined that Warin would help her this way.

"No," Warin said calmly, "much to my chagrin. No, Prince Ranulf, Lady Claire is promised to her love, Trian of Cathmara, King's Guard and future Lord of Chevring."

"I see," Ranulf stated flatly. But Claire wasn't so furious with Warin that she didn't miss the relief in Ranulf's expression. Warin took a step back and let the chaos ensue.

On the dais, Anwyl began to giggle. "Oh, thank heavens!" she cried, and Radha shushed her, causing Anwyl to laugh all the more.

Then Radha turned her wrath on Claire. "You'll have to break it," she ordered, stomping toward her. "You must realize how important this is. You could mean the difference between ending and saving thousands of lives! Ending the Blood Caste! The Fenrhi need a leader. And Nifolhad needs a queen of the bloodline. You are our last hope!"

"That is where you are wrong, Radha," Claire averred. "There is another option. One far better and greater than I could ever hope to be." Claire stepped back to allow Aghna to approach. Anwyl had finally stopped laughing, too curious to witness what would happen next. Madyan helped remove Aghna's cloak, drawing back the hood first, then exposing the beautiful gown underneath.

"Ooh!" Anwyl cried. "That one's my favorite!"

"Quiet, Anwyl!" Radha and Ranulf shouted simultaneously.

Aghna reached up and removed her veil, her hand trembling as she did it. When Ranulf saw her face, he choked out a sob.

"Milla," Radha demanded, "what is the meaning of this? Why are you dressed in one of Princess Claire's gowns?"

But Aghna ignored her. She was staring up into Ranulf's face with glistening eyes. Ranulf's hand shook as he reached up to cup her cheek. Anwyl had come to stand by Claire. She nudged Claire's ribs with her elbow. "Watch this," she conspired, and turned toward a sputtering Radha. "That's not Milla, cousin. That's Princess Aghna!"

Radha was utterly lost, and Princess Anwyl finally took pity on her. "Come on, Radha," she coaxed, suddenly the wisest person in the hall. "They need some time alone. That goes for all of you. I'm sure we'll get the full story later."

Then the woman Claire had thought so flighty, sensibly herded them all from the hall. Claire would have smiled at her, but was too infuriated by Warin. She turned to glare at him, but his dark glower put hers to shame.

CHAPTER FORTY-FOUR

Cargo

What was he about? Claire fumed. She had told him—no, begged him—not to speak of Trian. Did he have any idea what it would do to her to *use* Trian as an excuse against marrying Ranulf? She never would have believed Warin capable of such heartlessness. She charged out of the palace and into the gardens, hoping the flowers and trees would calm her ire. Before she reached them, she heard someone storming up behind her. Warin grabbed her shoulder and spun her around to face him.

"What on earth is *wrong* with you?" he demanded, giving her a shake.

She broke free of him. "*Me?*" she yelled back. "What is wrong with *you?* Do you not know what it does to me to be reminded of him? Of what we'll never have? Do you think me so hard that I have no feelings? That my heart doesn't break into a thousand pieces at the mere mention of his name?" She swiped her cheeks with the back of her hand, hating the tears that ran from her eyes. "It's bad enough that I dream of him, then wake aching for his voice. You, you…" He had put his hands on her shoulders again, this time gently, and steered her to a nearby bench. She collapsed on it, doubling over to sob into her hands.

"Claire," he called to her, and she ignored him. "Claire, look at me. I'm trying to understand. Are you afraid that Trian won't accept you now? Sure, your hairstyle is something to be desired, and you are marked, yes, but he loves you, Claire."

Claire's ears felt like the very air was pressing in on them. What did Warin mean? Was it possible that he did not know that Trian was dead? Didn't they find him in the valley? They couldn't think that he was alive, perhaps abducted as she had been.

"Warin, Trian was killed. He was killed in the valley," she choked.

"They must have hidden his body or you would have found him." No wonder he kept talking about Trian as if he yet lived. "I-I'm sorry. I thought you knew. He's gone, Warin, and I never even told him how I felt about him." She buried her face in her hands again and wept.

Over her sobs, she heard Warin pleading with her. "Claire. Claire! Look at me, Claire. Listen. Trian isn't dead. We found him. He's alive. Claire, please."

"Alive?" she breathed, her voice barely intelligible.

"Yes, Claire." He gathered her into his arms. "Trian is alive. We found him, and Grainne healed him."

"But I saw him dead, Warin. There was an arrow in his heart."

"It missed his heart, Claire. If you don't believe me, look at your dagger. The sheath is damaged. Look at the blade."

She pulled the knife free, noticing the gash in the metal.

"Your blade deflected the tip, Claire."

"But he wasn't moving," she persisted, even though her heart had begun to hope.

"A rock, Claire. He hit his head on a rock. Oh, my poor friend, all this time you thought him dead?" She hiccupped and stared at him with tear-filled eyes, and he pulled her into his arms again. "I would have set you straight right away."

"He's alive," Claire murmured.

"He's alive," Warin vowed to her.

. . .

Hours later, Claire sat in the council room with Warin, Aghna, Ranulf, Madyan, Etain, and Radha, even Pieter.

Ranulf cleared his throat. He stood beside a seated Aghna, and she reached up and took his hand. "Two miracles have occurred today," he started, "for two loved ones have come back to our hearts." He bent and kissed Aghna's fingers. "For you, Claire, we will do everything in our power to ensure that you reach the shores of Aurelia as soon as possible. But we were hoping, Aghna and I, that you would delay just a few days. You see, we have decided to marry immediately, before news of her vitality reaches Diarmait. And we would be honored if all of you were here to bear witness."

"Diarmait will attack when he hears," Radha warned. "Perhaps you should—"

"We expect him to," Ranulf revealed.

"Then Princess Claire should remain here," Radha asserted. "We will need her to control the Fenrhi." Claire started to rise in protest, but Aghna caught her eye and gave a slight shake of her head.

"Cousin," Ranulf chastised, disallowing any further debate, "do you imagine that we could secure the support of King Godwin if we held Princess Claire hostage? And if that is not argument enough, I am not so callous of heart that I would separate her from her love. She who returned to me Princess Aghna. Claire has done enough for Nifolhad, and with only her markings as recompense. A poor payment that you yourself had a hand in giving her."

"She'll be safer in Aurelia," Aghna added. "And no longer a pawn for Diarmait. We can have a ship ready for you in less than a month."

"That may be too late," Lord Etain warned. He pulled out a chart of the northern waters. "I guarantee you that news of Princess Aghna is already on its way to Diarmait. Our ships won't be fast enough to clear the Crags before he sends his ships to block the passage." He pointed to a broad section of the Kaldemer Sea where uninhabited rock islands stabbed up from the depths. "Passage from Sophiana to the Crags—" on the map, he drew an arc from one location to the next "—will take at least a month. The currents, while working against a west-east route, will favor Diarmait."

"So even if they departed today," Radha stated hopefully, crushing Claire's in the process, "they would be intercepted. I'm sorry, Claire, but it isn't safe for you to return to Aurelia either."

"Still, we'll not stand in your way if you wish to try," Ranulf vowed. "The choice is yours, Claire. I only wish my ships were faster."

Warin was poring over the chart, tracing his finger over the Crags. "I could do it; I have a ship faster than anything Diarmait might float. We could sail north of the Crags, passing well beyond his reach. He would never suspect it."

Claire's mouth dropped. "You have a ship? Couldn't you have said so earlier, Warin?"

"I assumed you knew. I *am* a son of Pheldhain, after all."

She studied the area of the chart that remained blank. "You're sure you can sail those waters?"

"My captain has done so already."

"I don't like it," Lord Etain cautioned. "This time of year, there are too many storms for any captain to risk it."

"Ah," Warin boasted with a sly smile, "but my captain is a shipmaster from the Southron Isles, home to the worst tempests in all the seas. And I'm counting on the storms of the Kaldemer to carry us swiftly to Aurelia." He pointed to the chart. "We'll catch one, say, here, and then ride it all the way to Ragallach. Diarmait won't even realize that we've passed him by."

"Especially if we let it slip that you are headed to the Crags. And perhaps, Rani, you could send a decoy ship," Radha suggested. She smiled at Claire. "I wish you would stay to help us. But I concede that Ranulf is right; we do not need a war on two fronts." She turned back to address Ranulf. "Remember what we discussed as a gift to Godwin for Princess Claire? Now it can stand as a gift of goodwill from you and Aghna instead. If Aurelia is ever able to help us against Diarmait, they must be prepared."

"A smuggler's vessel?" Ranulf guessed, looking at Warin.

"We prefer to call them trading ships."

"Call them whatever you want," Ranulf jibed, sounding quite pleased. "We'll need every inch of cargo space."

"What for?" Claire asked. "And what did Radha mean about preparing King Godwin? Oh! Of course, pihaberries."

"Not just the fruit," Ranulf amended, "but the trees as well. Forty in all. Pijala trees exist only near the cliffs in the northwest of Nifolhad, a day's ride from Sophiana. King Godwin will have to find a sustainable clime, for pijala trees will grow, but are temperamental when propagating. My sister has been arranging the transplants for months. They are ready for transport even as we speak. Where is your ship now, Warin?"

"In your port. Where else would she be?"

"Perfect," Anwyl added. "The trees have been specially crated. We planned on shipping them when you accepted Rani's hand, Claire, but all the better that you go with them."

Ranulf put an arm around his sister's shoulder and turned to Claire and Warin. "There's something else we'd like you to take with you. Or rather, someone else." He stared down at his sister. "Aghna and I discussed this at length, Anwyl. You see, we want you delivered to the safety of Aurelia."

She shook her head in protest. Before she could speak, Aghna took her hands. "We need you to be our ambassador."

"And besides," Ranulf added, "there is no one else we can trust with the trees."

"Fine," she capitulated. "But I'm taking my horse."

"I'm taking Jia'ma," Claire threw in. "So I can't see why you shouldn't take your horse."

Warin rolled his eyes. "Heaven help us," he swore under his breath.

Madyan stole a glance at Aghna, then stepped forward. "I'm coming, too. We've already discussed it, Claire. I'll help you get to *Cathma'ra*," she stated, pronouncing the territory in her Nifolhadian accent. Then she turned to Warin, and his expression grew even more beleaguered. "I'm bringing at least three horses."

"Of course you are," he lamented. "Any other cargo I need worry about?"

• • •

Bowen watched until the ship vanished into the horizon. He'd left Phelan in Brynmara to wait for Lady Claire alone, though the man still believed he was looking for Lady Aubrianne. His father's right-hand man would be waiting a long time, for the Chevring woman had somehow managed the impossible: she'd crossed the Fyrost and survived. Most likely, she was already aship and on her way back to Aurelia.

Bowen had tried explaining this to Phelan, but the man had refused to countenance it. He'd demanded to know from whom Bowen had received his intelligence. Bowen, of course, had lied, stating that it was a rumor that one of his men had overheard. He'd had to. It was the only way for him to hie to Kantahla, bringing his spy with him. And now that very informant was on Bowen's fleetest ship, heading for Aurelia.

The mere idea that Lady Claire had outwitted him made him want to rip apart Phelan with his bare hands. Thwarted yet again by a Chevring woman. Well, his spy had all but guaranteed that Lady Claire would be brought back to Nifolhad, or die trying to resist.

CHAPTER FORTY-FIVE

Ties

The Kaldemer Sea

For twelve days, they sailed the uncharted northern region of the Kaldemer Sea. Claire watched as the sailors fearlessly climbed the rigging, swinging from spar to boom to mast in graceful sweeps through the frigid air. Each day began and ended with rain, but thus far, no storm had come to push them east. And worse, the farther northeast their route, the colder it became. The rain had given way to sleet and ice fogs, coating sails and sailors alike. When the sun finally broke the cycle of freezing rain, the men were quick to toil, slapping the hardened canvases with what looked like giant rug beaters. Great sheets of ice crashed to the decks below only to be swept overboard. Behind the beaters, the darners waited, ready to repair any tears. Claire stood at the bow of the ship. Somewhere, out of view to the south, was the northernmost point of the Crags where Diarmait's ships were sure to be scouring that part of the sea.

Before they'd set sail, Radha had come to see her. Alone. Though she was one of the Artists, she was also Kena and had some talent as a seer. She had overheard Rhiannon voicing her foreboding about Claire returning to Aurelia and, knowing Claire could see nothing of her own future, reached out. It was true that her homecoming would herald a bloodletting, but Aurelia required Claire's return. As for Trian, Radha had predicted that he loved Claire but that he would fall in love with someone else as well. And to fully heal, he would require both women.

Claire shivered and pulled her woolen cloak tighter just as Warin came to join her.

"This is taking too long," he grumbled. "We've been both lucky and unlucky: not a single ship sighted, but neither is there a storm to ride."

"You sound disappointed," Claire teased. "Whether because of the lack of an engagement or the crashing around of the horses in a storm, I'm not sure."

He turned around, leaning his elbows back against the railing. "Don't remind me of our cargo. Between keeping the hold warm with braziers for the trees, tending to the horses you insisted on bringing, and avoiding the princess, I'm about to abandon ship."

Claire smiled; Anwyl liked to tag along behind Warin only, it seemed, because she knew it annoyed him. "Where is she now?" He pointed skyward, and Claire's eyes flew to the rigging. It took her a moment to locate the anomalous figure among the sailors. Anwyl was sitting on the topsail's yard chipping away at ice. "What on earth? Who let her up there?"

"Captain Grieg. She pestered him all morning. She's relentless, Claire. I was so thankful that she wasn't after me about the trees or the horses that I'm afraid I threw the captain to the wolves. I shunted the decision to him."

"I heard the crew cheering earlier," Claire recalled. "No wonder. Come to think of it, Madyan did mention that Ranulf hired Umbren women to train Anwyl in their art." Warin suddenly looked terrified and Claire followed his gaze. The person in question was hanging upside down, attempting to reach a particularly iced block.

"How am I to keep my word to Ranulf if she is so set on killing herself?" As he spoke the words, Anwyl grabbed a line on the shroud and flipped over so that she was upright again. One of the sailors shouted to her to make sure the breach was free of ice on the block she'd been clearing. "I should never have agreed to take her to King Godwin," Warin snarled. "She's a child who needs a nursemaid, not an escort. Gah, she makes me feel ancient with her acrobatics."

Claire elbowed him. "Warin, Anwyl is my age. You're not exactly old either. The same age as Trian, yes?" He rubbed his chin and ran his hand roughly through his hair. "I'll talk to her for you," Claire promised.

"Thank you," he replied. "Now, speaking of Trian, have you given any thought to what you will do when we make Aurelia?"

It was all that she'd been thinking of since she discovered that her love still lived. Warin had detailed the strange betrothal customs of the Cathmarans. She would be sure to face competition once she arrived and made her intentions clear to Trian's family. The hopeful brides would face three challenges, each created to ensure that her bloodline would only enhance that of the Cathmaran she wished to wed. The challenges centered around family: protect, provide, enrich.

Protection would showcase any defense or fighting skills the bride might have. Provision ensured that the bride could bring food and resources to her family. But Claire was at a loss when it came to enrichment. Art, music, weaving, carving, and so on. All ways that Warin cited as acceptable methods of proving that the bride would be able to enrich her family. Claire could heal, yes, but healing fell under protection. And she wasn't sure where using her specials talents would fall, but she couldn't imagine that her sight could enrich the life of anyone, at least not in the sense that the Cathmarans expected.

She turned and rested her hip against the rail so that she could face Warin. "I've a couple ideas, but I'm stuck on enrichment."

"Er, Claire, there's something I haven't told you."

"I knew it! Every time we talk about Cathmar and Trian, you get this look in your eyes. It can't be *that* bad. What is it? My competition? Is there someone else? What?"

"No, no. Nothing like that. I just couldn't figure out how to say it."

"Just tell her," chimed in a voice from overhead. Anwyl hung from a line in the rigging; she dropped down gracefully before Claire and Warin.

Ignoring her, Warin continued, "Grainne wasn't sure if it was the crack to his skull or the poison, but, well…Trian doesn't remember you."

Anwyl punched him. "I didn't mean like that, you oaf," she maligned. "Men! I'm sure he doesn't mean that Trian forgot you. Right, Warin?"

"Warin?" Claire asked.

He ran his fingers through his hair, a gesture Claire had noticed him doing more and more since taking responsibility for Anwyl. "It's not good, Claire. When I left him, he could remember that you were Anna's sister, but he thought you murdered along with your parents. Grainne

231

believed he would recall more as his head healed. At first, he didn't even know that Lark and Anna had Celeste, let alone that they were married. It was as if the past few years had been excised from his memory.

"He was still at Stolweg when I visited him," Warin continued. "He was making progress, recalling things about Anna and Lark. But of you, he had nothing but a scrap of linen to hold on to. Your handkerchief." Warin turned around to stare across the water. "He knew that he had lost something. I gave him my word that I would bring it—you—back."

"So, you don't know how much of his memory has returned?"

"No, I've no idea. As for the challenges, I can prepare you as much as possible while we are at sea. But once we make Ragallach, I must take the princess with all haste to King Godwin."

Claire studied Warin for a moment. "I have to be in Cathmar the day of the equinox or I forfeit any right to press my suit," she clarified. "And the challenges begin the next day?"

"Starting with *protection*," Warin reminded. "There will most likely be an archery tournament, or knife throwing. But I wouldn't count on it, Claire. Trian has made a name for himself in Cathmara, and the women there will insist on fighting for him—quarterstaffs is a distinct possibility. You should also expect interest from farther afield, especially from the smallholds. He is a favorite at court and well respected by King Godwin. Still, you'll do well in this challenge, the second, too."

"It's the third that I'm worried about. I don't draw or paint. I can embroider and make gowns, but that won't impress in Cathmara."

"Why don't you help him get his memory back?" Anwyl threw in. "Surely that would enrich him." Then she sauntered off to instruct one of the crewman in the rigging.

Warin shook his head, then studied the sails. "Without the storms, we won't make Ragallach until mid-August. From there, it will take you at least five weeks to reach Cathmar fortress. You have almost two months to prepare."

Claire glanced skyward and cringed when she saw Anwyl swing on a line out over the sea and back over the quarterdeck railing to drop gracefully next to the captain.

"I don't even want to know, do I?" Claire shook her head.

"Warin," Claire asked after a moment, "do you…"

"What is it, Claire? You're not worried about what the others will think of you, are you?"

"Truthfully? Yes. Before, when I was with Trian, well, he loved my hair. And now I have barely any. And the markings, I can't spend my entire life hiding them. What if Trian can't see past them? The things he used to say to me, I understand now; he raised me up onto a pedestal. I'm not the same girl that I was before."

"No, you're not. But these marks," he said, rubbing his thumb over the back of one of her hands, "they don't define you. And they are not what changed you. Believing that Trian was gone changed you. Surviving everything that Nifolhad threw your way changed you. And coming to love your new friends helped to make you who you are now." He turned her so that she was facing the Kaldemer. "Look out at the water, Claire. Describe it for me."

She studied the sea before her, and spoke of the sunlight reflecting off the surface and the rhythm of the waves.

"Perfectly accurate, Claire. A year ago, if I'd been asked to describe you, I would've done the same as you just did. I would have related the superficial characteristics that made you who you were: a young woman of keen wit, beautiful, and oft times aloof. And I would have said that your stoicism was warranted considering how much you had lost when Chevring was destroyed." Claire turned away, but he cupped her chin to refocus her on his words. "Then, I watched when you first became aware of Trian. I was envious of you both; it was so beautiful to witness. Still, you covered your hurt by never slowing down, doing everything in your power to control the world around you."

He took a moment to marshal his thoughts. "I could explain who you were in two or three phrases: a tragic past, a secret used to both lure men in and keep them at bay, and so kind that even the Queen's ladies could find no fault. Then Trian came along and gave you his unique way of viewing the world. Though it strengthened you, it did not make you who you are. You were simply mimicking him and not being your own person."

Claire could feel the tears welling in her eyes. "Warin, I—"

"You, my dear friend, are finally your own person. You have such depth within you now. Have you noticed how you no longer order everyone about as you once did?" He smiled when she shook her head. "It's because you no longer need to control every detail to be secure.

You've grown, Claire. The truth is, as much as Trian may have changed by losing his memories of you, you have changed even more. You are not the same person he fell in love with.

"Maybe you're not afraid of what he'll see in you, or that he won't recognize you," Warin surmised. "Maybe you're worried that you won't need him."

"I still love him, Warin."

"I know you do, sweetheart." He put his arm around her shoulder. "And if he looks at you and does not remember you, or the impossible happens, and he finds that he does not love who you've become, then I will dog you every minute of every day until you agree to marry me instead."

His words drew soft laughter from her, as she knew he'd intended. "But I know Trian, Claire," Warin promised, "and he will love you even more."

A commotion astern caught their attention. "I'd better get her belowdecks. But before I go, I want you to look out at the sea again, and this time, try to imagine what's below the surface."

• • •

Cathmar

Adara had been watching her brother more closely, astonished by his sudden curiosity in what she had termed "the bride pool." Physically, he was stronger than before. He had been in constant training over the summer. He'd been sleeping better, she had been informed, for the maid who tidied his chamber no longer complained each morning of strewn blankets and mangled cushions. And when it came to his impending betrothal, even his mother commented that he was showing a little more interest. What was more, he had taken measures to make himself appear more attractive—not that he needed help in that arena. His beard was still full, but he kept it shorter. The biggest change seemed to be his wardrobe. He'd stopped wearing layers of clothing to appear bulkier. It wasn't his fault that he didn't take after his father and the other barrel-chested men of Cathmar. He was a leaner version and much in line with many of the King's Guard.

Adara eagerly anticipated Larkin's arrival to Cathmar, for he'd sworn to stand by Trian during the betrothal rites. It was too bad that his wife Lady Anna could not join him, though her excuse was a joyful one: she was with child again. Even though Larkin would arrive within the week, Adara wasn't content to sit on her laurels and watch her brother make a horrible mistake. With luck, he would be in his chamber and she could tease out what he was up to. She stood outside his door and rapped her knuckles against it.

"Come," Trian called from within, and she pushed open his door to step inside.

"Trian, could I—" She stopped speaking at the sight she beheld. Trian, turning this way and that, stood in front of a tall looking glass, a tailor waiting on a stool beside him. Was he preening?

"These will do just fine," Trian told the tailor. "Ah, Adara, tell me what you think."

Adara could feel her mouth opening and closing and could do nothing to stop herself. Heaven help the women of Cathmara if her handsome brother suddenly developed vanity. He shook his head at her, then stepped behind a partition to change out of the pinned-together leather breeches. Adara took the time to assemble her wits and sat down wearily on Trian's bed. She put her hands on her protruding belly, counting off the days in her head until her babe's expected birth. The tailor collected the contents of his etui, caught the breeches that Trian tossed to him, and said he would have everything ready in a few days. Trian stepped from behind the partition just as the man was leaving. Adara could hold back no more. "Trian, I can't take this a moment longer."

"You're not due for a few more weeks," he teased, sitting next to her, "so you don't have much of a choice in the matter."

"Not me!" Adara exclaimed. "You! What has gotten into you, little brother? And don't you dare look at me like I'm crazy. You've changed, and you can't deny it. Even Mother says that you are finally cooperating." He regarded her as if he had no idea what she meant, but then saw her glowering expression; *Don't infuriate a pregnant woman,* she was silently screaming at him.

"I feel better, Adara," he began after a moment's reflection. "I recall everything that I've forgotten. That is, everything except that I'm supposed to be in love with a woman named Claire. A woman who, I had finally come to accept, died at Chevring."

"Go on," Adara encouraged.

"I simply must face facts. There has been no word from Warin. Nor has she returned on her own. I have to presume that she won't make it back in time. And if she does, what then? Will I even recognize her?" He paused. "I figured, if I am to be wed, I might as well attract the best bride that I can, yes?"

"This doesn't sound like you. The brother I know and love wouldn't yield so easily."

"That's just it, Adara. I'm not the same as I was. My values haven't changed, nor my beliefs; it's the way I view things." He took her hand, and Adara could see how much work it was for him to speak of his feelings. "A marriage is inevitable. I'm not without hope that this *dream* woman of mine will return and that everything will come back to me. It's not that at all. It's only that I…" He fumbled for the right words.

"Need a backup plan," Adara finished, and he smiled guiltily. "What can I do to help?"

"Tell me about the circling sharks."

So Adara began, first with Marach and Argel, then with Deighlei, Snáw and Scúr. She finished with the few their mother and aunt had discussed who were coming from outside Cathmara: two from the smallholds and a young woman from Pheldhain. "There's even been an inquiry from one of Queen Juliana's ladies: a widow, childless by her first marriage, well dowered and still young enough to give you a family. I don't know her name." Her brother grimaced, imagining who it might be. "Trian, you mentioned your dream woman. Have you had any dreams of late?"

He shook his head. "Not in the last month, which is why I must be prepared for any eventuality. She might be…" He hesitated.

Adara's heart broke for her brother. "Just because you haven't dreamed of her lately doesn't mean Claire is dead." He turned away. "Look at me. She *will* return to you in time. And you *will* remember her. And your dreams, they are just that: dreams."

"How can you be so sure?"

"Because, Trian, the mere mention of her once filled you with joy. And I will see you that happy again. Besides, you're my favorite brother, so it has to be!"

CHAPTER FORTY-SIX

The Princess

"There's a light ahead," Madyan said, leaning forward in her saddle and peering out into the gloom. "An inn, perhaps. It would be nice to have a roof over our heads and shelter for the horses for once. The mares are lagging."

She was right. The horses, as splendid as they were, were growing tired. Ever since their path split from the others, they'd pushed forward harder than they had on their race across the desert, sometimes at breakneck speeds. They'd had no choice. The storm which they had anticipated on the Kaldemer Sea had never formed. They landed in Ragallach a week later than they'd hoped, and now had to call upon the endurance of Jia'ma and her brethren to make up the difference. Every few hours Claire and Madyan would dismount to rest, transfer their saddles to their reserve mounts, and start off again.

August was at its end; she and Madyan had traveled from Ragallach into Cathmara, the state of Marach, to be precise. They had spent many nights under the open sky, both in fair weather and foul. Crossing the border into Marach would hopefully see them with a hot meal in their stomachs, beds into which to climb, and fresh straw and grain for the horses. Claire patted the hidden pocket in her cape, thanking Warin for his forethought.

He'd realized that they would attract attention. Claire's hair had grown some, and though it hung just below her ears, it was shorter than even most men's. Her markings still peeked from her hairline and were visible on her neck, arms and hands. Throw in their exotic tunics, breeches, and the tall boots that they wore, and they could be immediately singled out as Nifolhadajans. Their horses, too, were a different breed than those in Aurelia, and the saddles were delicate with extensive tooling and design work. Warin had pointed this out when they'd made port in Ragallach. One night at the fortress, currently held by Ailwen and Tomas of the King's Guard, and Claire experienced firsthand the hostile stares from the servants living and working there. She couldn't blame them after what they had once endured under Lord Roger's yoke.

So Warin had written out a warrant, assuring Claire and Madyan of King Godwin's protection and right of free passage throughout the realm. She'd used it four times already. Some of it could have been avoided, Claire knew, simply by adopting the traditional garb of Aurelia. But Radha's words had impressed upon her that she must not present herself as Lady Claire of Chevring, but rather as a stranger. What better disguise than a Nifolhadajan named Milla? Perhaps it was as simple as adopting the persona to prevent bloodshed. And with Trian not remembering her, Claire had warmed to the idea even more. Traveling thus gave her an excuse to wear her hooded cloak and cover her lower face when in public.

Claire stared out over the crashing waves of the Kaldemer Sea. The road they had followed from Ragallach had skirted the shore for miles, at times taking them inland and at others, like now, paralleling a sandy beach. The light winking in the night was several miles away as the crow flew. But the road curved away from the shore, adding distance to their journey. It was low tide, and the sand gleamed under the moonlight. "We could save some time by riding on the beach," Claire proposed. "I can just make out where the road meets the shore again, close to those buildings."

"It is what our horses were bred to do," Madyan pointed out.

Claire kicked the flanks of Jia'ma, pulling the lead on her other horse. Madyan did the same. Jia'ma, sensing the day's journey was nearly finished, broke into a gallop, and the other horses willingly kept pace. The sand was dry and hard from the ebbed waters, and their passage over it was fleet. They slowed as they approached the buildings. One, thankfully, was an inn. A short climb over the dunes gave them access to the road, and they trotted into an empty, well-lit courtyard.

The stable boy poked his head from the stable door, saw the four horses, and jogged out to greet them. And although his eyes widened at the strange trappings on the horses, he welcomed Claire and Madyan. "There's eel stew tonight." He spoke very slowly as if worried that they would not be able to understand him. When he made squiggling gestures with his arm to further illustrate the stew, Claire stifled the urge to giggle. "You'll like the sauce more'n the eel, I s'pose. Hearty brown bread for sopping the gravy. And fresh fish is always available."

Claire lowered her veil. "Thank you," she replied, adopting the accent of a Nifolhadajan. Madyan snorted, and moved off to gather their saddlebags. "Are there any rooms available?"

The stable boy blinked, then blushed when Claire smiled at him. "Yes, m'lady. This time of year we're usually full, but with everyone traveling to Castle Cathmar for the betrothal tournament, we've more than one spare room." He bowed to her again as Madyan returned with their belongings. "If there is nothing else that you need, m'lady, I'll tend to your horses now."

Claire gave as regal a smile as she could muster and thanked him. Madyan started walking toward the inn. "This way, Princess," she directed.

Towing two mares, the stable boy jogged into the structure, calling to his mate, "Here now, take extra care with that mare. She's a princess's horse."

"Princess?" Claire murmured under her breath.

"Rumor is faster than any horse, even your little Jia'ma. Let the competition know there is a Nifolhadian princess in the running, and a few might be scared away."

• • •

They started early the next day. The autumnal equinox was nearly four weeks away; an entire week earlier than when they would arrive if they kept to their current route. But Madyan had found a way to make up time.

Marach's shipbuilders were unsurpassed in Aurelia, and the bay which cut into the heart of the state boasted hundreds of inlets and coves. To cross Marach west to east, travelers had to ride due south for a week, then cut back diagonally into Cathmar. Madyan had lamented this fact to the innkeeper, saying it would be a shame if the princess was disqualified due to geography, when he had proposed the perfect solution.

"Ferries?" Claire asked again, disbelieving of their good fortune. Madyan nodded. "And how much time will this save us?"

"More than a week. We will arrive a couple of days before the equinox. Enough time, I'd warrant, to state your intent."

As they rode east to where they could catch a ship, Claire's anticipation grew. More and more, she was glad that she was traveling in the guise of Princess Milla. The anonymity would serve her well. She did not want Trian to accept her out of some sense of duty. If he did remember her, he would have to come to terms with who she had become in Nifolhad. And if he didn't, he would need to choose her above all others based on the three challenges. But what if Trian chose another—what then? Could she marry some other man on King Godwin's list?

CHAPTER FORTY-SEVEN

Room and Board

Three Days Before the Autumnal Equinox

"Is it true?" Adara demanded of her aunt. "A princess from Nifolhad wishes to marry Trian?" She hadn't believed it when Trian had told her of his latest suitor. But her aunt's expression, one that had been growing more and more strained as the equinox approached, verified the rumor.

When Trian had demanded the right of tournament, and thereby extending what would have been a week's worth of guests to a month's, their mother had raged for hours. But no matter how much Lady Baranne threatened, begged, and bribed, Trian remained steadfast in his decision. It was Lady Cafellia who had put the argument to rest, stating simply that it was Trian's life and therefore his choice. Lady Baranne didn't speak to her sister for days.

"Where has Mother put her?" Adara asked, for that was what had preoccupied her aunt and mother for the last week. As each would-be bride arrived, they brought family, servants, horses, and more. The castle's rooms were already full to bursting. And while the Cathmaran families had their own provisions for a month-long stay near Castle Cathmar, the families who'd traveled from outside Cathmara came with the expectation that all food and lodging would be provided by and within the castle. Only the young lady from Pheldhain had been aware that she and her escorts would need to bring their own pavilion.

These outsiders, as Adara and Trian had dubbed them, were at first indignant that they would be refused quarters within the castle. Even if space was available, it simply went against protocol and tradition. Not a single suitor would be given the advantage of sleeping under the same roof as her brother.

Her Aunt Cafellia growled in answer to Adara's original question. "We've finally finished tending to the needs of those from the smallholds and a certain Lady Caroline from court. Spoiled, they are, though the girl from Pheldhain looks promising. And now this! A princess, no less. We had only one tent remaining in storage, and it is so old and tattered, I'm not sure it will stand."

"Surely a princess would have retainers, tents, appointments," Adara assured her aunt. Her aunt was shaking her head to indicate the opposite.

"She's traveling with one escort, another woman, according to our sources. Well, she'll have to sleep on a dusty rug spread over a pile of straw. There is not a spare pallet to be found for twenty leagues. And because the best grounds have already been claimed, the pavilion had to be erected near the edge of the forest, where the nights are sure to be cold and damp. Hardly comfortable, even with the dented brazier we located to drive away this unusually cool autumn air. Your mother—" A great stir in the courtyard interrupted her. Horses, and the running feet of servants. Lady Cafellia wearily patted Adara's hand. "Let's go meet this princess."

On the way to the great hall, they met Adara's mother, Lady Baranne. She seemed even more harried than her sister. The men had certainly picked an excellent time to form a hunting party. While it was good to have them away from the castle the three days before the equinox, it meant that the thousands of details fell to Lady Baranne. Adara had been of little help, taking care of her new babe morning, noon, and night.

She had just taken her seat next to her aunt to await the princess when two exotically garbed women entered the hall. The first woman was attractive, deeply tanned with dark hair that was somehow bleached out by the sun at the same time. She wore a knee-length tunic woven of many dark colors, melding together into a shade of charcoal. A dark sash was wrapped several times about her slim waist, and long leggings tapered down her legs into knee-high leather boots that looked so soft that they appeared to be made of butter. Adara strained to hear their steps, but neither woman made a sound as they approached.

The other woman's tunic was of the same cut and style, but was the color of dust and trimmed with moss green and pale blue. Her leggings were charcoal-hued and likewise disappeared into her tall boots. About her waist was a beautiful sash the color of amber, and Adara could just make out that it was richly embroidered with multihued silken threads and seeded with pearls. She was tall and bore herself proudly. Aside from clothing, height, and build, Adara couldn't describe her, for across her lower face, the woman had affixed a veil. And the cloak that she wore thrown back from her shoulders allowed her to keep her head covered with a deep hood that shadowed her features.

Then Adara took note that both women were armed. Bow and quiver hung from shoulder and hip; daggers hung from their waists. They each held a staff in their hands. So natural were their weapons to their comportment that she had deemed them extensions of the women themselves. Adara glanced at her aunt; she was caressing the back of her hand with her fingers in a signal to her sister.

The woman garbed in dark colors bowed, not curtsied, before Lady Baranne. "M'lady of Cathma'ra," she declared, as the princess stepped forward, "permit me to present Princess Milla, cousin to Queen Aghna and King Ranulf of Nifolhad."

Lady Baranne motioned for the princess to approach. "Queen Aghna? We heard of the death of Princess Aghna. How comes she to be alive and crowned?"

"My cousin was in hiding these past years," the princess replied. "She was only recently able to escape the net of assassins commanded by the usurper Diarmait. She was reunited with her betrothed, Prince Ranulf, and newly wed to him." Her voice was steady and sure when she spoke—no mean feat, Adara credited her, considering how intimidating Lady Baranne could be.

"And now that she is married and crowned, she sends her cousin to Aurelia to win a husband," Lady Baranne intoned. "Without notice or word, I might add."

The princess nodded once, a graceful tilt of her head. "There was no time. Civil war will soon break out in Nifolhad. Queen Aghna wishes to renew and strengthen the ties between our two realms. In her place, would you not do the same?"

"King's Glen would be a better place to begin your quest, don't you think? For winning a husband from Cath-*mara*," she counseled, deliberately pronouncing the territory as one from Aurelia would do, "is not easily accomplished. I assume you remarked upon the pavilions when you arrived. My son's betrothal has caused considerable competition."

"He must be a treasure to have so many seek his hand," the princess's escort flattered. "This is pleasing to us, for nothing that is worthy of a princess should be simple to obtain."

Lady Baranne laughed at that, and Adara's aunt smiled approvingly. "I hope you have as much wit as your servant, Princess."

"Indeed," Princess Milla replied, "though my companion speaks not often, and sometimes not a whit at all."

"Very well," Lady Baranne acceded with amused grace. "I accept your suit for my son's hand. We heard that you were coming only of late, so I am afraid that we cannot accommodate you in the style to which you must be accustomed. There was but one tent remaining, and not a very good one. As there are only two of you, it should be spacious enough. We will send out food and drink for your sustenance and will provide an enclosure for your horses."

"Your offer is a gracious one, Lady Baranne. We gratefully accept the shelter, but we wish to cause you no more trouble than asking for feed for our horses. We have been on the road for many weeks and are capable of hunting and foraging what food we require. If we are given leave to do so in your woods and streams, that is."

Adara watched her mother assess the princess. "You have my leave."

"Then we will wait with our horses in the courtyard for someone to guide us to our accommodations," the princess pronounced, and then departed the room with her companion.

Adara turned to her mother to hear that which was not for the ears of the newcomers. "Your babe is asleep and with the nurse, I assume. Are you up to a walk through the tents?" Adara nodded to her mother. "Good. I want a detailed report on this princess. Her appearance is of great interest to me. If you take a liking to her, you may outline the coming challenges as we have to the others. I will leave it to your discretion." Lady Baranne turned to her sister. "What did you make of the markings on their skin?"

"I haven't seen the like since I was a little girl," Cafellia recalled. "The servant—we'll have to get her name—was marked only with dark-colored ink. But the princess, her skin is a work of art." Adara had noticed none of this and was silently berating herself.

"Did you note that the colors she bore were integrated together again in the embroidery of her sash?" Adara's mother shared. "The designs echoed the markings on her hands and wrists, right down to the honey-colored pattern."

Adara's aunt turned to her. "Don't look so forlorn, my niece. Your mother's observation skills vanished for nearly a year after you and each of your brothers were born. It's only to be expected."

"An entire year!" Adara bemoaned. "I was so caught up listening to their accents and admiring their weapons that I failed to note that which was before me."

"Weapons?" Lady Baranne demanded.

"Accents?" her aunt questioned at the same time.

Adara couldn't help herself and laughed, relieved that she was not the only one who had missed a pertinent detail during the petition. "First the accents," she addressed. "The princess's nameless friend spoke with the usual Nifolhadian rhythm. But Princess Milla's speech was precise. Her Aurelian accent was perfect, with only a hint of the foreign cadence."

"Maybe she had an Aurelian tutor," her mother supposed. "But the weapons, this is another matter. I only saw that they carried walking sticks."

"Quarterstaffs," Adara corrected. "Hawthorne, with markings similar to the ones made in Ragallach. The bows and quivers were of Nifolhadianmake, as was the companion's blade. But the dagger the princess wore, something about the sheath reminded me of work done in King's Glen. Perhaps it was a gift from her Aurelian tutor."

"And perhaps your observation skills are sharper than you think," her aunt declared. "We both missed that there were two well-armed Nifolhadajans in our midst."

"I'm not surprised," Adara informed them. "They wore their weapons as if they were extra limbs. Do you trust them, Mother?"

"I didn't get a sense that they are here for nefarious reasons. Did you, sister?"

"I believe her quest for a husband is honest enough," Adara's aunt replied, casting her stones. She frowned at the outcome. "She *is* hiding something, I just don't know what it is. Adara, try to get a glimpse of her without her hood and veil. In the meantime, I'll have food and drink delivered to their tent. You cannot hunt wine, nor can you forage for cheese and bread."

Adara took her leave, having already decided to discover that which the princess was too modest to reveal. She was determined to protect her brother and would see him married to an honest woman. She met them in the courtyard where already a mob was gathering. The princess's eyes crinkled at the corners when she tilted her head for Adara to lead the way to their accommodations. If they noticed the murmurings and stares of the men and women they passed, they held themselves above it.

Adara groaned at the sight of the tent assigned to her charges and began assembling an apology. "It was all that we had left—"

"After sleeping under the stars for weeks, this is a luxury," the companion replied nonplussed.

The princess was very pleased with the makeshift rope-and-post corral that had been crafted for their horses. The two women removed the saddles and tack from their mounts and let them loose in the pen. When Adara bent over to pick up one of their packs, Princess Milla stopped her. "You shouldn't do that so soon after having a baby."

"How do you know that I just had a baby?"

"Come inside," the princess proposed. "You can sit and rest and interrogate me to your heart's content. Besides, we are attracting another crowd."

Adara went inside, and was relieved that her aunt had been exaggerating, at least when it came to the sleeping arrangements. There were two overstuffed pallets and a pile of thick blankets. The ground had been covered with a waxed tarp to keep out the damp, and there were several small rugs spread about. There was a covered brazier set in the center under a vent in the tent's roof. The addition of a small dining table with two benches, a pitcher of fresh water, and a large washing basin completed the appointments. The entrance flap let in a goodly amount of light, and Adara noticed two oil lamps had been brought into the tent for the nighttime hours.

While the princess's companion lit the lamp on the table, Adara and Princess Milla sat on facing benches. "So, you would like to know how I divined that you recently had a baby? It was easy, really. Dark circles under your eyes, your hand traveling to your abdomen over and again, and if that is not enough, there is spit-up on your shoulder." The princess's friend chuckled in the background. She was rummaging through one of the packs.

Adara couldn't help but smile herself; she'd been thinking that perhaps there were spies in Cathmara. The other woman set a small wooden bowl filled with dates and a bottle of mead on the table, and she then handed out wooden cups into which the princess poured the beverage. "Thank you, Princess Milla," Adara said.

"Please, Milla is fine. No need for the princess bit."

"And what is your friend's name?"

Milla glanced at the other woman, then spoke. "In Nifolhad, the giving of a woman's name is—"

"Madyan," the other woman provided. "My name is Madyan." She tipped her head to her princess. "The customs are different here. And this tent is not the temple."

Adara picked up a date and bit into it. "*Ooh*, delicious. These grow in Nifolhad?"

Madyan nodded. "In the Fyrost desert."

Adara finished the date and took a sip of the mead. "Now, this is from Aurelia, I'd wager."

"You would win," Milla replied. "It is from Ragallach."

"As are your staffs," Adara noted. "Why sail to Ragallach when you could have sailed directly here?"

"King Ranulf sent a gift to King Godwin," Milla started. "His emissary needed to travel a more southern route than ours."

Adara studied the two women, and decided her tack would be honesty. "My mother wants me to find out as much as I can about you."

"Naturally. As I am sure you do, since I am vying for your favorite brother's hand. We will entertain any query put forth."

"Will you uncover your face? Surely you're aware that the women in Aurelia do not hide themselves. And Madyan wears no veil."

"Will my appearance make any difference to your brother?"

"I can't say until I see you, can I?" she replied unapologetically, but grinned. "I only have Trian's best interests at heart. If you are asking if beauty will be a determining factor in his decision making, I would have to say no. Still, I would look at your face."

"Then I will remove my coverings for you, Adara. But I will not do this for any other save Trian, and only if he chooses me. Will your family respect this?"

"You have my word."

Milla pulled back her hood. She had brown hair that shimmered like silk, falling straight down to just above her collarbone. She reached up to remove her veil. The markings on her skin were elegant; even her scalp had been inked. Colored tendrils reached down the princess's neck and disappeared beneath her tunic's collar.

"What do they signify?" Adara asked, reaching out to touch Milla's temple but stopping when she realized what she was doing. "Madyan has them too."

"As you are now aware, Queen Aghna was in hiding for several years. Outside of Sophiana, there is only one place in Nifolhad that is safe for women, and that is the Fenrhi temple. I was there as well." Milla gave a brief description of the Fenrhi, how they were divided into castes, and how each Fenrhi was marked with the color that represented her calling.

"But you have every color."

It was Madyan who answered for the princess. "Some women are adept at more than one art. The princess excels at them all: duty, protection, intuitiveness, and enlightenment."

"And the amber? The red on your sash?"

"Honor and sacrifice," Milla provided in a hushed voice.

"Your callings should stand you in good stead during the tournament." Neither woman seemed surprised that there would be a contest, so she continued. "My mother, Lady Baranne, tasked me with the responsibility of telling you what must be done to win the hand of Trian. Succeed or fail, you must swear to never repeat what you hear to anyone not born of Cathmaran blood." When they agreed to her terms, Adara instructed them on the three trials. The details of the first, protection, would be presented to all on the morning of the equinox.

"The second challenge is straightforward, no mystery involved," she continued. "Each woman is required to show that she can provide nourishment for her family. She is allowed a second to assist her. Hunting for game, fishing, foraging, all are accepted.

"The third challenge is decided by you, the suitor. You must show that you are capable of enriching the Cathmaran culture by giving a gift to Trian and his family. Here is where outsiders are at a disadvantage. Those from our territory have come prepared; some have worked on their gifts for months, years even. Embroidery and weaving are just two examples," she went on. "Once the third challenge is finished, Trian will be called upon to make an immediate decision. Now that you have all of the details, do you still desire to press your claim, Princess Milla?"

"I do," she said. "But I must beg one question of you."

"You may ask."

"We heard that your brother had been injured." The princess suddenly seemed nervous, surprising Adara. "Is he well?"

"Would it make a difference if he was not?"

"No," Milla answered. "But I might be able to help him, whether or not I am successful in winning his hand."

"That is very kind of you," Adara acknowledged. "He is well. He was injured, but he is physically stronger than he was before."

Milla's eyebrows drew together. "Physically?" she asked. "Is there more?"

"Nothing that should worry his future bride," Adara reassured, feeling guilty for not being completely truthful. She sighed. "Trian is healthy in body and mind. He will respect and honor whoever wins his hand."

"But not love?" the princess asked.

Adara was so surprised that she nearly confessed to the women that Trian's memory was compromised. "His marriage will be an arranged one, but love is always possible, is it not?" She rose to leave.

"Queen Aghna has sent your family a gift from Nifolhad," Madyan said, rising too. She handed Adara a basket filled with the dates they had shared. She lifted the cloth over the fruit to reveal a small pouch on top, then quickly covered it, concealing it from her princess. "Make sure to give some to your aunt."

As Adara bid the women goodbye, two servants from the castle arrived carrying crates of food and drink. "From my mother," she said on her way out. When she turned back, Milla's veil and hood were back in place.

• • •

"That went well," Madyan stated after the servants had departed. "If your Trian is anything like his sister, I will like him, too."

"She was very kind, wasn't she," Claire allowed, removing her hood and veil again and running her fingers through her hair. "Smart, too." She gazed about their sparsely furnished quarters. "Her mother was not happy to receive us." Madyan yawned; it was late, and Claire stretched. "I'm looking forward to sleeping tonight," she said, eyeing the pallet. She opened one of the crates to find smoked meat, cheese, a loaf of crusty, brown bread, and a jar of honey.

"When I checked, the mares had been fed and watered for us," Madyan added, as Claire prepared two servings for their dinner. "I say we eat, then go to bed. There will be nothing for you to do tomorrow except work on the third challenge; I might as well reconnoiter the area, catch what game I can find in the woods."

Claire was thoughtful for a moment. "Madyan, how difficult would it be to sneak into the castle tomorrow night?"

"With every corner of the castle and grounds occupied, extremely difficult." She smiled slyly. "But not impossible. Let me sleep on it."

Claire grinned, then reclined on her pallet. She had some reconnaissance in mind; there was no better person than Madyan for the task.

CHAPTER FORTY-EIGHT
The First Challenge

The Equinox

"Are you ready?" Madyan asked as Claire adjusted the tighter-fitting Umbren hood covering her head. Her lower face was veiled. She shifted the quiver of arrows at her hip and lifted her bow over her shoulder so that it was slung across her back. Her dagger rested at her waist. Madyan handed her the hawthorn stave.

"It matters not if I'm ready, for the horn has sounded, and it is time to begin."

They left their tent, walking side by side. Claire could easily pick out the Cathmaran women, for they each walked with only their second. The other suitors were surrounded by their families. At least temporarily, for when they reached the gate to the inner bailey, the families were instructed to take a different route. Each suitor would only be allowed one person to accompany them.

Being in the farthest tent, Claire was last to line up with the others. She passed by ten small pavilions, one for each of them. To either side of where she waited with the others, men and women sat in viewing stands. Before her was a grand dais with chairs and tables, and retainers were on hand with refreshments. Trian was seated next to his father and, not yet ready, Claire forced herself to regard the others first. Lady Cafellia, Lady Adara and her husband, then, she assumed, Trian's older brother Terrwyn and his wife, and finally, Lady Baranne. After Claire reached Trian's father, Lord Adalwulf, she continued to put off looking at Trian and skipped to the far right. Trian's cousin Cordhin occupied the end

251

chair. She resumed her study of the group, and was astonished to espy her brother-in-law, Lark. And then, finally, she set her eyes on Trian.

Her heart nearly faltered at seeing him alive and breathing. He was even more beautiful to her than before, for his ordeal had marked him, giving him a gravity that drew at Claire's breast. She'd felt that same weight and wanted nothing more than to step forward and declare herself.

Madyan touched her elbow. "Steady," she whispered.

Around them, some of the suitors were whispering nervously to their seconds. "We won't have to actually fight, will we?" came a plea from one of the young women. Someone down the line snickered, probably from Snáw or Scúr.

Claire stood tall, widened her stance, and planted her staff determinedly in the mown sod of the outer bailey. Those on the dais browsed the women, most of them pausing on Claire the longest. All but Trian, Claire realized. He looked bored. His gaze flitted over her without pause, just as it had the others. It took all of her will not to tear off her hood and run to him, but Rhiannon's warning remained fresh in her mind.

It dawned on Claire that the challenges could work to her advantage. Trian needed to choose her as she was now, not as she had been. By his insouciant demeanor when he leaned over to say something to Lark, he seemed much altered as well.

Lark stood, and all chatter ceased. "Trian has requested that I stand for him during the tournament," he called out to the crowd. "It is therefore my duty to make known that which he has determined to be the first challenge. Should you choose to withdraw due to the nature of this task, you may do so when I finish speaking." He took a moment to pause his address to the assembled women and their seconds, then began anew. "Today's challenge will determine how well you will be able to protect your family. Your goal this morning is simple: you must try to stand upon this dais. Each of you have a half an hour to prepare, then another to accomplish the task."

A group of forty Cathmaran men, each with a staff in hand, trotted forward, forming a stout line between the suitors and the platform. Lark held up his hand to halt the discontented grumblings coming from the spectators. "Before the preparation time begins, you may each ask one boon from Lord Adalwulf to help you in your goal." He turned on his heel and resumed his seat as shouts arose from the assembled families.

When Lord Adalwulf stood, a hush fell upon all. "This is an unconventional challenge, but it is what my son has declared, as is his right. As Lord Larkin announced, any who wish to withdraw their suit should do so now." One of the women from the smallholds, dressed in a hunting gown, turned and walked haughtily away.

There were only nine suitors remaining. "M'lady," Madyan softly assured her. "You will score well in this, I think. At least better than some. After the lessons I've been giving you, you could simply use your staff to sail right over their heads and onto the platform."

"No, Madyan," Claire whispered excitedly. "I've a better idea." When it was her turn to ask her boon, Claire spoke into Madyan's ear. Trian may have forgotten her, but she knew what he was trying to do with this challenge, and thanks to him, she had the skills to succeed. As Claire turned to go to one of the pavilions, her friend stepped forward to address Lord Adalwulf.

"Princess Milla requests some of the wine that is being served on the dais. If you would be so kind as to send one of the retainers to her tent."

"Does the princess withdraw?" Cordhin shouted with a laugh.

"No, she does not withdraw. There are three challenges; should she not win today, she will prevail tomorrow."

Lord Adalwulf tilted his head to her, looking slightly bemused. He turned to one of his servants, directing him to take wine to the princess's tent.

• • •

What was the Milla doing? Adara looked to her aunt, but there was no help there. Cafellia was studying her cast stones. She scooped them up over and over, tossing them onto the table, then shaking her head in confusion. And looking at her brother, Adara was sure that his bored expression was a façade. Trian was only concealing his disappointment that Lady Claire had not appeared in time.

The horn sounded again, and the suitors who had not yet stepped from their tents did so now. The flap on the entrance to Milla's tent remained closed. The challenge began, and Adara watched as eight women tried to cross the barrier of men. Snáw and Scúr, as Adara called them, had unintentionally teamed up. Together, they were pushing at the guards and decreasing the twenty foot gap between them and the dais. Cordhin was barking with laughter watching Lady Caroline flirt with the men who blocked her way. Heaven help Trian if that woman succeeded; though they maintained their ground, the men were furiously blushing.

"Seems like you are beneath the princess's attention," Cordhin jeered. "She must've found you undesirable and figured that your challenge wasn't worth the effort." He slapped his knee and guffawed, jostling a servant who'd been about to pour him more wine and causing the already tipped pitcher to be fumbled. Cordhin jumped up, sputtering, but the servant kept his head down and was smart enough to move away from Adara's blustering cousin.

The half hour passed quickly, and no one had attained the dais, although Lady Caroline was only a few feet away, as were Snáw and Scúr. The Pheldhainian girl had shown a surprising talent with her staff and had also come close. The other five women had made no headway. Princess Milla had never appeared, and Adara couldn't help but feel disappointed. Did she really think the challenge was beneath her, as Cordhin had claimed? Adara did not want to believe she had misjudged the woman. She glanced at the tent just as the flap opened, drawing even Trian's bored gaze. But it was Madyan who stepped forward, not Milla. The horn sounded the end of the challenge.

Lord Adalwulf stood, commanding everyone's attention. "Lady Shan of Snáw and Lady Reiga of Scúr came closest to attaining the dais and are declared the winners of the first challenge." He sat down and held up his cup to be refilled.

"Pardon, m'lord," Madyan called out. "The princess was under the impression that the goal was to stand upon the dais in the allotted timeframe."

"This is true," Trian's father proclaimed, "but she should have tried harder than simply sipping wine in her tent."

Madyan stepped forward again, dragging another person from the tent. It was a young man, and he'd been gagged and stripped down to his undergarments. There was a collective gasp from the other servants standing the dais, then pandemonium. All had turned to stare at the veiled servant pouring wine into Lord Adalwulf's cup. Those seated jumped to their feet. Everyone but Trian, Adara noted. Had he suspected all along?

Cordhin was another matter. Only Adara's pleased laughter and clapping stilled the hand of her cousin as he reached for his sword. The servant removed his coat, revealing that he was actually Princess Milla. Her father and mother exchanged shocked looks, but quickly recovered. Lady Cafellia looked relieved. Adara glanced again at her brother; his expression was no longer one of ennui. He walked over to Milla and removed the retainer's hat that she'd donned over her own head covering.

Milla cast her eyes downward. "Will you show yourself?" Trian asked.

Adara stepped forward. "I have given Princess Milla my word that we will honor her realm's customs and that she need not show herself unless you have chosen her to be your bride." Her edict was met with silence. "Do you choose now, brother?" Adara felt a touch of guilt that she had called Trian to task, but his feigned disinterest had driven her to it. He turned to Lark for support, but his friend seemed preoccupied.

"I…" Trian started, switching back and forth between Adara and the princess. "No." He turned and left the dais, Lark only steps behind him.

Her father was speaking to Lady Baranne. They nodded to each other, and he stepped forward. "Princess Milla was clever enough to reach the dais; she is declared the winner of the first challenge."

Terrwyn was first to congratulate her. Even the women from Snáw and Scúr seemed impressed. "I know only one other who could accomplish such a feat," Terrwyn admired, "and that is Trian himself."

Adara agreed. "I watched you, or rather the wine steward, leave your tent. I swear that nothing seemed amiss. How did you manage it?"

"Everyone was waiting for a princess," Milla pointed out. "A servant would be given only a cursory glance, if not ignored all together."

"I do not trust this Nifolhadajan. Princess or no," Cordhin blustered, his hand still grasping the hilt of his sword.

Everyone on the dais tensed, and Adara saw that Madyan was hurrying forward with Milla's staff. But with a gesture of the princess's hand, she slowed. The princess stepped closer to Cordhin rather than retreating from his veiled accusation. "You were thirsty and only observed what you wanted," Milla contended, her hand resting comfortably on the pommel of her dagger. Then, she did the most extraordinary thing: she held out her hand, and Madyan tossed the staff to her. Before any could say a word, she planted the end into the dirt before the dais and cantilevered herself through the air in a neat somersault, landing gracefully on the ground with the other contestants and proving to all that she could have won the challenge both by grace and by guile.

Adara's father announced that the next challenge would begin at dawn. Each contestant would have the remainder of the day and the night to prepare and plan. Milla and Madyan had broken away from the rest and were on their way to their tent. Next to Adara, Cordhin fumed.

"She should not be allowed to compete," he seethed. "There must be something wrong with her. Why else would she hide her face?"

Adara was saved from having to respond when her aunt came forward. "You are only angry that she stained your new tunic with wine, Cordhin. If you recall, you were insulting the princess and your cousin when the mishap occurred. Now, go with Terrwyn and try to be useful for once."

"You look relieved, Aunt," Adara observed, walking behind the others as they returned to the castle. "More so than when you were casting your stones. What did you see in them?"

"They gave me good odds that Princess Milla would succeed where the others would fail. When it seemed that she wasn't going to try, I was at a loss to interpret my throws." She stopped suddenly, and stared out to where the suitors were filing out the gate. "Adara, if you visit the princess later, please thank her companion for the dates. Tell her they are a wondrous gift indeed, and I will put them to good use while she helps her princess on the hunt."

"What are you not telling me, Aunt?"

"Nothing that you don't realize already in your heart. Give it time, Adara," Lady Cafellia counseled. "You'll come to it eventually."

"Has Larkin guessed?"

Her aunt looked startled at first, then she grinned. "He may have. Now, no more questions. You can trust this princess, Adara. No matter your cousin's protestations."

• • •

"So, that is how you escaped the ship in Naca'an," Madyan exclaimed. "I would have never believed it had I not just witnessed your transformation with my own eyes."

Claire smiled at her friend. "That wine steward would've never parted with his clothes if it hadn't been for your arrow pointed at him."

"Oh, I disagree. He knew I was bluffing. He wanted to see if you could manage it. Think of the stories he'll be able to tell! Besides, there were no arrows pointed at him while he waited."

It had been a good ruse, Claire thought, despite Cordhin's blustering. "We'll have to pack tonight and be ready to leave at first light. Our destination is a five-day ride, a hard one at that, if this map that you copied from the one in the castle last night is accurate." Madyan had been successful in her midnight excursion. If Claire was to succeed in the next challenge, she needed to find the quickest route to her quarry.

"I'll go check the horses," Madyan announced.

Claire, standing at the table, was engrossed in the study of the map that Madyan had replicated when her friend returned after only a few minutes. "Did you forget something?" she asked without looking up. When there came no reply, Claire stilled herself, put her hand to her dagger, and slowly turned around to face the intruder. She remembered too late that her head covering was on the other side of the tent.

"Claire?" Lark whispered. "It is you, isn't it?"

She nodded.

He rushed forward and lifted her from her feet. From the corner of her eye, she saw Madyan enter with knife drawn. Just as quickly, her friend ducked away.

Lark studied her skin where the markings had been inked. He lifted her hair to examine her neck. Grabbed her wrist and pushed up her sleeve. Then his eyes traveled back to hers.

"How are you, Lark? And Anna? Celeste?"

"We are well, all of us. Anna misses you. She never once believed that you wouldn't return. Even when we heard nothing from Warin." Worry filled his eyes.

"They're safe," she assured him. "Warin found me after I fled the Fenrhi temple. He's on his way to King's Glen, escorting Ranulf's sister Anwyl to King Godwin. Ranulf and Aghna want to protect her from the war that is coming. They'll ride through Stolweg first, to Anna and to you.

But you are here." Claire realized how fast she was speaking, and forced herself to slow. "You know that Aghna is alive and proclaimed queen?"

"Yes, I've heard." He was still caught up in studying the designs on her skin. "Are you—were you hurt when you were there?"

Claire thought about the ship and its crew, about nearly losing herself to the Kena, and then the forced marking of her body, the men in the Blood Hall. "I've recovered," was all that she could manage.

"Why don't you start with the princess charade," he suggested, then sat at the small table where Madyan's map was spread.

"Ah," Claire confessed. "But it's not a charade. You, my dear brother, are married to a princess of Nifolhad." She apprised him of what she had learned about the source of her family's lineage.

"But Claire, now that you have returned, why not use your own name? Why this ruse? If Trian could just see your face, he—"

"He would what? Miraculously remember everything? Or, he might not. I am not the same woman he fell in love with, Lark. I love him still, this is true, but I have changed."

He set his hand atop hers. "I'm listening."

She started the same story over again: the abduction, the Fenrhi, the race across the desert and the sea, even Rhiannon's prophecy. "I mean to win Trian's hand, Lark. And he must come to love the woman I am now, not the one I was."

"Are you so different? What does it matter that your skin is covered with designs? It doesn't change who you are inside."

"Yes, it does," she asserted quietly.

"But Trian *will* choose you, Claire. He still loves you."

"And if he chooses another? I've thought a long time about this. I won't marry someone else just because King Godwin decrees it. I would rather return to Nifolhad than be forced yet again to endure something against my will. Can't you see the pattern, Lark? Roger, Diarmait, then the Fenrhi, and even King Godwin's ridiculous list. And don't ask me about Chevring, because it is nothing to me without Trian at my side."

"Anna and I will support any choice you make, Claire," he pledged. "Now, what can I do to help you win Trian?"

"Nothing, for I suspect that even now, you may be breaking some Cathmaran rule that could disqualify me." His grimace confirmed her suspicion. "By the way, how did you see through my disguise?"

"There's only one dagger like the one you are wearing, Claire. I've admired the weapons and armor that go with it enough times on Anna." He stood, then glanced down at her map, tracing the route. "Cross here," he recommended, placing his finger slightly east of where she had marked the map. "Then travel south a half day. It's a longer route, but it will save you a day's ride if you skirt Deighlei's plain instead of the switchback foothills east of this peak."

"Thank you," Claire told him, rising as well.

He pulled her close once more. "It is so good to finally know that you are safe, Claire." He let go and walked to the tent's flap just as Madyan reentered. "One last thing," he added. "Trian could have picked any challenge he wanted. He chose one that only he, and you, could accomplish. His mind might not remember you, but his heart does. And that is something that I have been waiting to see for months." He nodded to Madyan, then slipped from the tent and out into the night.

CHAPTER FORTY-NINE

Mud

Two Weeks After the Equinox

Trian couldn't keep his mind from dwelling on the strange princess from Nifolhad. He paced back and forth on the dais. So far, five of the eight women vying for him had completed the second challenge and had returned. Lady Caroline was one; she'd ridden in triumphant with an enormous stag strapped to her packhorse. The suitor from Marach had caught a shark, an impressive feat until one remembered that as a woman from Marach, she'd probably been born asea with a fish spear in her hand. From Deighlei and the smallholds, a copious number of pheasant, rabbits, and quail had been snared or shot. All of this bounty would eventually supply his wedding banquet.

Cordhin had returned earlier. He'd been missing for more than a week, and had refused to tell anyone where he'd gone. Probably to meet some young maid. It was just as well, Trian thought. Cordhin had been expressing an unhealthy interest in Princess Milla. His cousin had flourished at King's Glen, but he had slipped back into his usual truculent mood upon his return to Cathmar.

Scouts had reported that the prospective brides from Snáw and Scúr would arrive within the hour, and when the horn sounded, all eyes turned toward the gate. The two women rode in side by side, some disagreement fomenting between them. They crowded their horses together, bumping stirrups and trying to knock each other out of their saddles. Examining their quarry, he understood why. Each had hunted and killed a wild boar. Trian ignored them; instead he listened for the hoof beats of a rider that would come to tell them that the princess had been spotted.

"How are you feeling today, nephew?" his aunt inquired, offering him one of the stuffed dates from her seemingly inexhaustible supply.

"I'm well, Auntie," he replied. His mind did seem clearer of late. The change had been so gradual that he hadn't noticed at first. He was remembering things, like taking Cordhin to court and returning to Stolweg with a dagger. He'd been informed that the dagger had been meant for Claire, but he still could not recall the details.

It occurred to Trian then that it no longer mattered, for even if she lived, Claire hadn't made it back in time, and he would soon be married. What would he do if she returned one day to find that he hadn't waited for her? Usually, this line of thinking made his head throb. However today, he felt lighter of mind and heart. For some reason, he was no longer worried about his impending nuptials.

His only concern now was that the princess would not return before the horn blasted the end of the second challenge. She intrigued him. Trian could still not understand why he'd chosen the first challenge as he had. He only knew that it had been the right task to assign. The moment that the wine steward had stepped from the tent, he'd realized it was the princess in disguise. It was exactly what he would've done, so he had played along to see the ruse to its end. And when she had poured wine on Cordhin, something had stirred inside him. Though it was brief, he was familiar with the sensation: attraction. If only Adara had not given her word that the princess could remain veiled. And what did it say about him that he felt no guilt that his eye was drawn to another when his heart supposedly belonged elsewhere?

"I think we have to call it a day," his mother proclaimed, looking at the setting sun whilst his father settled the argument between the two boar hunters. "The princess had only until sunset to return." And just as Trian rose from his chair, a horn sounded. An excited chatter filled the bailey as the princess and her friend cantered through the gate, pulling their pack horses behind them. The babbling gave way to snickers, then outright laughter. The princess, her second, and their horses were coated head to foot in caked-on mud.

Despite the filth, she sat proudly in her saddle, and he was pleased to see that she was an excellent rider. The laughter gave way to curiosity when the two mud-encrusted women dismounted and walked confidently to the pack horses. It took a moment to remove what appeared to be two small, dome-shaped baskets. Everyone stretched their necks to get a better view.

The princess carried the baskets up onto the dais, setting them down before Trian's mother and father. He heard a flutter of wings underneath the cloth, and his cousin snorted.

"At least her catch is fresh," Cordhin teased, laughing at his own jest. "I'm not surprised; look at her. Too weak-stomached to kill and dress your own game, Princess?"

Princess Milla ignored him. She grabbed a handful of each cloth, bowed to his parents, then pulled the fabric from the domes. Trian's mother gasped. His father jumped to his feet. Trian was so astounded, he couldn't speak. Each basket held a fledgling rímara falcon. A male and female, and very alive and healthy. At the sight of the raptors thought extinct, the crowd roared its approval. Trian's father had tears in his eyes as he thanked her for the gift.

And this time, when Trian glanced at the princess, she didn't look away, but returned his gaze. She lifted her filthy hand to her head and pushed back her hood, revealing her short hair, hanging in heavy clumps of dried muck and swamp weed. She jumped to the ground, then swung up into her saddle as lithely as a cat. And as the knots of her hair swung out, something inside Trian's gut clenched. He had the feeling that underneath the mud, her hair would feel softer than silk. He glanced at his best friend, but Lark only raised an eyebrow at him. "How did she know, Lark?"

"Know what?"

"Where to find the rímara. I never told a soul."

His friend shrugged, then rose to view to magnificent birds that the princess had brought.

Trian caught one last glimpse of her as she rode out the gate. Images of tresses sifting together in a silky fall of golden brown, just like the waterfall where he'd once found the same birds that she'd captured, teased the edges of his memory.

When he returned to the castle with the others, his only thought was for the next challenge. Princess Milla's first two achievements had plucked at something in his heart, and he was impatient to see what she would do next.

• • •

"It was him," Madyan seethed when they made it back to the privacy of their tent. "I swear it. He cut the horses loose while I gathered reeds and branches for the baskets." She brushed ineffectually at her mud-caked garments. "*Agh.* It's even in my teeth."

"You can't be sure it was Cordhin; we were too far away to get a clear look at him," Claire peeled off her filthy cloak. She knew Trian's cousin was always causing trouble for Trian, but Cordhin had never been malicious. Whoever had run off their horses did so with the intent of making Claire miss the challenge's deadline. Someone had unhobbled their mounts, and the branch corral they'd built had been dismantled. They'd spent two days tracking their horses through fen and bog alike. If Lark hadn't shown her the faster route, they would have been disqualified for being late. "It's more likely that it was one of the other families vying for Trian," Claire rationalized.

"Tall, barrel-chested, the way he moved," Madyan argued. "Exactly like the man standing next to Trian today. And did you see the way he frowned when we rode into the bailey? Something is off about him."

There was a noise outside their tent flap, and Madyan went to greet whoever was outside. Moments later, servants carrying not one but two portable bathing basins entered the tent. Behind them trailed a brigade of water bearers. The pavilion was soon filled with steam and the floral scents of oil and soap. "Compliments of Lady Baranne," one servant explained. "If you give us your soiled garments, we'll see to it that they are cleaned. Your horses will be tended to by the stable master himself." She then ushered everyone from the tent, departing before Madyan and Claire could even voice their thanks.

Claire examined her hands and the black muck under her finger-nails. "I hope this is enough water to get us clean," she jested. They stripped and eased into the tubs.

Closing her eyes, Claire thought about Cordhin. His instincts had had his hand racing to his sword hilt when she'd revealed herself as the wine bearer. She could think of no motive that he would have to cause trouble. Perhaps it was the old conflict between him and Trian: jealousy. "We'll keep an eye on him, Madyan," Claire promised.

CHAPTER FIFTY

Friendships, Past and Present

Claire was seated at her table going over her creation for the third challenge—a poem—when she heard a feminine cough outside the flap of her tent. She pulled her veil into place, and Madyan rose to give the visitor entry.

"Good morning, Princess," Lady Caroline greeted. Claire had shared some of the more ribald stories of Lady Caroline's courtly escapades with Madyan when they had first heard that she was seeking Trian's hand. Madyan beat a hasty retreat from the tent.

"I hope I am not disturbing you," she said, watching as Claire covered the poem she had been studying. "Oh, no need to worry that I might find out what your final gift will be. I myself was going to play the harp."

"*Was?*"

Lady Caroline's laughter tinkled like bells. "Yes. You see, I've pulled out of the race. A smart woman knows when she's been beat."

"Oh." Then, remembering her manners, she gestured to Lady Caroline to have a seat. "Wine?" Claire offered, then poured a small cup when Lady Caroline nodded.

"You've caused such a commotion that there are now only two other competitors remaining. One of the boar hunters, from Scúr, I believe, and the girl who caught the shark. After you left, there was quite a debate as to whether or not your falcons could be interpreted as providing sustenance for a family. Luckily, the woman from Snáw settled it."

"Did she?" Claire asked, not bothering to hide her surprise.

Lady Caroline was in her element, Claire realized, having discovered that she had a virgin ear to whom she could relate her gossip. "She did. And quite honorable of her to do so. I wonder," she mused, "with the right gown, and some help with her hair, she could be an attractive girl. I might just take her back to court with me. If I am not gaining a husband after investing so much time here, I might as well start a new project. Let me think…oh yes, I have it. Lady Shan from Snáw. A very pretty-sounding name, too.

"But that is neither here nor there," she continued, waving her hand in the air as if erasing her last comments. "I have come here to offer my assistance to you. And by the way that you covered whatever it was that you were working on, I see that my timing is perfect."

"Why would you help me? An outsider?"

"That's just it," Lady Caroline conspired. "You and I, and the Pheldhainian girl, for the others from the smallholds have already decamped, we three are all outsiders. It irks me to no end that these Cathmaran women have the advantage. Did you see the stag I brought down? A fish and two pigs were equal to that?"

Claire laughed at Lady Caroline's audacity. It was one of the woman's better qualities, along with her humor and intelligence. "I'm still not sure how you can help, but all right, I accept."

"Good. I like you, Princess. You remind me of someone very sweet that I once knew, though she lacked your competitiveness." The flap to Claire's tent lifted again and another woman entered. "Lady Murel of Pheldhain, allow me to introduce you to Princess Milla of Nifolhad."

"My pleasure," the Pheldhainian woman said, but her hands cried the opposite. Claire watched as she twisted and pulled at her kerchief.

"Murel," Lady Caroline exclaimed, observing the woman's distress. "For goodness' sake, what is wrong with you?"

"Here, sit and I'll pour you some wine," Claire said.

"Thank you, Princess. I'm fine, really. It's just that ever since I heard you were from Nifolhad, I have been dying to ask you something. Ere now, my family would not allow me to visit you."

"Just ask," Lady Caroline ordered, exasperated with the young woman.

Murel took a deep breath. "My cousin sailed off to Nifolhad to chase after a woman. We have had no word from him in months. I wondered if you might have heard of him. He was on a—" she lowered her voice to a whisper "—*smuggler's ship*."

Claire couldn't help herself and giggled beneath her veil. "You must mean Warin of Pheldhain."

Murel's smile lit her face. "Is he well? Where is he?"

"On his way to King's Glen, I suspect," Claire replied, describing how she had met Warin in Sophiana, and that it had been his ship that had transported her to Aurelia. Different context, different truth, but she had made no false claims. Murel was so happy, she jumped up and hugged Claire.

Lady Caroline smiled as well. "I am glad to hear it. We have missed your cousin's antics at court." She turned to Claire. "Now that that is settled, tell me, Princess, what have you planned for the next challenge?"

"I'm reciting a poem," she mumbled glumly.

"Oh dear," Lady Murel opined.

"Let's see it," Lady Caroline demanded. Claire shook her head.

"The princess wishes for it to be a surprise," Madyan divulged, coming back into the tent. "And, it isn't a poem. It's a song. One that she is refusing to sing."

"A song!" Murel cried. "But that's perfect! The Cathmarans love a good song. I would know; we have one in Pheldhain. A Cathmaran, I mean. Married to another cousin of mine. It's how I knew to bring something that I'd made. He's singing all the time. Songs about rivers, and fish, and rocks, and—" Lady Caroline raised her hand to stop Murel.

"You must sing then," Lady Caroline declared. "Come, let me hear your voice."

"But I don't sing," Claire argued. "I can't."

"You can't sing?" Murel asked incredulously.

Madyan was smiling at her, and Claire narrowed her eyes at her friend. "I *can* sing; I just do it so poorly." Under her veil, she felt the heat rush to her cheeks.

Lady Caroline glanced at Madyan. "Her song, I assume it's good."

"I've never heard better. It's a heartsong."

"Excellent, a love ballad," Lady Caroline approved. "Stand up, Princess. I am going to teach you to sing." For the rest of the afternoon, Lady Caroline made Claire sing notes, then scales, then simple verses. Claire felt ridiculous, instructed to stretch her mouth wide, make large *o* shapes with her lips. She was poked and prodded, had her shoulders pulled back for her by Murel, and her abdomen and ribcage pressed in by Lady Caroline. When it was time for the two women to depart, Claire was exhausted.

"We will be back first thing tomorrow to resume your lessons," Lady Caroline declared. "For tonight, I want you to put your song to a tune. Practice all night. You have a very pretty voice, so you mustn't fret."

"But I'm not confident that I can put it to a melody," Claire confided.

"My dear princess," Lady Caroline assured her, "the melody will come from your heart. And if the song rings true, so will your voice."

Claire rounded on Madyan after the women left. Her friend smiled innocently at her. "What have you done, Madyan? You have no idea how beautiful Trian's singing is. I sound like a crow compared to him!"

"Claire, you won't. Your words are beautiful."

"I can't do it," Claire asserted.

A strange gleam came into Madyan's eyes. "You don't know, do you?"

"Know what?" Madyan took her wrist, stroking the markings on Claire's skin. "These designs? They won't help my voice, Madyan."

"Sit down, Claire." Madyan sat as well and poured them each some wine. "Not the designs, but the background. The honeycomb. Why do you think the Mothers were marked this way?"

"A net to bind the castes together. Control?"

Madyan shook her head. "The pattern represents the Mother's ability to *unify* the castes. The color represents truth and clarity. And harmony, Claire. When you sing, it won't matter if you croak like a frog because your words will soar. They will touch everyone who hears them." Madyan sighed. "I assumed that Radha and Aghna had taught you about the six castes."

"No, just the four."

"So, you know nothing of the truth of Blood Caste either?" Claire pressed her hand to her waist where the linked chain had been inked. "Blood Caste was never meant to exist the way it does now. The red ink represents passion and everything that flows from it: birth and mother-hood. But it is the honeycomb that will help you to focus the love you feel for Trian, and you will sound like an angel. Try it; you will see."

Claire uncovered the song she'd written. She stood in the center of the tent, put her hand to her abdomen, then sang the first verse. When she finished, she looked at her friend.

Madyan stared at her, her eyes shining with tears. "Don't sing the rest right now," she begged. "I don't want to hear it until you sing it for Trian. I'll go check on the horses so that you can practice."

"Madyan, what's wrong?"

"When people hear your words, they will be touched. Believe me, Claire. I was."

Madyan slipped from the tent, and Claire stared down at what she had composed. She had memorized the words days ago. She started with the first verse again, then stopped. Something wasn't right. The singing of the verses should come honestly and not be rehearsed, Claire realized. She would not sing it until she stood before Trian.

• • •

The next morning, Lady Caroline and Lady Murel arrived with breakfast and a large trunk. "It seems there are more nuptial traditions the Cathmarans have forgotten to disclose to you," Lady Caroline began immediately.

"I only knew about them because my cousin married a Cathmaran, and my mother attended the wedding," Murel piped in with enthusiasm. "Incidentally, it was my mother's idea that brought me to Cathmara. I'd just as well remain unwed for now. Not that Trian isn't—"

"Murel," Lady Caroline interrupted. "Please tell the princess what you told me."

"Oh, yes. Well, it seems that once the *winner* is proclaimed, the wedding takes place immediately."

"Excuse me?" Claire asked, not quite sure she heard correctly. "As in the next day?"

"Er, no. Immediately, as in directly after."

"But I'm not…I don't even…And besides, I have nothing to wear," Claire finally managed.

"That's why we brought my trunk!"

Lady Caroline made a point of scanning the meager belongings in the tent. "If you'll pardon me for saying, Princess, we noticed that in your haste to leave Nifolhad, you neglected to pack a few basics." Murel clapped excitedly and bounced in her seat. "Luckily for you, Murel packed too much."

"No, I couldn't. Really," Claire stammered. "I'll be quite comfortable in what I wore when I arrived."

"Oh no, Princess," Madyan proclaimed. "You must."

"Traitor," Claire accused under her breath. The notion of wearing a gown as she had before, with the constraining stays and molding bodice, filled her with dread.

"Your friend—I must really get your name—is correct. You cannot let these Cathmarans have the upper hand," Lady Caroline all but ordered, then paused and regarded Madyan expectantly.

"It's Madyan."

"Excellent. Now, open the trunk, Murel."

When Murel pulled the first garment out, Claire blushed under her veil. There was nothing to it. In fact, it was so similar to what Queen Aghna had worn in Sophiana that she had to ask, "How come you to have a gown from Nifolhad?"

Murel laughed. "I'm sure my cousin Warin has filled you in on his favorite pastime." Lady Caroline gave an unladylike snort. "I'm talking about smuggling! Well, mostly. Let's just say that in Pheldhain, we dress for comfort. It can be very warm in the south. And humid."

"I'll bet," Lady Caroline quipped, plucking out another gown. "You need to come to court with Lady Shan and me. And you must bring this trunk."

"Anyway," Lady Murel chattered on, trying to ignore Lady Caroline but unable to hide her interest at the mention of court, "as a princess of Nifolhad, shouldn't you dress like one?" She held up a gown.

It was bright blue, the color of cornflower blooms, and made of the lightest silk, with delicate yellow beading on the hem of the skirt and at the neckline. Nothing adorned the sleeves, Claire saw, because the dress was sleeveless. She snuck a glance at Madyan to gauge her reaction to the gown. Her conservative friend's lips had a touch of *I told you so* in their smile. Ladies Caroline and Murel pulled out several more garments, all sleeveless and all in what Claire learned was the style worn in Pheldhain. While they were busy laying out one gown after another, Claire wandered toward the entrance of the tent, gazing out at the pen where their horses waited. Perhaps she and Madyan could take them on a ride later. They would need the exercise, and Claire had nothing to do until the next morning. Madyan came to stand next to her, throwing her a questioning glance.

"It's not the markings," Claire said, trying to make Madyan understand. "I've accepted that they are a part of me. Perhaps a sleeveless dress is just the thing. Better to show Trian who I am now."

"Then what?"

"This is almost over, and I'll have to reveal myself."

"Claire," Madyan whispered, "Rhiannon might be wrong. She—"

"Come, Princess," Murel urged excitedly. "We're ready!"

Claire gave Madyan a meaningful look, and then stepped over to her bed to see what they had chosen. The gown was made of honey-colored silk, heavier than the summer weight of the first dress. The waistline was not fitted, and Claire worried over the billowy cut until Lady Caroline brought over her Fenrhi sash, wrapping it around and around, just under the bodice and about the gown's waist. The seeded pearls on the sash matched the pearls on the gown's neckline. Like the others, the dress was sleeveless. The effect was both innocent and seductive. Claire frowned.

Murel was about to say something, but stopped when Lady Caroline held up her hand. "Madyan, Murel was just telling me how much she wanted to look at your horses. Would you mind showing them to her?" Madyan nodded, then escorted Murel to the corral. When they left the tent, Lady Caroline stepped over to the table and poured two glasses of wine. She handed one to Claire. "Princess," she started, "I have, as have many others, made note of the designs on your skin. Can I assume they are part of a larger pattern? Because if you are worried—"

"I'll wear it."

"Excellent," Lady Caroline exclaimed in surprise. "I'll leave you to try it on. And to relieve Madyan of Lady Murel." She paused at the pavilion's egress. "One last thing, Princess: the young woman you remind me of, she would never have worn that gown. Nor would she have been able to do the things you've done here. And as much as I am glad to see her well and safely returned to our shores, I am more pleased that I can now call her my friend."

Before Claire could comment, Lady Caroline slipped from the tent. Claire couldn't help noticing that Lady Caroline had changed as well. For she had discovered the biggest secret in the realm, and she hadn't told a soul.

CHAPTER FIFTY-ONE

Heartsong

Claire lifted her arms while Madyan adjusted the sash. Its amber-colored bands complemented the lighter-hued silk better than Claire had imagined they would. Madyan handed her the dagger that had stopped the arrow from piercing Trian's heart, and she secured it to her waist.

"Do you have your song?"

"I don't need it."

Madyan held out her cloak, and Claire turned around so her friend could drape it over her shoulders. A horn sounded from the castle, a single note signaling that there was one hour remaining before the third challenge was to begin.

"Did you eat something?"

Claire smiled; her friend was behaving like a worried mother hen.

"I guess you probably shouldn't. Eat, I mean. You might...never mind. You're almost ready, just the veil to put on," she said, helping Claire. "So, should we wait here?"

Claire looked around at the dilapidated tent that had been their home. When the other families from the smallholds had packed their things and departed, some purloining actual appointments belonging to Trian's family, Lady Baranne had sent Adara to offer them one of the larger and more luxurious pavilions. They'd declined, stating that they were content with their current accommodations. "Madyan, do you realize that last night might've been our final night in this tent?" Her friend nodded solemnly. "If I fail today, I do not wish to tarry in Cathmara. We'll come back here, right away, and pack our few belongings. I won't want to stay for his wedding. We'll ride for Stolweg. You'll like my sister, and she'll love you."

"You won't have to return here," her friend assured.

"If I succeed, could you come back on your own and bring our things to the castle? The horses will have to go to the stables; we can't leave them here alone. It'll be a week at the most before we can travel to Stolweg. In the meantime, I don't believe that Lady Baranne would want you to remain out here by yourself. They'll find you a room in the castle, I'm sure."

Her friend's face brightened. "I haven't asked you," Claire continued, "because I assumed you would, but will you come to Chevring to live there? Whether Trian chooses me or not, that is? The castle is being rebuilt, and there will be so much to do there. Say you will, at least until things are more settled."

"Yes!" Madyan affirmed, and threw her arms around Claire's shoulders.

Claire hugged her back. "We might as well start toward the castle. I've been last to arrive for everything I've done here. For this third and final challenge, I would like to be first."

"Better first," Madyan teased. "If your voice cracks during your song, we can make a hasty retreat while the other two present their gifts."

"Madyan, you made a joke!"

"Today, Princess, anything is possible."

• • •

They were laughing as they exited the tent, and didn't notice that they'd been the victims of an eavesdropper. They had led a merry chase, these two. Queen Aghna might be safe, but the Chevring girl and her Umbren friend were not. If Lady Claire failed in gaining a husband, she and her companion could be dealt with in the mountains. No one would suspect they'd been assassinated because, thanks to Lady Claire's insistence that her name was Princess Milla, no one would suspect that she'd made it back to Aurelia. It had been her undoing, using that name, for the news of Princess Milla had spread like wildfire, available to any interested ear that wanted information.

In the case that Lady Claire succeeded in securing the Cathmaran's hand, she could have her one night with her groom. Then, the very next day, she would be relieved of her life, her husband first, before her eyes. And all by the unlikeliest of attackers. Perhaps a few more of the Cathmaran family could be removed in the same fell swoop.

• • •

Adara noticed two figures walking through the gate and into the area before the dais. Surprisingly, it was Princess Milla and her companion. There was no sign that they carried a gift with them. A hush fell over the assembled crowd, but when nothing happened, the chatter of idle conversation filled the air once more. There was yet another half hour before Lady Reiga of Scúr and Lady Taishal, the youngest daughter of the Lord and Lady of Marach, were required to arrive. Two women broke free from the spectators to greet the princess and Madyan. Now, this was interesting, Adara thought. A friendship seemed to have formed between Lady Caroline, Lady Murel, and the two women from Nifolhad.

Trian, Lark, and Cordhin arrived and took their seats. Her Aunt Cafellia was next, and she made a beeline for her nephew. Again with the dates. Trian took one happily, nudging Lark to try one. Cafellia hesitated, but then offered him the plate. Before Cordhin could try for one, she whisked them away and came to sit next to Adara.

It appeared that her aunt had stuffed the dates with nuts and dried fruit. "Go ahead, try one." Adara hesitated, took one, then sniffed at it. "Oh for heaven's sake, Adara," her aunt complained. "Just eat it. It'll do you good."

"Tell me, Auntie, do they have anything to do with the pouch that Madyan had me smuggle to you?" Her mother sat down and, with an appreciative smile, took two dates, one for herself and one for Adara's father. Adara waited patiently while her aunt gauged how much information she was willing to impart.

"You were always too smart for your own good—in that regard, she takes after me, Baranne. To answer your question: yes. Madyan gave us an invaluable gift: these dates have been stuffed with fruit from the pijala tree."

"What is so important about the pijala tree?"

"Wait for a moment; perhaps you'll remember some of the plant lore I taught you as a child."

Adara chewed her date and tried to come up with a rejoinder.

"Pihaberries," she recalled. "With special properties to aid in clearing the mind. Oh!" Her brother was staring at the four women gathered some twenty paces from the dais.

"Auntie, what have your stones predicted about the princess? Will she win Trian's hand?"

"Alas," Cafellia whispered with a grin, "only Trian's love can win his hand."

"But Lady Claire isn't here, and…" Adara trailed off, stunned by what had been before her eyes all along. "Oh!" she exclaimed again, loud enough that those on the dais glanced her way. But only one person held her gaze, and he was smiling the same satisfied grin that her aunt wore. Lark must have already guessed. "But—"

"Hush now," her mother commanded. "The others are arriving. Cafellia, let's have the princess go first. Lady Caroline sent word that it would help to put the others out of their misery, though she wouldn't tell me why."

All three competitors stepped toward the dais, and the assembled spectators fell silent. Lady Reiga put one foot forward to take the lead, when Lady Baranne announced, "Princess Milla of Nifolhad was first to arrive, so she shall be first to present her gift." Reiga, Taishal, and their retainers moved off to the side, leaving the princess with Madyan.

Madyan helped her to remove her cloak, hood first. There was an audible gasp from the crowd as everyone craned their necks to get a good look at the princess's gown. It was of the Pheldhain style, and the beautiful sash that Adara had admired was wound around the princess's waist. The only other adornment was a small leather pouch that hung around her neck.

But the sleeveless sheath wasn't what had caused the stir. It was the exquisite designs marked upon the princess, everywhere, it seemed, except her face. Before the onlookers could start their chattering, the princess—Lady Claire—took another step.

She lifted her hands, showing they were empty, and every person on the dais leaned forward in their seats, including herself, Adara realized, to hear what the gift would be.

• • •

"If she's the gift," Cordhin extorted to all, "you could have her now, and still marry one of the others."

It was uttered so meanly, even by Cordhin's standards, that it wasn't possible not to react. Lark may have beat Trian to his feet, but Trian's fist was faster. There was a satisfactory crunch of bone as Cordhin's nose was broken, and he stood there dazed for a moment before falling backwards like an axed tree. Lark had returned to his seat, and Trian noted the neat little smile on his lips.

He turned toward the princess. Her eyes had widened, though not in surprise. Perhaps Cordhin had already made a fool of himself before her. "My apologies, Princess Milla," Trian called out, then bowed to her. He pulled a handkerchief from his tunic to wipe the blood from his knuckles. It was the kerchief with the forget-me-nots embroidered upon it. And, as he sat down, he paused halfway, noticing the pouch hanging about the princess's neck.

"Trian?" Lark asked.

But Trian held up his hand, trying to grasp at the threads of his tattered memory. It was almost within his reach, he could feel it. Like a word on the tip of one's tongue. He shook his head to make the elusive image clearer, but the strand dissolved. Deflated again, he sat down. "Forgive the interruption, Princess Milla," he apologized again. "My cousin is not feeling well today."

She took a step closer, hands outfaced as before, and spoke. "I came to Aurelia with naught but my friend, our horses, and a change or two of clothing. This dress, even, is borrowed." Trian watched her take a nervous breath, her veil puffing out. "I have nothing to present to you, nothing but a song. And though it is not much, it is from my heart." She turned then, directing her words to Lady Baranne and Lord Adalwulf. "Do you accept this gift?"

Trian couldn't help himself, and craned his neck to hear their response. His mother wore a smile that shimmered with a happiness he hadn't seen on her face in over a year. Not since the day he had confessed to her that he wanted Claire as his bride.

"Lark," Trian whispered uncertainly, and his friend gave him a sharp look. "Claire…?"

"Don't try to force it, Trian," his friend counseled, placing a concerned hand on his arm. "Let it come back of its own accord."

"A greater gift for a Cathmaran there cannot exist than that of the gift of a song," Lady Baranne declared. "You honor us by offering one from your heart." The assembled crowd began bobbing their heads in approval. Even the families from Scúr and Marach.

The princess inclined her head, then walked so that she stood in front of Trian. Her hands lifted to her heart, covering the leather pouch that lay there. When the crowd went silent, she began in a voice that lifted somewhere between song and speech: a simple lilt to the words, until the melody grew.

> There was once a maid so sorrowful
> Her tears no longer flowed
> Her loss at a kingdom's heart did pull
> Hard'ning hers 'til all love erode
> Hold strong, ye maids, ye lords
> Hold strong and note the flowers
> Love may blossom, love may die
> And alight the funeral bowers.

Her voice was sweet, Trian thought, though untutored and lacking strength. But there was emotion behind her verse; he could almost see the maiden of her song grieving for all that she had lost. He glanced at Lark and was surprised to find him moved to tears. When she started her second verse, Trian felt as if he were in a dream. He stared at the woman as she sang, shifting to the edge of his seat as everything around him blurred. Only she stood before him.

> A lord so fair, so strong was he
> From early age, he did know
> For his heart the lass who held its key
> But to speak it aloud he did forego
> Hold strong, ye maids, ye lords
> Hold strong and smell the rose
> Love may wilt, love may wane
> Yet with tender care it grows
>
> A more stoic lass there will never be
> The young lord passed without her note
> But by fortune's fate and royal decree

Provide safe passage he did devote
Hold strong, ye maids, ye lords
Hold strong and bard against the sting
Hive is smoked, and love's most tender
When honeybees take wing

O'er honeyed wine and boisterous voice
By his song, her first tears were wrought
As revelers cheered and made rejoice
She dabbed her cheek with forget-me-not
Hold strong, ye maids, ye lords
Hold strong, safe keep a fallen token
Love can nest and begin to grow
Quiet ways will stitch the heart that's broken.

Trian blinked as memories awakened one by one. He stared down at the threadbare scrap in his fist, and Warin's words echoed in his mind. His thoughts shifted again: a tavern, a song, a sad young woman dropping her kerchief. He could smell the fire in the hearth, and feel the vibrations of chair leg and footfall on the wood-planked floor, transported there by her voice and words.

With patient kindness did he attend to she
And observed she concealed more than her heart
So he gave of himself by lessons three
And she accepted and learned his lifelong art
Hold strong, ye maids, ye lords
Hold strong, ye must adapt
Love took ahold and bound itself
'til two souls became enwrapped.

Trian rose from his seat, ignoring everything but the princess. He jumped down from the dais and strode toward her. Three lessons he had taught the woman that once he loved: observe, conceal, adapt. The princess had named them all. She was singing his song, and that of Claire.

Fate stepped in 'fore intents declared
Foul plot did deadly quarrel seize
Maid's lord was gone, and she despaired

> While borne away on stormy seas
> Hold strong, ye maids, ye lords
> Hold strong, tho' fate deprive
> Strength is found in remem'b'rance
> Of love with tutored skill survive.

He stopped and stood before her, hardly able to breathe, afraid his tenuous hold on the deluge of memories would break away as it did each time he woke from one of his dreams. She was staring back at him, her eyes shining with unshed tears, and her veil fluttered as she began to sing again.

> Hark now and hear how maid was shown
> The truth about her love through friends
> And tho' art transfigured, herself did own
> She escaped asea and now pretends
> Hold strong, ye maids, ye lords
> Hold strong and let love live
> Love will triumph if given hope
> A princess's ruse forgive.

Her last words seemed a mere caress to his ears, but he was sure everyone had heard, for no one spoke a single word. Around him, it was as if the entire world had come to a halt. He gazed at the princess with fresh eyes. He studied the colored ink playing its game of hide and seek with her hair, promising more if one parted her locks. The lines grew bolder as they trailed along her neck, snaking down her shoulders and arms, reaching farther to mark her fingers with indelible jewelry. His eyes met her eyes. They were the same eyes he knew and loved, only now they carried more in them. An assuredness, as if no matter his decision, she could and would endure and live without him.

He lifted his hand to remove her veil, and she stood perfectly still. Gently, he released it, and the gauzy fabric drifted away, uncovering the face he'd dreamt of for over a year. "Claire."

• • •

Here stood the man she loved, the same, yet different. He was leaner, harder. And his eyes as he had approached her during the last verses were wild. Like a starving man who'd come across a banquet and not been permitted to eat. And when he whispered her name, she understood that her marks mattered not. She had been so determined to remain strong should he deny her that she was at a loss as to what to do when he didn't. It must have shown in her eyes, because he caressed her cheek. She sobbed, just one small hiccup, and the forgotten spectators heaved a collective sigh. This moment, this very public reunion, the ridiculousness of it threatened to make her laugh. And she sensed in Trian similar feelings. When a tear finally broke free and slid down her cheek, he wiped it gently away.

"Claire," he repeated, and she nodded. He touched her locks, letting them slip in a cascade through his fingers, and smiled at her the way he had done before. "You cut your hair."

She nodded, then noticed for the first time the woven strings he'd once worn in his hair were gone. "You've cut your hair, too, I see. And your beard is shorter." She searched his eyes, realizing that the young, idealistic man had been replaced with a much more mature soul.

He wore his clothes in a tighter cut than before, no longer trying to disguise his lean muscles. She ran her hand over his shoulder and down his arm, trying to gauge his weight. "New wardrobe, too."

"I could say the same of you." His eyes flitted to her hairline, her neck. He took her hand in his and studied her fingers and wrists. "These changes, the ones on the surface, they don't matter, do they?" Claire shook her head. "The deeper ones, though," he started, and searched her eyes for understanding, "I am looking forward to discovering them together."

"We are the same—"

"—and different," he finished, then leaned in to kiss her.

Claire felt the press of his lips against hers, and it was as if the last year that they had been apart had never happened. Could the solution to Rhiannon's vision be that simple, she wondered? She had not returned to Aurelia as Lady Claire of Chevring, that girl who'd lost so much and then survived. She had returned as a different woman.

A great cheer rose up around them, and they reluctantly broke the embrace. Trian's family and Lark were first to reach them and offer their congratulations. And when the crowd threatened to separate them, Trian's hand found hers and pulled her closer to him. Nearby, Lady Caroline handed a kerchief to Madyan. Neither woman was dry eyed. Lark was grinning, as were Adara and Terrwyn. Trian was laughing at something his father said, and when Claire turned, she observed Cordhin standing several paces behind his family. Strangely, his bruised face was blank. The crowd shifter closer, and when Claire looked for him again, Cordhin was gone.

Finally, it was Lord Adalwulf who called everyone to order. His booming voice thundered over the crowd. "I am assuming that there are no objections to a wedding between my son and the princess, Lady Claire of Chevring." The well-wishers laughed at that, and the families of Taishal and Reiga bowed with good grace. To Claire and Trian, their felicitations were genuine. "Excellent," Trian's father declared. "The union will take place—" His words were drowned out when the crowd roared its approval and lifted Trian and Claire up into the air, carrying them to the castle.

Through it all, Trian never once released her hand. And when they reached the hall and were set on their feet, he managed to pull Claire to the side and into an alcove. Madyan and Lark stood at the opening facing the gatherers, their gazes pleasant, but set against anyone daring to interrupt the private moment between the reunited hearts.

"Claire," Trian worried. "Is all of this—"

"Marry me, Trian," Claire proposed, loud enough for Lark and Madyan to hear. "Marry me. Right now. Right here. I don't care about customs or traditions. Our friends can bear witness."

Trian smiled at her then, and the worry and pain and fear that they would never find one another evaporated. "We'll need a cord of some kind," he stated.

Lark drew his dagger and cut a length of roping from the alcove's curtain. "Will this do?" He passed the cord behind him while warding off the well-wishers at the same time.

"It will," Trian confirmed. "Claire, your dagger, please." She handed it to him. Trian drew the sharp blade across his palm. A crimson line welled, and he looked at her expectantly. Claire lifted her hand to him, and he made a similar shallow cut across her skin. He clasped his to hers and then bound them with the cord.

It was perfect. No priest, no church, no crowd, just the two of them. She held Trian's hand, felt his excited pulse against hers. As he wound the cord, tying them together, the rhythms of their heartbeats synced.

"I, Trian, pledge my heart and my soul to you, Claire," he vowed. "I have loved you forever and will continue doing so until the end of time itself."

"And I, Claire, pledge to cherish and love you always, Trian. With every part of my being. Heart and soul."

"Kiss her," Lark called over his shoulder.

"Quickly!" Madyan pressed.

Trian's free arm snaked around her waist, pulling her solidly against his long body. She tilted her chin and met his lips. The kiss was incendiary, scorching her to her bones. Her body burned, molten against his.

"Here they are!" Terrwyn's voice boomed. The noise of the hall flooded the alcove as Lark was shoved aside. "What's this? You'll have time for kissing later. First, you must be wed!" But Claire and Trian grinned at him, then raised their bound hands high above their heads for all to see. "Good, it's done!" Terrwyn roared. "Now to feast!"

CHAPTER FIFTY-TWO

Heart's Blood

Trian set her on her feet, then kicked shut his chamber door and threw the bolt in place. He traced the thin cut on her palm, and Claire shivered. "There's something I have to tell you," Trian insisted. "Something you need to know."

"It's all right, Trian. The changes in us don't matter, remember?"

He shook his head. "No, Claire, it's not that. I want you to know…I love you. I should've said it before. Maybe if I had…"

She held his cheek. How many times had she regretted not telling him the same? All those months when she'd believed him dead; it was the thought that had tormented her every day until Warin had told her the truth. And here Trian was. No more regrets, Claire resolved. "I love you too, Trian." He touched his forehead to hers. When his knuckles brushed the pouch that hung next to her heart, he lifted it from around her neck.

"When I thought you'd been killed, I lost myself for a while. But your gift was there, reminding me that you would have wanted me to survive."

Trian pulled a worn square of linen from his pocket, and she recognized the remnants of embroidery that she'd once stitched on the corner. "Damn if Warin wasn't right," he whispered.

"Warin?"

"Oh, nothing, it's not important." He kissed her cheek. "It was your song, Claire; it woke me from my nightmare."

"And now I feel like I'm the one who is dreaming," Claire confessed. "Show me. I need to be sure that this isn't just some figment of my imagination, that your heart was truly not pierced." She pushed his tunic from his shoulders, letting it drop to the floor. He lifted his arms, and she pulled his linen shirt over his head. She let it fall on top of his tunic. Her eyes roamed over the broad expanse of his chest before lifting her hand to cover his heart. No scar marked him, and she let go the breath she'd been holding.

She traced her fingertips down the ladder of his stomach and back up his sides. "I've dreamed of this so many times." She placed her hand on his heart again, feeling it beat wildly against her palm.

His fingertips found one of the colored tendrils marked on her skin as it peeked out from behind her ear, and he traced it down her neck, over her shoulder, picking it up again along her arm. "I, too, have waited and dreamt about this. Somehow, I always knew it was you in my dreams. I don't know how, but I remember this." He ran his finger along the design on her wrist.

"I need to see you. I need to see what they did. Because, Claire, it's driving me insane to not know where all of the swirls and patterns go."

Her sharp inhalation was the only answer his hungry demand required, and he tugged at the sash wrapped around her. The silk and pearls were heavy, and the bands uncoiled from her waist of their own accord, falling around her ankles in a spiral. Under the gown, Claire's chest rose and fell in anticipation. But Trian took her hand and led her to his bed. There, he pushed the silk from her shoulders, and the gown slithered to the floor.

"Beautiful," he breathed, walking around her in a slow circle. "Later, you can tell me what it all means. But for now, I just want to touch you. Everywhere." His eyes dropped to the crimson links inked around her waist, following the chain to where it disappeared. Fire ignited in her belly and a slow, sweet burning grew. He dropped slowly to his knees, eyes level with the red chain on her skin.

And when, with just one finger, he touched the pattern, Claire gave a surprised gasp as pleasure speared through her. He smiled up at her, and her breath caught in her throat. With both thumbs, he brushed the blood-red chain that ran across her hipbones. His fingers he wrapped on either side of her waist, curving over and covering the line. Then he gently pulled her forward and set his lips to the first link that hung down. He kissed her there, using lips and tongue and teeth, and Claire moaned. One link at a time, he dragged his mouth downward until she was delirious with need. He steered her against the post of his bed, and she grabbed at it for purchase.

Never breaking contact with the blood-colored ink, he lifted her higher against the post. And when he pressed his face between her legs, Claire nearly came apart. Relentlessly, he licked, and sucked, and laved, and the tension inside her built and built. She'd die if he didn't stop, and die again if he did. Her cries filled the chamber as he devoured her. And when her legs threatened to collapse, he lifted her thighs onto his shoulders to support her. When he didn't immediately resume his ministrations, Claire dared to open her eyes. He'd been waiting for her to do so, for he smiled wickedly and bent his head to his task once more.

Everything inside her coalesced. Waves of pleasure cascaded through her body, faster and faster, and she arched her back with need. She vibrated with it until, when he plucked at her bud with his tongue, drawing it languidly into his mouth, she shattered. She didn't notice when he eased her past the bedpost and onto his bed. Slowly coming to her senses, Claire stretched, nearly purring with contentment. Trian took a moment to strip bare, then eased himself next to her. His fingers made light, delicate tracings on her skin, following the myriad designs forever marked upon her. She rolled toward him so that she was half on her side, and he let her hands roam and explore that which he'd prevented her from doing in the past.

Rediscovering Trian was a thought that had filled her restless nights since she'd heard that he still lived. "Hmm," she hummed, enjoying the way his skin stretched over rock-hard muscles.

He chuckled, then touched the red chain on her waist, and Claire gasped as her pleasure spiked again. "This one I want to know about first."

She pushed his hand away. "Wait, please," she begged. "I still need to touch you. To feel that you are real, that we are here. Together." She leaned forward and kissed the spot over his heart, then resumed her perusal. She lowered her gaze. He was hard, and long, and ready for her. She drank in the sight of his arousal, and this time, it was she who smiled wickedly at him. But then she found it, the proof of the attack from over a year ago. An angry, bright red scar marred his perfectly made thigh.

Claire frowned. "This is too ragged to have been caused by a quarrel tip." She touched it gently. His wince was so slight that she almost missed it. "It bothers you, even now?"

"Sometimes. When the puncture refused to heal, Grainne had to cut away some of the flesh." He propped himself up on his elbows. "It doesn't hurt, not really."

"Hmm," Claire wondered to herself, thinking of the Sylvan designs on her skin. But before she could work out what she might do, Trian took hold of her wrist and pulled her down next to him. Her breath was stolen away when her skin connected with his. And notions of healing fled her mind the moment his lips caught hers in a passionate kiss.

Trian's hand skimmed down her waist, stopping when she moaned into his mouth. He broke their kiss, and murmured, "There's one change I'm going to love." He pushed her so that she lay on her back and stared down at her. Then slowly, sweetly, he caressed the course in red from her hip to her stomach. "Do you remember when you were covered in mud and bathed in the spring, and I touched you, here, like this?" His hand reached lower, cupping her between her legs. "I've been dreaming of doing this to you again." And as he spoke the words, he slid his finger into her already wet passage.

Barely managing to keep her wits, she reached down between them and stroked him. Slowly, up the full velvet length of him, to hover on the tip of his manhood before taking him fully in her hand and stroking again. "I've been dreaming as well," she breathed against his lips, and he moaned into her mouth seconds before his tongue delved in after. She matched her rhythm to his, until she began to lose her senses. "Trian," she begged.

He levered himself over her, settling his hips between her spread thighs, and though she tried to arch against him, he pinned her with his weight. She could feel the throb of him just at her entrance, and marveled at his control. "We're not dreaming though, are we?"

For the briefest moment, she felt what it must have been like for him, his memories stolen and locked away. She shook her head and touched his cheek. "No, my love," she promised, then tilted her hips, lifting them far enough from the bed that he entered her. His gaze seemed to lose focus for a moment, then he pressed himself in the rest of the way. Claire felt a pinch deep inside, and Trian strained to remain motionless as she stretched to accommodate him. She nodded to the silent question in his eyes, and he lowered his head to kiss her. He withdrew from her to slide in again, slowly, like the first thrust. Though they had stopped kissing, their parted lips still touched. Each time he slid into her, Claire exhaled, softly at first, but with more urgency as their pace quickened, and soon she was lifting her hips to meet him. Trian reached down and drew up her knee, opening her more, filling her deeper and deeper with each thrust. He smiled against her lips, and she moaned, knowing what was coming and not wanting him to stop.

She felt his fingers find her waist, searching blindly for the red ink on her skin, pinpointing the permanent chain by her increasing moans and gasps. He was so far inside her. When his breathing grew as harsh as hers, she convulsed around him, and he growled her name. He thrust into her one more time, as far as he could, and they held themselves sealed together as they both climaxed.

Forehead touching forehead, they remained still. She could feel him, high up inside her, throbbing as he spilled his seed, her own muscles clenching around him. The intensity of their release robbed them both of speech. So they remained still, until their racing hearts calmed, and they could once more breathe.

He rolled from atop her, but drew her with him so that he lay on his back and she on her side. Then he reached behind him, drawing a blanket over their dewy bodies. Claire fell asleep listening to the steady and strong beat of his heart.

She woke, hours later, to the feel of his fingers on her temple, smoothing her hair from her forehead. He was so incredibly warm and alive, and she snuggled closer to him. He would have questions, but for now he seemed content to simply touch her. "What time do you think it is?"

"The sun set about an hour ago. Are you hungry?"

"Famished," Claire admitted. "I suppose we must attend whatever celebration is being held." In truth, she wanted to be nowhere but where she was right at that moment, safe in Trian's arms. He chuckled, and she lifted her head.

"This is one Cathmaran tradition you'll like," he teased. "When a man and woman are united by tournament, they are locked together in a room for three days and three nights. Even if we wanted to join the others, we couldn't. The door is secured from the outside."

She propped herself up on one arm and narrowed her eyes at him, thinking he spoke in jest. But he just smiled at her. "You're serious! But why?"

He pulled her back down to him. "What better way to give the newlyweds a chance to get to know each other?"

"What will we do for food?" she worried, sitting suddenly.

He pointed across the room where wine, bread, cheese, and fruit had been set out, then pulled her back to his side.

Claire cuddled up against him, then sat up again. "Madyan was going to bring my things."

Trian pulled himself up on the bed so that he could lean against the wall. Then he reached for her, drawing her up so that she could sit next to him. "I believe your belongings are over there, atop that trunk. And since the trunk isn't mine, I can only assume that Adara, my mother, or my aunt, probably all three of them, have found some additional clothing for you."

"They are very kind," Claire said, and he smiled at her when he saw that she meant it.

He leaned forward to grab a cushion to place behind her. Then, he swung his legs over the edge of the bed. Before he stepped away, he drew the thick blanket over her. "Stay here," he ordered. "I'll be right back."

"Where are you going?"

He gave her a sheepish grin. "Well, er, nature calls." He disappeared behind the screen set in the far corner of his chamber.

But Claire was too hungry to wait. Bundled up in the blanket, she climbed out of the bed, then shuffled across the chamber to where the food had been set.

"I said to stay in bed," Trian murmured into her ear as his arms wrapped around her, pulling her against his body. She should have been startled, but wasn't. Only Trian could move so stealthily. She leaned back and turned her head so that she could kiss him.

When he disengaged, she watched him carefully as they returned to the bed. If she hadn't seen the scar on his thigh, she probably would never have detected the ever-so-slight hitch in his gait. He sat across from her, and she handed him an apple. "Tell me what you went through."

"There is not much for me to tell," he began. "While you were gone, though I recovered from my wounds, my mind was in a fog. It was as if I had stopped, and the world carried on without me. This morning, when I realized who you were, and what you meant to me, it was as if my love for you had always been there. But you, you thought I was dead. You went on living your life. What happened, Claire?"

And so, propped up on pillows with Trian seated across from her, Claire related to him all that had transpired. And unlike her narration to Warin and Lark, she left nothing out. At some point in her telling, Trian settled next to her. He stroked the skin on her hands, and then her arms and shoulders. She felt herself relax into the soothing rhythm of his motions.

He paused at her temple. "You have a scar here."

"I got that in the valley, after you'd been shot." She touched behind his ear, finding the smooth flesh she knew would be there. "I once dreamt of this," she said absently. He continued to massage her neck and shoulders, but when she brought up the sailor named Amal, he stopped. He didn't interrupt her while she spoke to him of the captain, and of Amal's death. When she finished, he resumed kneading her muscles.

"The worst part of it wasn't that I was helpless, Trian. The worst was believing you to be dead and never having told you that I loved you." She reached up and touched his face. "I lost that gift once, Trian. I won't take it for granted again. I will tell you I love you every day, and with each utterance, it'll be like I'm saying it for the first time." She leaned forward and pressed her lips to his. It was a sweet kiss, one he returned with equal tenderness.

"Those men from the ship are all dead," she promised him when the shadow of anger lingered in his eyes. "And I was glad when I found out. Not because the captain beat me, or Amal tried to rape me, but because they had taken you away. But even when I believed you dead, you were with me in my heart. You gave me strength; you helped me to survive what came next: the Fenrhi."

"Tell me about them," he asked, tracing his fingers down one of the patterns on her arm. "Was it the Fenrhi who did this to you?" She nodded. "Why?"

"Because everyone in Nifolhad wanted something from me. Diarmait, the Fenrhi, Ranulf, even Aghna." She looked at her hands. "I wasn't supposed to be marked this way. The women who did it thought they were giving me a gift." She spoke of the good of each caste, and the bad, and how the Fenrhi had lost their purpose. From Earth Caste to Kena and all the rest, including Blood.

"I'm so sorry, Claire," he blurted, rising from the bed and standing in front of her. "I would not have made light of the chain around your waist. I wouldn't have used it that way."

On the edge of the bed, she knelt before him and laid her hand gently on his cheek. "But you didn't, Trian. The Fenrhi have lost sight of Blood Caste's true purpose. The chain is not for controlling or restraining or even using. It's meant to show the connection a woman has to her mother, her children, and even her husband. It tethers me to those I love. It binds me to you, just as we bound ourselves together when we made our vows. And, when we just made love. Just as it will bind me to our children when I give birth. Always with blood." She smiled and drew away the blanket folded around her, baring herself to him. "These marks are nothing," she said finally. "Focal points to help me heal, and serve, and see, and protect. Without them, I would still be able to do those things. I had done so before leaving Aurelia." She placed her hands on his shoulders, drawing him closer.

"And if I do not touch the red links?"

"I will still be drawn to you, still desire you." She took his hand and placed it on her breast. "I want to feel you touch me, and feel your skin against mine." Her heart raced just imagining making love again, and she leaned forward, pressing her nakedness against his. He moved his hand to her back, and with his other, reached down and caressed her. Gently at first, watching her expression change from longing to hunger. Slowly, he reached farther, until he found the entrance to her desire. When he lowered his mouth to her breasts, she moaned, then gasped when she felt his teeth.

And still, he held her suspended before him. She screamed his name as he worked her. She was so close, but she wanted him inside her, and with all her strength, she rose back up. She saw his hand delving between her legs and was almost undone. A shudder wracked her body, and she reached between them to caress him in turn.

They took their time discovering how far they could push one another. And when Trian inserted a second finger, stroking her inside, she was unable to continue her attentions and grabbed his shoulders. He twisted them around, sitting on the edge of the bed so that her knees straddled his thighs. Then, he centered her above him, holding her there, gazing into her eyes. Slowly, she lowered herself down his length.

"Trian!" She gasped at how deep he rode inside her. He leaned back, intensifying the feeling of being completely filled. And then, he thrust his hips, bringing them impossibly closer.

Claire lifted nearly completely away, then slid herself back down, and it was his turn to call out. She lifted and lowered, doing it again and again, riding him and stroking him with her body. She wasn't shy and stared at him, savoring the way his muscles flexed and strained. She felt the tension building inside her, stronger than before. Trian sat up and, holding her waist, helped her lift and fall until she thought she'd go mad. She was so close, and she leaned forward, pressing her breasts against him. He pushed deep inside her, sealing them together, then threw his head back, crying out her name just as she shattered.

He fell back against the cushions and blankets, taking her with him. When he maneuvered them fully onto the bed, she slid from him to nestle against his side under the blankets that he'd once again pulled over them. She didn't want to fall asleep, not quite yet, and she would at any moment if she didn't move. So she levered herself up, felt his arm tighten about her waist. He was on his back still, and she stretched out on top of him, resting her forearms on his chest and her chin upon her hands. His eyes were closed, and she studied him. She liked his beard, loved how it felt when his mouth was on her. His lips curled when she made a sated noise deep in her chest.

"We have two more nights together," he teased, and she wondered how much rest he would need.

The sound of something being slid under the door caught their attention.

"I'll get it," she offered, lifting up from him. On the floor near the door was a folded piece of parchment. She retrieved it and returned to the bed. But Trian was up and had donned his breeches. He tossed his shirt to her, and she raised her eyebrows at him.

"Never in the history of my family has a wedding night been interrupted. Whatever is in that note must be important."

Claire shrugged into his shirt and followed him to the chairs near the fire. He sat first, and when she moved past him to take the other seat, he grabbed her by the waist and pulled her onto his lap. Before she could unfold the note, he tilted her chin and thoroughly kissed her senseless. When he broke the embrace, she was pleased that he was as shaken as she. He nodded to the folded paper in her hand, and she opened it. When she did, a smaller note slipped out, one with her name written upon it.

"The first one," Trian said, pointing to the script that had been scrawled across the paper. "It's from Lark." Together, they read the contents.

> *Claire and Trian,*
>
> *Soon after you retired this afternoon, a messenger arrived from King Godwin with dire news. Multiple ships bearing the mark of Nifolhad have been sighted along our coasts.*
>
> *Your family has spent all afternoon debating whether or not they should interrupt your time together. I'm afraid I have taken it upon myself to do so despite whatever decision they come to. I must return to Anna immediately, and will depart at first light. Neither of you need to ask why as you both have firsthand experience with Diarmait's treachery.*
>
> *I thought you should be afforded the opportunity to decide whether or not you wish to join me. I am hoping you do. Either way, your family is meeting in Lord Adalwulf's council chamber to discuss the King's message. I've taken care of the bar across your door.*
>
> *Your loving brother,*
> *Lark*
> *P.S. The second note is from Madyan for Claire.*
> *P.P.S. Avoid the great hall as your wedding celebration continues.*

Claire opened the second note and read it. "Madyan says that Lark has kept her abreast of the situation," Claire paraphrased. "If we join him, she can have our things packed this night. She's already made sure that the horses will be readied."

"If this has to do with Rhiannon's foreboding, is there any question that we go?"

Claire shook her head. "Thank you."

"No thanks are needed, my love." He hugged her. "Lark and Anna are my family now, too."

CHAPTER FIFTY-THREE

Pins and Needles

The meeting with Trian's family took less time than Claire had imagined it would. After Claire and Trian's arrival, they quickly settled to the business of discussing the King's message. There wasn't much content to it. Just a warning about the ships in the vicinity of the coasts of Ragallach and Cathmara in the north, and Pheldhain and Sterland to the south. The ships sailed parallel to the coastlines, not attempting to land. By the time Godwin's fleet had rallied to the locations of the sightings, the Nifolhadian ships were gone. Godwin had sent his message to all of the castles, keeps, and fortresses in Aurelia. He also noted the safe arrival of Princess Anwyl, King Ranulf's sister, and that she would be traveling through Aurelia with the King's Guard as escort, bearing gifts from Sophiana.

Claire knew what these gifts were: the pijala trees and a goodly supply of its dried fruit. And she, out of everyone present, had the most information to contribute. When Lord Adalwulf asked after their import, Claire tried as best she could to explain the Fenrhi, the Kena in particular, with their talent for persuasion.

"Before you arrived," Lark added, "Madyan and I explained to everyone why you had to disguise yourself. Perhaps the violence in Rhiannon's vision has been avoided. No one here seems to begrudge your union."

It was Lady Baranne, though she did it kindly, who asked that which Claire dreaded hearing. "These women from Kena, you said they can influence someone else's will to such an extent as to force them to do their bidding. Are you able to do this as well, Claire?"

Trian took Claire's hand in a show of support. But it was his aunt who made it easier to answer. "We are aware of your sister's talents,

Claire, and that you have your own gifts. It's in your blood; has been for generations. I too am able to divine certain things, but I must use my stones. And though he's never realized it, Trian can move people with his songs as you did today. If you can do that which the Kena are capable, you need not worry that we will think less of you. Quite the contrary, in fact."

"Besides," Adara added, "if my brother loves you, it is enough for us. You're family now."

Claire glanced at the expectant faces, relieved that Cordhin was not among them. "I can, yes, but I choose not to. When I was with the Fenrhi, I was tricked into believing that that kind of manipulation was something to celebrate, a thing to enjoy using. It was Madyan who made sure that I identified it for what it truly was. She gave me a pihaberry, and I began to understand. Taking away someone's free will is…it's unnatural." She shuddered, and Trian put his arm around her.

"If these pijala trees from King Ranulf are so valuable, then perhaps it is the trees that Diarmait is after," Lord Adalwulf posited. He rose from the table. "Terrwyn, we'll double the watch for now. And we should inform the other families. Until we hear more, there is not much else we can do." He stepped over to Claire. "I expect to see you in the great hall later. We've yet to dance together, you and I." After she agreed, he left his council chamber with his eldest son.

"One last question, Claire," Lady Cafellia begged, as Claire headed out the door. "Is there a way to discern if someone is being influenced?" Lady Baranne and Adara paused to listen in.

Claire thought for a moment. "Perhaps. There are only a few among the Kena who are strong enough to make another do their bidding. There are even fewer who can sense that it is being done to another person."

"Could you?" Adara asked.

Claire considered the Umbren woman who had attacked her in the barley field, and Diarmait's soldiers being pushed forward by Rhiannon's hatred. "If I were close enough in proximity, yes, I believe I could. But they would have to be actively pushing. It is mush easier for the Kena to plant a suggestion, then simply walk away." The three women looked disappointed. "Of course," Claire added, "if you ever suspected someone of being controlled, you could simply give them a pihaberry."

Lady Cafellia's face brightened. "Yes, of course," she said, and they all made their way out of the council room to where Trian and Lark waited to escort them to the great hall.

When they entered, Trian took Claire's hand and pulled her into their first dance as man and wife. As they spun around the room, smiling faces whirled past her. Lady Caroline, Lady Murel, Adara in her husband's arms, and countless others. Claire danced next with Trian's father, then Lark, then Trian again. She was just about to take a rest when she was pulled back onto the dance floor in swift twirl. She thought that perhaps it was Terrwyn, but when she looked up, she stared straight into the bruised face of Cordhin. He smiled at her, and expertly led her across the floor.

"I didn't realize that you were such a skilled dancer," Claire praised, hoping to keep their conversation polite.

"One of the many benefits of visiting court," he remarked. "Tell me something, coz, or should I say Princess?"

"Cordhin," Claire started, all the while searching for some relief on the crowded dance floor. He had maneuvered them into a throng of revelers that she did not recognize. "I'm feeling tired, perhaps we could stop dancing." She saw Madyan and tried to get her attention, but her friend was too far away and seemed intent on something else.

Cordhin ignored her, spinning her in another circle but keeping her well away from Trian and the others. "I'll bet you're tired," he whispered harshly. "Tell me, does Trian mind being wedded to a princess whore? How long was it that you were alone with your abductors? I'll bet the waves weren't the only thing bucking the ship."

Claire used all her strength to break free of his arms, coming to such an abrupt halt that several other dance couples collided. He leered at her.

"Well, Princess?" He was almost shouting now, and others stopped to listen and stare. "I'll bet you enjoyed your time in Blood Caste. How many men did you—"

She slapped him, hard. So hard that the resounding clap startled the musicians into halting midtune. Those closest to them gasped and stepped back, girding them on all sides. Gasps turned to screams when Cordhin took a swing at her. Claire was too fast for him, and easily dodged the blow, sending Cordhin into an unbalanced spin. He regained his footing quickly, and just as his family broke through the circle of shocked onlookers, Cordhin drew his dagger. He stared at her with such hatred, and Claire finally grasped what was happening: this wasn't Cordhin. "Stop!" she yelled to Trian and Lark as they pulled their own weapons. "He's not himself."

"Bitch!" Cordhin hissed.

"Get everyone out of here," Claire ordered. "Except family and Madyan." Adara and Lady Cafellia, along with Adara's husband and brother Terrwyn, moved to follow her instructions. And that's when Claire felt it, the triumphant gloating emanating from somewhere in the room. "No, wait. If you don't recognize someone, don't let them leave. Even if their family insists that they are with them."

"Doesn't matter," Cordhin growled. "Someone here will die. This pathetic man, or perhaps your new husband." He swung his blade toward Trian. "I warned you that there'd be blood."

Claire and the others watched as one by one, the revelers began arguing and fighting. Even the musicians started attacking one another. Cordhin swung toward her again, but this time, he put the dagger to his own heart. His eyes stared desperately at her.

"Why?" Claire shouted to the room.

"You know why," a voice screamed at her from off to the side. She turned to discover Madyan crumpled on the floor at the feet of a cloaked woman. "Do you even care what happened after you fled the temple? Bowen came and found his cousin murdered. Do you know how many women suffered because of you, Princess? You, and this traitor?" She kicked at Madyan. "And now Queen Aghna has been reborn in the eyes of her people, and Diarmait has taken more and more of the Kena. He blames us for not foreseeing her return."

"Please, you cannot wish for things to continue the way they've been. Not even you, Rhiannon."

"I have no choice," she screamed, and the intensity of it pushed at Claire. "Mother expelled me from the temple. Someone started feeding her pihaberries. She's sought assistance from Aghna." Rhiannon threw off her cloak, exposing her arms and neck. The beautiful designs of the Kena were covered in disjointed indigo lines. There was no discernible pattern as Radha, the Kena Artist, had left the Fenrhi temple. "I heard what the Artists gave you," Rhiannon hissed. "Well, now I'm stronger too."

Cordhin whined; his dagger had pierced his tunic, and blood soaked through the fabric.

"Enough," Claire commanded. She felt the push against her mind as Rhiannon tried to manipulate her. That the woman could do so much at once testified to her great power. But Claire was stronger. She turned to Trian's cousin first. "You can rest now, Cordhin." She motioned to Lark and Trian. Cordhin's face went slack, he dropped his knife, and, as his knees began to buckle, Trian and Lark rushed forward to lower him to the floor. *Peace*, Claire pushed out to them all. The fighting slowed, then halted. *I won't let you harm anyone here*, Claire directed to the Kena woman. *You know this.*

Rhiannon's mind screamed her frustration, and she drew a knife. Before Claire could stop her, she put it to Madyan's neck. "You can't stop me. She'll be dead before you take a step." The dagger sliced, and blood welled where the steel bit into flesh. Claire searched Rhiannon's mind for her intent.

"I'm sorry, Rhiannon." The blade pressed deeper, then stilled. Rhiannon's eyes widened, and she stared at her weapon. Claire felt a tidal wave of rage crash against her. "Let go, Rhiannon," she begged. "I don't want to hurt you."

"Hurt me?" Rhiannon yelled, and laughed. "As if you could. I'm too strong for you. All of your castes have diluted you. I'm completely Kena!"

"It doesn't work that way. Please, let me help you."

"Never!" Another wave of hostility broke in Claire's skull. She imagined it as a tide, and turned it back on its source. Rhiannon's eyes bulged, realizing too late how easily Claire had deflected her ill will. Her hand and arm went limp, her blade clattered to the floor, and she sagged against the wall before silently falling.

Claire rushed to Madyan. She covered the neck wound with her fingers; but the blood was dark and hot and coated her hand. Through it, the emerald designs of the Sylvan Caste blazed like stitches going in and out of Claire's skin. Trian had come to her side and pushed fabric into her hand. She pressed the cloth against Madyan's neck.

"What do you need, Claire?" he asked.

Claire focused. What did she need? Lady Cafellia had come over to help. "Bee balm," Claire told her. "And horsetail, if you have any. Or shepherd's purse. Bloodwort, too. And bandages." Claire closed her eyes, thinking about the wound. It wasn't spurting blood, so the main artery hadn't been severed. But it was so close. She pictured what she would need to do to stop the bleeding. "Silk thread, a needle, and light." Lady Cafellia called to Adara, and the two women raced from the great hall. "And honey," Claire yelled after them.

"She'll be all right," Trian promised her. "The wound isn't deep." Lady Caroline stood near; she'd torn some bandages from her under-skirt and handed them to Claire. She gave a handkerchief to Trian, who nodded his thanks. Keeping the pressure on Madyan's neck, Claire placed the new linen atop the old, now blood-soaked fabric. She was surprised when Trian used the kerchief on her. "Your nose was bleed-ing." He gently dabbed at her upper lip.

"I'm missing something."

"It'll come to you," Trian assured her. "Here, let me." He set his hand in place of Claire's. "You'll need your hands rested and free before you begin."

Madyan's face was the color of ash, but Claire could still feel a pulse, a strong one considering the blood loss. Her slumped position when Rhiannon had cut her had probably saved her life. That was it! Madyan had already been unconscious when Rhiannon had tried to slit her throat. "Trian, I need to check the back of her head."

Together, they repositioned Madyan. Someone—Terrwyn, per-haps—handed her a tunic, folded neatly into a cushion for her friend. She inspected the back of Madyan's head, felt an enormous goose egg behind her friend's right ear. Rhiannon had struck her, or had made someone else do it. The skin wasn't broken, and when Claire probed Madyan's skull, she couldn't detect a crack. She wouldn't know for sure until the swelling subsided. "Let's lay her down," Claire recommended. Lark went to Madyan's other side, and helped guide her slowly and gently to the floor. Trian never released the pressure on her neck.

Nearby, Terrwyn and Lord Adalwulf were moving Rhiannon. Claire didn't know if she were alive or dead. And when Lady Cafellia and Adara returned, they also brought blankets. Adara tossed one to her father, who covered up the Kena woman. Dead then. Behind Lady Cafellia, Trian's mother was directing servants to bring hot water, lanterns, and candles.

Lord Adalwulf squatted down next to her. "You're doing fine, Claire," he encouraged. "We can handle the others who are injured."

And Claire realized for the first time that her skills might be needed elsewhere.

Lord Adalwulf gave her a fatherly kiss on her forehead. That gesture, more than anything the others did to help her save her friend, meant more than the world to her. Trian's family had watched how she killed Rhiannon, and still, they accepted her.

"I'd kiss you too, but I'm a mite occupied at the moment," Trian pointed out. Claire kissed him instead. Then, she went to work.

While Trian kept pressure on Madyan's neck, Claire threaded the needle, then began stitching the wound back together. She started from the farthest point back and moved stitch by stitch across the gash. Trian pulled back his hand in small increments while his aunt kept up a steady flow of clean bandages, patting at the seeping blood in between pulls of silk. The cut was a hand's width across and required over twenty tiny knots. When she was done, Claire sat back on her heels, then nodded to Trian to remove his hand. At first, small droplets of blood formed along the darned skin. Lady Cafellia continued to gently dab.

Claire stared down at her friend. Any movement might cause her needlework to pull and rip at the skin. If only she could seal it some-how. "Does anyone have a hairpin?" Lady Caroline drew one from the intricate pile atop her head. Trian took the thin piece of metal, intuiting what she needed, and held the tip over a flame until it was white hot. Then, he handed it to her.

With delicate precision, Claire touched the pin to the wound, in between the silk stitches to avoid burning them away. The smell of singed flesh filled her nose, but it was short work, and she was quickly finished. She next applied a thin layer of honey, followed by a layer of gauze. Adara had crafted a poultice of her requested herbs, and Claire used it, then wrapped clean bandages around Madyan's neck. Someone had brought over more blankets to cover her friend, for they could not move her from her position on the floor. "I'll stay with her tonight," Larkin promised.

"I will, too," Lady Cafellia volunteered. "I've had to cauterize wounds before, but have never witnessed anything like what you just did. You saved your friend's life, my dear."

"She has saved many lives this evening," Lady Baranne added when she came to see how they were faring.

Trian rose and held out his hand to her. Claire took it and stood, then searched for where she could help next. Surprisingly, the hall was empty of revelers. They had all been sent away to be tended to elsewhere. With a heavy heart, she walked over to where Rhiannon lay dead. She just stared at the covered body and only felt anger for what the woman had forced her to do. Her head began to hurt, and she felt a drip on her lip. She touched it, and found that her nose had started bleeding again. Unsteady on her feet, she reached out to the wall for support, but felt herself being scooped up and off her feet. It was Trian who cradled her in his arms. He carried her out of the hall and to his chamber. He settled her in his bed, and she fell asleep before her head hit the cushions. She did remember, though, Trian whispering that he loved her, and she was almost sure that she said it in return.

Epilogue

Chevring, the Following Summer

She sat beside her sister on the sloping hill to the east of the castle. Celeste played amidst the spring flowers a few strides away. Claire's new home was near completion. True to his word, King Godwin had commissioned the best builders and architects. Below them, the roof of the new stable gleamed in the sunlight. The paddocks were full. Chevring mares and their foals grazed peacefully on the clover that grew in abundance on their lands. To the south, Pieter was bringing back one of the small herds he'd been exercising. And to the north, a small group of dainty mares grazed: Jia'ma and her sisters, along with the Nifolhadian stallion that Aghna had sent to them as a wedding gift.

Anna had fallen in love with Claire's little mare, so Claire had promised to send to her sister the very first foal that was born. Madyan, with Pieter's guidance, was learning about the breeding and training traditions at Chevring. She had recovered from her ordeal with only a thin scar to show for it.

Claire heard the whinny of her own stallion Rebel in one of the paddocks. An answering neigh came from one of the other stallions, Tullian or Rabbit. Or perhaps Pepper, the Chevring steed reared at Stolweg and gifted to Trian from Lark and Anna to replace his lost Culrua.

Around the castle and stable and paddocks, a curtain wall had been erected. From their vantage point, it was an enormous belt circling the castle and its grounds. While Claire had been in Nifolhad, the wall had gone up, then the stable. Garden beds had been prepared and planted, too, and now in their second year, were already established. The orchards would take some time to regrow, and Claire homed in on the newest addition to the stands of fruit and nut trees. The pijala trees had been planted; only time would tell if they would thrive in a climate unlike that of Sophiana. Warin had been tasked with escorting Princess Anwyl around the realm, where she gifted the trees to the many territories in Aurelia. Claire smiled, remembering their last visit. She had seen what Warin couldn't, at least not yet.

"Daddy!" her niece squealed. Claire and Anna turned to find Trian and Lark walking up the other side of the hill toward them. Celeste ran to her father, and Lark caught her, swinging her high into the air. Trian sat down behind Claire, and pulled her back so that she was reclining against him. She hoped that, one day, they would hear the voice of their own little girl or boy call out in delight. But as it had always been, she could never see anything regarding her future or Trian's.

"It's hard to believe that the castle is almost complete," Anna observed, and Claire nodded. Her sister adjusted the swaddling blanket around her new baby boy. She and Lark had named him Gervaise after Claire and Anna's father. "Mother and Father would've liked the changes."

Claire had been thinking the same thing. "You'll have to leave soon, won't you?"

"After the solstice," Anna replied, watching Lark set Celeste on her feet. He got down on his hands and knees and proceeded to show his daughter how to play rolling pin on the hill. He stayed in front of her, not letting her go too fast. She was laughing the entire way down, until she came to a stop at the bottom and hit her knee on a rock. Lark scooped her up, but Celeste wailed for her mother. Anna grinned at Claire and Trian. "Watch," she predicted, "by the time I get down the hill, Lark'll have Celeste in giggles." Her sister stood and, carrying her new babe, walked at a more sedate pace down the slope. Celeste was full of laughter before Anna made it halfway down. Behind Claire, Trian chuckled at the spectacle.

She hugged the arms encircling her. "I would like to build bee hives," she mused. "There's so much clover growing here, and the pomeroi saplings from Stolweg are taking hold in the new orchards. Imagine all the honey." Trian made a noise of agreement in his throat, one that she could feel rumbling in his chest as she leaned against him, his breath warm on her neck.

Her hair had grown, and she had it pulled back in a short braid. Trian was taking advantage of her earlobe. He pulled on it with his lips, and when she felt the nip of his teeth, she shivered with pleasure. Anna, Lark, and Celeste and the babe had begun their trek back to the castle, and Claire wondered if Trian had persuaded Lark to make his family scarce. She turned her head to ask him, but when she tilted up her chin, his lips came down and captured hers. He fell backwards, pulling her with him to his side, then he rolled over and levered himself above her.

"Here?" She giggled when his hand skimmed up her waist. He rucked up her chemise, baring her breasts to his ravaging lips, and growled in reply. They were near the top of the hill, a few paces back from the crest that overlooked the castle, and unless someone came all the way to the top, they would not be visible.

He lifted his head to gaze at her with hungry eyes. His hand reached behind her, unraveling her braid so that her silken locks spread out beneath her. "Better," he murmured. "Something about all of this clover makes me want to do things to you." He plucked a green sprig and touched it gently to her nipple.

Claire felt the flush of heat course down her body. He smiled and bent his head back to her breast. The smell of crushed clover was all around them, as was the droning of bees. Her senses, normally under her strict control, broke free, and Claire was caught up in the billowing masses of the clouds floating serenely past in a sky the color of sapphires. Her thoughts drifted with the breeze, taking her miles away.

• • •

Trian knew exactly when Claire's attention had wandered. He was far from worried and paused in his tender ministrations, lifting his head to regard her peaceful expression. He was never sure if it was a vision caused by how he touched her or something else; she simply disappeared into herself for a few minutes every once in awhile. Over the last few weeks, her daydreaming had happened with more frequency. He rolled to his side, content to feel the warmth of her skin, and waited for her to come back to the moment.

Resting his head on his arm, he drew lazy circles and twirls on the areas of unmarked skin. Then he felt her fingers in his hair. "Something troubling you, Princess?"

Claire smiled as she stared up at the sky. "No, my love. I was only thinking of how happy I am right at this moment."

Trian had realized from the start how difficult it had been for her to forgive herself for killing Rhiannon, even though every person who knew the truth of how she had accomplished it assured her that she'd had no choice. Rhiannon would have brought down all of Cathmara, starting with his family and everyone else in the castle. Madyan would have most assuredly died. In her mind, Claire had known all of that; she had seen Rhiannon's intentions. She simply wished that there had been another way.

When the dust had finally settled, they had been unable to leave the next morning with Lark; Madyan could not travel. During the few weeks they'd been delayed in Cathmar, Cordhin had avoided Claire. Then one afternoon, Trian came upon them sitting together in one of the gardens. Cordhin was speaking, and Claire glanced away every so often. They stood, and his cousin stepped forward to give Claire a hug, but stopped when she stiffened. Trian watched him bow to her, quite respectfully, then walk away. Claire had never told him what Cordhin had said, and it had simply lost its importance as time unwound.

When Claire and Trian, with Madyan, had finally reached Stolweg, and Claire was able to speak with her sister, she finally let go of some of her guilt. Sisters in arms, they were. He would be forever grateful to Anna.

A cloud moved over the sun, and the temperature cooled. His wife touched his cheek. They leaned in and kissed each other, softly at first, allowing their passion to build. And as Claire reached down to undo his breeches, Trian's lips moved lower, nibbling the long column of her neck, stoking the heat lingering from moments before.

She took him in her hand and ran her fingers up and down the length of him. And somehow, Trian was able to remove her breeches. Her gasp as he entered her was almost one of relief, and he felt the same. Though they no longer had vivid dreams of one another, what they shared—the love and the attraction—grew stronger every day.

The clouds continued their march over Chevring, shadowing them, then moving on to allow the sun to bathe them in its warmth as they rocked together in the clover. Their breathing came in soft pants, and facing her, Trian was amazed again by how beautiful she was. She lifted up and kissed him, and he felt the tension in her build. His own heartbeat kept pace, and he pushed her further to the edge, thrusting deeper. The desire to touch her everywhere was strong, and he gave into it, stopping only when he cradled one of her breasts in his hand and noticing that it felt fuller and heavier than when they first were wed.

She was tightening around him, and her kiss grew more insistent. And when she arched one last time beneath him, he let himself go over the edge as well. He lowered his forehead to hers, and waited the moments it would take for them both to return to earth. When they did, Trian rolled again, bringing her atop him so that she was no longer pinned against the crushed clover.

She stared down at him, smiling at first, then laughing. "By next year, we should have all of Chevring covered," she teased, pushing herself up so that she sat straddling his hips.

Trian reached up to draw lazy circles around her breasts. They *were* fuller, he saw now, and her nipples were a darker rose than before. She watched him with a playful smile. He sat up, shifted her on his lap, and kissed her lips first, then each breast, taking time to appreciate their ripe fullness. She sighed contentedly.

Another cloud blocked the sun, taking with it the warmth of the early summer day, and Trian watched the hairs on Claire's skin lift. He searched for her chemise, finding it in a pile behind him. It was covered in green stains, and here and there scuffed with dirt. "We'll need to come up with an excuse for our clothes," he said, as Claire lifted her arms so that he could ease the garment over her head. He took her hips in his hands and regretfully lifted her from his lap. She laughed that his breeches were still about his ankles. Trian loved Claire's laugh. Especially now that she shared it with him more often than when he'd first pursued her.

Her breeches had been flung some distance behind them, and he rose to retrieve them. He held them out so that she could step into each leg, balancing herself by holding his shoulder. When both feet were through, he pulled them up and began to do the laces. That was when he noticed that he had to tug to make the ends meet. An idea burrowed its way into Trian's mind, one that would even explain his wife's drifting attention.

"Hopelessly stained," she agreed, oblivious to Trian's widening grin. She looked at the hillside where the clover had been crushed by Lark and her niece. "Maybe we should mimic Celeste," she suggested.

"And do what?"

"Something I haven't done since I was seven years old." She dropped back down to the clover and straightened out to roll down the hill.

"What? Claire, no!" He jumped over her and nearly fell headlong down the slope, but he managed to stop her before she completed a rotation.

She was on her back and laughing up at him. "Trian! What has gotten into you?"

He knelt down in front of her, not sure that she wouldn't continue on her way if he wasn't there as an obstacle. She was still giggling at what she must have perceived as ridiculous behavior on his part.

"Come on," Claire coaxed. "It is so much fun. Really." She sat up and tried pushing at his shoulders.

"You can't," he ordered, gently taking her wrists and laughing up at the sky. "Oh, my princess, you can see so many things for so many people, but you're completely blind when it comes to us, and to yourself most of all."

"Tell me something I don't already know."

"All right, I will. I know why your mind has been wandering more of late. It's what happened to my sister."

"And what was that?" she asked.

Trian grinned, and spread his fingers protectively over her stomach.

Her eyes widened at the implication. "I can't roll down the hill," she uttered softly, sounding slightly bewildered.

"No, Princess, you can't." She launched herself at him, and he held her tightly to his chest. "I love you, Claire."

"I love you, too," she told him. And as they proceeded down the hill, Claire completely forgot about their wrinkled and clover-stained clothes. She wondered how Trian had known she was with child even before she'd suspected it. "Observation," she mused aloud.

"Observation," Trian echoed, then placed her hand over his arm as they walked toward their new home.

Acknowledgments

I'm a lucky woman to have so many wonderful friends and neighbors, women and men who have been my cheerleaders during this writing process. Unlike my first book, I recruited no readers for *The Queen's Dance*—though a shout-out is required for Laura and Becca, who read a few chapters in the early stages, and who offered on more than one occasion to act as my ghost readers. During the writing of this second book, I felt the need to keep the characters close to my heart, not wanting to share them until they were complete. I realize that it was the loss of my mom that made me do this, and later, the loss of a good friend, a sadness shared by many in our ever-expanding circle of friends.

But grief makes room for joy, and I would be remiss if I did not thank my sisters for their exuberance and support. Lisa the gardening goddess, Patricia the healer, Kelli the champion, and Andrea the teacher. You are Earth, Sylvan, Umbren, and Kena, and I would not have made it this far without all of you. I am so happy that we have become close again, despite the miles between us.

As always, my love and thanks to my family: Dave, Patrick, Connor, and Tully the Dog.

Continued gratitude to Kae Tienstra, my agent, who found Diversion Books for me; it has been a joy to work with you.

To the team at Diversion Books—Randall Klein and Eliza Kirby, editors; Sarah Masterson Hally and her production team; the wonderful copyeditors; Taylor Ness; and now Nita Basu in marketing—my deepest appreciation for all that you do.

And finally, to you, the reader, for picking up a copy of my book. You should know that a percentage of the royalties that I receive goes to charity. For *Wild Lavender*, I chose a local organization that gives aid to people in need in my community—food, clothing, and more. And for *The Queen's Dance*, I have decided to honor my late friend Lucy by donating to her breast cancer support group, Beyond Boobs. I encourage my readers to find some personal way—be it a donation of time, goods, or funds—to give back to your own communities.

A graduate of the University of Michigan's College of Literature, Science and Arts, NICOLE E. KELLEHER studied French Literature and Language, Spanish and Mandarin while taking classes at UofM's Art School. She moved to France and attended the Université Catholique de l'Œest before relocating to Belgium to complete an internship at a fine arts and antiques auction house. During this time, she travelled throughout the countryside of Europe, immersing herself in its history, architecture, and art. Nicole lives in Northern Virginia with her two teenaged boys, her husband, and Tully the Dog.

Connect with Nicole:

www.nekelleher.com

www.facebook.com/Nicole-Elizabeth-Kelleher-854445384602371

@NKelleherAuthor

Newsletter: http://eepurl.com/cA1mBH

CPSIA information can be obtained
at www.ICGtesting.com
Printed in the USA
BVOW03s2304180417
481276BV00003BA/6/P

9 781682 308189